UFOs, Conspiracy Theories
and the New Age

Bloomsbury Advances in Religious Studies

James Cox, Craig Martin and Steven Sutcliffe

This ground-breaking series presents innovative research in theory and method in the study of religion, paying special attention to disciplinary formation in Religious Studies. Volumes published under its auspices demonstrate new approaches to the way religious traditions are presented and analysed. Each study will demonstrate its theoretical insights by applying them to particular empirical case studies in order to foster integration of data and theory in the historical and cultural study of 'religion'.

UFOs, Conspiracy Theories and the New Age

Millennial Conspiracism

David G. Robertson

Bloomsbury Academic
An imprint of Bloomsbury Publishing Plc

B L O O M S B U R Y
LONDON · OXFORD · NEW YORK · NEW DELHI · SYDNEY

Bloomsbury Academic

An imprint of Bloomsbury Publishing Plc

50 Bedford Square
London
WC1B 3DP
UK

1385 Broadway
New York
NY 10018
USA

www.bloomsbury.com

BLOOMSBURY and the Diana logo are trademarks of Bloomsbury Publishing Plc

First published 2016
Paperback edition first published 2017

British Library Cataloguing-in-Publication Data
A catalogue record for this book is available from the British Library.

ISBN: HB: 978-1-4742-5320-8
PB: 978-1-3500-4498-2
ePDF: 978-1-4742-5321-5
ePub: 978-1-4742-5322-2

Library of Congress Cataloging-in-Publication Data
Names: Robertson, David G. (David George), author.
Title: UFOs, conspiracy theories and the new age:
millennial conspiracism / David G. Robertson.
Description: New York : Bloomsbury Academic, 2016. | Series: Bloomsbury advances in religious studies | Includes bibliographical references and index.
Identifiers: LCCN 2015042312| ISBN 9781474253208 (hardback) |
ISBN 9781474253222 (epub)
Subjects: LCSH: Human-alien encounters. | Strieber, Whitley. | Icke, David. | Wilcock, David, 1973- | Conspiracy theories. | New Age movement. | Millennialism. | BISAC: RELIGION / General. | SOCIAL SCIENCE / Sociology of Religion. | FICTION / Fantasy / Paranormal.
Classification: LCC BF2050 .R625 2016 | DDC 001.942–dc23 LC record available at http://lccn.loc.gov/2015042312

Series: Bloomsbury Advances in Religious Studies

Typeset by Integra Software Services Pvt. Ltd.

Contents

List of Illustrations

Acknowledgements

Thanks are due to Steven Sutcliffe for nurturing this project to its completion; to Carole Cusack for many opportunities; to the committee of the BASR, and Bettina Schmidt in particular; to the Religious Studies Project, especially Christopher Cotter; to all of those whose company and discussion made this work a pleasure – Charlotte Ward, Ethan Quillen, Jonathan Tuckett, Beth Singler, Kevin Whitesides, Liam Sutherland, Asbjorn Dyrendal, Egil Asprem and many others; to Aileen, of course; and to Teddy and Rex, because if they really are Indigos, then we are truly doomed.

Prologue:
'And the Truth Shall Set You Free'

This book began for me the first time I saw a prophet on the TV. Even at the age of 14, it was obvious to me that people should not have been laughing at David Icke, the former sports broadcaster turned Green Party spokesperson. It seemed to me that there were two possibilities; he had had a religious epiphany or a mental breakdown. Either way, mockery was inappropriate. I felt then, as I do now, that Terry Wogan and the audience of his prime-time BBC chat-show were simply cruel. There was certainly a lesson to be learned, however, about the ease with which the crowd will respond with anger to the strange.

Or did it begin when I discovered a mysterious book years later? In my early twenties, while working as a musician and songwriter, I spent part of 1998 in a residential recording studio in Lincolnshire. Separated from all friends and family excepting the other band members, which can obviously become claustrophobic, I worked my way through every book I could find. Mostly they were the kind one might find in a charity shop, with anything collectable or valuable having been stolen long ago. The exception was Robert Anton Wilson's *Cosmic Trigger* (1977 [1986]), which was falling to pieces, clearly read many times but never stolen – left deliberately, perhaps, for others to find and have their minds opened. In it, Wilson describes his experiences of what appeared to be channelled messages from the star Sirius, and although the subject matter was apparently bizarre, Wilson was self-reflexive and sceptical, with a natural and humorous writing style, and I became a fan. As a lifelong atheist, it never seemed any odder to me that people speak to aliens than to Jesus nor to believe in the Illuminati's hand behind events than God's.

This led in turn to an ongoing fascination with another of Wilson's major concerns, conspiracy theories. While I have never been a subscriber to any conspiratorial narratives, and remain highly sceptical to this day, my involvement has been long enough to notice that certain elements – such as the existence of the Bilderberg group or, more recently, the extent to which security agencies are monitoring private communications – had passed from conspiracy theory to fact during the period in which I had been researching them. I began to wonder if the term's meaning was not as obvious as it might at first appear.

Later – as so often seems to happen in this milieu – a coincidental meeting turned out to be far more meaningful. In July 2005, when I had just turned thirty and two months before starting at University, my girlfriend and I went to Rennes-le-Chateau in the Languedoc region of France, following the sites of Baigent, Leigh and Lincoln's *The Holy Blood and the Holy Grail* (1982). I had first read about the conspiracy theories surrounding Bérenger Sauniére's church in a Robert Anton Wilson book (1995, 96) (along with my first exposure to 2012 millennialism) and later in *Nexus* magazine; as briefly as possible, Sauniére managed to earn an awful lot of money while serving as the Priest of Rennes-le-Chateau. Possibly he found some coded parchments, although others argue that this was a cover for his profiting from the sale of indulgences. However, his tale became embroiled with some documents found in the Library National which alleged the existence of an organization called the Prioré de Sion, whose grandmasters allegedly included Leonardo da Vinci, Isaac Newton and Jean Cocteau. Later still, with the publication of *The Holy Blood and the Holy Grail*, the story came to involve the existence of Jesus' ancestors – the scrolls Sauniére discovered were evidence of this, the story goes, and he was paid handsomely for his silence as a result. Our visit was several years before Dan Brown's incredibly successful novel *The da Vinci Code* and while Rennes-le-Chateau had yet to become the tourist attraction it became after the novel's success, when the themes of conspiracy and the spiritual seem to have become firmly entangled in the public imagination.

In order to get there in these pre-blockbuster days, we had to catch a train at 6 am, walk five miles up the hill, arriving hours before anything opened for business. We explored the village, rather disappointed, and trudged down the mountain again. Back at the hotel, we sat down for pre-dinner drinks under an ancient Elm. Most of the tables were occupied by a French family whose very organized approach to sing-alongs included folders containing the lyrics of the songs. Impressed, we laughed along with the English-speaking couple on the table next to us and quickly found ourselves in a conversation. When our table in the restaurant was ready, they invited us to join them, which we happily accepted.

John Millar was a striking figure, with long, straight, white hair like a wizard and one hand concealed in a white glove. I later learned that he had lost it as a young man, although this disability had not stopped him from being an ace shot, even competing in the Olympics for Estonia, if accounts are to be believed (Dawes 2005, 133). Joy, on the other hand, was exactly what you would expect a middle-aged teacher on holiday in the Languedoc to be – except that she and her husband were secretary and President respectively of the Sauniére Society, dedicated to investigating the mysteries of Rennes-le-Chateau, and that their eldest son was Rat Scabies, drummer of the well-known UK punk group, The Damned. In short, they were charming company, not least for their insistence that we sample all of the local wines. Joy and I talked a great deal about conspiracy theories, and John told us that von Däniken had stolen the research for *Chariots of the Gods?* – the influential 1968 book which popularized the 'ancient astronaut' thesis (see Chapter 3) – from him.

As the evening wound on, and more of the wines were sampled, talk turned to why I was about to embark on a Religious Studies degree. They were both confused by why I wanted to study religion when I was an atheist, insistent that I was wasting my time, that religion was only part of the repressive system. Yet while adamant that religion was 'just dogma', we had just spent several hours talking about spiritual beings, UFOs, and so on. So what are your beliefs, I asked, religious or spiritual? 'I count myself as a Gnostic', he told me. Their grandson had been born severely handicapped, and the parents were now embroiled in a custody battle over a child who would not live long. They did not want to talk about it, but it so absorbed them that they couldn't help it. The world was evil, he said. Existence was suffering. The Cathars had it right.

In a sense, my story is the argument in this book. Starting out with an interest in 'New Age' millennial literature, I was introduced to conspiracism. The thing they had in common was UFOs. Whether protecting the planet from malevolent forces, as Icke claimed, beaming messages into Robert Anton Wilson's brain or helping to kick-start human civilization in prehistory, UFOs were ubiquitous. I began to wonder why this was.

Introduction: Aquarian Conspiracies

In *The Aquarian Conspiracy* (1980), one of the seminal 'New Age' source texts of the 1980s, Marilyn Ferguson described a 'benign conspiracy' of individuals working towards a similar aim of significant, foundational and lasting change to the social order (1980, 25). These individuals were working together to change society for the better, 'challenging the establishment from within' (23):

> One by one, we can re-choose – to awaken. To leave the prison of our conditioning, to love, to turn homeward. To conspire with and for each other ... You are a seed, a silent promise. You are the conspiracy. (417)

By the 1990s however, the milieu in which Ferguson moved was beginning to acknowledge that such social change was not demonstrably occurring. As Introvigne writes, 'it could not be maintained that a new age of general happiness was in fact manifesting, notwithstanding any evidence to the contrary' (2001, 60). Moreover, narratives concerning conspiracies acting against such social change were becoming widespread. Ferguson's benign 'New Age' conspiracy was replaced by the suspicion that other, malevolent conspiracies might be working against such utopian ideals. The 1980s, on both sides of the Atlantic, were a period that celebrated the self-interested pursuit of wealth and saw a resurgence of Right-wing political rhetoric. As Barkun writes, '[s]ome New Agers may well [have felt] contempt for a society that has failed to transform itself spiritually in line with their aspirations in the 1970s' (2003, 299). Between 1984 and 1994:

> Aquarian-age optimism transformed into a dark new-age despair ... Interest in the mind has shifted from speculation about the mind's as-yet unrealized powers (ESP, for example) to absorption in the belief that evil beings, UFO aliens referred to as the Grays, are implanting mind control devices in the

brains of thousands of Americans. And they are doing this, my informants believe, with the cooperation of elements of the U.S. government along with the internationalists bent on creating a one world government. (Milligan, quoted in Kay 2011, 61–2)

This book is an examination of that change. I ask how conspiracy theories came to find common ground with 'New Age' millennial narratives in the late 1980s and 1990s, as evinced in the work of Whitley Strieber, David Icke, David Wilcock and others. I here term the resultant field *millennial conspiracism*: a field where conspiracy narratives concerning the machinations of hidden agencies (the 'New World Order', the 'Illuminati' or reptilian extraterrestrials) interact and combine with popular millennial discourses concerning imminent global transformation ('New Age', 'Aquarian Age', 'Ascension', '2012'). In millennial conspiracist discourse, utopian narratives of a better world to come are mixed with accounts of humanity's imminent destruction; the government is actively working against our 'spiritual development'; and extraterrestrial beings created religions to enslave humanity. Accounts concerning UFOs – and often encounters with their extra-terrestrial occupants (ETs) – were instrumental in this change, acting as a bridge by which ideas crossed between conspiracist and popular millennial fields.

It is important to note at this point that the term millennial conspiracism is entirely my own etic[1] construction, intended to enable analysis of this particular discourse and in no way intended to signify any kind of 'movement'. Indeed, as my discourse analytical approach (described in Chapter 2) implies, I do not intend to reify the term as a distinct field in any way; rather, I employ the term essentially as a form of shorthand, in order to facilitate analysis.

Succinctly, I shall argue that in the early Cold War period (1947–c.1959), UFOs are given a primarily 'physicalist' construction – that is, they were understood as physical craft, initially enemy weapons and latterly ET spacecraft. However, others were simultaneously constructing UFOs within a post-Theosophical tradition of 'channelled communication' with occluded Masters, including the founders of the proto-'New Age' Findhorn community (Sutcliffe 2003a, 65–85). The booming counter-culture in the 1960s drew upon this post-Theosophical tradition as evidence mounted against the possibility of life elsewhere in the solar system, undermining the physicalist construction, and this 'supernatural' construction became the dominant one. With the thawing of the Cold War in the 1980s, UFOs once again became a prominent feature of the conspiracist milieu, at the same time that the 'New Age'[2] milieu was undergoing a 'crisis' – essentially the realization that their millennial prophecies had failed to manifest. Conspiracist and millennial discourses had several concerns in common, particularly – though not exclusively – UFOs. As a result, there was fluidity between conspiracist and popular millennial audiences, and from around 1990, the boundaries of the two discourses become notably indistinct as the UFO narrative facilitated cross-fertilization. 'New World Order' conspiracist works such as William Milton Cooper's *Behold a Pale Horse* (1991) shared shelf space with millennial channelled texts such as *The Ra material: An ancient astronaut speaks* (McCarty, et al. 1984) on the grounds that both involved UFOs. The result was that the conspiracists' battle against powerful, hidden agencies increasingly incorporated popular millennial narratives of personal and planetary transformation. On the other hand, these same hostile agencies provided a ready answer to why the predicted 'New Age' had – thus far – failed to materialize. UFOs, then, are in this study constructed as the primary *discursive object* between millennial and conspiracist fields; that is, in the negotiation of the differing constructions of 'UFO' in these two fields, common areas of concern were revealed between them and an exchange of ideas was facilitated. I describe this process of *discursive transfer* in depth in Chapter 2.

Sociological studies of UFOs as religious phenomena began with *When Prophecy Fails: A Social and Psychological Study of a Modern Group that Predicted the Destruction of the Modern World* (Festinger, Riecken and Schachter 1964 [1956]), which became the cornerstone of the sociological study of UFO religion for the next thirty years. Later works examining New Religious Movements, including the Raëlians (Palmer 2004), Uranius Academy (Tumminia 2005), and others (Lewis 1995; Partridge 2003), have broadly followed its focus on small groups of marginalized individuals drawing predominantly from Theosophical tradition (Denzler 2001, xiii–xiv). The authors gained admittance to a small group who followed the messages that 'Marian Keech'[3] claimed to be channelling from ETs, including the claim that the world would end on 21 December 1954. The work attempts to explain how the group could continue to believe in the face of the apparent failure of this prediction. They found that for some, though not all, proof against a belief could actually strengthen that belief (Festinger, Riecken and Schachter 1964 [1956], 3) and that the group would collectively and individually find strategies to reduce the *cognitive dissonance* between their belief and apparent reality (Festinger, Riecken and Schachter 1964 [1956], 229). Cognitive dissonance is 'the existence of nonfitting relations among cognitions' (Festinger 1957, 3) – that is, contradictory knowledge or opinions held by an individual.

Although the book does not clearly lay out the various strategies, four can be established from the text:

> *Miscalculation* – in either case, the prophecy did not fail but was somehow garbled during its reception or interpretation.
>
> *Spiritualization* – the prophecy was correct but happened on the spiritual plane rather than in the everyday, physical world.
>
> *Aversion* – because of the actions of the group, the prophecy was avoided and a new status quo established.
>
> *Privation* – the prophecy did not fail but was only for the insider group, not everyone.
>
> To this list, however, I would argue for a further strategy:
>
> *Prevention* – a hitherto unsuspected agency prevented it from happening.

More recent sociological and ethnographic research has demonstrated that UFO and abduction discourse is not limited to small and marginal groups, however. Jodi Dean's *Aliens in America: Conspiracy Cultures from Outerspace to Cyberspace* (1998) reflects this, focussing on how UFOs and ETs have infiltrated popular culture in recent decades. She charts the changes in the ET contact narrative following the Cold War period (46–54). 'UFOlogy is political', she writes, 'because it is stigmatised' (1998, 6). Belief in UFOs marks one as being in opposition to epistemic norms, particularly for those who claim to have experienced contact with ETs. For such individuals, the subjective experience discredits claims to science's objectivity and therefore the alien comes to operate as a symbol of the perceived boundary between the objective and the subjective. Rather than reflecting widespread irrationality, she suggests, the currency of ET and UFO beliefs 'points to the widespread lack of criteria for judgements about what is reasonable and what is not' (1998, 9), a theme continued in Brenda Denzler's *The Lure of the Edge: Scientific Passions, Religious Beliefs, and the Pursuit of UFOs* (2001). Jeffery Kripal's *Authors of the Impossible* (2010) and *Mutants and Mystics* (2011) go further. In chapters on Jacques Vallée (in the former) and Whitley Strieber (in the latter), Kripal seems to be saying that accounts of anomalous experiences in the work of these and other authors describe emergent or potential psychic capabilities of the human mind. Kripal thus presents the UFO narrative as essentially a form of trans-humanism; that by writing about how humankind *might* evolve, these writers prefigure and even affect how humankind *will* evolve. UFOs are described as neither entirely subjective nor properly objective.[4]

This theme of UFOs symbolising a liminal space between the subjective and objective – so challenging the strict dualism inherent in post-Enlightenment thought – brings us to the mythological approach. In 1958, the elderly C. G. Jung published *Flying Saucers: A Modern Myth of Things Seen in the Skies*, which treated UFOs as mythological entities. Jung's interpretation was that UFOs were archetypes from the collective unconscious being projected out into the physical world. They were 'technological angels', emanations from our collective unconscious dressing in technological garb in response to modernity. Thompson (1991) developed Jung's approach by arguing that the physical existence of UFOs was of lesser import than their function as carriers of meaning. He argues that they act as archetypes which express the specific concerns of particular societies in symbolic form.

Therefore, UFOs are particularly relevant because they frequently signify epistemic uncertainty and issues of epistemology will emerge as being of particular concern in this discursive field. I will not, however, attempt to cover every twist and turn of the UFO narrative. There may or may not be spacecraft visiting this planet, but I do not have the faculties to assess that nor is it my principle concern. The UFO narrative is the McGuffin of this book, guiding the actor's actions but never the point of the story. Rather, I seek to answer two questions. Firstly, what is the common mechanism that facilitates hybridization between conspiracy narratives and popular millennialism? What is it that has brought these two apparently very different fields together? I argue that the answer is an epistemology that acknowledges sources of access to knowledge – here termed *epistemic strategies* – not acknowledged by the epistemic authorities of the contemporary Anglophone world. The dominant epistemic strategies of the contemporary Anglophone world are the *scientific*, which is the domain of the academy, and *tradition*, appealed to by institutions, both religious and of the state. These strategies are not denied in millennial conspiracist discourse but are appealed to alongside appeals to *experiential, channelled* and *synthetic* knowledge (that is, in which many small pieces of discrete information are combined to reveal 'the bigger picture') – strategies which I call *counter-epistemic*. I unpack these five epistemic strategies fully in Chapter 2 and give specific examples of how these appeals are strategically made in Chapters 4, 5 and 6.

Secondly, I ask what the appeal of millennial conspiracism is for its subscribers. How do these narratives serve the individuals who produce or utilize them? Even more simply, why is the idea that malevolent extraterrestrials secretly run the world attractive? By adding a conspiratorial counter-agency to popular millennialist discourse, millennial conspiracism offers its subscribers a *theodicy*. Theodicy – from the Greek *theo*, God, and Latin *dike*, justice – addresses injustice; if the universe is proceeding according to the plan of some benevolent agency, why does suffering exist, and why is it apparently distributed unevenly? Theodicies attempt to resolve the tension 'between the expectations that world-views create in people and the experiences they actually undergo' (Campbell 2001, 73). Christian theological responses, framing theodicy as 'the problem of evil', have argued variously that suffering is inevitable in a cosmos which allows free will (O'Conner 2008, 50ff) or that what we perceive as suffering on our earthly individual level may be part of a necessary, if regrettable, course of action towards a greater good (Davies 2006, 19). Within holistic 'New Age' discourse, however, 'good' and 'evil' tend to be constructed as two polarities within a larger whole. Hanegraaff writes, 'holism is incompatible with the very idea of a system of morality: the latter, after all, should be able to distinguish "good" from "evil", while the former cannot accept such distinctions as absolute' (1996, 276). Therefore, '[i]t is in fact the dualistic idea that evil is something which exists and should not be, that according to "New Age" sources, prevents us from seeing the universe as one benevolent entity. "Whatever is, is right", it is us who need to learn and to adjust'

(Hanegraaff 1996, 277–8). However, I suggest that malevolent agencies have been constructed in such discourses to a greater degree than scholarship has tended to accept.

Moreover, millennial conspiracism's theodicy has a distinctly Gnostic flavour. What little we know of Gnosticism – if it in fact ever actually existed outside of Christian hereisiology – comes from polemical writings by the Church Fathers in the second to fourth centuries (Smith 1988, 549). Academic tradition has followed them in constructing Gnosticism as a heretical Christian tradition which sought direct knowledge of God. Such knowledge was apparently called *gnosis* by many early Christians and Platonists (Merkur 1993, 112–3) and probably by some of the classical Gnostic groups themselves (Williams 1996, 33). The typical English translation as 'knowledge' is inexact; *γνοςισ* (*gnosis*) refers to knowledge which is experiential, as contrasted with *ἐπιστήμη* (*episteme*), indicating theoretical knowledge. *Anticosmism* – the idea that the physical world is malevolent, false or intrinsically flawed – was a recurrent theme of Gnostic texts (Culiano 1992, 60; Williams 1996; Pearson 2007, 12–13). In anticosmic texts, the world is described as the creation of an insane 'demiurge', a miscegenated lesser deity, misidentified as being the supreme deity. Gnosis was constructed as offering an avenue to escape the false world of the demiurge. Taken together, the anticosmic trope that the world is not as it should be and the concept of soteriological gnosis offer a striking parallel to millennial conspiracist discourse.

Two assumptions underlie discursive theoretical approaches and are therefore taken as axiomatic in this book. Firstly, discourses do not come from nowhere; rather they grow out of concerns that are to some degree widely held in culture more broadly. Secondly, the statements and practices of individuals and groups emerge from propositions that benefit them in some way, or perhaps more accurately, address their specific concerns. There is nothing intrinsic about the UFO narrative as it developed in the late 1940s that meant it would continue for more than sixty years; rather, it has continued because it has proven useful in certain discourses. Specifically, it has been useful in conspiracist and popular millennial discourses, as it symbolizes and perhaps validates the use of counter-epistemic strategies.

Conspiracism and religion

The relationship between conspiracism and religion has been less frequently investigated, but there has been an emerging scholarly awareness of the prominence of both millennial discourses in the conspiracist milieu, and of conspiracist discourses within the popular millennial milieu, in recent years. Keeley's 'God as the Ultimate Conspiracy Theory' (2007) argues that there is an implicit epistemological similarity between religion and conspiracism – specifically, that both posit a non-falsifiable agency orchestrating events in the world. In these two cases alone, he argues, 'absence of evidence is not evidence of absence' (2007, 145). Thus, any evidence against the narrative is interpreted as evidence of the occluded agency's attempt to conceal itself, not only rendering the belief non-falsifiable but creating a cycle of reinforcement.

Several scholars have pursued the comparison between conspiracism and esoteric discourses.[5] The construction of a complex network of correspondences underpinning reality mirrors the 'esoteric correspondences' of Faivre's influential definition of esotericism (1994, 119–20).[6] Dyrendal highlights 'the parallel ways in which knowledge, history, and agency are constructed' in these two discourses; where there is knowledge and there is special knowledge, 'real' history may be 'occulted', and the cosmos is not Manichaean but tripartite (2013, 224).

Barkun's *A Culture of Conspiracy* offered a groundbreaking historiography of the adoption of UFO narratives in Right-wing conspiracist discourse (2003, x). He argues that this has led conspiracism to adopt millennial narratives in eclectic and individual combinations, a milieu which Barkun calls improvisational millenarianism (2003, 170–7). Barkun utilizes a broadened conception of Colin Campbell's *cultic milieu* ([1972] 2002). Campbell's seminal essay was an examination of the well-known classification of religious formations, developed by sociologists from the work of Troeltsch, into *church, sect* and *cult*. Both sects and cults are constructed as small, novel and to some extent heterodox, but sects are collectivist, strongly structured, exclusive, stable in terms of belief and organization and tend to persist for long periods of time, while cults are individualistic, relatively unstructured, inclusive, unstable in beliefs and structure and generally short-lived (Campbell [1972] 2002, 13–14). Campbell attempted to explain why it is that although cultic groups constantly schism and collapse, new ones always spring up in their stead: 'whereas cults are by definition a largely transitory phenomenon, the cultic milieu is, by contrast, a constant feature of society' ([1972] 2002, 14). However, in Campbell's exposition, the cultic milieu is a 'space bounded by a religion-science axis' ([1972] 2002, 16). Barkun is considering the adoption of millennial discourses in conspiracist groups and therefore presents a broadened conception of the cultic milieu in which political heterodoxies as well as the religious, what we described above as challenges to the epistemological authorities (2003, 26; c.f. Partridge 2004, 4). Barkun calls the contents of explanations that challenge the epistemic authorities *stigmatized knowledge*. This includes knowledge which has been *forgotten*, that which has been *superseded, ignored, rejected*, or most pertinently, *suppressed* (2003, 26–9). In positing that we broaden Campbell's model to include political heterodoxies, he presents us with a milieu in which stigmatized political views mingle with unorthodox religious and scientific ideas. As we shall see, this is precisely what has happened in recent decades, with the ET discourse allowing the stigmatiszd political beliefs of the far right to be adopted in popular millennial discourses. However, Barkun's terminology reproduces epistemic judgements based on the primacy of particular epistemic strategies; which knowledge is defined as *stigmatized* depends entirely on one's acceptance of particular epistemic positions and will be relative to different socio-historical contexts. Therefore, I refer to counter-epistemic positions and strategies rather than stigmatized knowledge.[7]

Goodrick-Clarke notes the 'endemic spread of conspiracy theories in the New Age milieu' since the 1990s, focussing on *Nexus* magazine and David Icke (2002, 299). In his account, concerns about globalization, immigration and corporate power among the middle classes in the 1990s led to the increasing acceptance of conspiracy tropes in popular millennial discourses:

An anarcho-libertarian interest in tracing CIA mind-control experiments, federal government covert operations and links with UFOs and aliens can suddenly switch into a pessimistic discourse of hidden elites, the

Council on Foreign Relations, Trilateral Commission the Bilderbergs and Rothschilds, leading to reprints of the *Protocols of the Elders of Zion* (Goodrick-Clarke 2002, 299).[8]

More recently, Ward and Voas have outlined what they term *conspirituality* (2011). Focussing on popular culture and the internet, they argue that 'world-affirming, cultic "New Age" and world-rejecting conspiracy milieu have merged into a world-accommodating – arguably mainstream – hybrid' (Ward and Voas 2011, 116). Despite its limitations (see Asprem and Dyrendal 2015), the paper brought millennial conspiracist discourse to academic attention for the first time.[9]

My own work has attempted to advance this historiographical work to include analysis of the structure and function of these discourses in the field. Of particular relevance is my analysis of the use of prophecy in conspiracist discourse, focussing on Texas-based radio host and filmmaker, Alex Jones, arguably the most influential conspiracist in the world today (Robertson 2013). I argued that Jones exemplifies a particular method of claiming epistemic capital which has become apparent in the conspiracist milieu since the mid-1990s with the development of the internet and 24-hour television, although with hindsight can be seen to have been utilized on a slower scale previously in print.[10] *Rolling prophecy* entails making small prophecies on a regular and ongoing basis, although tied to a larger teleological narrative, in Jones' case that a Satanic Elite are covertly attempting to reduce world population to some tens of millions. The more successful elements are emphasized and the less successful quietly dropped; over time, the impression of successful prophecy is established, and moreover the cognitive dissonance produced by a failed prophecy is avoided (2013, 215–6). Rolling prophecy allows Jones to amplify his prophetic success, and thereby increase his capital in the field. This strategy is frequently employed in the millennial conspiracist field also, as will be shown in the case studies.

Locating millennial conspiracism

Millennial conspiracism is part of a broader cross-fertilization between the popular religious and conspiracist fields over the latter half of the twentieth century. This is a two-way process; as conspiracist discourse has increasingly included millennial narratives, popular millennial discourse increasingly adopts conspiracist counter-agencies, including such New Religious Movements (NRMs) as Aum Shinrikyo (Repp 2004, 168–9), the Nuwaubians (Palmer 2010) and some Rastafarian groups (Partridge 2005, 318). At the same time, some Christian groups have adopted conspiracist discourses, perhaps as a reaction against the growth of international governance and financial agencies in the post-war period (Boyer 1992, 263–72; Webster 2013).

Conversely, conspiracists increasingly adopt millennial discourses, talking of a 'global awakening' or 'transformation' (Ward and Voas 2011, 112). Texas-based radio host and filmmaker Alex Jones, for example, describes himself as the 'tip of the spear' in the war against the globalist conspiracy and states repeatedly that we are at the cusp of a mass awakening where the masses will rise up against their purported oppressors.[11] As we will see in the case studies in this book, these trajectories come together in millennial conspiracism.

UFOs became the central discursive object in millennial conspiracism as a result of symbolizing the perceived limitations of scientific and traditional epistemic strategies. Other discursive objects played a role, however, albeit a less instrumental one. 'Holistic' narratives of the interconnectedness of all beings, widespread in contemporary popular religious discourse, for example Gaian ecological narratives or Jungian 'synchronicities', are paralleled in conspiracism by discourses in which every event is the result of the machinations of an *occluded agency*. Occluded agency signifies explanations of world events in terms of agents who are not readily interrogatable through scientific means and who furthermore seek to conceal their actions and intentions (Keeley 2007).

In millennial conspiracist discourse, political, social and religious structures are constructed as the result of the machinations of these occluded and – importantly – malevolent elite who aim to keep the masses ignorant and subservient. Of particular importance here is the identification of *malevolent* occluded agencies, and indeed, a significant aspect of my book here is to argue for the introduction of a malevolent counter-agency to popular millennial discourses. Note, however, that both malevolent *and* benevolent agencies may be alleged to be in operation simultaneously.

Exposure to alternative health care through chronic ill-health is a frequent path through which individuals are introduced to 'popular', 'vernacular' or 'alternative' spiritual beliefs and practices.[12] It is little noted, however, that alternative health care is also a common feature of conspiracist discourse. Alex Jones' websites and radio show are supported by manufacturers of vitamin supplements, 'monatomic silver', genetically unmodified food and filters to remove fluoride from drinking water, a narrative which is signified by the term *big pharma* (Robertson 2015; Singler 2015). As Jones puts it in an advert promoting spin-off site selling alternative healthcare products infowarshealth. com, 'You can't stand against the machine if you're sick, tired and obese.'[13] Books such as *What Doctors Don't Tell You* (McTaggart 1996) – now also a popular magazine – appeal as much to individuals who subscribe to a 'holistic' worldview as those who believe that there exists a grand conspiracy to weaken, stultify or even eradicate the majority of humanity.

Similarly, alternative archaeological narratives concerning Atlantis, Mu and other lost civilizations are frequently encountered in these fields. From the millennial point of view, it makes sense that one might believe a golden age existed previously when one already believes that one is imminent. For the conspiracist, on the other hand, if one believes that what we are told about the present is a lie, it makes sense that the past would be a lie too. In both cases, however, appeals to history and tradition are a powerful strategy for legitimizing these discourses (Lewis 2012, 202).

Despite the bleak prognosis, however, millennial conspiracist discourse remains firmly focussed on the possibility of salvation. As well as stretching back into the past, these narratives construct predictions of the future. The conspirators can be overcome, this discourse states, if enough people 'wake up' to the 'truth' that the world is not as it seems. In other words, knowledge (or certain types of knowledge, at least) is constructed as capable of transforming and possibly even liberating the individual. In millennial conspiracism then, through questioning epistemological norms, accumulating information and making connections between anomalous events, individuals claim to begin to see through the false reality imposed by a postulated occluded malevolent agency or agencies. As Icke puts it in the title of his book, the truth shall set you free (Icke 1995).

Teleological narratives of the End Times in the conspiracist milieu are traditionally *apocalyptic* – that is, they posited destructive scenarios with a negative outcome for humanity. However, popular religious discourse is frequently *millennial*, positing transformative scenarios with a positive outcome (I define these terms in more detail in Chapter 2). 'New Age' discourse is one very clear example of these millennial narratives, although as we will see, far from the only one. In millennial conspiracism, however, these two narratives form a dialectic that is simultaneously millennial and apocalyptic; while the occluded agencies move forward with their plans for the enslavement of humanity, an increasing number of individuals are becoming aware of their enslavement. When a critical mass of individuals is reached, according to this narrative, there will be a gestalt shift in which the masses will realize the means of their liberation, a teleological motif which is currently most often referred to as the *global awakening*. In this hybrid belief system, ETs are indeed proof of a higher reality, but the evidence for the existence of that reality is being actively suppressed by the global conspirators; the eschaton will come only when enough of the population of the world realize this and resist. For example:

> The information we are making available, along with other events, will hasten the end of the economic system and the empires of the churches, and will shatter the very foundations of contemporary so-called scientific thinking. It will set humanity free. (Icke 1993b, 29)

Millennial conspiracist discourses can be found in magazines like *Nexus, New Dawn* and *Atlantis Rising* – available on the shelves in high-street newsagents – mixing a fixation with UFOs with speculation on ancient monuments, psychical phenomena and alternative healthcare, bound together with an undercurrent of spiritual and often millennial significance. In the United States, syndicated radio shows such as *Coast to Coast AM* and *The Alex Jones Show* get listeners numbering in the millions on multiple AM stations,[14] and while Europe does not have the same market penetration, these shows and local productions like Sweden's *Red Ice Radio* (tagline, 'for the seeker') gain considerable listenership over the internet. The traditional 'New Age fair' has begun to merge with the academic stylings of UFO conferences to produce events such as the *Shadows, Secrets and Spirits* symposium, *Contact in the Desert* and the events described in the anthropological sections of the case studies in Chapers 4 and 5. Even the Glastonbury Symposium – for many the home of 'alternative spirituality' in the UK – now advertises itself with the tagline 'An annual three-day conference of mysteries, truth and new frontiers' and includes 'conspiracies' and 'truth issues' among more traditional concerns including 'crop circles', 'astrology' and 'the environment'.[15] 'UFOs' remain near the top of the list, however.

Popular albums like Muse's *The Resistance*, Megadeth's *Endgame* or the eponymous *Conspirituality* (all 2009) encoded the message musically and less overtly, Black Eyed Peas' *Where Is the Love?* (a number 1 recording across the world in 2003) accused the CIA of being 'terrorists', stating that 'Wrong information always shown by the media ... war is going on but the reason's undercover, The truth is kept secret, it's swept under the rug ... If you never know truth then you never know love' (2003). The overarching narrative of *The X-Files*, broadcast from 1993 to 2002 and regularly watched by up to twenty million people (Goldberg 2001, 62), mixed Fortean phenomena, government suppression of UFOs, the Illuminati and *ancient alien* theories into a prime-time entertainment package. Dan Brown's novel *The da Vinci Code* (2003), which broke a number of publishing records and spawned numerous imitators, concerns a conspiracy by the Catholic Church to repress the 'sacred feminine', the revelation of which is described with millennial overtones.

The internet is an important medium for the dissemination of millennial conspiracist discourse, and each of the writers highlighted in this book – David Icke, Whitley Strieber and David Wilcock – maintain websites that attract large amounts of traffic. Podcasts including Strieber's *Dreamland* and *Red Ice Radio* are highly popular, and as streaming technology improves, internet-based videos are becoming the dominant medium. Films including *Zeitgeist* and its sequels (Joseph 2007, 2008, 2011), *Thrive* (2011) and *Sirius* (Kaleka 2013) achieved widespread audiences without any traditional cinema distribution. *Thrive* is a particularly interesting example of this field; it seeks to answer the question 'what went wrong?' Why are there still wars and millions starving? What happened to the post-War dream? The answer presented is that extra-terrestrials visited the earth in pre-history and continue to send messages to the earth in crop circles concerning 'free energy' technologies which could solve all of the problems associated with overpopulation and global warming. However, the 'corporate media' are suppressing these technologies because a small number of elite families have secretly co-opted the system for their own financial gain, effectively repeating the decades-old New World Order (NWO) narratives of Right-wing conspiracy theorists such as Pat Robertson and Alex Jones.

The degree to which the internet has nurtured millennial conspiracist discourse is unclear. It is commonplace for scholarly and journalistic pieces alike to begin by remarking that the development of the internet has nurtured the development of contemporary conspiracist discourse (e.g. Knight 2000; Bratich 2004). The internet is typically considered to allow fast and low-cost communication with a worldwide potential audience and to be (relatively) free of regulation from governmental and academic authorities, factors considered as benefitting the dissemination of alternative ideas. On the other hand, Clarke has argued that, while the Internet has aided the dissemination of conspiracy discourses, its hypercritical atmosphere has in most cases actually prevented such discourses from developing into properly articulated theories capable of challenging accepted narratives (Clarke 2007). My own position is that the internet has not so much encouraged the growth of counter-cultural ideas but rather, made them more visible. The internet allows for the formation of marginal group identities beyond the confines of geographical proximity, making them more identifiable, but I have seen no evidence that such ideas are any more or less widespread than they ever were.

Online or off, these discourses are largely Anglophone, and predominantly centred on the UK, North America and Australasia, although I am aware of significant outlets for this material in Scandinavia, Russia and South Africa. However, concrete socio-demographic data on subscribers to millennial conspiracist discourse is unavailable, as quantitative research has not been carried out. I was presented with the opportunity to hand out short questionnaires at the Strieber and Icke events, however, intended to enable cross-comparison between the two audiences. Although limited in scope, they do suggest some patterns in the demographic makeup of subscribers to millennial conspiracist discourse.[16]

Interestingly, gender balance was close to an even distribution. In the Icke group, twelve male and nine female, a ratio of 57 per cent male to female, but not in serious disagreement with my findings from Dreamland which was split exactly evenly (twenty-eight of each gender, with one not identified). This gender balance is supported by data gleaned from Google's advertising programme, which suggested that millennial conspiracist websites (including davidicke.com and divinecosmos.com) are visited by women and men in roughly equal numbers (Ward 2012).[17] Previous research on conspiracism has suggested an audience that is predominantly – but by no means exclusively – male (Stewart and Harding 1999). On the other hand, quantitative studies by both Heelas and Woodhead (2005) and Rose (2005) have found a predominance of females in groups with practices often considered 'New Age'. This raises an interesting question: is millennial conspiracism's gender balance a result of its appealing equally to male and female audiences, or rather, are its female subscribers more drawn to the millennial aspects and its male subscribers to the conspiracist? In fact, many of the authors we consider in this book work in close partnership with wives and partners (including Icke and Strieber), although typically with the male partner more prominent.

Discourses on conspiracy beliefs have typically been constructed as taking place within a politically Right-wing and religiously conservative Christian context (Stewart and Harding 1999, 293). However, recent studies suggest that their appeal have broadened considerably in recent decades, with significant audiences amongst working class and ethnic minorities, particularly black Americans (Waters 1997; Melley 2000). Moreover, some popular contemporary conspiracist narratives are prominent in Left-wing discourse, most notably conspiracies concerning the 9/11 attacks (Sapountzis and Condor 2013, 737). On the other hand, popular millennial discourses have tended more towards a Left-wing political position and tend to be religiously pluralistic and in the UK at least even anti-Christian.

In the questionnaires I circulated at the Icke and Strieber events, the question on 'religious affiliation' produced further interesting results. In the UK context, from fifteen respondents, two responded as 'Christian' and one 'CofE'. One responded with 'spirituality'; everyone else answered 'none' (although two qualified it with 'alternative' or "spiritual" in parentheses).[18] Perhaps more surprisingly, however, given that statistics frequently inform us that, unlike Europe, some 80 per cent of US respondents will identify as Christian (Newport 2012), only fourteen of the US respondents did so (roughly 25 per cent). Thirty (over 50 per cent) wrote 'none' (although interestingly none identified as 'atheist') and a further five identified as 'spiritual'. To summarize, in both UK and US contexts, the majority identified as neither 'religious' nor 'spiritual' (at least in response to the specific question of religious identity).

This trajectory of detraditionalization continued in the question regarding political affiliation. In the UK context, Icke's group, of fifteen nine identified as 'none'; the remainder were one 'voluntarist', one 'conspiracy nutter', one 'truth/conspiracy theory' and one 'spiritual'. In Strieber's group, only two identified as 'republican', with four further identifying as 'conservative' or 'libertarian'; on the left, nine identified as 'democrat', five as 'liberal' and two as 'moderate'.[19] But the majority, twenty-seven, put 'none'. Given the common connection between conspiracy beliefs and the political Right-wing, this was somewhat surprising but supported the argument above that conspiracist narratives have a broad socio-cultural appeal in the contemporary Anglophone world.

How I went about this study

The theoretical approach of this book is discursive and critical; that is, based in the analysis of how the field is constructed through the use of language by the actors within it and concerned with how such discourses are related to power relations (the background and theoretical implications of this approach are unpacked fully in Chapter 2). The data that my analysis uses is primarily historical and drawn chiefly from the primary sources of Strieber, Icke and Wilcock, who were chosen to cover the post-Cold War period, 1988–2010.[20] Each case involves multiple works spanning one or more decades, and I have taken great care not to simplify and conflate the accounts presented in each work into reified narratives, following the archaeological approach outlined in Chapter 2. Secondary literature has often been thin on the ground, and in several cases I have been forced to draw to an unusually large degree on the authors' own accounts; here, I have opted for the earliest account, and have not reproduced the authors' own interpretation of the biographical data. I have furthermore found it necessary to draw on journalistic sources to evaluate the authors' own accounts.

In each case, I also utilized video material, presentations and interviews, where relevant, and each of these authors disseminates their work through the internet, with online communities focussed on their websites – davidicke. com, unknowncountry.com and divinecosmos.com. A full study of these sites and their associated forums over an extended period is beyond the scope of the present study; however, Chapter 6 focusses on Wilcock's use of the internet to promote his millennial conspiracist narrative and uses such an approach to a limited degree.

This historical dataset was supplemented by three short periods of anthropological fieldwork at events where the authors in question interact with the communities they have developed around them. Strieber is not a frequent public speaker, but does hold an annual 'Dreamland Festival' for which one hundred and thirty tickets are available for a weekend of lectures by himself and his associates. I attended the event in Nashville, Tennessee, in July 2012 as a participant observer and was able to speak to both attendees and presenters in person. David Icke is a frequent public speaker, and I attended his Wembley Arena presentation on 27 October 2012. This was very different in structure to the Dreamland festival, as it was attended by 6,000 people with Icke as the only speaker, making it less collegial and more akin to a popular music concert. In order to interact with the subscribers, I also attended two smaller periphery events, an informal party after the event and a small discussion group the following afternoon. As this had covered both the US and UK contexts, in the Wilcock chapter I instead focus on the internet. While Wilcock has in the past been a frequent public speaker, his events (called 'Convergences') have become less frequent recently as his career has developed; however, he has made an internet version available and therefore the ethnographic portion of the chapter describes my experiences undertaking his 'Online Convergence'. Although not a feature of his published work, Strieber offered the Dreamland insiders meditation as a practical technique to access some of the counter-epistemic sources he utilises. Icke, on the other hand, does not offer any practical technique, beyond a vague exhortation towards synthetic knowledge through 'doing your own research'. As Wilcock's events are based around teaching techniques designed to make counter-epistemic sources of knowledge available to the participants. This section also explores how the internet is used by both producers and subscribers to engage with this material. Wilcock's presentation is more concerned with *methods* of accessing counter-epistemic sources than Strieber or Icke's events were, so Chapter 6 focusses more on myself as subject.

The aim of this ethnographic research was to interact with the typical subscriber to this material, rather than its producers. It asks to what the degree each author's ideas are accepted by subscribers, and if there is a significant degree of challenge, whether the audience is made up entirely of 'believers', or whether a significant proportion are there for entertainment or other reasons, and whether there is significant crossover between these audiences or, for that matter, animosity between them. In short, they address competition for epistemic capital in the millennial conspiracist discursive field. The subjects of the historiographical sections are the producers of this material and have demonstrated a mastery of the epistemic capital of the field. On the other hand, the ethnographic sections concern individuals who do not possess a high degree of epistemic capital but look to figures such as Strieber, Icke and Wilcock for guidance. Moreover, the historical sections offer a diachronic perspective on the field, whereas the ethnographic sections offer a synchronic perspective. Hence, the historiographical sections are in the third-person and past tense; ethnographical sections, in contrast, are first person and present tense.

During this fieldwork, I was open about the fact that I was approaching the subject from an academic position. Inevitably, there was some scepticism about this, though not as much as I had expected. To a degree this was because I made it very clear that I was not concerned with the truth or otherwise about the phenomena being described but rather in accurately describing what was said and how it was engaged with. This meant that I generally was not seen as a threat by the participants, perhaps because I was not challenging the epistemic strategies being employed. Nevertheless, I did whatever I could to build trust; talking about my children, drinking alcohol when they did, helping out in the kitchen and making self-deprecating jokes. For example, my opening gambit at the David Icke meeting in London was to say 'I admit it – I am an academic.' Although I stressed my personal lack of belief in the subject matter, I was twice told that I was 'meant' to be doing this research, which I took as a compliment. However, one concession I made was to change my terminology to some degree; concerned that terms like 'religion' and 'conspiracy theories' might not find a receptive ear among insiders, I described myself as a 'social scientist' looking at 'popular spirituality' rather than doing 'religious studies'. On the other hand, I found that my rejection of 'conspiracy theory' as a meaningful category (see Chapter 2) was well received.

At Dreamland, I benefited from Strieber's decision to vouch for me to the panellists and attendees at the beginning of the event, which was remarkably trusting as we had communicated only briefly and I had not at that point published anything upon which he could base this conclusion. However, I was challenged by two of the panellists. Marla Frees, a 'transformational psychic medium', told me that she was concerned that I would be 'defining' her and the group and accused me of being a 'sceptic' during her presentation. Chip Wilkins, however, seemed simply suspicious about my motives. He asked, 'Have you found what you're looking for yet?', and I laughed and answered in the negative. 'I have', he said, not smiling.

On the other hand, my overtures to the discussion group on Icke's website were completely ignored, and while an initial email to his management looking to arrange an interview received an initially positive response, subsequent follow-ups were not answered. When I got in touch with the organizer of the David Icke discussion group, she suggested that I give a presentation to the group, and I reluctantly agreed on the assumption that by making myself vulnerable, the attendees would feel more comfortable talking openly. I have remained in touch with a number of the subscribers through Facebook and email, and in some cases, this has led to more focussed exchanges where I have been able to elicit more detailed explanation of their position. In either case, I have changed their names in order to preserve their anonymity, excepting the few cases where the name was in the public domain already.[21]

Any study concerning conspiracism, millennialism or UFOs faces serious definitional issues, but I wish to make it clear that I am analysing *terms* and not *things*. I discuss the implications of this approach in the following chapter, and Chapter 3 presents a genealogy of the 'UFO' narrative. Appearing in 1947, they were originally understood as secret military aircraft, although by the 1950s the idea that they had an extraterrestrial origin was well established. However, the 1970s saw the UFO narrative adopted simultaneously by a resurgent post-Watergate conspiracism, in which they were constructed as evidence of suppression of information by the state on a vast scale and by the popular millennial milieu, which adopted them as an emblem of cosmic intelligence, which played a significant role in the early development of 'New Age'. The two audiences therefore encountered each other's literature, and the UFO narrative became the focal point around which millennial conspiracism formed in the late 1980s and 1990s. This sets up the socio-cultural and historical context for the chapters which follow, addressing the post-Cold War period (1986–2010) with which the book is primarily concerned. On the micro level, each of these presents a specific genealogy in which the UFO narrative acts as the primary discursive object between conspiracist and millennial fields. On the macro level, however, each represents a stage within the larger narrative from the end of the Cold War to the present day.

Chapter 4 takes us from 1986 to 1995, and concerns Whitley Strieber, a horror novelist whose 1987 non-fiction work *Communion* popularized the *abductee* narrative in popular culture. I examine the emergence of the abductee narrative at the same time as the Satanic Ritual Abuse scare (SRA) and argue that the abduction narrative was instrumental in popularizing the conspiracist narrative that a section of the US government is concealing from the public the fact that they are working with ETs.

Chapter 5, which takes us from the mid-1990s to the mid-2000s, is an account of the life and work of David Icke, former goalkeeper, television presenter and Green Party politician. Icke is well-known in the UK for publicly claiming to be the 'son of God' in 1991 but is now best known internationally for his theory that reptilian ETs covertly control the affairs of the world by interbreeding with elite families. Icke's ideas developed from a background in Theosophical literature and retains a firmly millennial position today.

Finally, Chapter 6 concerns channeller, writer and musician David Wilcock and takes us up to the present day. Wilcock demonstrates the continuity of the '2012' millennial narrative with earlier 'Aquarian', 'New Age' and 'Ascension' narratives. Moreover, his work demonstrates a tension between appeals to channelling and appeals to the scientific epistemic strategy in order to gain epistemic capital.

The concluding chapter attempts to 'connect the dots' and explain the function of millennial conspiracism. My answer is twofold. Firstly, millennial conspiracist discourse appeals to the full range of epistemic strategies and as such represents a broadened conception of what counts as knowledge. Therefore, in positing that the conspiratorial elites gain power by limiting access to counter-epistemic strategies, millennial conspiracists construct themselves as a *counter-elite*, defined by control of epistemic rather than economic, capital.

Secondly, millennial conspiracism discourse offers an answer to the problem of the failure of the various prophesied golden ages to arrive, by positing that they were *prevented from arriving*. In short, it adds a malevolent – and importantly, occluded – counter-agency to popular millennial narratives. As a result, millennial conspiracism offers a theodicy which reconciles the utopian vision of millennial discourses with the pessimism and mistrust of modern global society which conspiracist discourses demonstrate. In this cosmology, the earth is seen as a literal battlefield between benevolent and malevolent forces – a Gnostic war in which 'the Truth shall set you free'.

Approaching Millennial Conspiracism

The critical study of religion

In a review of Pierre Bourdieu's (1930–2002) *Outline of a Theory of Practice*, an anonymous scholar wrote that 'the most significant feature of his work for the historian of religion is the constant meditation on the epistemology of the anthropological informant and his speech' (quoted in Rey 2007, 128). The purpose of this chapter is to establish a way to ensure that this is what I am doing in my analysis. In analysing my operative terms – conspiracism, millennialism and religion – discursively, I demonstrate their relationship to power structures. As my research demonstrates, the reclaiming of epistemic capital from institutional authorities – religious, epistemological and political – is a recurrent feature of the field. Indeed, the relationship between knowledge and power is constitutive of the whole field. As I shall argue, the fundamental commonality between conspiracist and popular millennial discourses is the appeal to strategies for gaining knowledge that lie outside those accepted by the epistemic authorities, that is, traditional religious institutions and academia. In the second part, I outline five *epistemic strategies* which are encountered in millennial conspiracist discourse, the mobilization of which I demonstrate through Chapters 4, 5 and 6.

Discourse analytical approaches are based on the analysis of the use of language (in the broad sense of systems of communication through symbols) and have become increasingly dominant in the social sciences and humanities since the so-called 'linguistic turn' of the 1960s (Moberg 2013, 4). Underpinning them, however, is the epistemological paradigm of *social constructionism* – that our understanding of reality is constructed in language through our social interactions (Moberg 2013, 6; Hjelm 2014).[1]

Bourdieu's central concern was to challenge studies of society which he saw as either placing undue emphasis on the rational, conscious choices of individuals or, alternatively, reducing individuals to 'simple epiphenomena of structure' (1998, viii). Rather, he understood society as a network of temporal relations between individuals, a constant negotiation between the individual and the social. As Rey puts it, 'Bourdieu's theoretical project is a critical scientific analysis and explanation of the social influences on what people do and why they do what they do, and of how what they do contributes to the reproduction of these very social influences' (2007, 40). Indeed, Bourdieu attempted to bridge the epistemological divide between the subjective and the objective in the social sciences and 'to move beyond the antagonism between these two modes of knowledge, while preserving the gains from each of them' (1990a, 1).

Bourdieu's approach, often referred to as his 'theory of practice', can be reduced to three fundamental and interrelated concepts – *field, capital* and *habitus*. Bourdieu envisaged culture as a multidimensional space in which all factors which differentiate different individuals – or *agents*, as Bourdieu generally preferred – from one another may be plotted. Elaborating upon the work of Marx, Bourdieu named these differentiating factors *capital*. Capital can be understood as specific knowledge and/or skills that confer power within a particular discourse, and which individual agents compete over. In advanced societies, Bourdieu writes, the two principal factors of distribution are *economic capital* and *symbolic* (or *cultural*) *capital* (1998, 6). Economic capital is simply how much wealth a person has; it is therefore a measure of the ability of that person to influence other agents in the field, for example by paying them to work for their aims, employing the best teachers and lawyers and purchasing companies and therefore affecting their output. Symbolic capital, on the other hand, refers to knowledge and skills. Specific knowledge and skills – for example, skill with a musical instrument or weapon or knowledge about art history or pop music – may confer advantages in particular fields in particular societies. Although there may be practical advantages to these skills or knowledge, for example knowledge of hunting in a society where food is scarce, this is not what concerned Bourdieu. Rather, the symbolic capital of hunting skills would come from being perceived as an authority in a field in which such skills are highly regarded; for example, the ability to eloquently discuss art would be a form of cultural capital that could confer status, and therefore power, in middle-class groups (Barker 2004, 37).

To this, Bourdieu later added social capital, which he conceived of as consisting of resources generated through a 'durable network' of interpersonal relations (1985 248; c.f. Bourdieu 1980; Montemaggi 2011, 69). Thus social capital is power through *who*, rather than *what*, one knows or one's ability to purchase influence. Putnam influentially described social capital as a kind of 'connective tissue' holding societies together, thus normatively constructing it as an analogue of 'civic virtue' (2000, 19).

To this triumvirate, I add *epistemic* capital. Maton describes epistemic capital as 'the way in which actors within the intellectual field engage in strategies aimed at maximising ... epistemic profits, that is, better knowledge of the world' (2003, 62). Maton introduces the term in an attempt to mobilize Bourdieu's call for *reflexivity* in the social sciences – that is, to make visible the 'objectifying relationship between subject and object, knower and known' (2003, 57). However, I think the concept can be usefully utilized to map out not a sub-set of symbolic capital but a third axis (or dimension?) in the broader cultural field. Epistemic capital, in this instance, does not map *what* you know but *how* you can know. In academia (theoretically, at least), epistemic capital is accrued through the appeals to science and reason, but in many other fields, appeals will be made to experience, tradition and supernatural agents such as gods or extra-terrestrials. Actors in the millennial conspiracist field jostle for control of epistemic capital through such strategies, as well as admonitions as to how the scientific and academic authorities are restricting purported evidence countering materialism. This is all essentially to establish that they are able to draw from a larger source of information than 'the mainstream'.

Bourdieu called these areas of culture in which specific forms of capital are the differentiating factor *fields*. It is only within a specific field that specific capital acquires its value; the relative claims which groups or individuals hold over these forms of cultural capital constitutes their positions within the cultural field. According to Bourdieu, fields are hierarchical: the contemporary religious field is itself within the contemporary cultural field, and so on. They may also overlap, as in the present case, where the field of millennial conspiracism overlaps with the religious field. The field is both a field of forces, whose necessity is imposed on agents who are engaged in it, and a field of struggles within which agents confront each other, with differentiated means and ends according to their position in the structure of the field of forces thus contributing to conserving or transforming its structure. (1998, 32)

The mechanism by which the field is both imposed upon and reproduced or transformed by the agent was named *habitus* by Bourdieu. While habitus is generally translated as 'disposition' and sometimes as 'tastes', it is perhaps clearer to consider words with which it shares an etymological root: habit, habitat or habit, as in a monk's garments. Although we remain generally unconscious of it, our habitus

Make[s] distinctions between what is good and what is bad, between what is right and what is wrong, between what is distinguished and what is vulgar ... Thus, for instance, the same behaviour or even the same good can appear distinguished to one person, pretentious to someone else, and cheap or showy to yet another. (1998, 8)

In Bourdieu's model, individuals in the same socio-economic class will share similar habitus because they share many formative experiences, the dynamics of their family lives and the occupation and political convictions of those they interact with, for example. While the field represents a structure within society, the habitus is an incorporated structure – that is, the underlying and largely unconscious set of value-judgements that the individual draws upon to guide their actions and choices. Yet the habitus also allows for the individual and the field in which they are engaged to be involved in a dialectical relationship. The individual internalizes the rules of the field through their habitus, yet it is the actions of the agents within the field which define those rules. This is what Bourdieu refers to when describing his overall approach as 'generative structuralism' (Bourdieu 1990b, 14); through our habitus, fields have power over us as agents, but at the same time, our actions as agents shape the fields. Ultimately then, Bourdieu's analysis is an analysis of power. All fields are examined in their relationship to the broader *field of power* (Rey 2007, 55). In monopolizing the specific capital of a field, an agent is then able to exert power over the other agents in the field.

This concern with power relations links Bourdieu to Michel Foucault (1926–84) who argued that the epistemological categories by which we order the world are ultimately instruments of power, through which the social order is maintained. His argument was based on analysis of *discourses*, that is, of groups of statements sharing a common object, concept, theoretical theme and/or discursive style (Foucault 1969 [2002], 41). Burr defines discourses broadly as 'a set of meanings, metaphors, representations, images, stories, statements and so on that in some way produce a particular version of events' (2003, 64). Foucault himself defined a discourse more specifically as 'the group of statements that belong to a single system of formation; thus I shall be able to speak of clinical discourse, economic discourse, the discourse of natural history…' (1969 [2002], 121). Underlying all of these definitions, however, is the social constructionist paradigm that our language does not merely *represent* pre-existing 'things' but rather *constructs* them.

Furthermore, discourses are not static but 'constantly mutate and cross-fertilize' (Moberg 2013, 10), and Foucault sought to uncover discontinuities and disagreements within specific discourses that led to transformations in how the object or concept in question was understood. For example, *Madness and Civilisation* (1977) considers the transformation of insanity during the eighteenth century – how the insane came to be construed as ill and their subsequent incarceration. These developments were not a necessary and inevitable part of the evolution of society along rational lines but rather, a reflection of the increasing institutionalization of society and its appeals to positivism:

> What we call psychiatric practice is a certain moral tactic contemporary with the end of the eighteenth century, preserved in the rites of asylum life, and overlaid by the myths of positivism. (1977, 14)

Foucault described his approach as an *archaeology*, as opposed to a *history*, of ideas (1969 [2002], 151). As in an archaeological dig, where each strata uncovered reveals new structures built upon the old, so we see each strata of the idea as a new development, adaptation, appropriation or embellishment (1969 [2002], 23). The task of the scholar, then, is to dig out the field, disputes and all:

> Rather than seeking the permanence of themes, images and opinions through time, rather than retracing the dialectic of their conflicts in order

to individualise groups of statements, could one not rather mark out the dispersion of the points of choice, and define prior to any opinion, to any thematic preference, a field of strategic possibilities? (Foucault 1969 [2002], 40)

In uncovering these conflicts, and being able to place the adoption of certain strategic possibilities within their broader social context, Foucault sought to demonstrate that all of our knowledge is situated within the field of power, that

> Power produces knowledge (and not simply by encouraging it because it serves power or by applying it because it is useful); that power and knowledge directly imply one another; that there is no power relation without the correlative constitution of a field of knowledge, nor any knowledge that does not presuppose and constitute at the same time power relations. (1977, 14)

Kocku von Stuckrad suggests that Bourdieu's model can be combined with Foucault's to address what he considers to be the problems made manifest in contemporary Religious Studies by the linguistic turn (2003, 255).[2] His suggestion is that religious studies should focus upon the analysis of *fields of discourse*; that is, rather than attempt to define categories substantively, we should focus on analysing 'the public appearance of religious propositions' (2003, 268) and particularly the debates which surround them. Thus, discourses collectively establish the meaning of the cultural capital of fields, which furthermore may 'contain a number of competing and contradictory discourses with varying degrees of power to give meaning to and organize social institutions and processes' (Pinkus 1996).

They furthermore enable *discursive transfers*. In a discursive transfer, the meaning of a particular term is negotiated and often transformed when it becomes part of the discourse of more than one field (von Stuckrad 2005, 85). I here refer to these negotiated terms as *discursive objects* (McCutcheon 1997, 25; Potter and Hepburn 2008, 275).[3] Discursive objects can be differentiated from discourses themselves 'because discourse [...] is about how a certain object is constructed, whereas the [object] is the object of discourse (what is talked about)' (Taira 2013, 29). For example, the discursive field 'shamanism' contains 'healing, soul, nature, therapy, or consciousness' as discursive objects (von Stuckrad 2013, 13). In this book, I analyse how 'UFO' has acted as discursive object in conspiracist and popular millennial fields of discourse, thereby facilitating a discursive transfer between them.

Definitions

Here, I apply this discursive approach to the important terms of this book. It begins with an examination of how 'UFO' has been constructed in different ways, although this is relatively brief, and this narrative is considered in considerably more detail in Chapter 3. Importantly, I apply a critical approach to understanding 'conspiracy theories'. Despite the tendency in academia to construct 'conspiracy theories' as irrational, over-simplistic or ill informed, the category is revealed to be entirely contingent on 'official' or sanctioned accounts by the epistemic authorities. 'New Age' has presented considerable challenges to substantive definitions, but a discursive approach suggests that we can usefully consider 'New Age' as one particular taxon within a broader popular millennial discourse – moreover, a discourse predicated upon appeals to channelled and synthetic counter-epistemic strategies. Finally, I examine the terms 'religion' and 'spirituality' and argue that they too are constructed in relationship to epistemic norms and thus represent a challenge to institutional authorities over epistemic capital.

UFO

The meaning of the term 'UFO' has changed markedly over time. As will be discussed in Chapter 3, the public imagination was seized in 1947 by *flying saucers*. UFO, an acronym for 'unidentified flying object', was originally a military term for any sky-borne object which could not be immediately identified by observers (Air Force Regulation 200–2, 1) but was later adopted by witnesses, researchers and the broader public. For these groups, its meaning as a negative identification declined and its usage as a positive identification of an extra-terrestrial (or otherwise non-human) spacecraft increased (Saler, Ziegler and Moore 1997, ix). This semantic drift reflects the little-noted fact that in 1947 the general assumption was that flying discs were of terrestrial origin, products of secret military tests or unknown natural phenomena, whereas today, the majority of US citizens assume their extraterrestrial origin (Saler, Ziegler and Moore 1997, 6–7).

An important terminological distinction to raise here, however, is to differentiate between *physicalist* and *supernaturalist* interpretations of UFOs.[4] When I refer to physicalist accounts, I am indicating that the account in question views UFOs as physical, nuts-and-bolts spacecraft and by implication, subject to the laws of physics as *currently* understood, including the impossibility of faster-than-light travel and time travel, etc. That this is the *current* understanding of the limits of the universe reflects that, as noted in the literature review, the UFO is frequently constructed as representing the edges of current knowledge, in both emic and etic discourse. The socio-historical development of UFO discourse is examined in depth in Chapter 3, so I will not dwell on it here.

Conspiracism

It is fitting that we owe the term 'conspiracy theory' to Karl Popper, the twentieth century's preeminent philosopher of the conjectural nature of scientific knowledge. In his 1945 work, *The Open Society and Its Enemies, Vol. 2*, he outlines what he calls his 'conspiracy theory of society', namely

> the view that an explanation of a social phenomenon consists in the discovery of the men or groups who are interested in the occurrence of this phenomenon (sometimes it is a hidden interest which has first to be revealed) and who have planned and conspired to bring it about. (1945 [1957], 94)

Apparently prefiguring Keeley's argument regarding occluded agencies (2007), Popper describes conspiracy theories as a 'result of the secularisation of religious superstition', with the gods 'abandoned' and replaced with 'the Learned Elders of Zion, or the monopolists, or the capitalists' (1945 [1957], 95). Although the implied criticism of Nazism is obvious, the reference to 'monopolists' is likely a reference to Communism, which he accuses of peddling a 'Vulgar Marxist Conspiracy Theory' (1945 [1957], 101), that is, a simplification of Marx's more sophisticated theory which sees both the proletariat and bourgeoisie as equally trapped by the capitalist system (1963 [2002], 167, f.n. 3). For Popper, conspiracy theories of society must necessarily fail, because '*nothing ever comes off exactly as intended*' (1963 [2002], 166; emphasis in original). Indeed, Popper saw the very task of the social sciences to be '*to trace the unintended social repercussions of intentional human actions*' (1963 [2002], 460; emphasis in original).

However, the term has had a much broader application in the years since. The approach taken by most scholars, particularly those with a psychological background, states that conspiracy theories should be taken as evidence of mental ill-health, specifically paranoia or irrationality, most influentially in Richard Hofstadter's *The Paranoid Style in Politics* (1964).[5] Such an approach assumes a fundamental difference between proven conspiracies such as Watergate and unproven conspiracy theories such as the moon landing having been faked. This assumption is particularly obvious in the argument by Sunstein and Vermeule, who state that conspiracy theories 'create serious risks, including risks of violence'; that they 'spread as a result of identifiable cognitive blunders'; and propose a programme of 'cognitive infiltration of extremist groups', which appears to involve undercover agents engaging with such groups, either online or in person, and attempting to challenge the factual basis of their beliefs (2008, 1).[6]

Other psychological accounts (notably Kruglanski 1987; c.f. Byford 2011, 141) focus on the 'scapegoating' function of conspiracist narratives – that is, inasmuch as they reinforce group identity through identifying 'the Other' and therefore externalize a group's hostility and culpability. However, such a model sees the conspiratorial group as necessarily marginal and inevitably failed and therefore reproducing etic discourse. A more constructive and even-handed approach is to see conspiracism not as a rationalization of failure but as an attempt to fight back, challenging the authorities over control of epistemic capital, as I shall here attempt.

Others with a more philosophical bent insist that the conspiracy theorist need not be actually ill, but merely irrational, building on Popper's conclusions. Fredric Jameson's oft-quoted description of conspiracy as 'the poor person's cognitive mapping ... a degraded figure of the total logic of late capital, a desperate attempt to represent the latter's system' (1990, 356) is actually an aside in the penultimate paragraph of an essay concerning Marxism and modernity. Like Popper, Jameson is saying that conspiracism is an oversimplification of the complexities of the capitalist economy, perhaps even a degraded version of the Marxist interpretation of the socio-economic system. However, the assumption of stupidity even appears in works which aim to present a critical and disinterested analysis; for example, Byford concludes that the causes of 'the problems of society ... are more diverse and more complex than any conspiracy theorist can imagine' (2011, 156).

Baurmann, on the other hand, writes that conspiracists exist in a state of 'epistemic seclusion' in which only views which agree with one's own come to be trusted, and as a result, dissenting views become increasingly seldom encountered (2007, 161–2). This does not make them more or less irrational than the general public, however: 'Both kinds of individuals trust their authorities on the basis of common sense plausibility, the epistemic rules in their group and the testimony of people whom they trust socially and personally' (Baurmann 2007, 164). Nevertheless, Baurmann stresses that the conspiracist has overestimated the degree to which 'official accounts' are produced by epistemic authorities; rather, 'social knowledge is produced collectively' (2007, 157). To extend this, then, the committed conspiracist has, through an ever-tightening loop of epistemic seclusion, drifted from a position of acknowledging conspiracy beliefs that do not disagree with *most* epistemic authorities (such as Watergate) to acknowledging beliefs which do (such as that ETs were recovered from a crashed UFO in New Mexico). It also must be noted that not all epistemic authorities are created equal. The social knowledge produced by a government would seem to rest on less steady foundations than that of the physical sciences, for example.

Some conspiracy theories are patently untrue, but this is not what leads them to be labelled 'conspiracy theories'. In fact, many now-accepted historical events have at one point been regarded as conspiracy theories. Numerous examples might be marshalled: the US President, Richard Nixon, was complicit in organizing a break-in at the Watergate hotel; the British Intelligence dossier on Iraq's weapons was rewritten to exaggerate the threat posed in order to make the case for a US-led invasion in 2003 (Norton-Taylor 2011); working-class black men were refused syphilis treatment between 1932 and 1972 so doctors could learn about the disease (Jones 1981). In the last decade, the existence of the Bilderberg Group, the use of drones in overseas countries by the US military and the widespread interception of civilian telecommunications by intelligence agencies have all moved from being discussed only by conspiracists to widespread coverage by mainstream news media outlets. On a more mundane level, political 'spin' – how a party regulates its public image through control of how information is released – is now a ubiquitous part of popular discourses on politics. Olmsted goes further; popular conspiracy theorizing was a direct result of the tendency of the US government to posit conspiracies plotting against the American people, be they Germans, communists or Iraqi terrorists (Olmsted 2009, 9).

Moreover, a conspiracy theory cannot be taken simply to mean a theory which alleges a conspiracy. Conspiracy can be defined simply enough: it is 'an agreement between two or more persons to do something criminal, illegal, or reprehensible' (Oxford English Dictionary) or more simply, '1. the act of plotting in secret. 2. a plot' (Chambers English Dictionary). However, to take one example, both the official and conspiracist explanations of the events of 11 September, 2001, involve conspiracies as thus defined, yet the Al Qaeda theory, as presented by the 9/11 Commission report, is never referred to as a conspiracy theory (Coady 2007a, 132). In other words, a theory concerning a conspiracy in not what constitutes a 'conspiracy theory', and we cannot, therefore, define a conspiracy theory substantively, that is, by its contents (Pigden 2007, 222).

Rather, as suggested by the preceding example, the term's ultimate function is *rhetorical* (Coady 2007b, 202; Pelkmans and Machold 2011). In the wake of 9/11, President George W. Bush stated, 'let us not tolerate absurd conspiracy theories', firstly underlining my argument that although the official version of events itself posited a conspiracy in the legal sense by Al-Qaeda, it represents an epistemic norm and is therefore not a 'conspiracy theory'; secondly, and more importantly, implying that a good citizen should never question the government. As employed in political discourses, then, a conspiracy theory is understood to be 'an explanation that conflicts with the account advanced by the relevant epistemic authorities', and therefore the term is ultimately concerned with power (Levy 2007, 181; Sapountzis and Condor 2013, 732). Hofstadter's attempt to label any challenge to epistemic norms as pathological was in effect 'an excuse for neglecting, equating and even repressing political protest of all sorts' (Fenster 1999, 21). In short, by labelling an account a conspiracy theory, epistemic authorities including governments and scientific institutions seek to marginalize that account by portraying it as inherently irrational.

Rather than irrational, superstitious or anti-modern, conspiracy theories should perhaps be understood as a direct product of the ongoing process of modernity (Aupers 2012). The modern scientific approach which the Enlightenment established rests on both 'the inductive accumulation of proofs' and 'the methodological principle of doubt' (Giddens 1991, 21), and scepticism has been an intrinsic part of the process of modernization. For Aupers, conspiracy theories are 'a radical and generalised manifestation of distrust that is deeply embedded in the cultural logic of modernity' (2012, 24). Similarly, Latour sees in conspiracism a watered-down version of critical social theory:

> What's the real difference between conspiracists and a popularized, that is a teachable version of social critique inspired by a too quick reading of...Pierre Bourdieu ...?...in both cases again it is the same appeal to powerful agents hidden in the dark acting always consistently, continuously, relentlessly...I find something troublingly similar in the structure of the explanation, in the first movement of disbelief and, then, in the wheeling of causal explanations...it worries me to detect...many of the weapons of social critique. (Latour 2004, 229–30)

As Aupers suggests, academic studies which condemn conspiracy theorists as *a priori* irrational are an attempt to reclaim epistemological authority for the academy by drawing a rigid boundary between good, objective, rational science and its supposed bad, subjective and irrational counterparts (2012, 24). In fact, value judgements about what is sane, rational, 'true' or otherwise should have no place in the study of cultural meaning, and this is a strong reason to consider conspiracy theories from a Religious Studies perspective. In theory at least, Religious Studies scholars are specialists at 'bracketing off' truth claims, and as such, this book will contain no attempts to evaluate the truth or otherwise of particular conspiracy theories or ET contact. Indeed, my discursive approach prevents me from doing so. Rather, my concern is to, firstly, present a nuanced and historically located description of this field and secondly, to attempt to account for its popularity by considering how it serves its subscribers.

Therefore, I cannot use the term 'conspiracy theory' in good conscience. I shall therefore use Barkun's terms *conspiracy belief*, denoting a discrete unit of belief (that, for example, '9–11 was an inside job') and *conspiracism* for a world-view made up of a number of interconnected conspiracy beliefs. Barkun defines a 'conspiracy belief' as the belief that 'an organisation made up of individuals or groups has acted or is acting covertly to achieve some malevolent end' (2003, 3). When unpacked, this definition consists of three factors: (1) that an individual cannot constitute a conspiracy alone; (2) it must operate in secret; and (3) the thrust of the conspiracy must be to malevolent ends. These 'malevolent ends', of course, are culturally determined and therefore open to interpretation; the promotion of policies concerning centralized world government or gun control may be viewed as benevolent by left-leaning groups, at the same time as forming the malevolent agenda of the New World Order in Right-wing conspiracy beliefs. Conspiracism, on the other hand, underlines that more is involved than simply conspiracy beliefs: conspiracies certainly happen, but conspiracism involves the additional belief that they are the principal motivating force in history (Byford 2011, 34).

'New Age' and popular millennialism

In this book, I employ 'popular millennialism' as an alternative to 'New Age' and other related taxons. In order to understand why, I must first outline the issues with the existing terminology.

The earliest academic accounts of 'new age' sought to construct the category 'New Age' as a 'movement' (Lewis 1992; York 1995; Heelas 1996). Problematically, however, their attempts to create a bounded definition were unconvincing. Heelas' description is loose enough to allow him to include such NRMs as Soka Gakkai and Transcendental Meditation in the category (1996, 63), whereas York's solution is to include 'New Age' under the broader category of the equally ill-defined and loosely bounded 'holistic movement', which includes feminism, Neo-paganism and the ecological movement (1996, 330).

Hanegraaff's *New Age Religion and Western Culture* (1996) was a more theoretically rigorous attempt to establish a bounded definition of the category. Based on an analysis of material drawn from over one hundred books, he conceptualizes 'New Age' as a 'commodified' version of "western esotericism", including a rejection of the strictly dualistic scientific-materialist tendencies of modern western thought (1996, 515–7). Invoking Colin Campbell, he describes 'New Age' as signifying 'the cultic milieu having become conscious of itself as constituting a more or less unified "movement"' (1996, 17). The major trends he identifies as signifying this movement are 1) channelling, 2) healing and growth, 3) 'New Age science' (in which he includes holism) and 4) Neopaganism (1996, 19–20). I would reject this last category, as neopagans have not only a well-defined organizational structure and ritual practice but self-identify strongly, and are thus very different from the diffuse and diverse composition of the milieu as Hanegraaff describes it. Neither channelling nor 'healing and growth' are unique to 'New Age' discourses, and furthermore the final category is tautological; to define 'New Age' as 'that which contains New Age science' is equivalent to defining France as 'that which contains French people'. Therefore, Hanegraaff's definition does not provide any real analytical purchase on the category. However, Hanegraaff's model introduces the distinction between a 'New Age' *sensu strictu* and a 'New Age' *sensu lato* (1996, 98–103). *Sensu stricto* ('New Age' applied in a restricted sense) refers to the early movement of the post-World War II period, closely connected to Theosophy and highly millennial (Hanegraaff 1996, 518). *Sensu lato* ('New Age' applied in a general sense), on the other hand, refers to eclectic, cross-cultural explorations in popular religious beliefs and practices post-1980s.

Sutcliffe's genealogy of 'New Age' (note the quote marks – unlike earlier studies, Sutcliffe is analysing the use of a particular term within a popular religious field, rather than a bounded movement) is broadly in agreement with Hanegraaff's periodization. However, rather than a transformation in the central idea of a movement as Hanegraaff presents it, Sutcliffe argues that the change was due to the term 'New Age' being passed in the late 1960s and early 1970s 'from subcultural pioneers to counter-cultural baby boomers' (2003a, 112). This second generation were considerably younger and had quite different beliefs and aims, and in their writings the construction of 'New Age' shifted from 'apocalyptic *emblem* of the near future' to 'humanistic *idiom* of self-realisation in the here and now'

(2003a, 5). Sutcliffe argues that this transfer of meaning was accompanied by a distinct shift away from a millennial position (i.e. where the 'New Age' was painted as an imminent, cataclysmic event) towards a construction of 'New Age' as a shift in consciousness which individuals had to realize for themselves (2003a, 114–7).

On the other hand, Sutcliffe rejects completely the idea of 'New Age' as an identifiable movement. Sutcliffe argues that 'New Age' cannot be of any use as a heuristic analytical construct because it 'lacks predictable content … and fixed referents' (2003a, 29). That is, if we cannot say what 'New Age' is or is not, nor point to one belief or authority that its adherents have in common, in what sense is the term analytically meaningful at all? Sutcliffe's suggestion is that 'New Age' could be used to signify one discourse within the broader field of Anglo-American *popular* religion: 'the field of religion labelled "New Age" is the popular religion of our own backyards' (2003b, 24).

The problem in Hanegraaff and Sutcliffe's periodizations is that they conflate emic usage ('New Age', a term used in popular millennial discourse) with etic ('New Age' as employed by scholars and the media to describe some broad countercultural movement). Hanegraaff attempts to establish an etic category that changed over time, using a self-selected group of texts of which few even mention a 'New Age'. Sutcliffe, while being careful to differentiate emic and etic usage in the early post-war historiography, nevertheless seems to shift focus from emic to etic as his thesis shifts from 'emblem' to 'idiom'. However, if we focus entirely on emic usage, any identifiable 'New Age' discourses have largely disappeared by the 1980s. Etic usage has since applied the term to all manner of popular religious practices, alternative health therapies and even travelling communities, despite the lack of a clear definition.

I suggest here, therefore, that studies of 'New Age' could usefully be refocussed as analysing a particular popular millennial discourse, as its name would suggest (Mayer 2013, 263). I conceptualize 'New Age' as one discourse within a larger popular millennial field, which existed before 'New Age' and, as my case studies have demonstrated, continue in the post 'New-Age' world. Therefore, in this book, I refer to *popular millennialism*, a field of discourse in which the nature and immanence of the eschaton is the central concern. By 'popular', I indicate that I am referring to discourse that takes place outside of formal religious institutions and traditions. I am aware that by using 'popular millennialism' where scholars would typically use 'New Age', I risk upsetting preconceptions concerning the category, particularly on those occasions where we are used to reading 'New Age' rather than 'popular millennial'. This is deliberate: by untethering us from our usual terminology, it may be easier to consider the data anew.

I suggest that if my admonition that 'New Age' be abandoned as an academic category is heeded, we might avoid on the one hand making overly broad statements about the novelty of the field, and therefore its social implications, but on the other hand allow us to usefully extend our analyses beyond the 'New Age' taxon itself.

Prophecy and eschatology

Eschatology refers to narratives which posit an end-point in time (*eschaton*). This may be terminal (i.e. time ends) or transformative (i.e. one period of time ends and another begins). Broadly speaking, eschatological narratives take two forms: the apocalyptic and the millennial. In this book, when I use the term *apocalyptic*, I refer to eschatological systems in which the outcome of the end time is total and destructive, with the righteous being taken up to heaven and the remaining world consumed by flames, for example. Conspiracist eschatologies have typically been apocalyptic, because the narrative is predicated upon the belief that sooner or later the globalist conspirators will achieve their ultimate goal of the suppression and/or destruction of the rest of humanity.

When I use the term *millennial*, however, I refer to eschatologies in which the world is not destroyed but transformed, and a better world is instigated. The term is taken from the Christian prophecy of the return and thousand-year reign of Christ in Revelation; popular millennial narratives include 'New Age', 'Ascension' and '2012'. This terminological distinction is my own; Cohn counts 'apocalypticism' as a form of 'millenarianism' (1970, 19–21), whereas Landes differentiates between 'millenarian' (transformative) and 'eschatological' (destructive) teleologies, with 'apocalyptic' taken to refer to imminentist expressions (2006, 6–13). Neither of these schemas is universally employed, however, and my own distinction, I feel, is simpler and closer to common usage.

Eschatological prophecies are also a prominent feature of conspiracist discourse and have become increasingly millennial since the 1990s (Robertson 2013, 210–11). Although, as Barkun notes, there is no 'systematic connection' between conspiracism and millennialism, they are often connected because '[c]onspiracy theories locate and describe evil, while millennialism explains the mechanism for its ultimate defeat' (2003, 10). An interesting feature of millennial conspiracist eschatology is that it is simultaneously millennial and apocalyptic. The conspiracist apocalyptic discourse is tempered with a more millennial discourse which sees the masses becoming increasingly aware of the conspirators' plan and resisting it. This is frequently described in terms of a Manichean battle between forces of darkness working towards a conspiratorial apocalypse and forces of light working towards a millennial societal transformation. This dialectical eschatology is often referred to in emic discourse as the *global awakening* (Ward and Voas 2011, 112).[7]

Prophecy, the prediction of future events, is inevitably eschatological, that is, concerned with the end of time (*eschaton*). Date-specific prophecies (i.e. those which state that a specific event will occur on a specific date) were a feature of the UFO religions which flourished in the 1950s and 1960s. The Unarius Academy, Ashtar Command and the Aetherius Society all included channelled messages from extraterrestrial Masters predicting imminent cataclysm (Palmer 2004, 20–22). *When Prophecy Fails*, discussed in Chapter 1, describes such a group in detail (Festinger, Riecken and Schachter 1964 [1956]).

Religion and spirituality

At the highest level of discursive analysis, we analyse how the field itself is constructed. As Moberg notes, 'a basic starting point for a discourse analytic approach to religion must be to regard the very category of 'religion' as an 'empty signifier' that has no intrinsic meaning in itself' (2013, 13; c.f. von Stuckrad 2003, 166). It follows then that this book will not offer any definition of 'religion' but takes it as a socially constructed category.

I am concerned with analysing how the category is constructed in millennial conspiracist discourse. Millennial conspiracists make no claims to be involved in a 'religion' nor even a 'religious' discourse. Indeed, the majority of those I have identified reject 'religion' as a tool of the conspiracy:

> Spiritual for me means a reconnection with the One Consciousness, an understanding of our part in the eternal scheme of things and our potential for love and creation. Religion has hijacked spirituality and largely abused its name to build empires of myth and power, engineered and perpetuated by the manipulation of fear and guilt. (Icke 1994a, 12)

As we will see, however, emic sources do partake in a discourse concerning *spirituality*, however, and this is a recurrent feature of alternative forms of popular religion through the twentieth century and into the twenty-first (Sutcliffe 2003a, 213–6). Despite widespread popular and, more problematically, academic usage, no consensus on what 'spirituality' actually signifies has yet to be reached (Flannigan and Jupp 2007; Huss 2014). I suspect Sutcliffe is correct in stressing that its function is ultimately dissident; 'of finding or constructing an alternative to institutional religion' (2003a, 216). In other words, use of 'spirituality' rather than 'religion' is a discursive strategy, given that the spirituality discussed by emic sources frequently concerns supernatural beings and realms, typically considered the standard object of 'religion' in popular and much of scholarly discourse, yet so thoroughly rejects religious institutions.

A corollary to this, however, is to compare how these emic constructions relate to academic constructions of 'religion' and 'spirituality'. Broadly speaking, we can identify two dominant approaches to defining 'religion' in Religious Studies; substantively, in terms of descriptive attributes such as systems of belief or ritual, and functionally, in terms of what religion does for the individual or society. However, if we define religion substantively, that is in terms of specific attributes, a pertinent example being E. B. Tylor's assertion that religion is belief in supernatural beings (1958 [1871]; c.f. Spiro 1966; Cox 2007), then millennial conspiracism is certainly involved in a 'religious' discursive field. ETs could certainly be considered supernatural, and they often are (Robertson 2014); so from this point of view millennial conspiracism could be considered 'religious'. Alternatively, substantive definitions can refer to structural contents like ritual, myth, doctrine, sacred architecture, etc., as in Ninian Smart's *Dimensions of the Sacred* (1996); as

I shall demonstrate, millennial conspiracism possesses an eschatology, a cosmology, a theodicy and an occluded *primum movens*.

Functional definitions, however, as exemplified by Durkheim and Marx, apply much less easily to millennial conspiracism. Outside of websites, millennial conspiracism lacks institutions, and if it could be argued to possess rituals (going to David Icke's events, for example, or 'pilgrimages' to sites like Roswell in New Mexico, although I would not argue this personally), they are incidental, optional and ill-defined. Indeed, it is the case that it is the institutional aspects of religion which are most often rejected in millennial conspiracist discourse, as demonstrated by the quotations above. Although often *sub rosa*, there was a great deal of competing for position within the field between figures like Icke or Strieber with a higher degree of authority, as well as within their subscribers, as I record in my ethnographic chapters. Furthermore, the existence of a millennial conspiracist habitus was clear from both the existence of common assumptions accepted *a priori* (such as that extra-terrestrials exist and are in contact with humans) but differing according to social context (for example that Christian narratives were far more critically received by UK than US individuals).

Therefore, in the millennial conspiracist field, emic uses of 'religion' fit with functionalist etic definitions of 'religion', whereas emic uses of 'spirituality' fit well with emic substantive definitions. This book in fact offers significant supporting evidence that emic discourses are constructing 'religion' as necessarily institutional and doctrinal, as opposed to 'spirituality', constructed as personal and malleable. Therefore, the emic construction of these categories again takes place in terms of the relationship to epistemic norms and the reclaiming of epistemic capital from institutional authorities.

Epistemic strategies

We have established, then, that this book takes epistemology – that is, what we know, and perhaps more importantly, *how* we know it – as socio-historically contingent and tied to regimes of power. Foucault describes such a specific, contingent 'configuration' within the epistemological field an *episteme* (1970 [1966], xxii). Yet the hegemony of one episteme implies the existence of other 'epistemes' which 'may co-exist and interact at the same time, being parts of various power-knowledge systems' (von Stuckrad 2010, 159). To build on the concept of epistemic capital, then, I must demonstrate that there are different epistemes in operation in contemporary Anglophone culture. These epistemes – knowledge systems – must therefore allow differing strategies for the accessing of knowledge, and in this section, I outline five specific strategies I have identified. These will be demonstrated in the case studies that follow, and I reconsider the specific uses of these strategies in the conclusion in more detail.

Put simply, epistemic strategies are used to defend and construct the object, and different strategies mobilize different forms of epistemic capital. When an individual cites research or invokes personal experience in an argument to persuade others, they are mobilizing particular epistemic strategies in order to gain epistemic capital within the field. Yet the particular strategies which are acceptable is contingent on the particular field in which the discourse takes place; channelling, for example, may be taken as authoritative in millennial conspiracist discourse but may actually decrease authority in academic discourse. Indeed, academic discourse is – in theory, at least – entirely predicated upon the scientific discursive strategy; in society at large, however, *tradition* may be appealed to as often in practice, due to the continuing influence of religious institutions, civil institutions including the law and political parties and identification with ethnic or national labels. Furthermore, the particular degree to which these various strategies are mobilized will vary significantly according to socio-historical context. In short, in each context, certain strategies are supported by the epistemic authorities, and others are not; I here term these *counter-epistemic* strategies. It should be pointed out, however, that counter-epistemic does not necessarily indicate a minority position; surveys consistently indicate a high degree of belief in paranormal phenomena (Newport and Strausberg, 2001; Moore, 2005), and belief in reincarnation is very broadly attested even within Christian congregations (Stringer 2008).

Olav Hammer's *Claiming Knowledge* (2001) outlines three strategies frequently employed in what he labels the 'Esoteric Tradition'; tradition, science and experience (44–5 and ff.). The following section builds off his model but elaborates upon it by adding two further strategies; *synthetic* and *channelling*. The first two (tradition and science) are strategies which are most typically mobilized in western Anglophone discourses and should be familiar to my readers; the latter three, however (experience, channelling and synthetic), I refer to collectively as *counter-epistemic*: that is, they are strategies which are rejected by the epistemic authorities of the contemporary Anglophone world.

It will be noted that there is no specific 'religious' (or for that matter 'spiritual') epistemic strategy listed here. This is deliberate; as discussed above, I am not concerned with any substantive definition of 'religion' or 'spirituality', instead seeing them as categories which are constructed in various ways and to various ends by various groups at various times. However, these constructions almost always appeal to the strategies of *tradition* and *experience*; the former is prominent in both functionalist etic definitions and emic constructions of 'religion' and the latter in some substantive etic definitions of 'religion' and emic constructions of 'spirituality', as we will see.

Tradition

In many ways, appeals to tradition underlie every human society. Systems of law, government and economy are generally founded on tradition, whether explicitly (e.g. UK law being founded on Roman law and the Magna Carta) or implicitly (with economic systems building on previous systems rather than being periodically reconstructed from the ground up). Perhaps the most obvious example of a discourse which employs the strategy of tradition, however, is 'religion'; not only do we talk of 'religious traditions' but the etymology of the world 'religion' itself is sometimes said to derive from *relegere*, meaning to reread or retread and thus implying traditions of behaviour or thought.

Appeals to tradition necessarily involve the construction of histories. As already mentioned, and demonstrated often in the case studies that follow, emic histories in the millennial conspiracist field can be markedly different from etic historiographies of the same period. Most obviously, ancient alien discourses construct historical narratives which stretch back to the very beginning of human culture and even further in some cases (e.g. Sitchin's *Twelfth Planet* [1976] and sequels).

Conspiracist narratives frequently appeal to historical precedent, for example arguing that the existence of 'false flag' attacks in history makes their existence in the present more likely. Appeals are made to forerunners of those who 'see through' the conspiracy too, often including claims that they were silenced for it; notably for this book, the Gnostics are frequently cited as such a case.

In all of these cases however, whether counter-epistemic or reproducing epistemic norms, the basic thrust is towards creating a grand narrative in which the epistemic position of the individual or group is not contingent but inevitable;

> Behind the construction of traditions lies a grand totalizing project aimed at showing that the local traditions are mere reflections of a *philosophia perennis*, an ageless wisdom. (Hammer 2001, 44)

Scientific

It is almost redundant to point out that in the supposedly secular modern age, appeals to science and rationalism are the primary strategy encountered in popular discourse. However, it is also the case that many of these appeals are in fact appeals to tradition rather than science per se, as what legitimately distinguishes 'science' from other epistemic strategies is not always understood.

Although there have been a number of proposals for how to demarcate science, none of them have been an unproblematic match with commonsense understandings (Dolby 1979, 9). Karl Popper's thesis that science could be separated from metaphysics through the *falsifiability* criterion has the most support today; he suggested that only claims which could potentially be falsified – that is, that evidence which would disprove the claim could be posited – were legitimately the purview of scientific inquiry (1959, 78–92). Nevertheless, Popper's model is not without problems. Firstly, anomalous experimental results that appear to falsify theories are regularly rejected when the weight of other evidence is against them; and secondly, there are numerous claims that could be falsified in many non-scientific discourses, including the established religions, alchemy, astrology, and so on, and by Popper's criteria, these would count as scientific (Gordin 2012, 8–9).

Despite frequent claims to the contrary, conspiracy beliefs and millennial narratives typically present themselves as falsifiable and make clear appeals to scientific legitimacy. Indeed, a date-specific prophecy is the epitome of a falsifiable claim. Yet as I argue, these claims are bolstered with epistemic capital drawn from other sources; discourses on occluded agencies of whatever variety can be constructed through appeals to experience, channelling or synthetic knowledge, even when they cannot be through science. Their epistemology is not anti-rationalism per se; rather, scientific rationalism is simply one of a number of sources of epistemic capital from which they can draw.

Indeed, many of the popular texts in alternative culture during the high-water mark of 'New Age' discourse were similarly concerned with the putative line between scientific inquiry and other epistemic strategies; for example, Capra's *The Tao of Physics* (1975), Bohm's *Wholeness and the Implicate Order* (1981) or Zukav's *The Dancing Wu-Li Masters* (1979). The academic merits of these authors vary, but they certainly represent a popular concern with what science can – or perhaps more importantly, *cannot* – explain. As noted in Chapter 1, the UFO is frequently wielded as a symbol of such epistemic uncertainty, representing an emergent tension in western thought between absolute faith in scientific rationalism and continuing beliefs in 'things that science rejects as "merely" subjective or, at worst, as serious threats to the intellectual progress and continued well-being of humanity' (Denzler 2001, xvi–xvii). UFOs, therefore, represent the position that scientific materialism is fundamentally limited in its ability to explain reality.

Importantly, however, Asprem notes that such popular appeals to science undergo significant changes in their transmission from the academic to the popular fields of discourse. As he argues, the more counter-intuitive an idea, the less likely it is to be transmitted into popular religious discourse. At the same time, more complex ideas are reduced to illustrative metaphors, which are then retransmitted, further simplifying the discourse. These ideas are then married with existing theologies into new systems of meaning-making (Asprem 2015).

Experiential

A third major discursive strategy is to make appeal to personal experience. UFO, spiritual and conspiracist accounts all place enormous import upon eyewitness accounts. Essentially, the argument states that, as I have had an experience which defies scientific rationale, science is either wrong completely or fails to take some things I *know* to be correct into account. In such accounts, typical of millennial conspiracism, experience actually trumps simple scientific positivism. Arguably, this epistemological position is not so unusual. In contemporary consumerist society, individual experience is central, so for these individuals, personal experience can override collective facts. Hammer considers this discursive strategy to have grown in importance in recent decades:

> Only within the latest generation of Esoteric thought has personal experience risen to the fore as a major discursive strategy – perhaps *the* major discursive strategy. (2001, 339)

However, he adds:

> Any claim that such an experience 'should' be interpreted in one specific way is imbued with rhetoric and power over discourse. (Hammer, 2001, 339)

This is an important observation. Experiences do not passively happen to us but gain significance through their *post hoc* construction and that construction will necessarily take place within specific discourses as inculcated through our habitus. As Clancy notes, abduction experiencers typically start out as dubious about the nature of the experience but gradually come to be certain as their exposure to the narrative develops (2005, 52 and 57).

Another aspect of this argument is to take the eyewitness account as proof – if the individual reporting the account can be presented as someone reliable and therefore unlikely to have made it up, this is taken as proof that something *actually* happened to them. This is, of course, not the case; it merely proves that the person *thinks* something happened to them. Nevertheless, appeals to 'insider accounts' – essentially the experiential discursive strategy one (or more) steps removed – are frequently employed in millennial conspiracist discourse. As well as assuming that the first person accounts of others are necessarily authoritative, it assumes that some testimonies are more important than others. Such narratives assume the accounts of a few 'insiders' trump, or at least seriously call into question, the accounts of thousands if not millions of other individuals.

Indeed, conspiracist narratives often begin as rumours, which become 'solidified' over time when they are picked up by the mass media (Byford 2011, 140). A recent example of this was a list of names of influential individuals allegedly being investigated for paedophilia which was circulating on the internet and which was presented to UK prime minister David Cameron on live television. Research on rumour suggests that as well as the social function of providing information that for whatever reason is unclear in the official account, it also functions to make the speaker seem 'in the know', thereby increasing their social and epistemic capital (Byford 2011, 140).

Synthetic

I have described a fourth strategy as *synthetic*, as it involves creating structural-level analyses through piecing together many smaller pieces of information to reveal the 'bigger picture'. However, emic sources often prefer the term 'intuitive'. Often this strategy takes the form of long lists of names of individuals and organizations – often widely separated across time, geography and language – accompanied by their alleged hidden connections, creating a sweeping but highly suggestive narrative – 'connecting the dots' (Dyrendal 2013, 213–4, 218).

As Barkun notes, this is a technique employed by prophets of a certain type who, rather than channel from postulated non-empirical beings, instead read 'signs of the times' in the events of the day (2013, 17). Such individuals' claims are typically referenced with mainstream media sources, albeit often with a somewhat oppositional reading reflecting their particular world-view. Religious texts are also frequently marshalled, claimed as containing hitherto unnoticed prophecies concerning the present day. Michael Drosnin's *The Bible Code* (1997) is perhaps the clearest recent example of this.

Alternative historical narratives, including the *ancient aliens* thesis detailed in the following chapter, are an example of this synthetic strategy:

> Every conspiracy theory provides a narrative to legitimate its account of contemporary society, offering a view of how things got to be as they are. Conspiracy theory provides archaeology in narrative form, locating causes and origins of the conspiracy, piecing together events, connecting random

occurrences to organise a chronology or sequence of sorts, and providing revelations and denouements by detailing the conspiracy's plans for the future. (Mason 2002, 43–4)

Channelling

By channelling, I refer to claims of the direct transmission of information to an individual from a postulated, non-falsifiable source. Examples of such sources include supreme beings (God, Allah) or forces, intermediary beings (angels, spirits, demons) and, particularly relevant here, extraterrestrials. Channelling is typically considered to involve indirect contact, that is, the communication takes place telepathically – directly from mind to mind. However, it is not quite as simple as this. For example, channelled communications with ETs might be constructed as utilizing an advanced technology. In other cases, the channeller may claim to be receiving physical communications with the beings, in the form of meetings or messages via telephone or letters.[8]

These prophetic practises can be related to the prophetic types Barkun identifies, as mentioned above: direct communication from a deity; those who decode messages from the 'signs of the times'; those who channel from a transcendent source other than a deity; and those who make predictions from a the position of 'secular empiricism', such as those warning of environmental catastrophe (2013, 17). Type 1 and 3 are not in any substantive way different; as with his use of 'stigmatised knowledge', Barkun reproduces discourse which prioritizes dominant epistemic positions. Therefore, we can conflate these two types and find that we have three types which correspond to the epistemic strategies as outlined above; 1st and 3rd types, channelling (whether or not from an institutionally-sanctioned agency); second, synthetic; third, scientific.

Each of these discourses is constructed in terms of their relationship to epistemic norms. UFOs are constructed as symbolizing uncertainty about the limits of scientific knowledge; 'conspiracy theories' are constructed as those which challenge 'official accounts'; popular millennialism is predicated upon appeals to epistemic strategies not accepted by scientific or religious authorities; and 'religion' is constructed as limiting and repressive institutionalization of 'spirituality'. This begins to suggest that the underlying commonality between these discourses – the *meta-discourse*, perhaps – is the appeal to counter-epistemic strategies. Therefore the authoritative agents in the field – including Strieber, Icke and Wilcock – are those who have most successfully mobilized these strategies in the accumulation of epistemic capital and most successfully convinced others of the benefit of doing so themselves.

'Trust No-One': UFOs, Conspiracism and Popular Millennialism during the Cold War, 1947–87

'Wonder weapons': UFOs and the Cold War

From Communist secret weapon, to millennial space brother, to abusive abductor to agent of the secret government – the UFO follows broader epistemic trajectories during the years between the end of the Second World War and the end of the Cold War. In 1947, a year and a half after the Second World War ended with the detonation of two atomic bombs, the most destructive technology ever used, Chuck Yeager became the first man to achieve supersonic flight. In the same year, ENIAC, the world's first digital computer, was switched on (Pilkington, 29). For many, it seemed that a new world was emerging.

For some, this new order was a new alignment of the superpowers who had fought the Second World War; with the fascist Axis defeated, the communist bloc became the principal threat and Other for the United States and the UK. As early as August 1945, Churchill had expressed concern in the House of Commons about the UK's allies:

> Sparse and guarded accounts of what has happened and is happening have filtered through, but it is not impossible that tragedy on a prodigious scale is unfolding itself behind the iron curtain which at the moment divides Europe in twain ... I cannot conceive that the elements for a new conflict exist in the Balkans to-day. I am not using the language of Bismarck, but nevertheless not many Members of the new House of Commons will be content with the new situation that prevails in those mountainous, turbulent, ill-organised and warlike regions ... for almost everywhere Communist forces have obtained, or are in process of obtaining, dictatorial powers. (1945)

The rhetoric developed from concern into open opposition, and in April 1947, Democrat Bernard Baruch stated before the South Carolina legislature: 'Let us not be deceived, we are today in the midst of a cold war.' Baruch's statement was followed in June by the Marshall Plan, an ambitious programme of aid to all European countries, announced by former General and newly appointed Secretary of State, George Marshall (Ball 1998, 9). Implicitly, the plan would include the agreement to support both US foreign policy and a free-market capitalist economy. Stalin, not without some justification, perceived this policy as a coalition of capitalist states to marginalize the USSR (Ball 1998, 12). In September 1947, the Soviets launched a new policy directive, advocating a 'no diplomacy' initiative towards the West, and the creation of an Eastern European bloc entirely under Soviet control (Ball 1998, 25). Together, these initiatives would make Europe a political and ideological battleground for more than forty years.

Academic studies of the Cold War – largely western, although this is beginning to change – have vacillated between portraying a heroic US defending Western Europe against an aggressive, paranoid and expansivist Stalinist USSR, and portraying US foreign policy as desiring economic and military domination aiming to isolate and demonize the USSR (Ball 1998, 1–3). Besides the US-centric perspective, these accounts all assume the Cold War to have been a US–USSR conflict. Yet the UK and, latterly, China were also important players, and Berlin was a major site – and with the erection of the Berlin Wall in August 1961, symbol – of the conflict. Furthermore, Korea, Cuba and Vietnam all became theatres where the Cold War played out physically.

The Cold War was fundamentally an ideological conflict between a leftist statist model and a rightist capitalist democratic model. The ideological aspects were echoed in religious terminology of a battle between light and dark, with the United States defending liberty against the 'evil empire'. This Manichean weltanschauung would later facilitate the hybridization of Right-wing 'New World Order' conspiracism with Christian fundamentalism, and the UFO narrative was a primary discursive object in that discourse.

Although some writers have sought to demonstrate that the UFO sightings are a perennial phenomenon, citing wartime sightings by pilots known as *foo fighters* (Pilkington, 6), nineteenth and early twentieth century sightings of anomalous airships (Pilkington, 24–6) or even accounts by Swedenborg (Partridge 2003, 7; Hammer 2001, 288), the narrative as we know it today properly begins in that same year, 1947. On 24 June, deputy Sheriff and businessman Kenneth Arnold flew over the Cascade Mountains in Washington and reported seeing nine silver crescents flying with an odd movement like saucers skipping across water or speedboats in rough water (Saler, Ziegler and Moore 1997, 6 and 133–4). The misreported phrase 'flying saucers' piqued the public imagination, and a flurry of other reports of flying discs began to appear.

One of these would later become perhaps the second most significant event for the later changes of the construction of the UFO narrative within the conspiracist field. On the 14th of June, ten days before Arnold's report, a New Mexico rancher, William W. 'Mac' Brazel, found 'bright wreckage made up of rubber strips, tin-foil, a rather tough paper, and sticks' covering an area some 180 metres in diameter, although it was almost three weeks before he returned and gathered some up (Roswell Daily Record). The following day, 5 July, Brazel went into the nearby town of Corona, where he heard about Arnold's sighting of 'flying saucers' and speculating that one may have crashed on his farm, resolved to inform the sheriff during a trip to Roswell to sell wool on 7 July. Roswell Army Air Field sent two senior officers to Brazel's farm to examine the debris. Like Brazel, they were confident it was not a weather balloon or anything else they could identify and took the debris to the Base for further examination. On the morning of the 8th, a statement was issued by the Base's public relations officer stating that they were in possession of a flying disc, which was unsurprisingly picked up by local and national press. However, in the meantime, the debris was sent to Fort Worth Air Force base, where a weather officer was able to identify it as the remains of a balloon-borne radar reflector, and a second statement was issued, retracting the first (Saler, Ziegler and Moore 1997, 6–9). Although it was not a well-known event at the time, it would later become a central element in the UFO's re-engagement with conspiracist narratives in the 1990s, principally through Berlitz and Moore's *The Roswell Incident* (1980), which alleged that there had in fact been a crash and a successive cover-up by the military.[1]

Flying saucers were certainly a success; by the end of the decade, less than three years later, reported sightings were commonplace and flying saucers were a frequent and popular feature of cinema and television (Partridge 2003, 5). The apex of sightings came in 1952, during which there were 886 reported sightings between June and October, including a well-documented flap over Washington DC, more than the total number to have been reported since 1947 (Pilkington 2010, 79).

Some of this public interest may have stemmed from a resonation with the political situation. During these early years of the Cold War, the US public and their leaders were still reeling from the physical attack on their territory at Pearl Harbour, Hawaii, on 7 December 1941. Japanese submarines continued to patrol US waters, and after several skirmishes with US boats, an oil refinery at Ellwood, California, was shelled in 23 February 1942. This created the impetus for Japanese Americans to be interned. The following night, multiple individuals in Los Angeles reported that they were being attacked by enemy aircraft, the so-called Battle of Los Angeles, an event which has been frequently cited by UFOlogists as evidence of pre-1947 UFO phenomena. However, the photo was heavily retouched, and the recently surfaced original does not show a UFO. Later, we will see that attacks on US soil have had a particularly marked effect on the national psyche, and on their construction of the Other.

It is an under-acknowledged fact that during its first decade, very few interpreted flying saucers as having extra-terrestrial origin (Gallup 1972, 666). In fact, given that the war had ended only two years previously and Baruch's 'Cold War' speech was given less than two months previously, military secrecy was a far more likely explanation for most. In fact, Kenneth Arnold's motivation for reporting his epoch-making sighting was that the craft might be of Russian origin (Kripal 2010, 151); Brazel, who lived close to a military airfield, also assumed that the debris he had found and Arnold's saucers were a secret military project (Saler, Ziegler and Moore 1997, 6). The characteristics of the early flying saucer underlines that they were not thought of as miraculous messengers but rather as 'wonder weapons'; they look like planes but not exactly, they fly like planes but do things planes cannot, they do things that earthly enemies would, such as monitoring military bases. They are beyond contemporary scientific capability *but only just*. Clearly, they represent the limits not of technology but of the popular human imagination.

Although Mao would famously denounce the United States's own wonder weapon, the atomic bomb, as irrelevant to international politics, a 'paper tiger' (Ball 1998, 37), the Soviets were quick to frame the growing Cold War in terms of a struggle over stockpiles of nuclear *materiél*, as reflected in their political rhetoric through the 1950s (Ball 1998, 72). This reached a peak during the Cuban Missile Crisis of October 1962, arguably the nearest the Cold War came to becoming a full-blown nuclear conflict.

Communism was an internal as well as an external threat. In the 1930s, Stalin had created a network of spies in the United States, both Russian and US, and during the Second World War their efforts to infiltrate the projects developing the atomic bomb were ultimately successful (Olmsted 2009, 86–7). As a result, in 1947 the US president Harry Truman signed Executive Order 9835, commonly known as the Loyalty Order, which gave the FBI the mandate to investigate all current and potential federal employees for communist sympathies (Pilkington 2010, 36). FBI head J. Edgar Hoover had long believed that communism was 'the most evil, monstrous conspiracy against man since time began – a conspiracy to shape the future of the world' (quoted in Olmsted 2009, 89), and was determined to expose what he believed to be a vast network of communists working to undermine the United States. The November 1945 defection of Elizabeth Bentley, a Connecticut-born Vasser graduate who had been running a Soviet spy ring since 1943, gave Hoover the apparent means of doing so. The case was entirely based on her testimony, however, so the FBI tried having her work as a double agent, unsuccessfully, as the Soviets were informed of her defection by British double-agent Kim Philby and immediately shut down their operations (Olmsted 2009, 90). She seems to have grown impatient, and in 1948 contacted a reporter from the *New York World-Telegram*, who published her sensational story on 20 July (Olmsted 2009, 94). She testified before the House Un-American Activities Committee (HUAC) the following month, where her testimony would eventually lead to charges against Harry White and Alger Hiss, both of whom plead not guilty, but who were, it is now agreed, in fact guilty of espionage (Olmsted 2009, 95–8). Truman tried to calm the public's concerns, but on 23 September the Soviets detonated an atomic bomb, which was shortly afterwards revealed by British Intelligence to have been the result of information leaked from spies in the United States, including some named by Bentley (Olmsted 2009, 98–9).

The public's concerns were shared by the Republican Senator for Wisconsin, Joseph McCarthy, who used his chairmanship of the Senate's Subcommittee on Investigations to launch a campaign to root out communists covertly operating in the United States – and even worse, atheist communists (Byford 2011, 59). He described a 'fifth column' of communists working within and against the establishment. Thousands working in the arts, the media and academia were 'blacklisted' as 'communist sympathisers'; films were banned, and books were removed from libraries (Byford 2011, 59). In the UK, too, intelligence agencies were monitoring prominent figures for evidence of their Communist leanings.

The post-World War II 'Red Panic' had three consequences of import. Firstly, its narrative of a widespread conspiracy against the American people helped inculcate the conspiracist worldview in broader US culture. Secondly, because the US government were using its greatly enlarged secret agencies to investigate large numbers of the public, the US government and its agencies would increasingly become the focus of those conspiracy theories. US conspiracism began to shift from discussing external threats to discussing internal threats. Thirdly, as Byford notes, it marks a shift towards an Other identified as an ideology, rather than a marginalized group per se (2011, 59). It is clearly more difficult to identify a group through ideological rather than racial – which is to imply, physical – traits and thus the move to the Other as identified ideologically enabled that group's otherness to be implied rather than obvious, and therefore hidden.

McCarthy's rapacious tactics eventually alienated even his staunchest supporters. Thalmann traces how the reaction from Left-leaning academics and journalists against the legitimacy granted to these anti-communist conspiracy narratives led directly to the claim that *all* conspiracy beliefs were necessarily irrational (2014). By the mid-1950s, conspiracist discourse had once again become the currency of small Right-wing groups such as the John Birch Society (Byford 2011, 60; Thalmann 2014, 4–5). Here it would largely stay until the end of the Cold War in the late 1980s. These groups sought to distance themselves from anti-Semitism, whether to broaden their popular appeal or through a genuine reassessment of their earlier position in the light of the holocaust, and internationalist bodies became the new power behind the throne. Boyer charts how the post-war development of international governance bodies and financial agencies led Christian millenarian writers in the United States to be increasingly concerned with global conspiracy (1992, 263–72). Bodies like the United Nations, the Trilateral Commission and the Council on Foreign Relations replaced the Jews, the Communists or the Illuminati (Byford 2011, 60–1); although the names had changed, the discourse largely remained the same.

On leaving office in 1961, President Eisenhower brought this discourse into mainstream political discourse with the following statement:

> Our military organization today bears little relation to that known by any of my predecessors in peacetime … This conjunction of an immense military establishment and a large arms industry is new in the American experience. The total influence – economic, political, even spiritual – is felt in every city, every Statehouse, every office of the Federal government … we must not fail to comprehend its grave implications … In the councils of government, we must guard against the acquisition of unwarranted influence, whether sought or unsought, by the military-industrial complex. The potential for the disastrous rise of misplaced power exists and will persist. We must never let the weight of this combination endanger our liberties or democratic processes. We should take nothing for granted. (1961)

When his successor, John F. Kennedy, was assassinated in Dallas on the 22nd of November 1963, and perhaps unsurprisingly, conspiracist discourses quickly laid the blame at the feet of that newest occluded agent, the 'industrial-military complex'. Interestingly, many of the leading investigators promoting a conspiracy narrative were Left-wingers but were prepared to deal with Right-wing conspiracists in order to get to 'the truth' (Byford 2011, 66–7). Indeed, many of those who alleged that the Warren Commission was covering up a government plot had previously been blacklisted by McCarthy (Olmsted 2009, 137; Byford 2011, 66). Conspiracy beliefs about the assassination are the first point in this genealogy in which conspiracist discourse spreads beyond an exclusively Right-wing sphere of influence. Significantly, a number of these writers (including Jim Marrs and William Milton Cooper) would later incorporate UFO conspiracy beliefs into their work.

Building a New World: UFOs and the 'New Age' in the Cold War

McCarthy and his ilk were attempting to protect the social and political order, but for many others in the immediate post-war years, however, the war was seen as proof of the brutality, stupidity and corruption of western civilization, and their aim was not to defend the old world but to build it anew. Technology was progressing rapidly and was frequently eulogized as offering a utopian vision of a world where it had overcome all problems. In the UK, the National Health Service, arguably the world's most successful social welfare system, was founded in 1946. The United Nations was formed in 1945 with the express aim of preventing international war, 'which twice in our lifetime has brought untold sorrow to mankind', and to promote human rights, social progress and 'better standards of life in larger freedom' (United Nations 1945, Preamble).

For many, this desire to rebuild the world had ramifications which went beyond the merely political. Alternative communities sprang up in the post-war years and shared a belief that western civilization was corrupt and sick (Hanegraaff 2007, 27–8). Within these communities, practices and doctrines derived from Theosophical (and other heterodoxic) traditions merged with a pioneering, anti-establishment spirit to produce what Partridge calls 'the essential features of westernised Eastern spirituality' – that consciousness is the essential spiritual factor of human beings; that it can be transformed by spiritual practices; and that teachers/masters/gurus have achieved this and can guide others (2003, 29).

However, of perhaps greater importance was their strongly millennial leaning, in particular, the idea of an imminent global transformation, typically described as a 'New Age', a term which seems ultimately to have drawn its millennial significance from British Theosophist, Alice Bailey (Hanegraaff 2007, 27–8). Around 1919, she claimed contact with a 'Master' called Djwhal Khul, D.K. or simply 'The Tibetan' and that he had begun to communicate revelatory messages for humanity through her. Bailey and her husband were forced out of the Theosophical Society in 1920 over questions about the validity of these messages and concerns that if genuine they might challenge Annie Besant's authority as leader (Hammer 2001, 65). She continued to claim contact with The Tibetan until her death in 1949, however, and published a series of books describing an elaborate taxonomic schema based on seven 'rays', essentially the spiritual principles upon which the physical world is built (Hammer 2001, 65). She strove to promote an ideal of 'service', developing humans of all races and nations who would promote the Tibetan's plan of the for Earth's spiritual, political and technological development. Her synthesis of Christian and Theosophical discourse developed into a millennial narrative of the imminent return to Earth of the 'Christ Spirit', which would be the dawning of a 'New Age' (Sutcliffe 2007, 68–71).[2]

Perhaps the best-known example of these communities is the Findhorn community in the Scottish Highlands, founded in 1962 by Eileen Caddy, a noted channeller, her husband Peter and their friend Dorothy Maclean. The community began as a single caravan on a patch of waste ground, and the impoverished residents attempted to improve the fertility of the soil through communication with the earth spirits, apparently with some success (Sutcliffe 2003a, 77–9; Chryssides 2007, 8). In the evenings, the group carried out meditations enabling them to act as transmitters and receivers in a telepathic 'Network of Light', a network of groups and individuals working to prepare the planet for Bailey's 'New Age' (Sutcliffe 2003a, 65–6). The Cold War seasoned their millennialism with an apocalyptic flavour, foreshadowing the dialectical millennial apocalypticism of later millennial conspiracist discourse. For Peter Caddy;

> There was a real danger of total nuclear holocaust if the wrong finger was on the wrong button at the wrong time. Planetary crisis on such a scale would affect the balance of the whole solar system, so certain contingency plans had been made by extra-terrestrial beings, among the more desperate of these plans was one in which groups of people were to be evacuated from chosen places around the world. (1996, 161)

In communities like Findhorn, then, the flying saucer narrative was incorporated into 'New Age' discourse through the Theosophical tradition of hidden Masters. The identification of the Masters as potentially extraterrestrials develops during the second generation of Theosophical writing (Hammer 2001, 389; Rothstein 2013). Leadbeater, who was to a large degree responsible for the elaboration and codification of the Masters narrative, claimed to have 'seen Visitors from other systems' (1925, 277). When the theological elaborations came into contact with the Flying Saucer narrative, it quickly developed into the *contactee* movement. The first and perhaps best known contactee was George Adamski (1891–1965), who had a history of involvement with various systems of post-Theosophal metaphysics, including his own Order of Tibet (Hammer 2001, 389–90). From 1953, he began publishing accounts of his contact with and messages channelled from humanoid extraterrestrials. Many contactees claimed physical contact with extraterrestrials, notably Adamski, Billy Meier and Daniel Fry, but channelled messages were and equally and increasingly important method of contact (Hammer 2001, 390–1). Works recording these messages include George van Tassel's *I Rode a Flying Saucer* (1952), Ken Carey's *Starseed Transmissions* (1986) and, pertinently, the *Law of One* series, channelled by Carla Rueckert from 1981 (discussed fully in Chapter 6). As I shall show, many of these communications concerned impending planetary change, whether for good or – increasingly – ill. By the 1960s, UFOs and the channelled messages of their occupants were a common feature of the discourses of proto- 'New Age' communities. In Australia, the Universal Brotherhood community, founded in the 1960s, had a particular concern with UFOs (Heelas 1996, 52–3), as did the Heralds of the New Age in New Zealand, founded in 1956 (Sutcliffe 2003a, 74). Findhorn founder Peter Caddy would often stay at the Edinburgh home of Sheila Walker, secretary of the Scottish UFO society, and the US contactee Daniel Fry was Findhorn's first residential guest (Sutcliffe 2003a, 84–5). Indeed, Sutcliffe notes that the early Findhorn community were similar in many ways to the group studied in *When Prophecy Fails* (2003a, 73). The significance ascribed to UFOs in popular religious discourse of the period is further demonstrated by their incorporation into many of the NRMs which emerged in the post war decade, including Heaven's Gate, the Aetherius Society, The People's Temple and Scientology, and later adopted into the Mark-Age/I AM tradition and the Nation of Islam (Partridge 2003, 13–21). Thus in the post-Theosophical abductee discourse, UFOs were increasingly constructed in a supernaturalist, rather than physicalist, framework.

The second major influence on religious discourse in the immediate post war period, particularly for those leaning to the political left, was Buddhism,

Zen in particular. Buddhism was introduced into western intellectual life by writers including Aldous Huxley, Pierre Teilhard de Chardin and Paul Tillich (Heelas 1996, 46–7) but began to enter popular culture through the writing of the *Beatniks*, or *Beats*. The Beats were particularly drawn to Zen's supposed technology of enlightenment; they wanted to break through the boundaries of everyday western consciousness, and Zen techniques such as meditation and non-attachment promised a means of achieving that. Of course, sex and drugs did too, and were probably practised with greater diligence. In several respects, the Beats foreshadowed the 1960s *Hippie* movement, particularly with their desire to live 'authentically' and according to one's 'true nature' and the resulting rejection of restrictive, 'straight' capitalist society. There are direct connections; for example, Kerouac's roman-a-clef *On the Road* centres on a fictionalized version of Kerouac's friend Neal Cassady, who later became the driver for Ken Kesey's Merry Pranksters and was a prominent character in Tom Wolfe's *Electric Kool-Aid Acid Test* (1968). The major difference was that while the Beats' 'dropping out' implied rejecting the world as illusory, the Hippies were more interested in changing the existing system through protest and creating alternative communities. While the Hippies were millennial to the extent that they believed that they could enact fundamental social change through force of numbers, the overtly imminentist ideas of the original Findhorn community – that UFOs would soon arrive and somehow-or-other help to establish a pacifist, socialist Utopia – became less dominant.

Scholars have tended to argue that the mixture of Theosophical millennialism and channelling with Beatnik drug-induced satori and Zen metaphysics in these communities fostered a significant shift in 'New Age' discourse; 'a "world-denying" eschatology gives way to a "world-affirming" idiom of human potential: apocalypse gives way to self-realisation' (Sutcliffe 2003a, 122). For Hanegraaff, 'New Age' is fundamentally transformed, moving from a millennial *sensu stricto* to a diffuse, worldly *senso lato* (1996, 95–8 & ff.). In other words, it is claimed that millennial discourse began to fall from favour in this field, and personal rather than planetary transformation became the primary concern (Sutcliffe 2003a, 127).

However, if we construct 'New Age' as one discourse within a broader popular millennial discursive field rather than as a discrete field in itself, as this book does, then we can uncover a somewhat different historical narrative. Rather than 'New Age' transforming, the *term* 'New Age' is gradually abandoned in millennial discourse as it is adopted in popular religious discourse more generally. This culminates in what Lewis and others have termed the 'crisis of New Age' in the late 1980s, as discussed below. However, popular millennial discourse continued unabated; it just did not use the term 'New Age' anymore.

As with the UFO narrative, the war casts a long shadow; the *baby-boomers*, the generation born in the post-war decade, was not only larger than its parents' but was the product of a very different set of social circumstances. During these years, the US experienced political dominance, and with it, unprecedented economic prosperity. They were the first to grow up with television and were considerably better educated than their parents (Brown 1992, 91). Furthermore, as the first of three generations not to be decimated due to war, through sheer numbers they were able to affect society to an unprecedented degree. Naturally, the young will reject the values of their parent's generation, and therefore pacifism, anti-capitalism and (of importance) anti-clerical attitudes towards religion were prominent. As a result, these communities began to experience a huge influx of new residents; between 1969 and 1972, Findhorn's resident population grew sixfold, from twenty residents to some hundred and twenty. The new residents were separated by more than just age, and there were clashes over the newcomers' attitudes to appearance, cleanliness and drug use (Sutcliffe 2003a, 118–9).

However, the three-year residency from 1970 to 1973 of the US writer David Spangler, often considered the most influential Findhorn figure after the original founders, sealed the transition of the community to a new generation. Hanegraaff, Sutcliffe and Melton ascribe different significance to this shift. Hanegraaff sees 'New Age' broadening its usage, becoming in his terminology, *sensu stricto* (1996, 94–103); Sutcliffe sees 'New Age' moving from emic 'emblem' to etic 'idiom' (2003a, 122); Melton (2007, 90) and Introvigne (2001) see the abandonment of the 'New Age' as an emic signifier. Yet in each case, they did not construct 'New Age' as inherently millennial. If they had, they would have realized that, no matter what the emic terminology, popular millennial discourse was alive and well. This is of significance to my argument; although the term 'New Age' was of decreasing importance as a signifier, other millennial narratives appeared to replace it. As I shall argue, while Sutcliffe and Hanegraaff were right that the discourses that were popularly and academically being identified as 'New Age' by the late 1970s were significantly different from the term's original emic usage, we should not therefore conclude that millennial discourse had declined in importance. In fact, a tradition of popular millennialist discourse can be traced from the inter-war years all the way to the present day.

UFOs and conspiracism in the Cold War

In 1947, following the passing of the National Security Act in reaction to the new political status quo, the Office of Strategic Services (OSS) became the Central Intelligence Agency (CIA) (Knight 2000, 28). This act, and the numerous intelligence agencies it created, including the Federal Bureau of Investigation (FBI) and National Security Agency (NSA) as well as the CIA, underline that the US government increasingly saw its aims as being most easily achieved by clandestine means, and in effect created what Wise and Ross later dubbed an 'invisible government' (1964, 1–2). The extent of 'black ops' – political operations by these agencies, unaccountable and unknown to the public, both at home and abroad – became clear during investigations in the 1970s and early 1980s, including the Church Committee, the Watergate investigations and the Iran-Contra hearings, which helped galvanize public opinion that the government was conspiring to keep some secrets (Knight 2000, 28–9). Pilkington goes further, claiming that the UFO narrative was entirely a product of the Cold War, a disinformation programme by the Air Force to provide cover for experimental aircraft. He cites the 1952 flap, which peaked with multiple sightings and radar tracking of fast-moving objects over Washington DC on the 20 and 26 July, as an example of the CIA deliberately creating a panic (Pilkington 2010, 78–98).

By 1952, then, the UFO narrative had already undergone a significant shift in construction: from an Earthly, physicalist 'wonder weapon' to an ET physicalist spacecraft. This is not to say, however, that the connection between UFOs and military intelligence in conspiracist discourse ceased – on the contrary. This section presents three examples of how UFO literature increasingly involved conspiracist motifs in the Cold War period: the *abductee* narrative, in which UFOs were alleged to be physically taking humans against their will; the *Men in Black* narrative, in which military intelligence operatives apparently visited UFO witnesses; and the narrative which developed from the alleged 1952 Presidential Briefing on the reality of UFOs, Majestic-12.

Abductee narrative

Contactees claimed to have been contacted by benevolent extra-terrestrials to pass messages to humanity, but during the 1960s a darker version of the narrative emerged. *Abductees* did not claim to have been chosen in order to pass on benevolent messages but for sexually tinged experimentation. By the 1980s, abductee accounts were arguably the most popular narrative in the UFO community.

Two cases in particular formed the basis of the later narrative. Firstly, Brazilian farmer Antonio Villas-Boas claimed to have been taken aboard a spacecraft in October 1957. He had been ploughing fields at night to avoid the fierce sun, and with his brother, witnessed a bright red light which would dart away when they tried to approach it. Two nights later, it returned, and was soon joined by a thirty-five-feet long egg-shaped craft. His tractor engine stopped, and he tried to run but was seized by several beings dressed in shiny overalls and carried aboard. There, he was washed before being seduced by a naked, blonde and apparently human woman, with whom he had sexual intercourse. Afterwards, she pointed to her belly and then to the sky, suggesting to Villas-Boas that she was bearing a half-human, half-extraterrestrial child. He was told to leave, and the ship lifted off. He staggered home, where his sister reported him to have vomited a yellow liquid and have bruising under his chin (Pilkington 2010, 108–10).

A few years later, in 1961, Betty and Barney Hill were driving in the mountains when they saw a bright object which appeared to be following them. They arrived home some two hours later than they had expected. Betty (who, it should be noted, was a long-time UFO enthusiast) soon began to have dreams about being taken on board a UFO, and by 1962 was giving talks locally describing her abduction. In 1963, the couple underwent hypnosis; it took four months for a coherent narrative of what had happened during the two missing hours to emerge, and even then, the account as recorded by John Fuller's bestselling *The Interrupted Journey* (1966) bore little resemblance to that in the hypnosis transcripts (Clancy 2005, 94–8). Nevertheless, the essential features of the abductee narrative are present in the book's account: nocturnal abduction, small, grey aliens with slanted eyes, medical examinations, missing time.

Although Villas-Boas' account takes place in the 1957, it did not appear in print until 1962 and not in English until 1966 in Coral Lorenzen's Startling Evidence, intriguingly the same year that the Hills' account was published. There followed a flurry of similar accounts, mostly from the United States, often involving children, frequently of dubious provenance, generally 'enhanced' through hypnosis and almost always involving imagery from the Villas-Boas or Hill accounts (Rogerson 1994). Clancy claims that abduction reports increased by 2,500 per cent in the two years following the 1975 broadcast on NBC of a TV movie of the Hill case, *The UFO Incident* (Clancy 2005, 99). The abductee narrative entered popular discourse following the publication of Strieber's *Communion* in 1987; I consider the abductee narrative in considerably more detail in Chapter 4.

Men in Black

One of the clearest examples of this connection is the *Men in Black* (MiB) narrative, in which UFO witnesses, contactees and abductees have reported being approached by a pair of darkly dressed individuals who warned them off talking about their experiences publicly. According to this narrative, people who report UFO sightings or contact are shortly afterwards often visited by individuals who identify as or at least appear to be intelligence agents. They tend to travel in pairs, often one male and one female, dress head to toe in black formal wear and drive large black cars. The earliest version of the narrative was reported to *Amazing Stories* days after Arnold's sighting by Harold Dahl, a harbour patrolman from Tacoma, Washington. After seeing five 'flying doughnuts' which emitted a black, molten metal-like material, Dahl was taken to lunch at a diner by a man dressed in black who knew every detail of his sighting and who warned Dahl not to talk about it (Pilkington 2010, 32). *Men in Black* next appeared in the 1956 book *They Knew Too Much About Flying Saucers* by Gray Barker (1925–84). As described by a former collaborator, Barker's talents lay less in historical objectivity than they did in mythic storytelling (Sherwood 1998). Sherwood further accuses Barker of believing the UFO narrative to be essentially a joke, albeit a lucrative one, and describes him as knowingly participating in fabricating material later used by Adamski, John Keel and others (Sherwood 2002). In the wake of abduction narratives in the 1980s, the high strangeness of the MiB narrative is stressed: they move oddly, as though they are themselves ETs or perhaps even 'programmed robots or androids of some sort – or beings under remote electronic control' (Barker, cited in Sherwood 2002); it is often stressed that the outfits retain Cold War fashions even as the MiB narrative becomes more reported in the 1960s, 1970s and 1980s, as though they were somehow out of time. This is significant as it demonstrates how existing conspiracist UFO narratives begin to adopt the more bizarre aspects of the more supernaturalist constructions, in this case the abductee narrative.

Barker's work was adapted into a comic book by Lowell Cunningham, beginning in 1990, which was in turn adapted into Columbia Pictures's 1997 Will Smith vehicle, *Men in Black*, cementing the narrative in popular culture (Westcott 1993).

Majestic-12

During the late 1980s, a number of books by leading conspiracists were published which connected UFOs and New World Order conspiracism explicitly. Over time, these books contributed to the establishment of a vast and complex narrative concerning the secret collaboration of ETs and the military. *The Roswell Incident* (Berlitz and Moore 1980) not only popularized the narrative that a UFO had crashed in New Mexico in 1947 but introduced the allegation that the government had covered it up. The book claimed that a UFO had been hit by lightning over Brazel's farm, producing Brazel's debris, before eventually crashing 100 miles north in an area called the Plains of San Agustin. The crash was alleged to have been observed on radar and that the military quickly arrived to find a crashed saucer, complete with its diminutive humanoid passengers. On the morning of the 8th, a statement was issued by the base's public relations officer stating that they were in possession of a flying disc, which was unsurprisingly picked up by local and national press. The authors allege that the statement, and its swift retraction, was designed to distract attention away from the San Agustin site (Saler, Ziegler and Moore, 6–9).

In 1987, Moore, Stanton Friedman (who had been the principal researcher for *The Roswell Incident*) and television producer Jaime Shandera released an alleged 1952 briefing on UFOs, prepared for President-elect Dwight Eisenhower, known as the Majestic-12 report, or MJ-12, which apparently confirmed and considerably developed their former account (Saler, Zeigler and Moore, 18–19). The briefing, stamped 'TOP SECRET: MAJIC EYES ONLY', concerning the crash, the recovery of four extraterrestrial cadavers and the cover-up controlled by a group called Majestic-12 (Olmsted 2009, 185). Their announcement received wide media attention, coming as the investigation into the Iran-Contra affair was suggesting that conspiracies were operating at the highest levels of the US government and military (Saler, Ziegler and Moore 1997, 18–19). The document was published in Timothy Good's 1988 book, *Above Top Secret* and became a firm fixture of UFO conspiracism for the next decade, including the works of prominent abductees like Strieber (1989; 1995).

However, the MJ-12 document has widely been considered a forgery since Moore's admittance that he had acted as a disinformation agent in his keynote speech at the 1989 Las Vegas MUFON Conference (Vallée 1991, 47). According to Pilkington, Majestic-12 originated with a counter-intelligence operation by the US Air Force Office of Special Investigations (AFOSI) against an engineer named Paul Bennewitz, an Air Force and NASA contractor who had begun seeing UFOs in 1979. Bennewitz' investigations into cattle mutilations in the Dulce, New Mexico, area led to his belief that there were ETs operating in the area from a secret underground military base (Pilkington 2010, 158–9).[3] After Bennewitz informed his employers of his conclusion, puzzlingly the AFOSI decided to begin feeding him faked government documents and other concocted evidence, which continued for more than a decade. Their contact with Bennewitz came through Richard Doty, who was also secretly in contact with Moore, from whom AFOSI received information about new and popular theories in the UFO community. Thus a sort of feedback loop was created in which the relative success of the stories being fed by the AFOSI to the UFO community was reported back to them, along with any narratives from other sources they could work from, which could then be amplified or elaborated further by releasing further faked documents into the UFO community through Bennewitz (Pilkington 2010, 11–13).

Many continued to believe in the existence of the Majestic-12 programme, however, presumably because it fitted their belief that a huge conspiracy was covering-up the existence of UFOs. One particularly influential example was *Behold a Pale Horse* (1991) by Milton William Cooper. The book, a loosely-structured collection of UFO sightings and documents including MJ-12 and the *Protocols of the Elders of Zion*,[4] alleged that the ultimate force behind the conspiracy were the Illuminati, who had been in contact with alien races long before 1947 (Cooper 1991, 76 ff.). He alleged that a total of sixteen UFOs had crashed during the Truman administration, forcing Truman into negotiating a treaty with the ET occupants (Cooper 1991, 200–21). Cooper even managed to include JFK, allegedly assassinated because he had threatened to go public on the existence of extra-terrestrials (Cooper 1991, 215–6). Cooper's story is of particular significance to this book, as it marks clearly a point at which UFOs have become, through the Majestic-12 narrative, perhaps the central discursive object in conspiracist discourse.

So, why did these ever more complex conspiracy narratives appeal to the UFO community at this particular time? Between 1980 and 2000, UFO discourses became increasingly concerned with constructing narratives that combined several discrete conspiracy beliefs into all-encompassing explanatory systems (Barkun 2003, 54–5). I argue that this development was a result of the end of the Cold War, for two reasons. Firstly, the collapse of the Soviet bloc caused conspiracists to look elsewhere for hidden Others, and as I argued above, these were increasingly constructed as an internal threat. The Majestic-12 narrative enabled a construction of the UFO in which the secrecy came not from the ETs but from the government. Secondly, the UFO was now firmly constructed as extraterrestrial in origin, rather than Cold War wonder-weapons, and therefore could be utilized in a wider range of contexts, and on a larger – even cosmic – scale.

As we will see, the UFO material in these conspiracist narratives would lead them to be encountered by individuals already involved with popular millennial discourses, including many who had formerly taken part in 'New Age' discourses and vice-versa. Due to the UFO narrative having a prominent position in both discursive fields, a discursive transfer was facilitated between popular millennial and conspiracist fields. A clear example of this was the development in the 1960s and 1970s of narratives which place UFOs in alternative archaeological discourses, which I discuss next. Not only do they construct conspiratorial 'hidden histories' which implicitly challenge the traditional epistemic strategy of the world religions but increasingly involve popular millennial discourse.

UFOs reconstructed

By the 1970s, the practical realities of space exploration and travel were well understood, and with the end of the Cold War, UFOs were less frequently interpreted as experimental military craft. This section charts the hermeneutic shift in the construction of the UFO narrative has shifted over seven decades, as their pilots have grown more distant, at first coming from other planets, then other stars and finally other dimensions or times. In short, in the face of mounting evidence against physicalist interpretations of UFO as wonder weapons or spacecraft, the UFO narrative has been opened up to more elaborate interpretations which construct ETs more akin to spiritual beings. From an emic point of view, then, the spiritualist hypothesis represents an ever more sophisticated explanation of the phenomenon, the reality of which is taken as self-evident. According to Jim Marrs:

> Back in the 1950s, the burning question among UFO researchers was 'Do they come from Mars or do they come from Venus?' Well, we got a little more sophisticated in the '60s and '70s and '80s, and the question became, 'Well do they come from Zeta Reticula 4, or do they come from Alpha Centauri?' Now it's the 2000s, and now we're even more sophisticated. Now the question is 'Do they come from another planet, do they come from another solar system, do they come from another galaxy, do they come from another dimension, do they come from another time?' (2012)

The 1950s saw the United States and the USSR began to conceive of space as the next frontier ripe for colonization and the Space Race begun. The USSR took an early lead, launching the first geostationary satellite, *Sputnik*, in 1957 and then propelling Yuri Gagarin to be the first human in space in 1961. However, the United States, with the help of Wernher von Braun and other former Nazis liberated by the OSS under the auspices of Operation Paperclip, would eventually prevail by successfully putting a man on the Moon in 1969 (Cadbury 2005, 334–9; Biddle 2009, 127–52). While the moon landing was undoubtedly a political boon for the United States, Neil Armstrong's words: 'A small step for man, a giant leap for mankind', show that for the astronauts, at least, the Space Race was bound up in the post-war dream of building a New World. The photograph of Earth was adopted as a symbol by nascent 'New Age' discourses, most obviously on the cover of the Whole Earth Catalogue and echoed on Icke's *Robot's Rebellion* (1994b). Yet this holistic vision of Gaia undoubtedly caused problems for the physicalist UFOlogist. If it took this much effort – not to mention luck – to travel just to our own satellite, how many orders of magnitude greater would the effort to travel to another planet be? And to what end?

In 1977, the United States launched the two Voyager probes with the express intention of studying the outer solar system. They bore plaques intended to relay information about their progenitors should they encounter extraterrestrial life. They did not, but their mission continues as of 2012, with Voyager 1 poised to become the only manmade object to leave the Solar System. It was therefore demonstrated that UFOs could not originate from our solar system; there were no diminutive green humanoids on Venus. For some, the answer was that UFOs came from nearby stars, rather than nearby planets. By 1969, Special Relativity was becoming well known, however, and with it, the physical impossibility of faster-than-light travel. Although popular science-fiction such as Star Trek got around it in various ways, relativity rendered an interstellar origin for UFOs extremely unlikely due to the length of time such journeys would necessarily take. Two alternative explanations seem to have suggested themselves. If UFOs come not from nearby planets or stars, could they come from other parallel realities? Alternatively, perhaps they were not extraterrestrial at all?

For example, some (including Strieber) suggested that the occupants of UFOs might be time-travelling humans, from far in humanity's future. As Pilkington notes, if one can accept the central premise, it offers explanations to several odd features of the UFO narrative, such as reports of human beings aboard UFOs, why they are monitoring us and why they might want to stay hidden (2010, 270–1). Jung's mythological interpretation, as detailed in Chapter 1, presents an alternative human-centric explanation. Jung understood flying saucers as expressions of archetypes found in the human collective unconscious and projected out onto physical reality. In Jung's interpretation, 'flying saucers' thus were being created – albeit unconsciously – by their human observers.

Jacques Vallée's interpretation, on the other hand, was *de-mythological*. While Jung sought to interpret the UFO phenomenon through traditional religious or mythical symbolism, Vallée inverted this to interpret traditional religious or mythological phenomena through the symbolism of the UFO phenomena (Kripal 2010, 162). For Vallée, UFOs and the beings of myth were one and the same, but not because UFOs were mythological but because they were physical. In this sense, Vallée's work follows Immannuel Velikovsky's *Worlds in Collision* (1950), which argued that the Genesis and Exodus describe a comet passing close to the Earth before settling into a solar orbit as the planet Venus and thus argued that it was a misunderstood historical account rather than mythology.

Vallée had a background in astronomy and computers but also in science fiction. His first novel, *Sub-Space*, won the Jules Verne prize in 1961, when Vallée was only 21. Vallée gained a PhD in computer science in 1967 but was described as a 'mystical man' by his latter employer J. Allen Hynek, a sceptical astronomer and academic (Kripal 2010, 150). Through Hynek, between 1963 and 1967 Vallée worked for Project Blue Book, the US Air Force investigation into UFO sightings, which ran from 1952 to 1970, albeit in an unofficial capacity (Kripal 2010, 152). He made his name in the UFOlogical community with 1969's *Passport to Magonia: From Folklore to Flying Saucers*, which argues for the numerous similarities between UFO encounters and encounters with supernatural beings earlier in previous eras. In UFOs, Vallée found a materialist explanation for spiritualist and mythological phenomena in history. Rather than creating new gods to suit the technological age, as Jung had suggested, Vallée argued that we had simply interpreted the same physical phenomena in a way which suited our epistemology at any given time (1975, 140). Vallée argues that as space travel had only recently become a possibility, earlier accounts could not have been interpreted as extraterrestrial craft. However, he claims that narratives of aerial beings communicating with humans, and sometimes abducting them, predated 1947 (Kripal 2010, 161).

Vallée also makes the radical suggestion that physically real UFO incidents may be staged; ETs may be messing with our heads, deliberately. 1975's *The Invisible College* suggests that 'UFO appearances may be part of a huge 'control system', a kind of mythological thermostat on the planet designed to adjust and control the belief systems of entire cultures over immense expanses of time' (Kripal 2010, 169). Vallée is never clear about the nature of that outside force, but it was certainly some kind of cosmic intelligence. It also seems that he was certain that the outside force was largely interested in problematizing scientific-materialist epistemology. Vallée, like many later writers on UFOs, rejected a strict dichotomy between science and religion (Kripal 2010, 144–5).

Vallée's work is particularly important in this book, as he was the originator of the discursive shift from physicalist to supernaturalist constructions, which saw UFOs increasingly seldom described as interstellar craft. He was a major influence on Strieber, who provided a foreword to Vallée's first post-*Communion* work, *Dimensions: A Casebook of Alien Contact* (1988). The book was the first in a trilogy meant as a summing-up of Vallée's work, continuing with *Confrontations: A Scientist's Search for Alien Contact* (1990), and concluding with *Revelations: Alien Contact and Human Deception* (1991). This latter work concerns conspiracies in the UFO milieu, both to cover genuine phenomena and to engineer fake sightings to manipulate public opinion. The first part concerns alleged crashed saucer stories, including Roswell (which he rejects) and the MJ-12 papers, which he similarly rejects as being a hoax executed by the intelligence services (1991, 39; c.f. 1979). He claims that he, Allen Hynek and Jenny Randles were approached to leak information in support of the MJ-12 narrative by intelligence operatives, but refused (Vallée 1991, 178). He had earlier claimed to have seen physical evidence of UFO activity in France being systematically destroyed (Vallée 1992, 48; Kripal 2010, 148). He concludes only with the admonition that, while the UFO phenomenon is real, the Majestic-12 narrative is a deliberate falsehood designed 'to convince the world that we are being threatened from outer space' (1991, 236).

Strieber's *Communion* (1987) also cemented a second subtle shift in the alien hermeneutic; not only were space travellers no longer from nearby planets, they had also changed appearance. The archetypical 'little green man' was now a little grey man with large, slanted eyes, perhaps representing their more shadowy nature, both in terms of their nefarious nocturnal activities and the epistemic uncertainty they seem to have come to represent, some grey area between scientific knowledge and intuitive knowledge. Undeniably, the shift recognizes a change in the way the public were conceiving of ETs, and I suspect that it was that they were increasingly likely to be constructed as inter-dimensional rather than interplanetary travellers. Certainly, the iconic image on the cover of Strieber's *Communion* was both a major marketing success and a catalyst for images of the ET in the future (Figure 3.1).

Ancient aliens

What about images of ETs in the past? If they were secretly operating in the 1980s or 1940s, could they have been operating in secret before this? An alternative demythological interpretation entered popular culture with the 1968 publication of *Erinnerungen an die Zukunft*, published in English the following year as *Chariots of the Gods?*, Erich von Däniken echoed Vallée's thesis of UFOs as a perennial phenomenon and that extraterrestrials have interacted with humans in the past. For von Däniken, extraterrestrials flew to Earth in flying saucers in prehistory, and their interactions with ancient humans are recorded in what are now interpreted as interactions with gods. The book claimed that certain archaeological sites were impossible to construct and therefore evidence of ET technology in the ancient world, while others were claimed to show prehistoric depictions of astronauts. Interestingly,

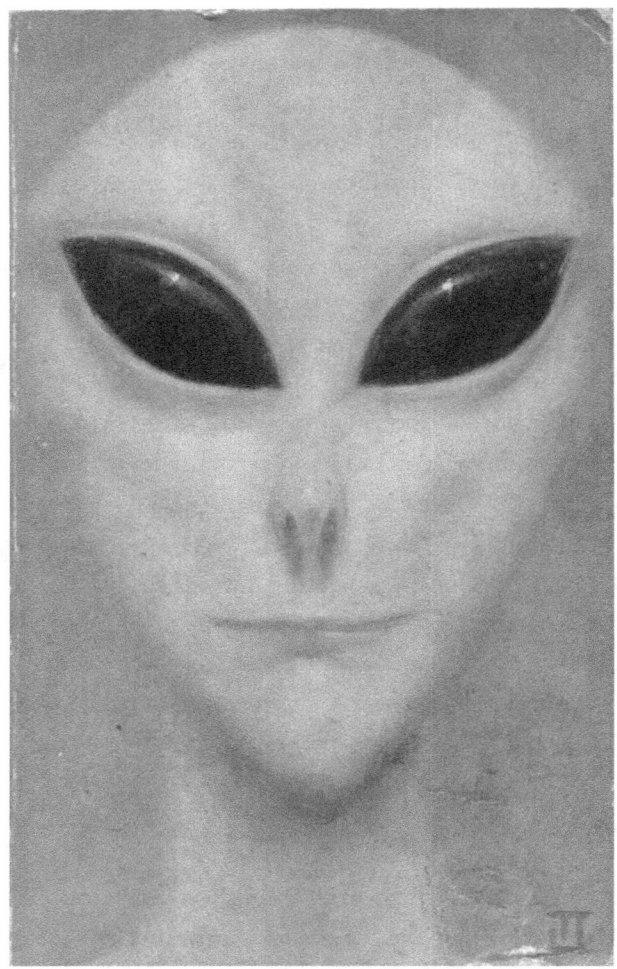

Figure 3.1 Painting by Ted Jacobs, from the cover of *Communion* (1987). Walker & Collier, Inc. Reproduced with permission.

von Däniken's images show *astronauts* rather than ETs per se, focussing on a very familiar and contemporary physicalist vocabulary of space suits, helmets and rockets, once again demonstrating that ETs represent the limits of *human* imagination.

Von Däniken's work, like Emmanuel Velikovsky's *Worlds in Collision* (1950) before him, seem to demonstrate a shift in the discourse about the boundaries of 'science' and 'pseudoscience' during the Cold War. From the 1950s, what he calls the 'pseudoscience wars' increasingly demonstrate 'the paranoid style of the moment', mobilizing the conspiracist motif that certain powerful scientists 'were engaged in a conspiracy to supress new knowledge' (Gordin 2012, 3; c.f. 190). During the late 1960s and early 1970s, Velikovsky lectured frequently on college campuses (Gordin 2012, 165–7). The link with the 'New Age' was made plain by a speaker at the 1974 Lethbridge Conference in Alberta, Canada:

> The veil of amnesia has been lifted, the result is the awakening of consciousness, whether the apocalyptic agent is perceived to be an extra-terrestrial jostling, or biospheric poisoning, atomic weaponary overkill, or overpopulation; or whether one has experienced the disintegration of his world view by chemical inducement – a magical mushroom of the fabled LSD. The generation of the *Whole Earth Catalogue* has experienced the catastrophe and, consistent with Dr. Velikovsky's amnesia theory, they no longer itch to re-enact the primordial paroxysm that heralded our present age – the bomb has gone off. (in Gordin 2012, 169)

Yet as Gordin notes, these ideas now appealed to both sides of the political spectrum. While Velikovsky challenged the hegemony of science and traditional epistemic institutions, appealing to the Left, he also promoted a literal reading of the Bible and an application of eschatology to Cold War political discourse which appealed to the Right (2012, 169).

Chariots of the Gods? was a huge success, eventually selling four million copies (Gordin 2012, 178). It was adapted into a documentary in 1970 by German director Harald Reinl, which was nominated for an Academy Award in the Best Documentary category. A re-edited version, entitled *In Search of Ancient Astronauts*, was broadcast on US television in 1973, with a new voiceover by host of popular *The Twilight Zone*, Rod Sterling (Whitesides 2013, 76). Sterling would also voice two sequels, *In Search of Ancient Mysteries* (1975) and *The Outer Space Connection* (1977). All three feature Mayan culture prominently, and the latter concludes with the first televised (or popular) reference to '2012' millennialism, to which we will return in Chapter 5:

> We know the Mayans left a calendar, one that stretches back more than 90 million years, long before civilized man walked the Earth, and forward in time to a day that will mark the close of a crucial cycle. An inscription

tells us that the modern period will end December 24, 2011 A.D. We may presume that they were computing the length of a space voyage and marking the exact date of return ... Christmas Eve, 2011 A.D. On that day they may return to seek the fate of the colony left on Earth. (quoted in Whitesides 2013, 77)

Von Däniken did not originate the ancient alien thesis, however. John Miller of the Sauniere Society told me – rather conspiratorially – that he had been working on the same thesis before his research was stolen from him by a Swedish woman working for von Däniken.[5] But he was apparently unaware that the idea had already been published by Pauwel and Bernier's *Morning of the Magicians*, which spoke of the possibility that ETs had affected the course of human history, and Brad Stieger's 1967 *The Flying Saucer Menace*, which argued that Atlantis was a global civilization founded by aliens (Trompf and Bernauer 2012, 110). Along with Otto Binder's *Aliens are Watching Us* (1968), these books establish a direct link between later ancient alien narratives and the 1966 publication of the first abductee accounts.

The ancient alien thesis seems to inevitably shade into speculation about ancient lost civilizations, particularly when speculations about apparently impossible feats of construction – the pyramids being the usual example – and their possible means of construction arise (Trompf and Bernauer 2012, 110). Although Atlantis' one-sentence reference in Plato's *Timaeus* was widely referenced in mediaeval works, most of the narratives surrounding it in millennial conspiracist discourse come from are derived from Blavatsky (Trompf and Bernauer 2012, 101–5). Indeed, von Däniken actually quotes *The Book of Dyzan* in *Return to the Stars* as though it was a historical document (1970, 154). The process can also be seen to run in the opposite direction, however. Authors such as William Cooper and, as described in Chapter 4, Jim Marrs, have presented functionally identical alternate histories without recourse to channelled material – at least, not acknowledged as so (Dyrendal 2013, 216).

Perhaps as a result of the degree to which his work penetrated the mainstream, von Däniken's work was widely criticized and much of his evidence convincingly discredited. However, a substantively similar theory, put forward by Zechariah Sitchin (1920–2010), an Azerbaijan-born US journalist with a degree in economics, has had more longevity (Fritze 2009, 210–11). After teaching himself to read cuneiform, he began promoting the idea that the Assyrian creation myth Enuma Elish contains an account of prehistoric contact between humans and ETs. In *The 12th Planet* (1976) and successive works, Sitchin argues that there is a planet unknown to human science which orbits the Sun on a 3,600-year elliptical orbit. Sitchin claims that the planet's occupants, an alien race called the Anunnaki, came to Earth and assumed control of human society, heralded as gods and founding dynasties ('bloodlines') that exist to this day. Sitchin later finds corroborating evidence in the Old Testament, and in the final book of the series, *End of Days: Armageddon and Prophecies of the Return* (2007) he draws in '2012' millennialism as evidence that an Anunnaki return is imminent (294–5).

The fall of the iron curtain and the crisis of 'New Age'

On his appointment as General-Secretary in March 1985, Mikhail Gorbachev set about restructuring the USSR's faltering economy by reducing military spending. In order for this to happen, he pursued a foreign policy intended to encourage 'civilised dialogue' between the two states and cooperation towards mutual benefits (Ball 1998, 221–2). Between 1985 and 1987, a series of meetings between Gorbachev and US president Reagan took place in which Gorbachev attempted to get the United States to commit to mutual reductions in nuclear weapons and troops in Europe. At this time, the United States was attempting taking the Cold War into space with the Strategic Defence Initiative, a system of satellite-mounted anti-missile lasers, popularly called 'Star Wars'. Gorbachev failed to get any such agreement, although Reagan nevertheless considered the meetings a step forward 'inconceivable just a few months ago' (Ball 1998, 225). A desperate Gorbachev announced in a speech to the UN in December 1988 that the USSR would unilaterally reduce its forces in Europe by half a million men by 1990 (Ball 1998, 226). In August 1989, Poland gained its first non-communist prime minister since the war, and the USSR did not retaliate. In September, Hungary opened its border with Austria. A growing number of East Germans took the opportunity and fled to the West German embassy, asking for asylum. West German Chancellor Helmut Kohl seized the moment and in November announced a programme to reunite East and West Germany, which happened less than one year later, on 3 October 1990 (Ball 1998, 237). The first section of the Berlin Wall was demolished on 9 November 1989, and the USSR itself ceased to exist as of December 1991. Thus ended the Cold War.

In January 1987, a television adaptation of actress Shirley MacLaine's autobiography *Out on a Limb* was a great success and stimulated the media's appetite for stories concerning 'New Age' discourses (Lewis and Hammer 2007, ix). The Harmonic Convergence, which called for 144,000 people to take part in coordinated meditation at various 'sacred' sites around the globe, took place on 16 and 17 August of the same year (Whitesides 2013, 80–1). The event was intended to guide the predicted eschaton in a millennial rather than apocalyptic direction and received extensive coverage in the media, although the actual number of participants is unclear (Whitesides 2013, 81).

According to some scholars, however, beneath the surface, 'New Age' was in crisis. It seems that the generational and ideological shifts described above had led to a good deal of self-reflection in 'New Age' discourse. By the end of 1987, a number of prominent figures were publicly acknowledging the failure of the event to appear; for example, David Spangler now stated that the 'New Age' was 'an idea, not ... an event' (Sutcliffe 2003a, 114), and Findhorn founder Peter Caddy wrote that '[a]ll that had been prophesied in the early years was no longer true' (1996, 262). There was a crash in the value of crystals and the closure of a number of shops dealing in 'New Age' paraphernalia (Introvigne 2001, 59–60; Melton 2007, 89–90) Most importantly, the majority of those still using the term 'New Age' dropped it altogether (Melton 2007, 90).

The foretold 'New Age' had failed to arrive, and as Festinger would have predicted, a number of strategies were mobilized to avoid the cognitive dissonance the apparent failure caused. Many argued that there had been no failure; rather, to use the schema presented in Chapter 2, there had been a *miscalculation* of the date. The arrival of the 'New Age' was a lengthy process, some, including David Icke, argued (e.g. 1991, 9); while the shift had begun, it would not be immediately obvious and would take a long time to complete. Others suggested alternative dates further in the future. One successful version of this strategy was the *Ascension* narrative of Montana-based channeller Solara, who was also involved in the Harmonic Convergence. Solara argued that a twenty-one-year window had opened, from 1992 to 2011, during which 'our world of duality and [that of] the Greater Reality' overlapped, and the opportunity was presented for humanity, individually or collectively, to take an evolutionary step forward (Melton 2007, 92).[6] She organized coordinated meditation and rituals to facilitate this through her *Star-Borne Unlimited* organization, although her symbol '11:11' is better known today. She suggested that when you see the symbol, you are seeing the overlap between the physical and divine realms (Melton 2007, 92), and of course, when people started looking for it, they began to see it everywhere – another version of Robert Anton Wilson's '23 Enigma'. Traces remain of Solara's terminology in millennial conspiracist discourse; *Thrive* was released on 11/11/11, and Wilcock frequently uses the term 'Ascension'. Indeed, '2012' millennialism was another example of this strategy and one which all three case studies have been involved with at one time or another. I return to 'Ascension' and '2012' narratives in Chapter 6.

For others, such as David Spangler, imminent millennialism was reinterpreted as a metaphor for personal (rather than global) transformation (Introvigne 2001, 62). As a result, Introvigne argues, there was a process of *privatization* – that is, while the prophecy may not come true for the whole planetary group, it could (or had) still come true for a smaller, elite group (2001, 64). This privatized narrative of personal transformation is clear in the works of popular 'spiritual' writers of the late 1990s such as Paulo Coelho, John Redfield and Deepak Chopra. However, it may also explain the movement by some groups to a hierarchical, organized structure more typical of 'cultish' New Religious Movements, such as Ramtha's School of Ancient Wisdom, led by channeller J. Z. Knight, or the Damanhur community near Turin (Introvigne 2001, 61). Moreover, if this strategy was interpreted as that the 'New Age' had indeed come true, just not for everyone, this could also be interpreted as the *spiritualization* strategy. I suggest that we see a third strategy at work; for some, the best explanation for the failure of 'New Age' millennialism was that a conspiracy – to whit, a malevolent occluded agency – prevented it from arriving (Hammer 2001, 400–1; Goodrick-Clarke 2002, 299).

The UFO narrative was discursively negotiated during the Cold War period, beginning with Kenneth Arnold's 1947 sighting up to the collapse of the Soviet Union in 1991. Initially constructed as mysterious but human 'wonder weapons', by the mid-1950s UFOs were typically interpreted as of ET origin. This was encouraged to a large degree by the discourse being adopted by theosophical thinkers to create the abductee narrative, which the space race guided towards an increasingly supernaturalist interpretation. By the mid-1980s, however, with the apparent collapse of both the Cold War and 'New Age' discourse, UFOs were once again open to reinterpretation. For the next decade, UFOs were generally interpreted within a Right-wing conspiracist discourse of government secrecy, yet this split genealogy made UFOs particularly suited to acting as a discursive object between conspiracist and millennial fields.

The three chapters which follow outline how this discourse developed over the following three decades. The next chapter examines the work of Whitley Strieber, which popularized and in some ways exemplified the abductee narrative. But as I shall argue, through his investigations into UFOs, his work increasingly incorporated millennial and conspiratorial motifs as it developed into the post-Cold War period.

Occulted Histories: Whitley Strieber and the Abductee Narrative

Whitley Strieber exemplifies that the trajectory I suggest is typical of millennial conspiracism; an individual involved with millennial discourse becomes interested in UFOs and through this encounters conspiracist material. Strieber had an active interest in UFOs, gained through exposure to alternative epistemologies in popular millennial discourse, and in particular involvement with the Gurdjieff Foundation. However, his abduction experience of 26 December 1985 led him to encounter the post-Cold War reinterpretation of the UFO material exemplified by the MJ-12 documents and thus the conspiracist material it contains. His books recount

> one man's journey out of the trap of ordinary life – and it is a trap, make no mistake. Because we do not understand our true past and cannot see our likely future, we are treading close to the edge, very close. If we don't wake up, I fear we may fall. (1997, xvi)

This quotation encapsulates several of the tropes which typify this milieu: alternate history, teleological and potentially destructive narratives of the future and significantly the motif of 'waking up' – recalling both Strieber's Gurdjieffian background and the acquiescent *sheeple* of the conspiracists. Strieber's 'waking up' – his *gnosis* – was his first encounter with beings he came to call *the visitors*, and the idea that such an event could lead one into questioning other accepted epistemologies is a recurrent theme of his work. For Strieber, even his own life was a lie, but in recovering his own occulted history, Strieber had the curtain drawn back on the occulted history of the world. At the same time, however, the visitors – 'a dark and highly active phenomenon that seems to inhabit cracks in the unconscious, cracks in space time, and cracks in history' (in Vallée 1988, vii) – are that convenient dot that allows him to connect all the others.

Whitley Strieber demonstrates a discursive transfer between millennial and conspiracist discourses, with UFOs acting as discursive object. This was facilitated by a hermeneutic shift in the UFO narrative towards supernatural constructions, driven by both the end of the Cold War and developments in the scientific understanding of the universe, as outlined in Chapter 3. Finally, that Strieber's conclusions and concerns regarding occluded malevolent agencies were shared by a significant number and broad spectrum of individuals in the Anglophone West and still are in the present day.

The fall of the Berlin Wall heralded the end of the threat of imminent and total nuclear annihilation, which as the previous chapter demonstrated, had been a popular concern since 1947. However, I suggest that it is not coincidental that as this threat abated, rumours of other threats, similarly internal yet undeniably alien, began to circulate in the Anglophone West at this time. It is significant for this book to note the apparent continuing need to perceive of a malevolent other in the sudden absence of the perceived Communist threat. Moreover, the abduction narrative was not the only such example to emerge in the immediate post-Cold War period.

Satanic Ritual Abuse

Reports that Satanic cults were abducting, physically and sexually abusing and sometimes murdering children first reached the US public through *Michelle Remembers* (1980), purportedly an autobiography by Michelle Smith, written with her psychiatrist and husband Lawrence Pazder. Pazder had begun treating Smith for depression following a miscarriage, but in 1976, after a session in which she allegedly screamed for twenty-five minutes before beginning to talk with a five-year-old's voice, he focused on using hypnosis to recover memories of childhood trauma. Over 600 hours, what was recovered was a history of physical and sexual abuse by members of a 'Satanic cult', including her mother, from the age of five. She alleged to have been locked in cages, forced to take part in rituals and been witness to several murders and even the incarnation of Satan himself.

Other first-person accounts by adults followed, notably *Satan's Underground* (1988) by Lauren Stratford, which described 'brood-mares', women who were selected to bear children specifically for sacrifice (La Fontaine, 36). Pazder became an adviser to the authorities, eventually working with the police on more than 1,000 cases. One of the most important was the McMartin Preschool trial, which was investigated from 1984 to 1987, going to trial with 321 charges of child abuse against forty-seven children being laid on several members of the McMartin family, proprietors of a Californian preschool. Due to lack of evidence, all charges were dropped in 1990, despite what was at the time the most expensive trial in US history. During this period, however, the Satanic Ritual Abuse (SRA) panic had produced over a thousand other allegations, and there was widespread public and official acceptance of the existence of a wide network to facilitate ritualized paedophilia. By 1988, SRA had spread to the UK, with reports in several newspapers including the Times and the founder of a children's charity publicly stating that over 4,000 children were being 'sacrificed' annually in the UK (La Fontaine, 1). Academic works were being published based on the existence of these unproven networks of abusers; for example, *Treating Survivors of Satanic Abuse* (1994) was criticized in one review as 'a startling, clear demonstration of the amazing ability of 20th century human beings to persuade themselves to believe firmly in utter claptrap and nonsense' (Underwager 1994).

In its most elaborate forms, proponents of SRA described a vast global conspiracy of paedophile Satanists. Cathy O'Brien's *Trance-Formation of America*, published in 1995, after SRA was generally recognized by the authorities as a moral panic, described her own alleged abuse both as a child and an adult as part of a CIA programme to produce multiple-personality 'sleeper agents'. No-one has ever been prosecuted of such crimes nor has any corroborating material evidence ever been produced (La Fontaine, 5), and as a result, SRA has generally been regarded as a baseless moral panic; nevertheless, these books and others similar were still on the shelf in the library of my university in 2012, and these claims were to be frequently reproduced throughout the fieldwork period of this book.

As Partridge notes, the 'alien abduction' phenomenon has a good deal in common with the SRA scare (2005, 260). Circular spaces and outdoor spaces, including forests and parks, are prominent in both cases, as are messages telling the victim that they are somehow special. In many cases, these narratives allege a series of abusive incidents reaching back into early childhood, often with sexual trauma prominent. They claim to involve 'screen memories' which replace traumatic incidents with innocuous imagery. As Whitley Strieber would later write:

> As I matured, the feeling grew that my ordinary life was not the whole story. It seemed a sort of outer theatre, an outer life that concealed another existence that was far more real, far richer, far more important than this one. (1997, xiv)

Regressional hypnosis was instrumental in the production of these narratives. However, its efficacy in recovering suppressed memories of genuine events is now widely challenged in clinical psychology literature (Baker 1982; Wagstaff 1984; Spanos 1996, 91–104).

At this time, the accounts of Betty and Barney Hill and Antonio Villas-Boas were popular in the UFO milieu. These accounts have many of the features associated with later abductee narratives, including lost time, high strangeness, hypnotic regression and the taking of physical samples. There are notable differences, however; their ET abductors typically look human, the spacecraft are entirely physical and there are no medical probes or implants. These proto-abductee accounts, therefore, bridge Cold War physicalist constructions and later supernaturalist abductee accounts.

With the 1987 publication of Whitley Strieber's *Communion*, the abductee narrative began to reach popular culture. *Communion*'s striking cover gave us the image of the ET with large black slanted eyes, small mouth and nose and a large head atop a willowy body, which twenty-five years later shows no sign of abatement as popular culture's idea of the physical appearance of an ET (see Figure 4.1). Indeed, the shift from 'little green men' to 'the Greys' (or Zetas, after their supposed origin in the Zeta Reticuli star-system) is a pivotal moment in the hermeneutic shift of UFOs from physicalist to supernaturalist – that is, beings from other dimensions rather than the physical occupants of spacecraft from other planets. Every one of Strieber's ET-themed books, both fiction and non-fiction, feature this image on the cover, despite not being typical of the beings Strieber describes encountering. Strieber has remained open-

Figure 4.1 Scarritt-Bennett Centre, Nashville (photo by the author).

minded about the nature of his experiences, but there is a tension in his work in his understanding of the beings he came to call the *visitors*; while he tends to reject physicalist explanations, he has an ongoing engagement with the mainstream UFO community.

Life and work of Whitley Strieber

Abduction narrative

Whitley Strieber was born on 13 June 1945, to a successful lawyer and his wife in San Antonio, Texas (Conroy 1989, 43). His father developed cancer of the larynx which took his voice several years before it took his life in 1977, leaving him unable to work and the family relatively impoverished (Conroy 1989, 47). Whitley is described as a bookish and thoughtful child, and his mother described him as very sensitive, 'cry[ing] at everything in sight' (Conroy 1989, 55). Although he presents himself in *Communion* as an 'indifferent skeptic' (1987, 13), Strieber had long been interested in UFOs and other types of unusual phenomena. Brother McMurtrey, one of his teachers from his sophomore year in High School, who Strieber would on numerous occasions describe as his biggest influence in choosing a career as a writer, noted that 'he was always interested in the occult' (Conroy 1989, 69). The interest in alternative spiritualities continued in later life.

In 1963, Strieber enrolled at the University of Texas studying law, before heading off instead to Europe with dreams of being a filmmaker, enrolling at the London School of Film Technique (Conroy 1989, 70–7).[1] After graduating in 1968, he worked in advertising until retiring to write full-time in 1977, at the age of 32 (Smith 2000, 110).

His first novel, *Wolfen* (1978), concerned a race of humanoid wolves that have been living secretly alongside humanity for millennia, hunting them. It was successful enough to be turned into a film starring Albert Finney, and his follow-up, vampire novel *The Hunger* (1981), was also filmed. His two subsequent horror novels, *Black Magic* (1982) and *Night Church* (1983), sold less well, and he next collaborated with James Kunetka on two speculative fiction books, *Warday* (1984), concerning nuclear warfare, and *Nature's End* (1986), on the subject of environmental collapse.

In 1986, as SRA was beginning to appear in the mainstream press, a draft manuscript of *Communion* was circulated around a number of publishers after Warner's, Strieber's current publisher, rejected it (Conroy 1989, 12). A successful bid was made by William Morrow, and the book became a New York Times #1 bestseller, staying on the list for almost a year, making it perhaps the most successful non-fiction UFO book in publishing history (Conroy 1989, 2).

It is not hard to understand why *Communion* was a success. Whether intentionally or not, Strieber gave *Communion* the atmosphere of a good horror novel: the narrator's self-doubt; the dawning sense of terror; the intrusion of strangeness and violence into everyday life; and the gradual, though never complete, revelation of the threat. Reading it late at night, I found myself jumping at the rustle of a curtain and seeing faces in the shadows cast by the lamp through the leaves of a pot-plant. Moreover, *Communion* contained many motifs familiar from his previously published fiction, notably the idea of a parasitic race existing in secret alongside humans. As a result, doubts were raised about the providence of the tale; *The Nation* accused Strieber of creating the story (Smith 2000, 114), while *Publisher's Weekly*'s review was entitled 'When Is a True Story True?' (Nathan 1987). As Anne Strieber later remarked, 'Poor Whitley–he's a horror novelist and the biggest horror novel he ever writes is not a novel but is something real.'[2] But if *Communion* was indeed a disguised fiction, then the plan backfired dramatically; his new role as a spokesperson for ET abduction in the media seriously stalled his career as a novelist.

As *Communion* recounts, on the evening of 26 December 1985, Strieber woke in the middle of the night and saw a small figure rushing towards him. He was taken out of the room by a group of squat, blue, identical beings and taken to first a depression in the nearby forest and then a brightly lit room where he encountered other beings, willowy, short and large-eyed. Probes were inserted into his brain and anus, and an incision was made on his finger. Then he awoke with a sense of unease and a vivid memory of seeing an owl through the bedroom window (Strieber 1987, 20–31). In the weeks which followed, he became withdrawn and hypersensitive. A report of a UFO sighting in the area led him to read *Science and the UFOs* (1985) by Jenny Randles and Peter Warrington, which he initially found frightening. It included a description of an 'archetypal abduction experience', which included both the depression in the woods and the memory of seeing an animal. Strieber then began to suspect that he may have been abducted himself.

He then made contact with Budd Hopkins, a leading figure in the UFO abduction scene, whose name he had found in *Science and the UFOs*. Hopkins was the popularizer of the motif of 'missing time', in which UFO witnesses discover that a period of time, often several hours, has passed without them remembering, as though their memories had been altered. Hopkins, suggesting that hypnosis might be useful in recovering the details of the event, organized a session for Strieber, during which more detailed memories of his abduction experience emerged.

Now believing that his memories of the event had been deliberately obscured, he then began to believe that an earlier event at the cabin had been a similar abduction event. Strieber (and later his wife, Anne) then recalled under hypnosis that they had been 'visited' during an earlier event which had taken place on the 4 November 1985. Strieber, his wife and son, and two friends had been woken by a mysterious bang and bright lights during the night. All had commented upon it the following morning, but it had not been discussed further, as though, Strieber hypothesized, their memories had been similarly 'screened'. During a second hypnosis session, Strieber spontaneously recalled a third event, seemingly occurring in 1957 when Strieber was aged 12. During a business trip with his father, Strieber became fevered during the return train journey. He awoke to find himself in a room where a number of GIs, in full uniform, were lying on tables, and were being touched by a tall, thin, black eyed being holding a copper rod.

Instead of the single abduction experience, then, Strieber now believed he had uncovered a history of multiple abductions, stretching back into his childhood. As a result, he starts to reconsider several other episodes of his life history for which his memories seem anomalous or missing altogether. Notable is the aforementioned European sojourn in which he claims days and even weeks are absent from his memory and those memories which remain are fractured and often strange. As a result, he starts to suspect that he has been continually and repeatedly abducted since childhood, and like the purported victims of SRA, a traumatic 'other life' begins to emerge from the cracks in his life history.

He contacted a senior psychiatrist, Donald Klein, in an attempt to establish if he were experiencing psychosis or temporal-lobe epilepsy; the former was ruled out, the latter deemed possible, though unlikely (Klein, quoted in Conroy 1989, 24–7). Strieber also underwent two CAT scans and a lie-detector test, all of which suggested his honesty and sanity (Conroy 1989, 24–35). From this, he concludes that something genuine happened to him. Strieber admits that he was at this time exhibiting many symptoms of depression or trauma, including alcohol abuse and undue aggression. *Communion's* narrative ends with Strieber meeting, through Budd Hopkins, a group of people who have had similar abduction experiences.

The latter third of the book is a lengthy meditation as to the possible nature of these experiences. He gives five possibilities; ETs, time-travellers, fairies, the dead, or the human collective unconsciousness (1987, 95). As a result of his uncertainty, he refers to the beings as the *visitors* rather than aliens. Importantly, given that *Communion* brought alien abduction into the mainstream, Strieber is careful not to state categorically that he believes the visitors to be physically real. He later wrote that, at the time, he was concerned that he had experienced 'a psychotic episode, possibly brought on by organic brain disease' (1997, xix). This latter section is rich with allusions to religious and mythological symbolism, demonstrating Strieber's obvious knowledge of these subjects (Kripal 2011, 293–4). *Communion*'s language of transformation, marriage and 'higher consciousness' were in keeping with the 'New Age' literature of the period, perhaps adding to its appeal (1987, 280).

On the opening page of *Communion*, he writes:

> At first, I thought I was losing my mind. But I was interviewed by three psychologists and three psychiatrists, given a battery of psychological tests and given a neurological examination … I was also given a polygraph by an operator with thirty years' experience and I passed without qualification. (1987, 13)

This is somewhat misleading. Strieber had had a lifelong interest in UFOs, and that it was reading a book on UFOs which set him to consider that his experience might have been an abduction, and therefore to seek out Budd Hopkins. Moreover, he had these tests only after he had 'recovered' his abduction memories through hypnosis by one of the foremost promoters of the alien abduction narrative. Hopkins was an artist by profession who had an interest in alien abduction, not a psychologist nor a medical practitioner of any kind, so would seem a curious first port of call for a man concerned primarily about his sanity. Although the hypnotist employed by Strieber and Hopkins, a respected psychologist named Donald Klein, was apparently selected specifically because he had not worked with Hopkins before (1987, 56), the mere knowledge of Hopkins' presence may well have influenced Strieber's 'recovered memories' along alien abduction lines. Indeed, this course of action suggests that he visited these medical professionals in an attempt to validate what he had recovered through hypnosis rather than to discover the root cause of his anxiety symptoms. Furthermore, while a polygraph test may indicate that one is not lying, it does nothing to prove that what you experienced was genuine. Strieber's career is marked by an uneasy ambiguity in his account of UFOs; despite the distancing of *Communion* and its sequels from the extraterrestrial origin thesis of UFOs, Strieber maintains an ongoing engagement with the mainstream UFO community, as we shall see when considering the Dreamland festival.

In fairness, however, Strieber was not alone in claiming to have experienced anomalous phenomena in the cabin during this period. As already mentioned, his wife Anne, their son Andrew and several of their friends also had anomalous experiences, and on one occasion, the Striebers were in their bedrooms, two of their friends (Raven Dana and Lori Barnes) were in the upstairs bedroom, a filmmaker in the living room and his crew bunked in the basement, and all are alleged to have reported some degree of anomalous experience (1995, 75–94). Most dramatic of these was Raven Dana, who claims to have made conscious physical contact with a visitor that night. She woke to find a being in her room, which, apparently uniquely among Strieber's circle, allowed her to touch it. She described it as feeling like chamois leather and suffered an allergic reaction afterward.[3] Yet this took place *after* Strieber had become famous for having been abducted. What's more, it is considerably more anomalous than the November 1985 event, which is reliant entirely on vague nocturnal recollections long after the fact.

Dana was one of thousands who contacted Strieber following the publication of *Communion* with their own experiences of abduction by seemingly sinister non-human agents. Anne, rather than Whitley, became custodian of these accounts, which allegedly eventually totalled nearly 140,000 reports. While there are striking similarities in these accounts (many of which are shared by SRA accounts), they are also dramatic and often puzzlingly idiosyncratic. In one case a woman reported a group of small humanoid beings, some with antennas on their heads, building a platform in a tree in her garden from which they began to film her (Strieber and Strieber 1997, 90–2); in another, the letter reported that the witness saw a large group of small blue men standing on the ocean, holding spears (Strieber and Strieber 1997, 99). This tendency to contain details which lie outside the typical has become known in UFOlogy circles as *high strangeness*, and for those in the milieu, their specificity adds to the veracity of the individual accounts; why would you make up something so obviously ridiculous?[4]

A flurry of other abductee works followed, capitalizing on *Communion*'s success in various ways: Bud Hopkins' *Intruders* (1987), with a cover reminiscent of *Communion*'s ET face (Smith 2000, 115), Jacques Vallée's trilogy *Dimensions* (1988; with a foreword by Strieber), *Confrontations* (1990) and *Revelations* (1991), Raymond Fowler's *The Watchers* (1990) and a reissue of his *Andreasson Affair* ([1980] 1988) with a new foreword by Strieber. Strieber capitalized himself with *Transformation* (1988), published eighteen months after *Communion*, describing his continuing visitor experiences. Strieber's experiences since completing *Communion* had begun to change his thinking about what the visitors might be and what they might be trying to achieve. Firstly, during another abduction, a being which resembled the one depicted on the cover of *Communion* but pure white, told him that he needed to stop eating sweets or he would die. It then allowed him to touch the hem of its garment, which produced a sensation which Strieber described as 'like an edge of heaven' (1988, 73):

> That being in white sitting on the edge of my bed and talking to me about death might have been a representative of the most powerful of all the forces that have shaped us … An Angel in my bedroom. (1988, 77)

This suggested to Strieber that the visitors' ultimate aims were benevolent, despite appearances. Two months later, he woke in the cabin to find his son Andrew absent from his bed. Rushing outside, he saw a light shooting up into the air. A voice in his head told him to go back to bed, and in the morning his son was present as always. Yet Strieber was struck by several mystical statements his son came out with in the days following, including 'Reality is God's dream' (1988, 25). Further communication came in the form of a series of nine knocks – grouped into three groups of three – which emanated from a point on his roof which he believed could not have been accessible without being heard or triggering the automatic lights and which allegedly terrified his cats (1988, 129–30). These events persuaded Strieber of both the physical reality of the visitors and their good intentions (1988, 141). He began to venture out of the cabin alone late at night in an attempt to provoke further visitor experiences and perhaps challenge the balance of power.

By this point, Strieber had abandoned hypnosis, concerned that untrained researchers were 'imposing their own beliefs on their victims' and that their use of hypnosis and other 'aggressive therapies' would lead to 'suffering, breakdown and possibly even suicide' (1988, 254). Perhaps as importantly,

Strieber and Hopkins disagreed strongly over Strieber's increasingly complex and millennial interpretation. For Hopkins, the visitors – which, tellingly, he calls *intruders* – are physically travelling across space (1987, ix–xi). He was also extremely sceptical about their possibly benevolent intentions:

> The technologically superior group [the visitors] apparently views itself as more genuinely needy than the more 'primitive' culture. One simply cannot reconcile the idea of kindly, helpful, all powerful 'Space Brothers' – *a* science fiction cliché now dear to spiritualist cults – with the ethically complicated reality of these unsettling UFO accounts. (1987, 240–1)[5]

Strieber, however, was constructing the visitors in increasingly supernatural and benevolent terms:

> I do not think we are dealing with something as straightforward as the arrival of a scientific team from another planet that is here to study us. Neither are we dealing with hallucinations. This is a subtle, complex group of phenomena, causing experience at the very limits of perception and understanding. It suggests to me that there may be quite a real world that exists between thing and thought, moving easily from one to the other – emerging one moment as a full-scale physical reality and slipping the next into the shadows. (1988, 9)

Here, Strieber was clearly influenced by Vallée's ideas, outlined in Chapter 3, which he acknowledges in *Transformation* (1988, 45). The visitors are beings which belong in fact to our world but are at the same time somehow Other, Strieber now argues. What's more, he understood the visitors to be the origin of stories concerning spiritual beings described in different cultures and traditions at different times, including fairies, goblins and succubae. Because we experience the world scientifically and technologically, however, he argues, that is how we presently experience them; or alternatively, that is how they choose to present themselves at this time. In *Transformation*, the straightforward horror of the abduction experience as presented in *Communion* was replaced by the more complex idea that the ugliness of the abduction experience comes from ourselves, not from the visitors (1988, 184). Strieber now argued that the visitors were in some way challenging us to overcome ourselves, but the nature of their benevolence was simply incomprehensible to us:

Whatever the visitors are, I suspect they have been responsible for much paranormal phenomena, ranging from the appearance of gods, angels, fairies, ghosts and miraculous beings to the landing of UFOs in the backyards of America. It may be that what happened to Mohammed [*sic*] in his cave and to Christ in Egypt, to Buddha in his youth and to all our great prophets and seers, was an exalted version of the same humble experience that causes a flying saucer to traverse the sky or a visitor to appear in a bedroom. (1988, 236)

Transformation also contained the first hints in Strieber's work of the discursive transfer between popular millennialism and conspiracist discourses, which was to become increasingly apparent over the following decade and a half. As discussed in Chapter 3, this discursive transfer was centred on the Roswell narrative, in particular its alleged cover-up by the government and the MJ-12 documents as 'revealed' by Friedman and Moore in 1987, discussed in Chapter 3. These came to the fore in Strieber's ostensible return to fiction in 1989. *Majestic* (tagline: 'The government lied') was presented as a fictionalized version of the Roswell crash and the events which immediately followed it, leading to the military cover-up of the truth. The novel concerns Wilfred Stone, a young Military Intelligence agent given the job of collecting the Roswell crash debris and controlling the release of information to the public. Yet a series of strange events, clearly drawn from Strieber's own experiences, make it clear that he too has long been in suppressed contact with the Visitors. In one memorable sequence, Stone, fleeing to Area 51 with the rapidly decomposing corpse of an ET in the back of his car, begins to feel sick and pulls his car over. Getting out, he crouches by the side of the road as a loud humming fills his ears. After a while, he returns to the car; only later does he discover that several people had seen him and his car being levitated into a UFO during that time. The novel uses multiple first-person narratives, has some remarkable descriptive metaphors and many passages of high strangeness.

However, Strieber today claims that *Majestic* is not really a work of fiction; rather, it was constructed from his own visitor experiences and the testimony of his uncle, Colonel Edward Strieber, and his commanding officer, General Arthur Exon. As he explained to me at the Dreamland festival, the two had worked together at Wright-Patterson Air Force Base in Ohio, where it is alleged that the debris from the Roswell crash was taken (Berlitz and Moore 1980, 75). As he could not persuade them to go on record, he published their insider account in a fictionalized narrative. Strieber was playing a risky game here, by publishing testimony-disguised-as-fiction only two years after being accused of publishing fiction-disguised-as-testimony.

A cinema adaptation of *Communion*, starring Christopher Walken and with a screenplay by Strieber, was also released in 1989. The film performed poorly both critically and commercially, and *Transformation* also sold markedly less well than its predecessor. Neither were Strieber's novels of the period successful – although interestingly, they all concern themes of abduction and transformation. In 1994, the Striebers could no longer afford their cabin and moved back to his recently deceased Mother's apartment in New York (Strieber 2012, 189).

Conspiracism and alternative histories

Strieber returned to the subject of the visitors in 1995, ten years after the initial event, during the height of the debates concerning the MJ-12 documents in UFOlogical circles.[6] In *Breakthrough: The Next Step*, the third volume of the series, Strieber claimed that the seven-year gap since the previous book was a deliberate withdrawal from public life in order to seek to understand the visitors and their motivations better. Strieber now describes himself as a willing participant in his visitor experiences, and as a result, is now completely convinced of their transformative potential. *Breakthrough* includes an astonishing sequence where Strieber describes a visitor physically cohabiting with him and his wife for a period of several months. Strieber and the being would meditate together every evening, although Strieber was apparently unable to collect any photographic or other physical evidence.

Conspiracist tropes also come to the fore, with Strieber writing that the US government were spreading disinformation 'horror stories' in an attempt to seem more in control of the situation than they really were. He suggests that the Military and Intelligence communities are aware of the abduction phenomena and are attempting to keep it covered up or perhaps are even working with the Visitors (1995, 214–5). Many of the visitor experiences recounted in *Breakthrough* involve mysterious black helicopters, a ubiquitous feature of NWO Right-wing conspiracism at that time (1995, 71; 127). He claims to have been given an implant in his right earlobe which broadcasts microwaves and moves to avoid being removed (1995, 222). He further claims to have been offered to work for the CIA, and when he turned the offer down, was stalked, harassed with telephone calls and eventually had his apartment broken into (1995, 227).

Perhaps more interesting, however, is 1997's *The Secret School*, which is essentially an elaboration of Strieber's childhood experiences with the visitors, first mentioned in *Transformation* (1988, 90). Subtitled *Preparation for Contact* and structured to parallel the three-by-three knocks of *Transformation*, it recounts his nocturnal experiences with the others during the summer of 1954, aged nine, in what he describes as a kind of school. While being filmed for a television show in 1995, he unexpectedly found what he believed to have been the site of this 'school' in the Olmos basin in San Antonio, marked by an ancient, misshapen oak tree, which caused further memories to re-emerge (xxi–xxiii). His memories of these gatherings are supported with references to Conroy's apparent discovery that others who had grown up in the area had similar memories (in Strieber 1997, 235–45).

The book contains nine 'lessons', each composed of a recovered memory followed by Whitley's commentary. After a dream in which the visitors introduce themselves to Strieber as 'the Sisters of Mercy' and give him a fantastical vision of a Sphinx on Mars, he met an old woman who ran an astronomy class, named Mrs Carter. After sneaking out after dark, Strieber became part of the class; suddenly, they found themselves in the Olmos Basin rather than Mrs Carter's house. He reports that buzzing sound again, and the smell of electricity (1997, 90), and then found himself simultaneously in Texas and ancient Rome (122–31), observing an antediluvian civilization awaiting the impact of a comet and building 'stoneworks that will survive the cataclysm and take with them a coded message to the future' (149) and finally an apocalyptic vision of earth's future (181–7). This narrative is intercut with incidents of apparent mundanity described in prose of spiritual wonder, including an electrical storm and a passage where a fevered Whitley literally danced with Death, personified as a boy younger than himself (61–5). In Strieber's account, these are memories of a complete, but forgotten, other life:

> In the other life, I had answers about the mystery of man, what is going to happen to us in the future, and who we really are. In this other life, I was a much more powerful human being, and I sensed that this was true not only of me, but of many other people, perhaps of everybody. (1997, xiv–xv)

Are Strieber's recollections an unusually vivid recalling of the interior life of a nine-year-old boy, or rather an unusually strong attempt by a mature man to narrate a life-story in which he is a powerful and unusual person?

The Communion Letters, a selection of the thousands which Whitley had been sent since the publication of *Communion*, was also published in 1997. It was edited by Anne Strieber, who had taken on the role as their custodian, a role she continues through their website at time of writing. The final publication of this second phase of the visitor narrative was 1998's *Confirmation: The Hard Evidence of Aliens Among Us*. Despite the affirmation in the title, seemingly chosen to recall the other *Communion* books, the book is actually a speculative discussion of what evidence would be needed to prove the reality of the UFO phenomenon, whatever its nature might be. Once again, Strieber is happy to continue his connection with mainstream UFOlogy, despite continuing to move away from the language of UFO abduction in other respects. In these later books, the visitors are portrayed as another race – although whether terrestrial or otherwise is uncertain – who exist alongside humanity, although hidden.

Strieber has become unambiguous in his insistence that the experience is ultimately positive, even transformative:

> [C]ontact with the Visitors is safe, though extremely challenging. I feel their coming is a call to change ... they might be what the force of evolution looks like when it applies itself to a conscious mind. (1995, 5)

My understanding of what Strieber means by such statements is that certain individuals are being particularly affected by an imminent evolutionary transformation which the visitors – whatever they might be – are somehow guiding. In other words, the visitors are nothing less than agents of a coming millennial event; '[i]f we face them, one way or another', he later wrote, 'we are going to find ourselves living in what amounts to a new world' (2012, 7). In statements such as these, Strieber ties his abduction experiences, and the UFO narrative more generally, to a popular millennial discourse.

Around this time, Strieber was interviewed for the first time by Art Bell on *Coast to Coast AM*. Created in 1984 by Art Bell, *Coast to Coast AM* is an influential and widely listened-to radio show covering paranormal and conspiracist topics. It continues to the present day, although it is now hosted principally by George Noorey, and Strieber remains a frequent guest and occasional presenter. Strieber and Bell struck up a friendship, and in 1997 they collaborated on *The Coming Global Superstorm*, a work of 'speculative non-fiction'. It was a return to Strieber's environmental concerns, as well as a continuation of his teleological thinking and argues that small, incremental increases in CO_2 production could nevertheless rapidly produce dramatic climatic changes. The book later became the basis of the big-budget 2004 disaster movie *The Day After Tomorrow*, for which Strieber wrote the novelization. In 1999, Strieber took over *Coast to Coast AM*'s sister show, *Dreamland*, from Bell, which covered similar topics but with a greater emphasis on ETs and spirituality and lacking the call-in format. The show is still broadcast weekly, albeit in an internet-only format, through Strieber's website, unknowncountry.com. So, although Strieber's social capital had fallen due to the decline in his career as a novelist, his position as an 'alternative' radio host introduced him to a new and potentially larger audience, with a younger and more rural demographic, which my fieldwork suggests significantly increased his epistemic capital. While sweeping, conspiratorial revisionist histories and ancient alien narratives are not overtly a part of Strieber's published work, they are a frequent feature of both *Coast to Coast AM* and *Dreamland*. Recent episodes include 'The Growing Presence from Another Dimension' (22 November 2013), 'Lost Secrets of Maya Technology' (14 June 2012) and 'The Last Pole Shift, Atlantis and Current Changes' (30 April 2012).[7] The Dreamland festival, which began in 2007, has now become an annual gathering for some 120 paying attendees and a panel of invited speakers drawn largely from Dreamland presenters and interviewees. Whitley and Anne are hosts, but the event is organized by William Henry, whose weekly internet radio show is hosted alongside Dreamland on unknowncountry.com.

Strieber's next book, the self-published *The Key* (2001 [2011], reissued by Tarcher-Penguin in 2010), purported to be a transcript of a conversation with a mysterious individual, identified only as 'The Master of the Key', who arrived, unbidden and late, at Strieber's hotel room on the 6 June 1998, during the promotional tour for *Confirmation*. 'I am here on behalf of the good', he said: 'Please give me some time' (2001 [2011], 182) and proceeded to make a series of enigmatic statements of a scientific and often prophetic nature. The conversation, lasting some thirty minutes, was reconstructed several months later from Strieber's scribbled notes and was published first in journal entries on his website, which differ in several ways from what appeared in the book. Strieber claims that, in part, the decision to publish privately was to allow the Master to identify himself and perhaps even offer corrections and clarifications (2001 [2011], 4–6). In the time between that publication and the 2010 reissue, Strieber became convinced that many of the puzzling statements he was given had been scientifically proven. An example is the Master's claim that 'gas is an important component to consider in the constructions of intelligent machines', which Strieber claims was proven in 2005 in experiments where nitrous oxide was made to store data as memory (2001 [2011], 7–8; references to specific research is not given). Strieber's introductions to both editions show that his concern with a man-made environmental crisis continues. They also make manifest his demythologization of the supernatural, claiming the supernatural is simply an unacknowledged aspect of science.

He returned to writing fiction during this period; this included two 2012-themed novels, *The War for Souls* (2007) and *The Omega Point* (2010). Like Icke and Wilcock, Strieber sees 2012 as emblematic of global transformation over a longer timescale rather than a specific teleological event. Nevertheless, it is typical of his incorporation of motifs from the counter-culture into his work, whether by accident or design. He also published two further novels which elaborate on the visitors, with similar themes of breeding and government secrecy. *The Greys* (2006) concerns a nine-year-old boy who is the result of decades of selective breeding by the visitors, a Colonel charged with keeping the visitors a secret and a telepath who can communicate with the one visitor remaining alive from the Roswell crash. *Hybrids* (2011), on the other hand, posits that abductions were carried out by visitors working with the military to collect sexual samples with which to create human-ET hybrids.

To some extent, 2012's *Solving the Communion Enigma*, the fifth in the official series, published twenty-five years after the original, is both a restatement and reassessment of the series. His ambiguity about the physicalist thesis of the UFO narrative remains, though elsewhere his position has hardened – he describes his original 1985 encounter unambiguously as 'rape', for example (2012, 4). It is also a catalogue of Strieber's favourite pieces of rejected knowledge, including crop circles and the 'face on Mars', both of which have fallen from favour in popular conspiracist discourse in recent years. However, the book does build on the themes of the series in two respects. Firstly, he now believes the abduction experience is not rare but perhaps universal; what is rare is remembering it (2012, 15). Secondly, the connection between the visitors and the dead introduced in *The Communion Letters* was made more central. He describes seeing a bright floating light outside on their last night at the cabin, which he recognizes as the being he had been living and meditating with:

> Certainly, I had been in a school ... But now the amazing purpose of this school was clear: it was to draw back the veil that stands between us and the world around us, and in so doing draw back the veil between the living and the dead .... On that night, I saw a dead man in his true state, shining with a living light ... he was, to my mind, what ordinary people-good people-become. This caterpillar had a glimpse of the butterfly. (2012, 191)

This, then, is Strieber's solution to the enigma posed by his apparent abduction on Boxing Day a quarter of a century before. The visitors are *us*, in our true, spiritual state. They – or perhaps, we – are helping humanity evolve to a higher state, against malevolent occluded agencies who do not want us to evolve. For Strieber, this is the biggest cover-up of all.

Demythologization of the UFO narrative

Strieber first understands his experiences in the typical physicalist framework of abduction, as evinced by his contact with Budd Hopkins. At the same time, he is aware of the mythological parallels, gleaned from Vallée's work. For

Strieber, however, the visitors must always be explicable through the scientific discursive strategy. Strieber is aware that the visitors, as he presents them, represent a 'demythologized' (1988, 241) take on encounters with mythical beings:

> There can be only one reason why the nature of the visitor experience is changing. They seem more realistic, more possible, than ever before. Conceived of as extra-terrestrials, they become almost understandable. Perhaps the prevalence of this concept is our way of admitting to ourselves that we can now understand ... Two hundred years ago a farmer might have come in from his plowing and said, 'I saw fairies dancing in the glen'. A thousand years ago he might have seen angels flying. Two thousand years ago it would have been Dionysus leaping in the fields'. (1988, 237)

The changing status of the physicalist hypothesis in UFO discourse can be read against his work, however. In *Communion* and *Transformation*, he finds the physicalist thesis possible, though unlikely, due to the limit set by the speed of light. By 1997, however, he was writing that 'the main objection to the presence of aliens in our midst ... [i.e.] the notion that the vastness of interstellar distance makes their coming so improbable' (1997, 106) was now gone, due to a couple of speculative papers in scientific journals which argued that the speed of light might not actually present an absolute barrier. This was restated in his keynote at the Dreamland festival in 2012, and such strategic mobilizations of the scientific epistemic strategy will be seen to recur in my other case studies. Strieber is happy to overlook decades of scientific work supporting Special Relativity and therefore the impossibility of faster-than-light travel to highlight one paper which supports his own position, gained primarily through counter-epistemic means. As I will restate in the conclusion, for Strieber, as with Icke and Wilcock and millennial conspiracist discourse in general, science is one epistemic strategy amongst others within a broadened conception of potential epistemic capital.

So far, this chapter has demonstrated that, for Strieber, the UFO narrative acted as the primary discursive object between popular millennial and conspiracist discourses. Furthermore, I have demonstrated that in the negotiation, there was a discursive shift in interpretation of the UFO narrative away from physicalist and interplanetary interpretations, towards more ambiguous interdimensional and/or supernaturalist ones. For my conclusions of this thesis to carry any weight, however, I need to demonstrate that his beliefs, and the manner in which they were reached, have a broader currency within the contemporary spiritual milieu. To what extent, in other words, are Strieber's beliefs typical of his readership and listeners? In the following section, I examine how conspiracism, popular millennialism and UFO narratives intersect amongst a group made up of committed subscribers to Strieber's work.

Dreamland Festival, 2012

The 5th Annual Dreamland festival took place in Nashville, Tennessee, on the weekend of the 18–20 May 2012. The venue was the Scarritt-Bennett Centre, 'a non-profit education, retreat and conference centre' with 'a strong commitment to the eradication of racism, empowerment of women and spiritual formation'.[8] It was a beautiful collection of Gothic-revival buildings set in ten green acres on the edges of the campus of Vanderbilt University (Figure 4.1). Other events being promoted included a 'Radical Hospitality Retreat', a workshop 'exploring the world of ancient women through song, story and creative interpretation' and various inter-faith dialogue workshops.

When I had decided to do fieldwork at the event, it had been scheduled for August, but due to high temperatures and storms in previous years, it was moved forward to May. As a result, I could only leave Edinburgh on the morning of the Friday, the first day of the Festival, so I arrived at the centre very shortly before the event began. My first task was to introduce myself to Whitley, which he'd asked I do in our email correspondence but which wasn't easy as he already had a queue of people wanting autographs and photos. Conscious that he must already be feeling rather harassed, I caught him just as he was preparing to start and said a brief hello. I also said that I was happy if he wanted to let the other guests know what I was doing.

Whitley took the podium and opened the Festival by welcoming everyone. To my surprise, he then asked me to come to the front, where he introduced me to the audience and told them that like Jeff Kripal (who had recently published a chapter on Strieber in *Mutants and Mystics* (2011), and with whom Strieber has become firm friends), I was 'doing important work'. He then introduced the speakers, most of whom were Dreamland regulars; Anne Strieber, official 'editor-in-Chief' of the website; Linda Moulton Howe, director of the 1980 cattle mutilation documentary *Strange Harvest*, occasional *Coast to Coast AM* presenter and Dreamland's 'science editor'; William Henry, proponent of 'stargates' and Revelations presenter; and Marla Frees, 'psychic medium and transformational therapist', who was to do readings of the room, as she had in previous years. There were also three guest speakers, and the differences between them exemplify the field. First was Jim Marrs, author of *Crossfire: The Plot That Killed Kennedy* (1989), one of the texts which the seminal conspiracist movie *JFK* was based on; *Rule by Secrecy* (2000), about alleged elite bloodlines; *The War on Freedom* (2006), about the 9/11 attacks; as well as *Alien Agenda* (1997), which he claims is the bestselling book on UFOs and abduction of all time. Secondly, Nick Pope, formerly employed by the Ministry of Defence to investigate UK sightings of UFOs and latterly turned author and speaker. Finally, Whitley announced that Sunday would include an unscheduled presentation by Free Energy proponent Charles 'Chip' Wilkins on an alternative health technology. The presenters therefore ran the gamut of the field, from mainstream UFOlogy to traditional conspiracism to more traditionally 'New Age' motifs of mediumship, health and holism. Indeed, that such a diverse range of speakers came together under Strieber's aegis underlines that the commonality is not UFOlogy per se but rather the epistemic uncertainty which the UFO narrative symbolizes.

The Festival proper opened with a presentation by Raven Dana, who as discussed above, claimed to have had physical contact with one of the visitors in Whitley's cabin. The festival was loosely themed around *Communion*, due to both the 25th anniversary of its publication and the recent publication of *Solving the Communion Enigma*. Dana, now describing herself as a 'Life Coach and Seminar leader', described a family history of questioning authority and how her grandmother would talk to the dead and that her grandfather had seen a UFO. Such a counter-cultural and – more importantly – counter-epistemic habitus is clearly a generational affair, as Dana claims her own children have had visitor encounters too.

When she had finished, I was approached by Tom, a farmer and metal-worker from upstate New York. He was keen on stone circles, had been to the

UK for the Megalithomania festival and told me he had had an inexplicable experience at the ring of Brodgar on the Orkney mainland. I have a fondness for the Neolithic myself, and we bonded. Tom would regularly refer to himself and the other Dreamland attendees as 'the Nutters' and liked to playfully accuse me of being a reptilian. When he invited me to join the Nutters for some food, however, I reluctantly declined, as it was already 4 am by my body clock and I was worried I'd fall asleep at the table.

Saturday

I woke at 6:30 am. At breakfast, Tom introduced me to some of the Nutters, including his daughter Jenny, Donny (so named because he looked a lot like Donny Osmond), Zack, a geologist, Mark from Canada and a younger couple called Brian and Carole, all of whom were welcoming. I also got talking to Bill, who had been a GI for twenty-four years before retiring and going into computer programming. He never mentioned if he'd seen UFOs or not but told me his big concern was with government secrecy. He talked about 'the removal of individual rights' and asked me if it was true that in the UK there were security cameras everywhere. This came up a number of times with different people, and I had to admit it was true. Bill then told me that he was concerned about the poor quality of food in the United States and about the use of GM produce and hormone supplements in cattle. I told him I thought it was interesting that in the UK security cameras are accepted but not GM, yet it's the other way around in the United States. He suggested the 'elites' might not allow GM and hormones in the food supply in Europe because it was their 'homeland', and they feared contamination.

Saturday had six presentations scheduled of between 60 and 90 minutes – a long haul by any standard. The first presentation (9 am) was by William Henry, who is firmly in the demythologizing tradition of von Däniken, Velikovsky and Sitchin. His particular angle is that ancient and mediaeval art portrays *wormholes*, 'portals and gateways to the stars, which have been preserved in the art and myths of each era and place. Advanced beings that came from the light of the vastness of the Milky Way, and beyond, did so through these gateways.'[9]

'We are now in the Last Days', he announced and stated that the United States and Iran are both preparing to publicly display the Ark of the Covenant in order to cause Armageddon. The Ark, he said, is 'one component of a larger supernatural device, called the Judgement Day Device', which would open a wormhole to 'Sion' – actually the physical centre of the Milky Way galaxy, home to spiritually evolved humans who have outgrown their physical bodies, also known as Seraphim or Archangels. He then showed slides of ancient Egyptian statues, Tibetan Buddhist icons and mediaeval Christian devotional paintings, each of which he claimed showed these wormholes. Henry suggested that both the United States and Iran were attempting to open one of these wormholes and concluded by pointing out that many had suggested that the logo for the 2012 Olympic games in London actually said Zion, wondering if that meant we would see the big revelation of the Ark there.

Anne Strieber, accompanied by Whitley, then gave a presentation entitled *Bumping into God*, telling the story of her recent hospitalization with an aneurism and complications. Whitley found her unconscious on the floor of their LA home and had forgotten that he was due to be interviewed on *Coast to Coast*; when the phone rang, the listeners heard him weeping in panic. She developed meningitis and pneumonia, and Whitley stayed by her bedside, 'praying constantly' and claimed that he and 'thousands and thousands of Coast listeners' were 'literally praying the oxygen levels up'. Anne survived to describe messages being 'beamed into [her] brain like little bolts of lightning', including the message that 'God is a mathematical formula', and in the months of recovery which followed she had a number of experiences which she understood spiritually, including 'meeting an Angel in a copy shop'. 'Look to the little things in these miracles and signs', Whitley concluded: 'Because they fill our lives but we miss them all the time.'

These two opening presentations encapsulated a microcosm of millennial conspiracism. Henry mixed ancient aliens with a fear of imminent apocalypse through war with Islam, whereas the Striebers talked of health and how the spiritual manifests in the mundane through symbols and coincidences. But for both, change was imminent, and in both cases, ETs were literally divine beings. Interestingly, both used Christian language and symbols – prayer, Angels, Sion, *Revelations*, the Ark – along with symbols and terminology from other religious traditions.

Jim Marrs was introduced by Whitley as 'the most conscious member of all the conspiracies [*sic*] I have ever known'. Jim was the antithesis of Strieber in manner; where Whitley is careful and measured, Jim is avuncular and playful. His presentation, an overview of his then-unpublished book, *Our Occulted History* (2013), was nothing less than a retelling of the history of human society, tying the ancient alien narrative to UFO and conspiracist narratives. He began with a retelling of Zecharia Sitchin's interpretation of the Enuma Elish, the Sumerian cosmogony, before moving to von Däniken territory, discussing depictions of flying deities, scientific anomalies like the Baghdad battery and constructions which pre-date the known societies of antiquity. He compared our knowledge of history to the story of the blind men and the elephant; 'we have pieces of prehistory but can't see the whole'. However, the data, like gigantic skeletons and Egyptian relics in the Grand Canyon, is being deliberately suppressed; 'The Smithsonian institute is a government agency ... [and] a major suppressor of information of our heritage.' Marrs suggests the reason for the suppression is that the so-called elite bloodlines are hybrids with ETs from Niburu. The big question, he said, is where did they go? His suggestion, echoing Icke's in Chapter 5, is that they're still here, with the financial system and religions being the control systems they put in place to cement their control. This concern with 'religion' as control system ('and I'm not talking about spirituality', he added, 'that's real'), would be repeated throughout this research, both in the fieldwork and in the primary sources. He ended by asking: 'Are they still here? Are they even us?' and showing a slide of a politician being revealed as a reptilian. I later asked him about that image and whether this meant a conscious identification with Icke's reptilian thesis; his reply was 'I do not believe I will win many friends or converts by publicly calling the Queen Mother a "200 year old Reptilian Cannibal". Having said that, I am not prepared to state definitively that he is wrong.'[10]

Marrs often touched on themes more common in mainstream, Right-wing conspiracism *a la* Alex Jones, for example, focussing on the Trilateral Commission and the Bilderberg group, critiquing anthropogenic global warming and describing vaccines and 'chemtrails' as part of a eugenics programme against the overpopulation of humanity. When he brought the Knights Templar into the mix, I could not help but be reminded of *Foucault's*

Pendulum. His account of the Khazarian origins of Ashkenazi Jews – and by extension, the Rothschilds and the wider association of Jews with money lending and their centrality to elite bloodlines – was surprising only in context, as such material is widespread in the conspiracist milieu (see Chapter 5 for more detailed discussion on this). While none of the other speakers would suggest such a thing, there was no dissension, and as we will see in the following chapter, these views are heard frequently in this milieu.

We broke for lunch. Mark, the young Canadian chap I had been introduced to at breakfast, was talking about *Majestic.* I told him I'd read it on the plane coming over and really enjoyed it. He told me that reading a passage in the novel which included a description of a buzzing sound said to accompany abductions had caused him to spontaneously recover a history of visitor experiences. He suddenly remembered ETs coming into his house through the porch, as he told them: 'Not now! Not now!' He says he realized suddenly: 'I'm an abductee!' In the interview he recorded with Anne Strieber about his experiences, he described himself as a 'Starchild' – as he put it, he was a Grey, spiritually, if not physically. He also described 'the Motel', where he had had experiences with the Greys since childhood, similar to Strieber's descriptions.

The session with Marla Frees involved her performing 'readings' of the audience, in some cases channelling dead relatives, apparently rather successfully. She is bubbly and attractive, clearly popular with the other dreamland staff, and I later learned that she had known Betty Andreasson personally. As I mentioned in Chapter 1, she also used her presentation to accuse me of being a sceptic, to which I indignantly responded: 'I'm not a sceptic, I'm a social scientist.' Despite Strieber's later support, I have since learned that several others thought I was less open to Frees than to the other sections of the festival. I wonder if this was because they realized that her work appealed to a greater degree to counter-epistemic strategies and therefore was more open to a critique based solely on a scientific position – as her describing me a sceptic seems to suggest she took to be my position.

Next, Linda Moulton Howe presented on 'ETs, Time Travellers and Self-Activating Machines'. Beginning with a brief recounting of her *Strange Harvest* material on cattle mutilations, she moved to discussing sightings of small, drone-like UFOs which began in 2007. Known as *dragonfly drones,* they are the size of a remote-control helicopter toy, and several photographs are clear enough to make out mysterious symbols on their extremities. She received an email, allegedly from an engineer who had worked for military black projects, which claimed the symbols were 'self-activating software for extraterrestrial craft'. He provided her with several documents showing the symbols as part of a programme to back-engineer ET technologies recovered from UFO crash sites. She compared the symbolic 'alphabet' to the patterns found in some recent crop circles and asked if crop circles are therefore also self-activating software. She then speculated on the connection to the 12,000-year-old ruins at Gobekli Tepi in Turkey, previously mentioned by both Whitley and Jim Marrs.

Like Marrs, her presentation connected anomalous events into a vast, alternative history, and I later learned that she'd given the same talk at a conference organized by *Nexus* the previous year. Befitting someone with awards for journalism and a background in broadcasting, her presentation was polished and relaxed and included a lot of audio and video material. Unlike Marrs, however, her narrative lacked cohesion, and I was never sure how her conclusion had been reached from where she had begun.

The final presentation of the day was of Whitley Strieber, who asked: 'How could they be here, if they are aliens?' He then surveyed several recent scientific theories which offered ways by which the visitors might reach earth without defying the limit set by the speed of light under special relativity, including evidence for parallel universes and wormholes. He also recounted a recent UFO sighting, in keeping with the *Communion* theme. Conspiracist narratives were a subtle but constant presence, with Strieber stating: 'There is someone here with an immensely subtle intelligence ... who do not want us to be free.'

Nevertheless, the thrust of his talk addressed 'spiritual' concerns; the process of physically travelling to the stars and the 'uniting the inner and outer lives of man' are one and the same, he claimed. When he talked of becoming a child again and living outside of time, I became acutely aware of the fact that I was listening to a man in his late 60s, who moreover had recently come close to losing his wife of more than thirty years:

when you ascend, you ... can reconnect to the infinite truth of ourselves, that is projected into these bodies of ours, living in the time stream. But only part of us is here, the rest is more vivid, more alive, more true and far more real. The rest is entangled with the whole of reality, with every consciousness, with every event, with all that has transpired in time and that will transpire in time, and beyond time, with the building, joyous, improbable and surprising truth. The true being, a body that encompasses everything, that contains every star, every atom, every thought, the shadows of the mind, losses, dreams and expectations of all of us, all worlds, alpha and omega. And *when you see this, and feel yourself as this, then you are free.* (emphasis added)[11]

I was frankly exhausted by the end of this marathon of stigmatized knowledge, so when Tom invited me to the pub, I accepted eagerly. In the end, a large group of us set out to find somewhere to eat, including all the Nutters from breakfast and some others including a lady called Bree who could not remember my name and so called me Edinburgh, and Christine, another Canadian abductee, who was modelling silver earrings made by Tom in the shape of the visitor face from the cover of *Communion*. Conversation flowed pleasantly and openly, and I got the courage up to be a bit more proactive. Tom and Brian both agreed that they enjoyed Icke's work but drew the line at the Reptilian thesis; Wilcock they were unfamiliar with. Jenny, on the other hand, knew of Wilcock but said she 'doesn't trust the Davids' (but added sweetly that I was an exception). What other sources did they trust, I asked? It turned out that they all listened to *Coast to Coast AM* on a regular basis. Only Tom had heard of *Red Ice* but regarded it highly, and none had seen *Thrive*, which I found surprising; I later learned that my knowledge of these sources helped to convince them that I was trustworthy.

Heading back to my room, I bumped into Bree, Mark and his mother, sitting outside with some drinks. Having seen notices about not drinking on campus, I was unsure about the etiquette but accepted the offer to join them. Whether due to the lateness of the hour, the smaller group or the more female-led situation, conversation moved to the more personal aspects of the day. I asked about William Henry's presentation; it seemed very negative to me, with all its talk of Muslims and Last Days and very much at odds with his 'spiritual' image. He also seemed to have disappeared soon after his presentation on Saturday morning. They agreed that he'd seemed unusually angry and mentioned that he had complained about being ill, so had gone back to rest. Mark's mum suggested his new English wife might be the problem; Leigh confided: 'He's very competitive.' This was the first indication I had had of any competition for authority at the Festival; Whitley's authority had seemed rather absolute, although implicit. Interestingly, due to Anne Strieber's health, no Dreamland festival was held in 2013, and William Henry organized an event which also featured Whitley Strieber and Graham Hancock (renamed the Revelations Symposium) in the same venue in May 2013. All, however, agreed that the overall tone of the conference seemed a little more downbeat than in previous years and speculated that this might have been to do with the financial situation. I suspect that Anne's health was also a factor.

By now, my head was buzzing. But I slept soundly and without visitor interference.

Sunday

After breakfast, Whitley led the audience in a guided meditation. Several of the attendees had told me this would be a highlight of the festival, and Strieber clearly relished the effect it had on the audience. Indeed, this session was the closest Strieber came to a traditional 'religious authority' at the gathering, and it was clear that many who were there regarded it as an event of 'spiritual' importance. At lunch with the Nutters later, Tom said he'd definitely 'felt something', while Jenny heard a voice saying her name behind her. Zack had the most profound experience of travelling down a tunnel, at the end of which was a scary human face, which he did not recognize.

The presentation which followed was by Nick Pope, who worked for the UK Ministry of Defence for twenty-one years, a number of those leading the department which investigated UFO reports, until it was shut down in 2009 as part of the programme of spending cuts. To me, he seemed somewhat out of place among the group, as his presentation, on the 1993 Cosford flap, was the only one which involved mainstream ufology, that is, limited to descriptions of sightings of apparently physical unidentifiable craft, without any postulation of the motives of ETs or wide-ranging revisionist histories. Indeed, he has been the subject of a conspiracy theory himself, when accused of spreading disinformation for the MoD and/or helping acclimatize the public for a coming 'false flag' alien invasion. He managed to keep a careful balance between tailoring the material for the audience (such as emphasizing that the CIA were still secretly investigating UFOs and arguing that whatever the broader public might think, governments were taking the possibility of UFOs very seriously) and not being drawn into speculation based on particular reported details in witness accounts.

Chip Wilkins, who is also a promoter of free-energy technologies, next demonstrated a health technology based on the book *Earthing* (Ober, Sinatra and Zucker 2010). The book argues that the human body needs to be connected to the electric field of the planet for optimal health; this, the authors suggest, is why it feels good to walk barefoot. They argue that because modern humans wear shoes with synthetic soles and walk on carpet or other floor-coverings, they have insulated themselves from these currents and that many of our chronic illnesses are a direct result. Naturally, the authors also market a range of products to circumvent this deficiency and Wilkins had brought along a mat which connects to the earth in a wall socket to demonstrate, along with a couple of stories about its efficacy (although stressing that he had no commercial interest in the products or the book).

The day – and the festival – closed with an open question and answer session with all of the presenters, bar Linda Moulton Howe (Figure 4.2). However, as it had already overrun, the session was short. The first few questions were about the Earthing mat, which Strieber got increasingly irritated by, eventually refusing to allow any more. This was another demonstration that his implicit authority was capable of becoming explicit when required. Strieber was then asked if he'd seen *Thrive*. His reply was no but was intending to, although he had reservations based on the retraction recently issued by some of the participants (see Chapter 5). There was just time for lunch with the Nutters before catching a plane home again.

From Raven Dana's opening presentation to Nick Pope's closer, and the grey alien logo on the official mug, UFOs were never far from the agenda at the Dreamland festival. It would be incorrect, however, to describe Dreamland as merely a Contactee get-together; barely half of attendees reported a close encounter, and the speakers covered a broad spectrum of positions within the counter-epistemic field. Wilkins and Frees never mentioned ETs or UFOs at all. Of the 2012 presenters, Jim Marrs occupied territory more

Figure 4.2 Closing panel by Dreamland speakers (photo by the author).

often associated with conspiracism; whereas Marla Frees and Chip Watkins occupied the more popular millennial end of the spectrum, at least as traditionally constructed. Strieber, Linda Moulton Howe and William Henry were all somewhere in the middle of the spectrum. Nevertheless, themes of cover-ups, hidden histories and a coming transformation of humanity ran through the whole conference.

Nick Pope told me later that he was well used to the presence of conspiracy beliefs among the UFO community:

> The idea that the government knows more about UFOs than it lets on is a central trope of ufology ... but I'd be hard-pressed to say whether belief in UFO-related cover-ups and conspiracies has gone up, down, or remained broadly the same. There should be numerous opinion polls out there that will help you with that, as a common question is something along the lines of 'do you believe the government is covering up the truth about UFO?' ... I've noticed ... that people who believe in one conspiracy tend to believe in others; so there's a fair degree of crossover between the UFO community and 9/11 'truthers', for example.

Jim Marrs agreed; there had always been conspiracy theories in the UFO community, he told me, it was all the 'New Age, love beads stuff' that surprised him. Yet, as we discussed in previous chapters, UFOs were a prominent feature of popular millennial discourse in the Cold War period, which leads me to suspect that Jim Marrs may be an example of someone who is drawn to the spiritual aspects secondarily, having come into contact with conspiracy beliefs principally. Others, like William Henry or Marla Frees, seem to have been drawn by the spiritual aspects primarily. Either way, the Dreamland festival demonstrates that the UFO narrative may bring together agents who otherwise might have stayed within the conspiracist or popular millennial fields.

One interesting statistic from the questionnaires was that as many of the attendees knew Strieber's work through Dreamland or Coast to Coast as they did through *Communion* and even fewer through his fiction. Therefore, Strieber's initial extraterrestrial abduction narrative is less important to his capital than his later mobilization of the full range of counter-epistemic strategies through his Dreamland website and podcast. Nevertheless, several ideas were held by almost all attendees. For one, almost every attendee answered the question 'Is there an environmental threat to the planet?' in the affirmative, with only four saying they were unsure and two not answering. Twenty-one (of fifty-eight) answered the question 'Do UFOs come from other planets?' using the term 'interdimensional' or a similar term.

UFOs as discursive object in Strieber's work

Strieber's association with UFOlogy may be the reason that the conspiracist and millennial aspects of his work have not frequently been recognized, but we should not ignore their importance. Like many of his generation, however, as this thesis argues, Strieber's millennial leanings became increasingly conspiracist since the 1990s. There is nothing overtly conspiracist in *Communion*, perhaps because Strieber is at this point unconvinced about the physical reality of the visitors. *Transformation*, however, includes speculation on the alleged UFO crash at Roswell and the first mention of the possibility of a 'government cover-up' of the existence of UFOs (1988, 117). The cover-up narrative is considerably elaborated upon in *Majestic* (1989).

As a result of his upbringing, Strieber's writing is steeped in Catholic imagery; indeed, Kripal has described *Communion* as a Catholic mystical text, noting that it describes a journey undertaken at Christmas which culminates in sexually-tinged congress with an apparently divine female figure (2011, 304–5). Strieber would later describe this being as 'a postindustrial vision of the mother goddess' (1995, 232). Strieber describes the visitors – or some of them, at least – using angelic imagery; they dress in white and are associated with the colour blue, emanate love, seem particularly concerned with children, come from the skies above, are jealous of the free will and individuality of humans (1987, 144; 261), and intervene in the lives of mortals to elicit spiritual progress and, on occasion, give life-saving information (1987, 65). Indeed, this function of the visitors as messengers becomes of particular importance, first in their warning about Strieber's need to stop eating sugar in *Transformation* and later in the idea that they are guiding humanity in a specific direction, developed in *Breakthrough* and *The Secret School*. He later wrote of:

a whole Marian subculture that exists within the phenomena, and one of which I am a part: At one point I was very much ready to believe that the strange being depicted on the cover of Communion was the prototypical mother of us all. (Strieber and Strieber 1997, 52)

Yet Strieber is also highly critical of the Catholic church, and as early as *Communion* he talks of 'the inescapable thought that some sort of failure had taken place to bring Catholics to the point of disaffection that so many of us had reached' (1988, 169). What exactly that failure was is not directly addressed, but one might speculate that it relates to the perceived inability of the Catholic Church to incorporate anomalous experiences of the type Strieber experienced. In *Communion*, he states that his adult life has been 'a rigorous and detailed search for a finer state of consciousness' and 'eager study of everything from Zen to quantum physics' (1987, 35). He has practised meditation at least since before the writing of *Communion*. He also has several Wiccan friends, including Margot Adler and Dora Ruffner, and has taken part in pagan ceremonies (Conroy 1989, 95). He appeared with Dora Ruffner and other pagans on a 1987 episode of the Oprah Winfrey Show, in which he defended witches against charges of Satanism and ritual sacrifice, and stressed that Christianity and Wicca need not be in opposition (Winfrey). His stressing of the importance of the divine feminine, made manifest in the Marian mysticism of *Communion*, is another common theme of the alternative religious milieu in the twentieth century, including both Wicca and popular millennialism. He has also had a long term involvement with the tarot, describing the cards as 'a sort of philosophical machine that presents its ideas in the form of pictures rather than words' (1987, 283).

The symbolism of the triangle, which he finds recurrent in abduction accounts, links his Catholicism to his fifteen-year involvement with the Gurdjieff Foundation, beginning ca. 1971 (1987, 254–81). George Ivanovich Gurdjieff (1866?–1949) was born in Russia of Greco-Armenian parents, and like Blavatsky, his early life is obscure and his auto-hagiographic accounts describe years of wandering in search of ancient knowledge. What is certain is that by 1913 Gurdjieff is residing in Moscow and has begun to teach. Although there were fragments of a complex cosmology in his teaching,[12] the bulk of his work was focused on 'waking up' his pupils. Gurdjieff taught that the vast majority of humans were literally asleep and that discovering one's 'true will' required a great deal of hard work and 'conscious suffering'. After several years of upheavals, he settled in France in 1922, where he was to remain until his death. He established his Institute for the Harmonic Development of Man at Fontainbleau-Avon that year, but it was formally disbanded only two years later in 1924 following a serious car-crash. Although it continued informally until 1930, Gurdjieff devoted himself to writing from then on (Moore 2006, 445–8). His proposed trilogy, *All and Everything*, was less an attempt to systematize his ideas than to produce the effect of the Work in the reader, as Gurdjieff seems to have lost faith that he would be able to sufficiently train a successor in the time and health remaining to him.[13]

Strieber left the group because he felt that a change in leadership was refocussing the group's concerns 'from matters of substance to matters of form' (Conroy 1989, 94), which I understand as meaning a move away from the practical towards the philosophical. Gurdjieff stressed the practical component of his teachings, and Strieber similarly rejects the idea of metaphysics, instead stressing the physical and scientific reality of souls and the so-called supernatural. It is probably worth noting that when Gurdjieff decided to publish his teachings, he did so in the form of an allegorical novel in which angels and demons are portrayed as extraterrestrials who travel to earth in spacecraft to work covertly in the service of a higher power, *Beelzebub's Tales to his Grandson* (1950 [1999]).

Strieber is aware of a 'spiritual' discourse in his work, even if the public are not necessarily. In *The Key*, he describes his style as 'warmed-over Catholicism and new-age mysticism' (2001 [2011], 196). Indeed, millennial concerns are constantly present in his writing, particularly those which form discursive objects in the field of millennial conspiracism. Perhaps most obvious is the theme of imminent ecological catastrophe, present in his 1980s novels, through the Communion books (particularly *The Secret School*), *The Key* and the book it inspired, *The Coming Global Superstorm*. His belief that the tarot cards 'reveal a hidden symbolic coherence of great purity that has more to do with order than chance' (1987, 282) underlines his belief in an occluded order underlying seemingly unconnected events. Furthermore, the teleological motif of the imminent transformation of humanity is frequently encountered in the Communion series:

> As we express ourselves into the *next age*, we will come to the prime moment of this species, when mankind gains complete mastery over time and space and lifts his physical aspect into eternity, including the ascension of the whole species into a higher, freer, and richer level of being. (Strieber 1997, 225–6; emphasis mine)

> [T]he human species is going down the proverbial birth canal. Right on schedule, it seems, as the Age of Aquarius is dawning, mother earth is spilling her waters … Mankind is going to die, one way or another, to the world that we know now. But, at the same time, mankind is going to be born-literally born again. (Strieber 2012, 202)

Ultimately, Kripal suggests, the visitors are 'channelled Masters of the American Millennial Tradition' and the *Communion* series and *The Key* fit nowhere so well as among the corpus of "western esotericism" and the 'New Age' (2011, 327). Yet the belief in the physical reality of the visitors, and their being the same entities behind religious and supernatural phenomena, only now describable in scientific terminology, does not lead Strieber to reject religion absolutely. In his foreword to Vallée's *Dimensions*, he states that Vallée

> places this modern UFO experience firmly in its historical context as the latest manifestation of a phenomenon that goes back at least as far as recorded history. Thus, at a stroke, he redefines it as a part of the fundamental mythology of human experience and enables us, for the first time, to begin to raise questions about it of sufficient depth and resonance to be meaningful ... He reveals an appalling truth: the phenomenon has been with us throughout history-and never, in all that time, have we been able to deal sensibly with it. (Vallée 1988, vi)

For Strieber, the idea that 'most major religions have emerged out of visionary experiences that are, in fact, understandable in the context of the UFO encounter' (In Vallée 1988, viii) does not lead him to reject the validity of those religions. Rather, it provides a way in which they can be relativized, seen as having a common source. More importantly, this common source can be reclaimed by the individual, back from priestly intermediaries. Even Marrs, the most traditionally conspiracist of the Dreamland presenters felt the need to preface his critique of 'organized religions' as mechanisms of oppression and control. He later clarified his position for me; '"Religion" refers to social structures largely created to control the human population ... Spirituality refers to the basic energy make-up of the universe with its wide range beginning with crude electrical energy all the way up to sentient, self-aware energy'.[14] Thus, his demythologization of religious experience through the lens of the UFO narrative is motivated by issues of power, and specifically, the mobilization of epistemic capital. I return to this theme in my conclusion.

At the close of *Breakthrough*, Strieber claims that the idea of malevolent extraterrestrials – an idea which, intentionally or not, he helped to popularize – was a result of Cold War paranoia and a received Judeo-Christian worldview. However, he adds: 'And then there are the awful Lizard-men who enter the picture, but there seems little to be served by discussing them' (1995, 235). Nevertheless, that is what the next chapter will do.

'Problem-Reaction-Solution': David Icke and the Reptilian Thesis

As Strieber moved increasingly towards conspiracist discourses, millennial discourse was itself changing; as described in Chapter 3, by the mid-1990s, many prominent 'New Age' figures were acknowledging that their imminent millennial prophecies had failed to pan out as predicted, and a number of strategies were mobilized to avoid cognitive dissonance.

Cometh the hour, cometh the man. On the back cover of Icke's *Heal the World* (1994a), early 'New Age' promoter and Findhorn supporter George Trevelyan stated: 'This is the man I've been waiting for, for many years.' Perhaps this was because Icke, unlike the majority of his peers, offered a solution as to why the prophecies had failed; something – some malevolent occluded agency – was preventing the 'New Age' from arriving. Trevelyan was apparently not alone, as today Icke commands a significant audience. His website steadily ranks in the top 10,000 worldwide, he has some twenty-plus books in copyright (three published during the writing of this book) and has lectured in at least twenty-five countries, in the type of venues more associated with major pop concerts (Lewis and Kahn 2005, 3). Icke, who Barkun describes as 'the most fluent of conspiracist authors', possessing 'a clarity rarely found in the genre' (2003, 163), has constructed a bricolage of popular millennial and conspiracist beliefs of staggering complexity. He is indelibly associated with the theory that a race of reptilian extra-terrestrials is in covert and malevolent control of society, here called the reptilian thesis. Astonishingly, a 2013 poll by Public Policy Polling indicated that 4 per cent of the US public believe that 'lizard people' control society.[1]

In the press, Icke is typically portrayed as either an eccentric or a dangerous anti-semite, a serious issue which I deal with at length below.

In the public mind, however, he is perhaps most often remembered for his 1991 Wogan interview in which he claimed to be 'the son of god' and as a result is sometimes considered as a 'cult leader'. In fact, Icke has never made any attempt to create any kind of formal organization, despite his significant audience; nonetheless, his particular and peculiar nonformative spiritual discourse has importance for scholarly analyses of contemporary popular religious narratives.

I begin with a historiographical overview of Icke's life and work; as with the previous chapter, the concern is not the factuality or otherwise of his claims but to bring out those aspects in which popular millennial and conspiracist discursive fields overlap and the way in which the UFO narrative functions as discursive object between them. Indeed, Icke's career represents an encapsulation of my argument in this book that with the perceived failure of 'New Age' discourses in the 1990s, the *prevention* strategy provided an explanation for this failure. Icke's early material is demonstrably drawn from Theosophical and 'New Age' sources; his move to conspiracism in 1993–4 coincides with the term's abandonment by many of its leading proponents; and UFO and ET narratives provide the discursive object between the two fields, most obviously his infamous reptilian thesis. Importantly, however, he remains as committed to millennialism as ever.

Life and work of David Icke

David Vaughn Icke was born in Leicester on 29 April 1952, the second of Barbara and Beric Icke's three sons (Icke 1993a, 28). Beric was a staunch socialist who had won a British Empire Medal during the Second World War for rescuing airmen from burning aircraft (Icke 1993a, 30) but was by this point working in a clock factory (Icke 1993a, 32).[2]

Like Strieber, David Icke describes himself as a nervous child and something of a loner, 'frightened of everything' (1993a, 37). He was influenced by the pacifism and idealism of the time, and his love for the music of the 1960s remains to this day.[3] A stronger personality began to develop when he became interested in football. After taking up goalkeeping in the school football team, he was selected for the Leicester Under-Fifteens

Team (Icke 1993a, 47) and was offered an apprenticeship with Coventry City upon leaving school in 1967, aged 15 (Icke 1993a, 48). During the next four years, he played for the Coventry Youth team, on the Coventry City reserves and briefly on loan to Oxford United, a period in which his career was hampered by injury, including a recurring swelling to his knees and ankles (Icke 1993a, 56–60). He was given a cartilage removal operation, as a result of which he was diagnosed as having rheumatoid arthritis, aged just nineteen (Icke 1993a, 60). That May, Icke met Linda Atherton; they were engaged by June and married on 30 September 1971 (1993a, 61). Although he had been fired by Coventry City, one of the directors, John Camkin, managed to secure Icke a month's trial for Hereford United, who would eventually sign him, and although part-time, gave him a higher profile than he had had with Coventry City (1993a, 61). However, the arthritis continued to spread and he was forced to retire in 1973, at the age of 21 (Icke 1993a, 69–70). This sets the pattern for which he was to repeat several times in the next decade: a mercurial rise in a career, followed by sudden and absolute abandonment within a few years.

He then began working as a reporter for the *Leicester Advertiser* (Icke 1993a, 75). After several other low-key journalism jobs, in 1975, shortly after the birth of his first child, Kerry, he got a job as a news and sport broadcaster with BRMB Radio in Birmingham (Icke 1993a, 82–3). This would eventually lead to as a presenter for BBC television, first with the local *Midlands Today* (Icke 1993a, 88–9) and eventually onto sports reportage for flagship programmes *Newsnight* and *Grandstand* in 1981–82 (Icke 1993a, 93–5). The couple's second child, Gareth, was born 12 December 1981. In 1983, Icke co-presented the launch of the innovative breakfast television show, *Breakfast Time*, on the 17 January 1983, with Selina Scott, Nick Ross and Frank Bough (1993a, 99–100).[4] His first book, a memoir of his football career was published later that same year (Icke 1983). Even at this point, Icke seems to have been an ambitious but restless and possibly difficult character (Icke 1993a, 102). In fact, as we go on, we'll see that he has fallen out with almost everyone he's worked with – the significant exception being his wife Linda, despite several severe challenges.

Icke's political views, perhaps typically for a working-class person living in the North of England in the 1980s, were Left-wing. When he became concerned about the amount of 'horrendous building applications' being passed, Icke decided to attempt to prevent this by entering local politics, and after considering joining the Labour Party, decided on the Liberals because of their manifesto commitment to environmental issues (1993a, 110). However, he quickly became disheartened, finding the political process to be dominated by 'gamesmanship' and dishonesty (Icke 1993a, 111). Instead, in mid-1988, he and Linda established an Isle of Wight branch of the Green Party, and Icke announced his intention to run as a candidate in the next General Election (1993a, 115). Due to his public profile, the branch soon attracted a lot of support, and Icke was invited first to be a 'regional representative' at the national party council (although, by his own admission, because he was the only person who put their name forward), and at the meeting was elected one of six National Speakers, who acted as spokespeople in an organization that eschewed formal leaders (Icke 1993a 116). Although he rejected speculation on his ambitions to lead the party at the September 1989 Green conference (Hoyland 1989), by the following April, Icke was widely considered *de facto* co-leader, along with Sara Parkin, and delivered a speech calling for a more organized structure which was received with a standing ovation from half the delegates (Linton 1990). In it, he admitted that he would accept the role of salaried spokesman if offered to him but opined that the notion of a party leader in the traditional sense would mean that the Green Party 'would be playing the same grey games the other parties play' (Linton 1990) (Figure 5.1).

Icke's forays into green issues seem to have awoken a hitherto dormant interest in millennial questions; 'The teachings of the traditional church had made little sense to me, and so the spiritual side of things had passed me by. But the deeper I travelled into Green politics, the more it became a spiritual journey ... Why were we here?' (1991, 13). He increasingly began to feel that 'the next step for the Green Movement is to encompass this spiritual dimension more completely' (c.f. Kemp and Wall 1990, 19; Icke 1991, 138). During a tour to publicize his book on Green politics, *It Doesn't Have to Be This Way* (1989), he stayed with a Nottingham couple who told him they had been asked to present him with an unidentified book by a 'spirit message' (Icke 1991, 14).

Part of his new found political conscience included refusal to pay the Community Charge (popularly known as the 'Poll Tax'), introduced by the Conservative government in 1989 in Scotland and 1990 in the rest of the UK. He finally paid the 'unjust' tax, telling the press that he had 'taken my protest far enough on behalf of those who cannot pay' (Anonymous 1990).[5] There were claims that his prosecution led to his dismissal from the BBC in 1990 (Christy 1991; Taylor 1997), although others speculated that the reason was that his prominent profile in the Green Party – including his candidacy for the Isle of Wight constituency – was seen to have compromised his impartiality (Barker 1990), perhaps a dubious claim given that he was a sports presenter. There have also been suggestions that the BBC had been forewarned that he was planning to use his BBC profile to promote his recent 'spiritual' experiences.

Icke describes that during 1990, he had begun to feel an overwhelming sense of a 'presence' accompanying him. In an oft-repeated story, he claims that during a hotel stay, he said to the presence: 'For goodness sake, if you are there, contact me. This is driving me up the wall' (1991, 14). In 1990, he visited a well-known psychic named Betty Shine for the first time, after coming across her book *Mind to Mind* in a railway bookshop (Icke 1991, 15). Although he was primarily seeking relief from his arthritis, he claims that from the beginning he was also attempting contact this other 'presence' (1991, 16). On his third visit, the 'presence' apparently made contact with the psychic, to whom Icke had said nothing in regard. She described him as 'Chinese in appearance' and dressed as a mandarin. He said his last incarnation had been in 1200 CE and gave his name as Wang Ye Lee, adding that 'Socrates is with me' (1991, 16–7).

Wang Ye Lee then made a number of prophecies:

There will be great earthquakes. These will come as a warning to the human race. They will occur in places that have never experienced them …

In the country which he lives… there will be a cultural revolution in five years' time. He was chosen as a youngster for his courage … He was led into football to learn discipline and training, but when that was learned it was time to move on. He also had to learn to cope with disappointment, experience all the emotions, and how to get up and get on with it …

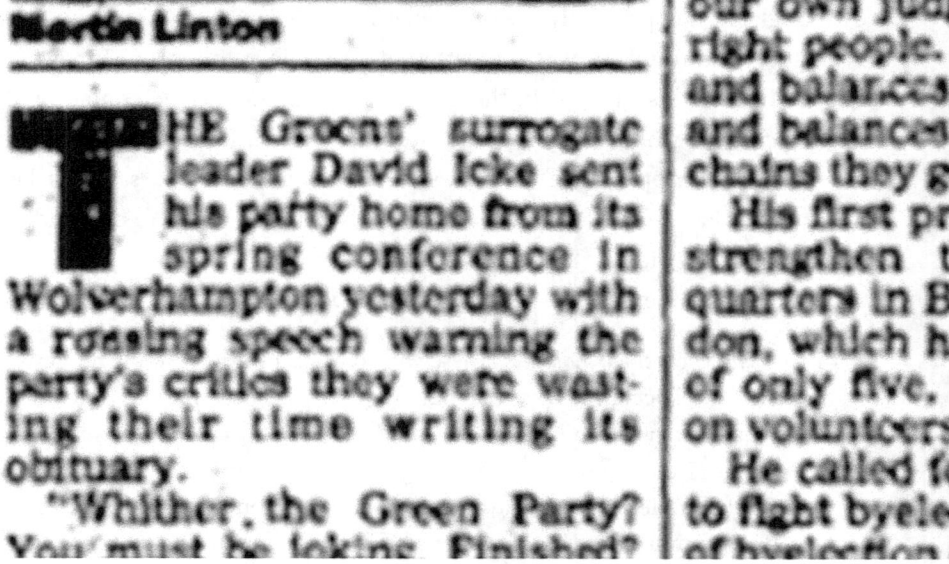

Figure 5.1 David Icke in *The Guardian*, 9 April 1990. Guardian News and Media Ltd. Reproduced with permission.

ing cry of 'We're on ou

their

e world's

to elect the
for checks
when checks
ne balls and
ar."

is clearly to
arty's head-
, south Lon-
ll-time staff
elies mainly

ational team
and a panel
ates

leaders' speech at the close of
the last session. He was given a
standing ovation by about half
the 600 party members. The
rest appeared unhappy at what
was clearly a speech by a de
facto joint leader — together
with Sara Parkin who left for
another conference on Friday
— of the party, even though
both disavow any belief in
party leaders.

There has been a grounds-
well of suspicion that the two

He is a healer who is here to heal the earth, and will be world famous.
He will face enormous opposition, but we will always be there to protect
him...Sometimes he will say things and wonder where they came from.
They will be our words... (Icke 1991, 16–7; emphasis mine)

By the time Icke was able to visit Betty Shine again, he had begun to see
an 'eye' everywhere he looked, and had furthermore begun serious reading
of Edgar Cayce's books (Icke 1991, 21). Wang Ye Lee, through Shine, made
another series of prophecies:

He will write five books in three years.
   Politics is not for him. He is too spiritual. Politics is very unspiritual and
will make him unhappy.
   He will leave the Isle of Wight. He will find closed minds there. It will
become difficult for people who need to see him to get to the Island, and he
will leave.
   One man cannot change the world, but one man can communicate the
message that will change the world. (Icke 1991, 22; emphasis mine)

Icke repeats sections of these prophecies in his current writings and talks,
though notably none of the passages I have italicized above, all of which
are patently falsifiable (e.g. Icke 2012, 9). This is a clear example of *rolling
prophecy*, as I described in Chapter 2. Icke produces a number of date-specific
prophecies, but those which are unsuccessful are quietly dropped – for example,
Icke continues to promote *Truth Vibrations* as prophetic by only mentioning
those passages of which have not been disproven. This process emphasizes
prophetic successes (or often, merely potential prophetic successes) while de-
emphasizing prophetic failures, thus increasing his epistemic capital within
the field. Here, Icke is stressing the importance of the channelling epistemic
strategy.

Icke then consulted an astrologer who confirmed Wang Ye Lee's
(or, arguably, Shine's) predictions and went on to outline several of Icke's
past lives (Icke 1991, 32–4). His book about these events, *The Truth
Vibrations*, was written in the latter months of 1990, while Icke's public
profile through the Green Party and the BBC was at its apex. It laid out
Icke's new millennial beliefs:

I have called these new energies the 'Truth Vibrations' because they will
affect – are affecting – our consciousness and understanding in such a

way that we will open our eyes to the truths about God and life, truths which have been forgotten for so long. (1991, 9)

In the book, Icke revealed that the presence which had contacted him was in fact only one of several Ascended Masters who were now guiding him, which he sometimes referred to as 'the guys'.[6] Many of the messages from 'the guys' came through a Welsh channeller called Janet (Icke 1991, 63). Chief amongst them was 'Rakorczy' (Icke 1991, 73), 'Racorczy' (1991, 74) or possibly 'Rakorski' (Icke 1992, 31), who was, in previous lives, Merlin, Joseph the father of Jesus, an Atlantean priest, Christopher Columbus and both Francis and Roger Bacon (Icke 1991, 74). This figure is clearly the 'Rakoczi' identified by Bailey in *Initiation, Human and Solar* (1951, 46, 49, 56–9, 61), *The Externalisation of the Hierarchy* (1957, 274, 304, 507–8, 644, 665, 667–9), and *Discipleship in the New Age vol. I* (1944 [1972], 730) and elsewhere referred to as 'Master R____' (1925, 455). Bailey refers to Rakoczi as 'Lord of Civilisation' (1944 [1972], 232), as does Icke (1991, 4). Bailey states that his specific 'task' is to establish the Age of Aquarius (1957, 667). Icke's description of the rays, seven visible and five hidden (1991, 121–2), follows Bailey's to the letter. Interestingly, Icke never mentions Bailey as the source of the name Rakorczy and the information about the Rays, although it is possible that this information came via Janet.

In February 1991, following his intuition and a series of coincidences, he travelled to Peru:

> I suddenly had a tremendous urge to go to Peru, although I had no idea where this came from … I kept seeing the word 'Peru' everywhere, on books, in newspapers and in travel agent windows … Everything I was doing since I had those first communications through the psychic was based purely on intuition. I didn't know why I was going to Peru, for instance, only that I had to for some reason. (Icke 2003, 16; c.f. 1993a, 175–85)

For their similar insistence on the meaningfulness of apparently random events, and the apparent importance of travelling to South America, it is worth comparing this description with the 'First Insight' of James Redfield's *sensu lato* best-seller, *The Celestine Prophecy*:

> Have you ever had a hunch or intuition concerning something you wanted to do? … And then, after you had half forgotten about it and focussed

on other things, you suddenly met someone or read something or went somewhere that led to the very opportunity you envisioned?...They feel destined, as though our lives had been guided by some unexplained force. (Redfield 1993, 17)

While in Peru, Icke had a revelatory experience in a circle of stones on a mound near the ruins of an Incan city. He heard voices and had the sensation of being flooded with energy, and felt that his consciousness had been irrevocably transformed (Icke 2003, 21–2):

My feet could not move. It was as if two giant magnets were pulling them down and suddenly my hands were thrust into the sky ... energy of incredible power poured through me from head to toe and vice versa. Then it began to pour out through my hands ... For well over an hour I stood there, arms to the sky, my feet never moving an inch, as the power built up. My head was pounding and it like a piece of music getting louder and louder ... Then I felt the first drops of rain and it was like a switch had been turned off. (Icke 1993a, 180)

At the beginning of March 1991, Icke, Linda and their children were joined in their home by Deborah Shaw, a channeller who, although resident in Calgary, had grown up in the Midlands of England (1991, 88). As part of the channelled communications during his Peruvian experience, Icke was told that he was to have a physical relationship with Shaw and that in fact he had already done so on the astral plane (1993a, 216–7). This ménage-a-trois was later nicknamed 'the turquoise triangle' by the press.

By 20 March, he had resigned from the Green Party, although it was publicly dismissed as 'merely a temporary thing' (Kennedy 1991). The Guardian interpreted his leaving as a power tussle, describing Icke as 'denying, without ever being able to silence, accusations of his leadership ambitions' (Kennedy 1991). The piece ends with the party spokesman saying that while the party would re-elect him if given the option, Icke replied by saying that not only would he be out of the country but 'at the centre of tremendous and increasing controversy' and that the publication of the 'apocalyptically titled' *Truth Vibrations* will be the cause of said controversy (Kennedy 1991).

One week later, 27 March, Icke, accompanied by Linda (now going by the name of Michaela), Deborah (now called Mari Shawsun) and daughter Kerry, gave a press conference to publicize the book (Ezard 1991). Icke, dressed in a turquoise 'shell' tracksuit, presented a number of prophecies including the imminent eruption of Mount Rainier in Washington State (Figure 5.2). When heckled about whether he and Shaw had a sexual relationship, Icke replied:

> If you resonate on the level of the world around us, then you see a man and two women and you say, 'Oh, there's a bit going on there, mate'. But if you resonate on this higher level then you see not two ladies, but two bodies with energy patterns. (Ezard 1991)

Icke stated that they were guided by messages delivered through 'voices and automatic writing. No one was more gobsmacked than I' (Ezard 1991). It is not hard to see why the press reported it as though they were dealing with a 'cult' in the popular understanding – a prophetic figure, the taking of new names, unusual dress and apparent polygamy. Indeed, while Icke is presently keen to distance himself from his behaviour during this period, it is worth asking whether at the time he *did* intend to create a more formal 'cult' organization but changed his mind when the public response quickly became overwhelmingly negative.

Given that he was a popular television personality, it is perhaps understandable that he seems to have thought that interviews in the popular press were the best way to disseminate his ideas. These included lengthy interviews on Nicky Campbell's *Into the Night* show on BBC Radio 1 and on ITV's lunchtime chat show *Coast to Coast People*, hosted by Fern Britton. Most famous, however, was his appearance on the prime-time BBC interview show *Wogan* on 29 April 1991, during which he was laughed at by the audience. Where Campbell was genially tongue-in-cheek and Britten compassionate but incredulous, Wogan's tone was reproachful:

> Icke: You know, the best way of removing negativity is to laugh and be joyous, so I'm delighted there's so much laughter in the audience tonight.
>
> Wogan: David, they're laughing at you. They're not laughing with you. (Wogan 1991)

This statement is not as openly hostile as it appears on paper, however. Wogan may have been warning Icke more than mocking him. After admitting that Icke's moral position is 'not entirely unreasonable', Wogan tells him:

Spreading the word . . . David Icke with (from left) daughter Kerry, Deborah Shawsun and Linda Icke PHOTOGRAPH: KENNETH SAUNDERS

'Son and daughter of God'
predict apocalypse is nigh

Figure 5.2 David Icke in *The Guardian*, 28th March 1991. Guardian News and Media Ltd. Reproduced with permission.

If I may say so, you have confused the message by an awful lot of predictions ... But if you don't give them any proof, if you don't give them any reason to believe you they'll dismiss you as a crank. Which is what they're doing. (Wogan 1991)

In the latter half of the interview, following the question regarding predictions, Icke increasingly fails to make any connection with the audience whatsoever. He insists, with absolute certainty, that there will be earthquakes and volcanoes during 1991 and that if there are not, then 'the Earth will cease to exist' (Wogan 1991). These events did not occur, and this is likely the reason the footage remains unavailable today. The Guardian asked why the BBC had allowed 'poor, mad Icke' to make a 'loony address to the nation', suggesting that they were taking revenge on a former employee who would not toe the line (Christy 1991). In the tabloid press, however, the controversy revolved around his statement that he was the 'son of god', which was interpreted as Icke claiming he was Jesus (Ronson 2001a: 147–8).

Interestingly, even at this point his later conspiracist themes were present:

[W]hen a child dies in this world of preventable disease every two seconds, when the economic system of this world must destroy the earth simply for that system to survive; when you see all the wars, and when you see all the pain, and when you see all the suffering, is it a force of love and wisdom and tolerance that is in control of this planet? (Wogan 1991)

This flurry of public activity led not to Icke's messages being broadly accepted but to almost total public ridicule, to the point where he claims he could barely walk down a street in the UK without being heckled and mocked. A few weeks later, the Times reported a crowd of more than 100 youths gathered outside his house, shouting 'Give us a sign, David!' (Anonymous 1991) The Green Party, already split by infighting, may also have been affected: their previous momentum was lost by the 1992 General Election in which they achieved only 1.5 per cent of the vote (Linton 1991; Anonymous 1992). National Speaker Sara Parkin put her resignation down to the decision to invite Icke to speak at a Green Party event in November (Wood 1992).

Icke has largely disowned the book he wrote during this period, *Love Changes Everything*, which drew principally from Shaw's channelled sources (1992, 11).[7] Nevertheless, *Love Changes Everything* is particularly interesting, as it demonstrates Icke's early millennial discourse and appeals to the channelling epistemic strategy. Icke explicitly identifies as 'New Age', despite the contemporary decline in the currency of the term and Icke's later explicit rejection of the term (1992, 85; 130). It is principally a detailed description of the evolution of the planet Earth along the lines established by Blavatsky and her later elaborators, beginning with Mu's 'Crystal Wonderland' where Wang Ye Lee originally incarnated (Icke 1992, 42), its destruction and replacement by Atlantis (Icke 1992, 45)[8] and the memory of these events on the 'Etheric level' (Icke 1992, 91). However, certain aspects of the narrative are more reminiscent of Gurdjieff, in particular the section describing the creation of the first Solar Logos and planets by the Godhead in order to learn about itself (33–4 and ff.). *Love Changes Everything* talks extensively about a fallen *deva* (essentially a Theosophical term for an angel without the Christian connotations) named Lucifer who became imbalanced and began to challenge the Godhead for control of the Creation, beginning with the Earth (55–9). He incarnated in a small, dying planet, which he propelled towards the Earth, devastating the rest of the Solar System in the process and destroying the Atlantean society (Icke 1992, 59–61). The Earth's energetic connections to Creation and the Solar Logos would have been completely destroyed but for the efforts of the Archangel Michael to prevent physical collision and to remove the malevolent force controlling what we now call the Moon (Icke 1992, 61–5).

Icke's relationship to Christianity is at this point complicated. On the one hand, he takes issue with the institutionalism of the churches for allowing 'dogma to turn thinking into heresy' (Icke 1991, 11). On the other, however, Icke is elsewhere using Christian imagery and language freely; 'The Way, the Truth and the Light' (Icke 1991, 17); the evil spirit is named 'Lucifer' (Icke 1991, 59), and later his 'physical aspect' is named Satan (Icke 1991, 101); Jesus 'set the standard to which we all should aspire ... that perfection of thought and action is possible for us all to achieve' (Icke 1991, 117); the parable of the prodigal son and the quotation 'become like little children' are used as metaphors for the spiritual path (Icke 1991, 25–6). In *Love Changes Everything*, Icke talks quite happily about – and sometimes *to* – Jesus, either as a historical figure or as an Ascended Master, as constructed in the Theosophical tradition (1991, 4). His stance was to become much more militant, however, as we shall see.

Another reason for Icke's rejection of *Love Changes Everything* may be the less-than-amicable end to his relationship with Shaw. Shaw bore Icke a daughter, Rebecca, in 1991 (Icke 1993a, 223). Icke claims that she had left the house on his bequest due to her increasingly divisive behaviour and emotional instability and that she only then revealed her pregnancy to him (1993a, 219–22). Others have suggested that Linda insisted that she leave the house as a result of the pregnancy (Taylor 1997). Either way, Icke saw the child only once before Shaw decided that she would raise her without any contact with him (Icke 1993a, 223). Icke and Linda's third child, Jaymie, was born in November 1992.

He set out on a speaking tour of universities and what were then still generally referred to as 'New Age fairs' around the country, which, except for a few mockers, were sparsely attended (Icke 2003, 22–3). Two further books followed in 1993, *Days of Decision* in July, and *In the Light of Experience: The Autobiography of David Icke*. *Days of Decision* is a slight (eighty-six pages) collection of material from his talks at this period, and as such, is useful to compare with later presentations. Like them, it starts with a defence against his charges of madness, is particularly vigorous in its environmental agenda and presents a Gnostic vision of a humanity programmed to believe an illusory cosmology:

> The human race is mind controlled to think that black is white and white is black. When you strip away all the diversions and illusions, it is this programming, especially in what we call the 'developed world', that is the real reason we are devastating the planet. (1993b, 4).

Days of Decision critiques the existence of the historical Jesus, who Icke describes as 'a myth prostituted as fact' for political reasons by the Roman Emperor Constantine (1993b, 23). He does not, however, deny the existence of the Theosophical 'Christ spirit' and restates that 'Jesus' (with quote marks) was a higher being who incarnated on earth (1993b, 38). While he defends channelling, he states that he now has 'ceased to work with channellers, and instead I "feel" the information being passed to me from other levels. The sources of information are those highly evolved intelligences that operate outside our own physical level, and who are guiding the earth and humanity through this period of great change' (1993b, 32). Among these higher intelligences are UFOs, which are described as being able to change vibrational frequency and thus apparently 'disappear' from our perception (1993b, 38–40). Thus although they are agents of spiritual or supernatural powers, Icke constructs them as essentially physical, albeit in a way not presently scientifically falsifiable.

The fact that the autobiography *In the Light of Experience* (1993a) was published by Warners underlines that despite all the ridicule, at this point Icke was still a household name in the UK. At 317 pages, it is considerably longer than his other works of the period and is a surprisingly candid account of his life, particularly focussing on the period 1990–93.

The pace continued into 1994, with the manifesto *Heal the World*, which is as slight as *Days of Decision* at only 101 pages of large print. Yet, as he acknowledges in the frontispiece, its publication fulfilled Wang Yi Lee's prophecy of five books in three years (1994a, 6).

Middle period: Conspiracism

1994 marks a second phase of Icke's thought, in which conspiracist narratives become increasingly prominent. *The Robot's Rebellion: The Story of the Spiritual Renaissance* (1994b) was immediately different in presentation to his earlier works, being the first (with the exception of *Days of Decision*) not to feature a somewhat saintly portrait photograph on the cover. It marks the beginning of the increasingly conspiracist direction Icke's work was to take over the following nine years, with Icke using conspiracist writings as source material rather than channelled sources and Theosophical texts. He connects them into a metanarrative concerning the enslavement of humanity by the Illuminati, who covertly rule the world by manipulating world events. Icke again alludes to his belief that it is the Illuminati who have prevented the arrival of the 'New Age';

> [T]his book is the story of a conspiracy to control the human race. That may sound fantastic to you at this stage, but read on and you will see that it is very real and affecting our lives every day. It is, however, a conspiracy that we can, and will, dismantle … At the heart of this attack on human freedom is the desire to keep us from the knowledge of the spiritual realities of our true selves and the understanding of our place in this wondrous web of life we call Creation. (Icke 1994b, xi)

The Illuminati narrative originated in a 1797 book by John Robison, Professor of Natural Philosophy at the University of Edinburgh, entitled *Proofs of a Conspiracy against all the Religions and Governments of Europe, Carried on in the Secret Meetings of Free-Masons, Illuminati and Reading*

Societies, etc., collected from good authorities. A Bavarian intellectual, Adam Weishaupt, founded an Order of the Illuminati in 1776 to promote rationalism and liberalism, but it was forcibly disbanded by the Bavarian government in 1785 (Melanson 2009). Robison was convinced that they continued covertly, seeking world domination, and had infiltrated Freemasonry (Partridge 2005, 273). The concept that a small group of families covertly seek to monopolize humanity is a highly significant conspiracist narrative and one of the clearest examples of Right-wing discourse crossing into popular millennial discourse; from National Socialist anti-Semitism to anti-Communism in the 1970s to anti-Globalism in the 1980s, which then makes the leap into popular millennial discourse through UFO and Ancient Alien narratives. In the 1990s, the idea that Illuminati dynasties originated in early civilizations such as Sumeria and Babylon hybridized with Ancient Astronaut theories and developed into the idea that the Illuminati were descended from extra-terrestrials, particularly through William Bramley's *Gods of Eden* (1990), to which *Robot's Rebellion* makes frequent reference.

Another significant source for Icke during this period was *Nexus*, a bi-monthly 'alternative news' magazine based in Australia but with offices in the United States, Canada, the UK and Europe. It is widely available in newsagents, has a bi-monthly circulation of 18,000[9] and describes itself as 'The world's No. 1 magazine for alternative news, health, future science and the unexplained'.[10] Nexus began publication in 1986, but its present form dates to 1990 when Duncan Roads bought it and assumed editorial duties.[11] Roads, like Icke, was heavily involved in 'New Age' circles prior to his interest in conspiracism, running (in his own words) 'one of Australia's largest new age bookshops' but had dropped the term by 1990.[12] *Nexus'* articles are seldom blatantly millennial in tone, and Roads claims he 'revived this magazine by deleting all articles on the new age, the occult, environment and similar subjects, and concentrating on what I call "suppressed information"'.[13] Yet the 'Statement of Purpose' states 'humanity is undergoing a massive transformation',[14] and furthermore, although they claim no affiliation to any religious or political groups, Roads states that the force 'behind' Nexus is 'God'.[15] In other words, Nexus retains a millennial perspective, despite distancing itself from 'New Age' discourse. The worldview presented therefore – simultaneously millennial and apocalyptic, holistic and counter-epistemic – is a clear example of millennial conspiracism.

Billed as 'the most explosive book of the twentieth century', ... *and the truth shall set you free* continued the trajectory of combining popular millennial and conspiracist narratives. It includes more detailed critiques of Illuminati control of the banking system, media, and politics, and notably, a chapter critiquing Zionism, although apparently in a form considerably toned down from the first draft (Honigsbaum 1995). Importantly, it also develops the idea, only briefly mentioned in *Robot's Rebellion* (Icke 1994b, 212), that the ultimate controllers of the Illuminati are extra-terrestrial. This is the reason, Icke argues, that the existence of UFOs is being covered-up; were the masses to accept the existence of extra-terrestrial beings visiting the Earth, the Illuminati's extra-terrestrial masters' cover would be blown (1995, 290–5). The book's cover was by artist Neil Hague, beginning a collaboration that continues to the time of writing, with Hague's representations of Icke's ideas, mixing bright oil paints with photo-manipulation, becoming increasingly prominent in his books and presentations.

At this point, Icke's efforts were focussed on the United States, where he seems to have found a more receptive audience. Perhaps, as Taylor suggests, there may be a peculiar susceptibility in the US psyche to claims of malevolent, possibly supernatural, forces (1997). Moreover, US audiences were not prejudiced by his familiarity as a television presenter and subsequent apparent descent into madness on the Wogan show. Perhaps most importantly, there was a history of New World Order narratives among Christian Right-wing groups in the United States which Icke's ideas were able to piggyback off. Whatever the reason, the initial printing of ... *and the truth shall set you free* is alleged to have sold out in four weeks (Brown 1995). Together with the following year's *I Am Me, I Am Free* (1996) (subtitled *The Robot's Guide to Freedom*, suggesting that it is a companion piece to *The Robots' Rebellion*), Icke introduces many of the terms and motifs for which he would become well known in US conspiracism.

Firstly he describes a process by which the Illuminati are alleged to guide the population gently in the direction they desire by creating false problems to which the solution demanded by the public is their intended outcome. Icke names this dialectic '*problem-reaction-solution*' (Icke 1995, 50). Part of this process is the creation of false opposites; for example, the funding of both Axis and Allies in the Second World War to provoke the creation of the European Union and the State of Israel (Icke 1995, 67). Icke calls these false opposites *opposames* (1996, 14–5) and compares them to modern business binaries such as McDonalds/Burger King or Pepsi/Coca-Cola. Through this process, Icke claims, society is gradually and almost without challenge being converted into a global totalitarian state under Illuminati control, which he names the *totalitarian tiptoe* (2002, 19).

Perhaps recognizing that his audience was at this point drawn more from the conspiracist milieu, Icke's writing in these books often attempts to sell millennialism to conspiracists rather than the other way around as his earlier works did:

> To understand the true nature of the conspiracy, we need to appreciate its esoteric foundation. Esoteric knowledge, often called 'the occult', is not negative in and of itself. It is just the knowledge of the potential to harness the energies of Creation for good or ill, and the understanding of the human psyche how it can be balanced, healed, or manipulated. (1996, 211)

I am Me, I am Free includes the prescient admonition:

> Cathy believes that holographic projections were used to give the appearance to her of people transforming into 'lizard-like' aliens? This relates to the theme in some UFO & extra-terrestrial research of a race known as 'Reptilians' operating on the planet ... What if these reptile-like extra-terrestrials can manifest in human form? I know it sounds fantastic, but with each month that passes I am more convinced that there's much to investigate here. I will expand on this in my next book. (Icke 1996, 69)

Before he could complete this work, however, there was another significant change in his personal situation. Icke met Pamela Leigh Richards, a fifty-two-year-old financial services worker from Phoenix, Arizona, in August 1997 at a speaking event in Jamaica. Three months later, they met again on Aruba, in the Caribbean, and they became romantically attached. Icke had approached her because he had recently been told by the English psychic Derek Acorah that he would meet an American lady who would invite him to dinner and with whom he would become inseparable.[16] Icke was at this point still living with Linda and their children in Ryde, but he divorced Linda (although she remained his business manager) and married Pamela in 2001 (Clarke 2012).

After five books in three years, it took Icke an unprecedented four years to complete *The Biggest Secret* (1999), perhaps as a result of these personal upheavals but perhaps also as a result of its controversial thesis. *The Biggest Secret* presents the thesis that the Illuminati are a race of extra-terrestrial bipedal reptilians who assume human appearance. Although originally from distant stars, they are also extra-dimensional, existing in a parallel but less dense, energy state to ours. They keep humanity in a state of fear and anxiety in order to feed on these emotions, which he alleges are sustenance to beings made of less dense matter. In effect, by making the Illuminati bloodlines originate with the Reptilian Anunnaki, Icke connects ancient alien narratives with mainstream conspiracism.

The Biggest Secret is comparable to Blavatsky's *Isis Unveiled* (1877 [1997]). Both books are breathless syntheses of the gamut of popular epistemic narratives, drawing on any source which fits the narrative, scientific, synthetic, channelled or otherwise. Icke's thesis draws heavily from three primary sources: Zecharia Sitchin (discussed in Chapter 3), alleged SRA victim Arizona Wilder and South African Zulu *sanusi* Credo Mutwa. Icke takes Sitchin's historical narrative but combines it with Mutwa's stories of reptilian and other ET races (in this case originating on distant stars rather than an undiscovered planet) interacting with humans in prehistoric Africa (Steyn 2003; Chidester 2005: 182–3). Mutwa not only reports being taught about ETs during his training as a sangoma but reports personal abduction and sexual congress with them (Steyn 2003, 84). As Steyn notes, Mutwa's stories bear little resemblance to other recorded among the Zulu people (Steyn 2003, 72) and that they should not be taken as historically accurate (Mutwa 1966: i). At the same time, however, aspects at odds with middle-class western culture, such as the efficacy of animal sacrifice, are downplayed by Icke and others (Steyn 2003, 85).

Like Strieber, Icke accepted the Satanic Ritual Abuse narrative without reservation, and it formed a major part of his thesis in *The Biggest Secret*. He had previously made use of O'Brien's *Trance-Formation of America* (1995), but late in the writing of *The Biggest Secret* he met Arizona Wilder, an alleged SRA victim whose testimony enabled Icke to make the connection between SRA and the reptilians. Her account, published by Icke as the video *Confessions of a Mother Goddess* (1999), agreed with Icke's reptilian hypothesis but gave him a great deal more detail (e.g. it is from Wilder that Icke got the material about the British Royal Family being reptilians). Wilder's accusations that Laurence Gardner, author of popular books expanding on the *Holy Blood and the Holy Grail* hypothesis that the Merovingian royal dynasty were descended from Jesus, took part in Satanic rituals involving human sacrifice, seems to have been the cause of the final break between Icke and *Nexus*.[17]

The reptilian thesis was new to the public but has a long tail. It seems to have been primarily a development of Hollow Earth theories. Sir Edward Bulwer-Lytton's 1871 novel *The Coming Race* described a subterranean humanoid race, the Vril-ya, who utilized an all-pervasive force called *vril* to provide light and heat, power machines and permit paranormal feats such as telepathy (Bulwer-Lytton 1871). Although legends of a sacred city in Tibet called Agartha (or something similar) have a longer genealogy; the French occult writer Joseph saint-Yves d'Alveydre was the first to describe it as being located underground, in 1910 (Goodrick-Clarke 2002, 112). Once again, the modern form goes back to Blavatsky, who, inspired by her contemporary Ignatius Donnelly, wrote that the Atlanteans had left a global network of 'subterranean passages running in all directions' (1877 [1997], 128). In the early 1930s, the motif of Atlanteans or other ascended masters residing in subterranean chambers was taken up by later Theosophists Guy Ballard, founder of the 'I AM' Religious Activity, and Maurice Doreal, founder of the Brotherhood of the White Temple (Barkun 2003, 114–5). The Hollow Earth hypothesis was popular among European esoteric groups too, becoming a significant part of Nazi mythology, both during the Second World War and afterward (Goodrick-Clarke 2002, 212–4 and 216).

The earliest known report of specifically reptilian subterraneans comes from mining engineer G. Warren Shufelt, who, as reported by the Los Angeles Times in 26 January 1934, sunk a shaft into Fort Moore Hill in search of tunnels inside. He alleges to have been told by Little Chief Greenleaf of the Hopi Indians (also going by the name L. Macklin) that the Hill contained a lost city, constructed by 'the Lizard peolpe' [*sic*] after a 'great catastrophe'

5,000 years previously. Shufelt was looking for golden tablets upon which the Lizard People had preserved the 'origin of the human race'. Shufelt's account contains many elements of later reptilian narratives; subterranean dwellings, technological advancement, a desire for gold and some connection to the origins of the human race (Bosquet 1934).

In 1945, the pulp science-fiction magazine Amazing Stories began to publish the work of Richard Shaver, an unknown writer who had previously spent a number of years hospitalized for unspecified psychiatric problems (Barkun 2003, 115). Shaver wrote a series of letters to the magazine's editor, Raymond Palmer, in which he claimed to hear voices through the welding equipment at his workplace, initially of his co-workers but later originating from a subterranean world, which he found he could telepathically travel to (Barkun 2003, 116). Palmer encouraged his literary endeavours, and Shaver eventually turned in a 10,000-word manuscript which Palmer reworked into a 31,000-word novella, entitled 'I Remember Lemuria!' (Shaver 1945). Although Palmer admitted to extensive revisions to make the manuscript fit the style and conventions of pulp sci-fi, their collaboration, collectively known as the Shaver Mystery, was both prolific and successful, being prominent in the magazine between March 1945 and 1948 (Barkun 2003, 116). The core of the scenario was the two types of beings who occupied the subterranean world – the good 'teros' and the evil 'deros', who had occupied the antediluvian caverns but were devolved by the radioactive machines they found therein. Shaver and Palmer alleged that the deros were creating chaos on the surface through telepathy, and Doreal wrote a letter to *Amazing Stories* in September 1946 in which he confirmed Shaver's account and therefore its compatibility with a Theosophical lineage (Barkun 2003, 117). The Shaver Mystery increasingly included UFO material from 1947, and when Palmer retired from *Amazing Stories* in 1948, he continued to advocate the belief that UFOs originate from within the Earth (Barkun 2003, 117).

Hollow Earth motifs continued their association with UFOs through the theories of post-war neo-Nazi writers who described an ever-more elaborate scenario in which the Third Reich survived by retreating to the Antarctic and constructing UFOs, often in collusion with inner-earth or extra-terrestrial powers (Goodrick-Clarke 2002, 156–72). By the 1980s, mainstream UFOlogical writers had picked up on these motifs, most importantly in the growing mythology around secret military bases reputed to be located in Dulce, New Mexico, and Groom Lake, Nevada, also known as Dreamland or most famously, Area 51 (Barkun 2003, 11–2). That this was happening at the same time that the abductee narrative was gaining traction through Strieber, Budd Hopkins and others, is likely not coincidental; as UFO and conspiracist discourses became ever more intertwined, narratives which had previously remained on the fringes – such as Inner Earth narratives were being drawn into the narrative too.

The motif of malevolent reptilian extra-terrestrials entered popular culture through the television series *V*, broadcast in 1983. The popular NBC series, also broadcast in the UK, depicted first contact with apparently friendly humanoid extra-terrestrials. In fact, their true reptilian appearance was covered by masks, and they were just as dishonest about their intentions, working to destabilize the US way of life through stealth. Its writers intended it to be an allegory of fascism, and multiple aspects of the plot and design are obvious references to the Nazis, from the costumes, the human characters being split into collaborators and resistance, and even a character who is a Holocaust survivor. A question: did *V*'s fascist allegory influence Icke's critics as much or more than Icke himself?

The reptilian narrative gathered steam through the early 1990s, appearing in a number of books which combined conspiracism with millennial narratives. Valdemar Valarian's *Matrix II* (1990) describes reptilians as one extra-terrestrial race among several at war across the galaxy, and John Rhodes had founded reptoids.com by 1994, which continues at the time of writing. Linda Moulton Howe's 1993 book, *Glimpses of Other Realities 1: Facts and Eyewitnesses* contains an account of Jeanne Robinson, who contacted Howe with the assertion that she had been abducted by reptilians since the age of four (1993). O'Brien's *Trance-Formation of America* alleged that she witnessed George H. W. Bush transformed into a 'lizard-like "alien"' during a ritual (O'Brien 1995, 133–4). Also influential on Icke's synthesis was Arthur Horn's *Humanity's Extra-terrestrial Origins; ET Influences on Humankind's Biological and Cultural Evolution*, in which he suggests that the Sumerian Anunnaki were reptilian ETs (1994). From 1997, Branton (a pseudonym) posted a series of articles to several internet sites describing reptilian extra-terrestrials living in vast subterranean complexes (of which Dulce et al. are the merest tips) and fighting a war on a cosmic scale against the forces of individualism and liberty, from which Icke would draw significantly (Barkun 2003, 122–3). Yet Icke's account was to be the one that caught the public imagination and brought the Reptilian thesis into the mainstream.

At the same time, it proved divisive in conspiracist circles. In 2001, Alex Jones described Icke as a 'con man' and the Reptilian thesis as the 'turd in the punchbowl' of his otherwise lucid conspiracist research (Ronson 2001b). Even active supporters of Icke, such as one-time Greenpeace activist Brian Selby, have sought to distract from the centrality of the Reptilian hypothesis, claiming that it 'confuse[s] things' (Ronson 2001a, 157–80). Icke himself admits, 'I wish I didn't have to introduce the following information because it complicates the story and opens me up to mass ridicule. But stuff it' (Icke 1999, 19). Yet he has never rescinded his thesis, although, as we will see, the degree of importance Icke places on it has shifted over time. 2001's *Children of the Matrix* develops the narrative that the reptilians are interdimensional as well as extra-terrestrial, although the book's impact would be overshadowed by events.

The 11 September 2001 attacks on New York's World Trade Centre, whatever their wider geopolitical effects, provoked an increase of discussion of stigmatized knowledge, both on the internet and in the media more broadly; there were reports of UFO sightings at the scene, and numerological analyses of the attacks were distributed widely via email (Barkun 2003, 158–61). Icke was quick to react, publishing on his blog that the attacks were orchestrated by the Reptilian-controlled US government as a reason to further restrict the freedoms of the population and to promote centralized government and war in the Middle East. Icke's interpretation fitted neatly with what had quickly become the conspiracist consensus (Barkun 2003, 161) and his book on the events, *Alice in Wonderland and the World Trade Centre Disaster* (2002), was one of the first to appear, and in the United States at least, his epistemic capital increased as a result. In it, he argues that the attacks were a 'false flag' attack – that is, an attack upon one's own people but blamed upon the enemy – in order to provoke public support for an attack on Afghanistan as part of the problem-reaction-solution mechanism.

Late period: Millennial conspiracism

Icke's work enters a third phase in 2003; as that year's *Tales From the Time Loop* put it: 'I knew that for me to take the story on and understand the even greater context in which this manipulation is unfolding, I would have to see into other dimensions of reality beyond the "world" that we daily experience' (1). The catalyst for this broadening of perspective was an ayahuasca experience in Brazil in January 2003. He had been invited to speak at a ten-day event in Manaus, during which participants would be offered ayahuasca, an extremely potent native psychoactive narcotic. He claims that he was invited because users often experience reptilian entities during their experiences. Due to travel delays, he ended up taking the drug apart from the rest of the group, alone with one of the organizers. After an hour of screaming, which he understood as a release of pent-up frustration from the days of mass ridicule in the early 1990s, he became calm and began to channel (Icke 2003, 322–5). He was told that

> all that exists is one infinite consciousness, which was referred to as 'The Infinite', 'Oneness' and the 'One'. In our manipulated, illusory, reality we had become detached from the One (in our minds, though not in fact) and therefore we viewed everything in terms of division and duality instead of seeing that all is connected, is the same infinite Oneness. This illusory sense of disconnection is the mind prison I call the Matrix. (Icke 2003, 325)

This experience seems to have affected him considerably, and from then on his work swings back towards the popular millennial and in fact seems like an attempt to reconcile his later conspiracist work with his earlier Theosophy-derived material. If we are all one, Icke asks his younger self, how can there be malevolent extra-terrestrials? His answer is that none of it is real; we created the reptilians just as we created the rest of the world we experience every day.

It is here that Icke's debt to Gurdjieff is clearest. Gurdjieff posited that humans had become spiritual sleepwalkers due to the presence of the 'organ kundabuffer', placed there by the Solar Logos to prevent a planetary catastrophe in prehistoric times, but that when it was removed by the higher powers, humans continued to act as though it were there and did not become reconnected to the energetic currents of the larger galactic system.

Icke's argument in these later works is very similar, except that the initial shutting-off of human awareness comes not from the Solar Logos but from humanity themselves. In *Tales from the Time Loop*, Icke outlines a cosmology channelled during his ayahuasca experience wherein the human collective subconscious projected a 'collective thought projection' – named, with Icke's typical populism, after the popular 1999 science-fiction film, *The Matrix* – to escape its fear of the unknown, and forgot that there was anything else beyond (2003, 326). Furthermore, the Matrix takes the form of a 'time loop', in which a finite set of events endlessly repeat, albeit with variations in detail (Icke 2003, 325–6). In other words, time itself is part of the trap which has separated humans from the realization that all beings are 'one consciousness experiencing itself subjectively' (Icke 2003, 353). This 'illusion… that humans believe[d] to be real' became self-actuating and began to manipulate and generate events to create more of the fear with which it was created (Icke 2003, 328–9). One expression of this manipulation was the creation of 'sentient programs' to act as agents within the Matrix – the reptilians (Icke 2003, 329). So on a macro level, Consciousness is responsible for both humanity and reptilians, on a day to day micro level, malevolent forces are indeed acting against humans. Reptilians are as real as our human bodies are; but they lack the connection to Consciousness – the spark of the Divine – which humans possess (Icke 2003, 239).

His presentations became less frequent in direct proportion to their increasing length – at this point six to seven hours, although his 2012 talk at Wembley Arena would pass ten hours. The basic structure was firmly established by now; Icke would begin with a conspiracist reading of a recent event – the death of Diana Spencer was an early favourite, later replaced by 9/11. By convincing the audience that they might be being lied to about one event, then that audience should then begin to wonder what else they may have been lied to about. So this discreet conspiracy belief moves seamlessly into a broader conspiracism and Icke's explanation of how the global elites work. As the basic presentation developed, it grew a longer and longer tail on the theme of interconnectedness and the motif that we are all parts of one consciousness. Around 1993, however, Icke flipped the basic structure of his presentations and began opening with the holistic consciousness material, moving to why this knowledge is suppressed and finally how that manifests in the real world. Which begs the question, was there a deliberate change of focus? Perhaps the death of his mother in 2006 provoked the swing back towards spiritual matters, as for the next few years, his talks included a description of seeing her corpse in the mortuary and his realization that it was a 'spacesuit' for her consciousness (Icke 2008). I discuss the structure of his presentations further below.

In 2006, Wogan re-interviewed him for a special 'Now and Then' series, and was apologetic regarding his former mocking interview. This paralleled a broader reconsideration of Icke's work in the UK, with Channel 5 also screening an unusually disinterested documentary entitled 'David Icke: Was He Right?' (Hull 2006). Icke's critique that 9/11 was a 'false-flag' attack was finding acceptance within more mainstream conspiracist discourse through films such as *Fahrenheit 911* (2004) and *Loose Change* (2005; see Chapter 1), and his references to reptilian extra-terrestrials and appeals to channelled communications either found a new audience or were ignored. Alex Jones also softened his position – or rather, capitulated to Icke's capital within the field – as Icke has become a frequent guest on Jones' radio show and continues to be so at time of writing.

Icke restructured his business operations in 2006,[18] and around that time channeller du jour, Carol Clarke, began to council Icke against Pamela.[19] By 2008, Pamela was no longer part of the business; Linda and Gareth are listed as directors, with Kerry owning 10 per cent and Icke having sold his stock (David Icke Books Ltd, 2008). Icke eventually filed for divorce in 2008, although it would be a further three years before a settlement was reached. Richards accused Icke in the tabloid press in the UK and on her personal blog of threatening her and her family and of accusing her of being a reptilian.[20] David Icke Books' first publication was *The David Icke Guide to the Global Conspiracy (and how to end it)* (2007) which, although a weighty tome of 613 pages in trade paperback format, was relatively slight in terms of new material. Interesting, however, is that conspiracy has moved back to the fore. Perhaps due to an expensive divorce and legal proceedings, it was simply a direct attempt to capitalize on his US conspiracist audience.

In June 2008, Icke mounted an unsuccessful political campaign in a by-election in the Haltemprice and Howden constituency. The by-election was triggered by the resignation of the then Shadow Home Secretary David Davies in protest at the passing of the Counter-Terrorism Act, which he felt unacceptably curbed civil liberties (Wintour 2008). Icke, claiming he had no intention of winning, ultimately lost his deposit.

Despite its 800 pages, the only significant new contribution in *Human Race, Get Off Your Knees: the Lion Sleeps No More* (2010) concerns the moon. Drawing primarily from *Who Built the Moon?* (2005) by Alan Butler and Christopher Knight, Icke argues that the moon is not a natural satellite, but a hollow artificial space station (2010, 299–307). Its primary function, he argues, is to act as an antenna broadcasting the Matrix' signal which humans perceive as reality (2010, 405–37). Here, his writing once again recalls Gurdjieff's description of (unconscious) life on Earth as 'food for the moon' (e.g. Ouspensky, 1949 [1987], 84–6). *Remember Who You Are* (2012) develops this narrative further; now Saturn is the control centre from which the moon's signal is originally broadcast (134–7). Saturn, he claims, is the origin of the single eye symbol (as in the eye in the pyramid of the Freemasons) (2010, 137–8), the Star of David (2010, 153) and the root of the words 'Satan' and 'Satanism'; 'Saturn is Satan so Satanism is Saturnism' (2010, 154). Throughout this period, he was on tour, presenting at major venues around the world, including New York and Melbourne, Australia. The tour culminated at Wembley Arena with what was almost certainly the largest gathering of millennial conspiracism to date. I described my fieldwork there below.

In 2011, Icke also contributed to Foster Gamble's *Thrive*, as described in Chapter 1. His contribution forms the bulk of the middle section of the movie, where the conspiracist material dominates, and Icke's contribution is a critique of the 'fractional reserve' banking system, i.e. where banks can loan (and therefore charge interest) on several times the amount of money they actually hold in their reserves. Importantly, *Thrive* does not mention reptilians, and indeed, describes extra-terrestrials as benevolent. Nevertheless, Icke's involvement is believed to have been the major catalyst behind ten of the other contributors, including Deepak Chopra, John Robbins and former astronaut Edgar Mitchell, to disown the movie in a statement issued 12 April 2012, in which they wrote that they were 'dismayed that our participation is being used to give credibility to ideas and agendas that we see as dangerously misguided' (Chopra et al. 2012).

Allegations of anti-semitism

Icke's work is not often taken seriously, by scholars or by the popular media. To a large degree, this must be due to the apparently outlandish nature of some of his claims. Furthermore, Icke's evidence is frequently drawn from non-scientific sources; channelled (or invented) documents such as Blavatsky's *Book of Dzyan* (2001, 92–3) or the *Emerald Tablets* (2005, 98–9); popular films, which are interpreted as coded fact (2003, 312); and discredited researchers such as Sitchin, although naturally Icke claims that the reason that they are discredited is that they are exposing the truth (2003, 17).

However, a far more likely reason why the *Thrive* contributors might describe Icke's work as 'dangerously misguided' is the widespread opinion that sees Icke's use of 'Reptilian' as a code word for 'Jew' (Honigsbaum 1995; Kalman and Murray 1995a, 1995b, 1996; Ronson 2001a, 2001b). The prominence of Rothschild and other Jewish families among the Reptilian bloodlines and his references to the Protocols of the Elders of Zion as the Illuminati's plan for world domination reinforce this impression. Milton William Cooper's influential *Behold a Pale Horse* (1991) claimed that the Protocols were actually an Illuminati text, published in a doctored form to cast suspicion on the most popular scapegoat of the time, the Jews (Barkun 2003, 59–60), a claim which many conspiracists have repeated, Icke included (e.g. 1994b, 138–41 and ff.; 1995, 54–5 and ff.). *Robot's Rebellion*'s frequent references to the Protocols of the Elders of Zion and alleged Holocaust revisionism in an early draft of his next book ... *and the truth shall set you free*, brought Icke to the attention of the Guardian and London Evening Standard, saw him heckled repeatedly at his Glastonbury presentation by Green Party national spokesman, David Taylor (Honigsbaum 1995) and banned from speaking at the Green Party conference in September 1994 (Chaudhary 1994). Indeed, it seems likely that this was the reason why Icke broke with Gateway and began publishing independently (Honigsbaum 1995). The book was eventually published by Icke's own Bridge of Love.[21]

As a result, Icke has been picketed by Left-wing activist groups during some public appearances, notably in Canada, as documented in journalist

Jon Ronson's documentary *Secret Rulers of the World* (2001b). However, as Ronson notes, this reading requires disregarding the many non-Jewish Reptilians named by Icke (2001a, 149). Ronson, in fact, comes to see the picketers as no more rational than Icke and decides that no matter how odd his thesis may be, Icke means it literally (2001a, 162). That has not stopped Ronson from being frequently cited as arguing exactly the opposite, however.

It is my opinion that Icke is not anti-Semitic, and I present my reasons here. Firstly, Icke was accused of anti-Semitism *before* there was any mention of reptilians in his work (e.g. Honigsbaum 1995; Kalman and Murray 1995a, 1995b, 1996). His split with Gateway publishing around 1996 seems to have been forced by disagreements over revisionist Holocaust material, as detailed above. Yet Icke continues to publish material about the Jewish people which, while not necessarily anti-Semitic, is certainly questionable; a good example is the chapter in *Tales from the Time Loop* which relates the theory that Ashkenazi Jews descend from the mediaeval Khazar kingdom of Eastern Europe (2003, 92–130). Yet elsewhere in the book he outlines his reptilian thesis. One simply cannot have it both ways; if he means 'Jews' when he says 'reptilians', who does he mean when he says 'Jews'?

Secondly, it requires one to ignore the many identified by Icke as reptilians who are not Jewish. These include many of his most famous identifications, including the British Royal Family, US Presidents including Clinton, Obama and both Bushes, and country singer Kris Kristofferson.

Thirdly, Icke identifies the supposedly reptilian ruling elites as being 'Aryan' in several places (1999, 40; 2003, 91). This would seem to directly contradict the thesis that 'reptilian' is code for 'Jew', given that Right-wing anti-Semites tend to identify with Aryanism. Similarly, he identifies Hitler as being in the employ of the reptilian Illuminati (2012, 234–5).

Fourthly, one must ignore Icke's frequent admonitions that he means Reptilians literally (1995, 125; 1999, 19; 2003, 226). He was asked the question directly in 2012:

Daily Bell: We've asked you this before. Is your work a metaphor–an allegory–even though it's not understood that way?

David Icke: I don't do allegory except when I'm using it to symbolize a concept. *I am certainly not using allegory when I'm talking about what's behind the conspiracy and the nature in which*

the conspiracy works. I only use allegorical symbolism
when I'm trying to use symbols that people can relate to,
to understand deeper concepts of stuff, but absolutely no
allegory otherwise. (Wile 2012; emphasis added)

He denies that his critique of Zionism should be taken as a critique of the
Jewish people:

Ask most people about Zionism and they'll say, 'That's the Jews'. The
Rothschild networks in politics and the media have successfully 'sold' this
impression – this image – as 'common knowledge' and 'everyone knows
that'. But it's not true. The terms 'Jewish people' and 'Zionism' are not
interchangeable as we are led to believe. Many Jews vehemently oppose
Zionism, and many Jews are not Zionists. Rothschild Zionism in its public
expression is a political ideology. (2012, 228)

As Barkun notes, he has never been a member of any Right-wing groups
(2003, 107) and has indeed criticized them on occasion for their Christian
fundamentalism (Icke 1994b, 466).[22] At Wembley, 2012, Icke denounced
racism as simply 'the ultimate idiocy'. It occurs to me that to interpret Icke
as meaning 'Jews' when he says 'reptilians' requires conspiratorial thinking in
itself, that is, that Icke's real meaning is available only to initiates. Ultimately,
it may simply be easier for most people to accept that he is anti-Semitic – a
worldview that they at least are familiar with – than that he believes that extra-
terrestrial reptiles control world politics.

Similarly, Lewis & Kahn's interpretation of his narratives as a satire of
rapacious avarice of free-market capitalism is similarly misguided (2005).
In interpreting Icke's ideas as satirical, they imply an authorial intent which
I do not feel they provide adequate proof of; although they demonstrate that
Icke's work *may* be interpreted in such a satirical manner, they fail to present
examples of where it *must* be. So while interesting, we need to consider it an
oppositional reading.

Perhaps a more fruitful approach would be to examine the reptilian thesis
in relation to a broader context of portrayals of Otherness, malevolence and
secrecy. Like Strieber, Icke portrays the reptilians as being the phenomenon
at the root of folk tales concerning fairies, angels and other supernatural
beings (2003, 297); however, Icke's descriptions of the reptilians are

unambiguously demonic, mirroring traditional religious descriptions of demonic figures in numerous respects. Most obviously, their resemblance to snakes seems drawn from Christian imagery relating to the Genesis serpent, who from the Middle Ages has been equated with Satan himself and who is also frequently portrayed with reptilian features (Barkun 2003, 123). What's more, Icke portrays them as living in subterranean cities and tunnels (1999, 37) and a chthonic origin for evil creatures, as well as Hell being located underground, is widespread in Judeo-Christian mythology (Partridge and Christianson 2009, 8–9). Shape-changing is another ability associated with demons, including the ability to appear in human form. Icke's reptilians can also control those with high levels of reptilian DNA, operating them remotely, a narrative that parallels accounts of demonic possession (Partridge and Christianson 2009, 8–9). Indeed, this idea of hybridization may also tie into the biblical demonic narrative of the *nephilim*, in which demons are the result of the interbreeding of human women with fallen angels (Flaherty 2010, 85–91).

Icke further portrays the reptilians and their hybrid bloodlines as partaking of paedophilia, child sacrifice and cannibalism, tying these accounts into those of the SRA scare through the accounts of Cathy O'Brien, Arizona Wilder and others. What is important to recognize is that these accusations form a common pool of images from which descriptions of Otherness may be drawn; the same accusations were made against those purportedly influenced by the Devil in the medieval witch crazes (Victor 1996) and, pertinently, against the Jews in Europe from the medieval period until the present day (Frankfurter 2006, 130). Thus, I think it is not only an oversimplification to reduce the reptilian thesis to anti-Semitism but may actually be perpetuating an anti-Semitic narrative of the Jewish people as cause, rather than victim, of the vocabulary of Otherness.

The question of Icke's potential anti-Semitism is serious and sensitive, and the points I have made above are not intended to close the subject once and for all but rather to problematize the automatic assumption that he is anti-Semitic based on second-hand information. I return to these issues of Othering and how it relates to popular millennial theodicy in the concluding chapter. For this book, however, we should note that this neatly parallels Gnostic theologies. Despite Icke's predictions of a 'global awakening', those awakened by his ideas remain a relatively small group. The following section examines how Icke's subscribers receive his ideas.

'Remember Who You Are', Wembley Arena 2012

As I was preparing for my trip to London, the recently deceased TV presenter Jimmy Savile CBE became major news. The initial trigger was an ITV documentary, *Exposure: The Other Side of Jimmy Savile*, broadcast on 3 October 2012, which alleged several cases of sexual abuse by Savile against teenage women. It quickly emerged that the investigator, Mark Williams-Thomas, a former police detective, had been working with the BBC to produce a report for their Newsnight slot but which was cancelled on orders from above. Further, a Newsnight piece on the investigation was also shelved, allegedly because the BBC was showing obituary material. While the BBC Director General resigned, it quickly became apparent that the BBC's misdemeanours were not the most serious issue. As I travelled to London, the latest was that Operation Yewtree had three investigations proceeding – Savile alone, Savile and others, and others. Arrests were being made daily, including the formerly convicted paedophile Gary Glitter. The links to the BBC, Prince Charles, and according to internet rumours, 10 Downing Street, suggested to many that paedophilia and sexual abuse more generally were endemic and institutionalized in the upper echelons of UK society.

Many saw this as a confirmation of (some of) Icke's claims; he claimed to have named Savile as a paedophile, Satanist and 'procurer of children for the reptilian elites' in 1999.[23] However, I can find nowhere where Icke names Savile prior to the ITV documentary. Essentially, this is another example of Icke mobilizing rolling prophecy – retrofitting his claims to fit present events. Yet rumours had been circulating for many years about Savile, so much so that Louis Theroux felt the need to address them in his interviews with Savile (Theroux 2000). Bizarrely, the story as reported by the tabloid press went even further into Icke territory, with the Daily Mail claiming that Savile was a practising Satanist (Fielding 2013; Figure 5.3). In essence, I was witnessing a miniature revival of the Satanic Ritual Abuse scare. As the story developed, rumours were spreading across the internet as to who else

Figure 5.3 *Daily Express*, 13 January 2013. Express Newspapers/N&S Syndication. Reprinted with permission.

was going to be arrested, culminating in Philip Schofield presenting a list of alleged paedophiles procured from the internet to PM David Cameron on live daytime television.[24] It would have been easy for Icke to make the story the crux of his presentation. He did not, but for his supporters that I met, it was of central importance.

It was bitterly cold when I arrived, and due to a broken ticket scanner, the queue was not moving. It did give me a chance to listen in to some of the conversations going on around me. A group of young men immediately behind me got talking to an older couple about Icke. This was their first time seeing him live, they said, although they had all watched his previous presentations online. Their friend had got them into it, they said, 'he's the real nutter'.

The chap from the older couple laughed: 'Well, we're all nutters here.' So before I'd even got inside, I heard insiders using the same term Jim and the others I'd met in Nashville had used. By inverting the language of sanity, they embrace their counter-epistemic status. When normal is crazy, to be a 'nutter' is to be enlightened.

'I'm surprised to see so many couples here', he then opined. 'Women don't tend to be so awake.' This was interesting for several reasons. Firstly, it echoed my findings about gender from the Dreamland research, as presented in Chapter 1, that millennial conspiracism is a middle-ground between female-centric popular millennial discourses and male-centric conspiracist discourses. Personally, I was more surprised that there was no negative reaction to his gender-specific statement, which there certainly would have been in the circles I generally move in.

We arrived at our seats just in time to catch the closing seconds of Gareth Icke's opening set. Icke had invited his son and his band to perform at the event, performing before each section of the event, and they had also recorded a single entitled *Remember Who You Are*, after the title of Icke's most recent book, published that January. The choice to have his son's band play at the gig was criticized later by a few people; they thought it was 'selling out'. The situation is certainly more complex than this, however; as already noted, Gareth is a director of Icke's estate, and it cannot be coincidental that he released the single at the same time as his father's book of the same title. Who instigated the cross promotion is unclear, however.

Although I had a clear view of the stage, the steep and already almost full arena made getting to my seat awkward. I tried to get a bit of chat going with the others around me, but unlike Dreamland, people were keeping themselves to themselves. In the seats around me were four couples, one in their 30s, one in their 40s and two in their 50s, several pairs of young men and a pair of elderly women, one of whom promptly fell asleep. In total, the audience was just below 6,000, with an unspecified number watching online. Icke walked on to cheering and applause. His first words were: 'The nutter is at Wembley Arena!'

Structurally, the show was typical of his later presentations; three sections, beginning with the 'spiritworld' material, through the Illuminati, into Reptilians and then back to the real world, with practical applications. The first section moved extremely slowly. As has been the case since his earliest books, we got a potted history of Icke's personal history, and a lot of speculative physics about the nature of the universe. Typically, mainstream science was vilified as 'the enemy', and being part of the conspiracy, except when it agreed with Icke's hypotheses, in which case it was held up as authoritative. The room was vast. Latecomers trickled in throughout the first hour. Someone had brought a baby, which cried throughout.

'This is where we enter the Twilight Zone.' Icke launched his second section by talking about the Illuminati, and the hijack of reality by 'entities which operate outside of human sight'. Some of the slides in this section, notably the diagram of the pyramidal structure of the Illuminati control system, date back to Icke's very earliest presentations. Reptilians were mentioned for the first time about an hour into this section. I was very interested in how the reptilian material would be received; was it, as several reporters have suggested, something which put people off Icke's other ideas? Well, my experience suggests otherwise. The room fell quieter than would be possible through random means. The lady next to me who had slept through the first section suddenly woke up; I saw several of the couples around me cuddling up. Two solutions suggested themselves: (1) the couples had bonded over the reptilian thesis, and the fact that they shared something dangerous was part of their shared identity or (2) the reptilian thesis provided a meeting point between those in the audience more drawn to the conspiracist material and those more drawn to the millennial material. Nor can this really be explained by the suggestion that people are drawn to the more outlandish material for entertainment; given that you could watch any of his previous presentations on the internet free, it would be an expensive night out, even if you lived in London to start with.

Towards the end of this section, he added some new material. *Human Race, Get Off Your Knees* had introduced the idea of the hollow Moon, and *Remember Who You Are* had added Saturn into the mix; Icke claims that Saturn is not only the origins of the term 'Satan' and 'Satanism' but also of the idea of the Black Sun, a term adopted by neo-Nazis as an alternative to the swastika and described as the power-source of the Aryan race (Goodrick-Clarke 2002, 3–4). Now, Icke claims that the Reptilian frequencies are broadcast from Saturn and amplified by the Moon, and this Saturn-Moon matrix is an important aspect of the mechanism through which we are controlled. Perhaps as interesting, although less obvious, was his increasing use of terms taken from Gnosticism. In particular, he several times referred to the highest powers of the Illuminati as 'archons', rather than reptilians. Was this a way, I wondered, of distancing himself from the reptilian thesis without abandoning it altogether?

At the break at seven hours in, I went to the bar next to the venue for a drink, along with many others from the event. The couple next to me were ordering their drinks, when the barman pointed out that there was a special offer on margaritas. The gentleman changed his mind and ordered a margarita. His girlfriend said: 'You're like the Sheeple.'

The final section proceeded as it has since 2003 or so – how his ideas could be taken into the real world. His suggested solution is 'non-compliance'; the many are only ruled by the few because they allow themselves to be. Peaceful non-compliance will disempower the elite, 'breaking the hypnotic trance'. Teachers, media and politicians need to 'shut the fuck up' about how people should live and what they should think; 'I am infinite consciousness, I will decide my reality!'

This particular performance added a new coda, however. A number of audience members came on stage, and they performed a 'non-compli-dance' to piped-in Irish music. He then led the audience in an allegedly 'Native American' chant entitled 'We Are All One' from a recording by Michael 'Red Buffalo Heart' Dimitri[25] and a folk song called 'I Choose Love'. He gave something between a prayer, a poem and a meditation over ambient, 'New Age' music on the same themes. I was frankly surprised at his energy, given that he was then sixty years old, suffering from arthritis and no longer slender. Moreover, it was a brave move given that this was his highest profile performance to date. It was also a reminder that his work continues to have a strongly 'New Age' aesthetic, with images of nature, children, the Earth from space, chakras on meditating bodies and 'native' peoples.

Highgate

I then headed across London on the Tube to meet a friend. Caroline and I had been in contact for a while, and I always enjoyed her perspective on this material. She'd had what she called either a 'spiritual awakening' or a 'mini-stroke' a few years previously and became involved with the Lucis Trust (founded by proto-New Age Theosophical channeller, Alice Bailey). This led her into a more conspiracist milieu, and shortly after I met her, she'd moved into a house she described as 'the centre of the Truth movement in London'. She had been researching the demographics of the millennial conspiracist milieu using web analytical tools and had been happy to share the data with me. I'd reciprocated by trying to involve her in a few projects, and we'd built up a level of trust. As a result, she invited me to the house. It was risky for both of us; if they didn't take to me, I would lose their trust and potentially find a lot of doors closed to me. Worse, Caroline could find herself accused of working with a 'disinfo agent'.

The house turned out to be a red-brick Victorian semi-detached in leafy Highgate. The decor was lived-in and slightly cluttered but highly individual – the kind of house I would expect a retired professor or novelist to own. It belonged to Belinda McKenzie, whose name I knew from her high profile campaign concerning Hollie Greig.

In 2000, Holly Grieg, then twenty years old, living in Aberdeen and suffering from Down's Syndrome, alleged that she had been abused by her father since the age of six. The story soon grew to allege that her father had shared her with a group of abusers including her brother, her uncle and a paedophile ring made up mostly of senior professionals, including a senior police officer and a prominent sheriff.[26] Investigator Robert Green became involved in 2009, and according to his account, his investigation was blocked at every turn, although the authorities insisted he was wasting public time and money on a non-existent case.[27] He has since been incarcerated, although the case continues. Belinda continues to operate the official website, www.holliedemandsjustice.org.

Although child abuse was Belinda's main concern, she has also been involved in the 9/11 Truth movement. Her house had become a hub for the confluence of conspiracy and spirituality in London. Kerry Cassidy from Project Camelot often stayed there, and when I petted a cat which had jumped onto the table, I was told that it belonged to MI5 whistle-blower and (later) self-proclaimed Messiah, David Shayler. He'd stayed here, along with fellow whistle blower and then girlfriend Annie Machon, between 2005 and 2007 (O'Neill 2006), until he'd become infatuated with Belinda, I was told. Rooms had been built in the basement (which the other guests called 'hobbit-holes') and a small film studio had been set up in a summerhouse at the end of the garden, in which a number of YouTube videos had been filmed.[28]

More surprisingly, she has also been prominent in promoting the 'Starchild skull' as genuine.[29] Currently owned and promoted by Lloyd Pye, the Starchild Skull is an apparently human infant skull with an abnormally large brain cavity which was allegedly found in Mexico in the 1930s. Although sceptics argue that it is likely a case of hydrocephalus, Pye promotes the thesis that it is a skull from a human-extraterrestrial hybrid.[30]

When I arrived, Belinda was working – presumably answering emails from her several websites – and Catherine and I opened a bottle of wine and got caught up. When she came through, I learned that she was hosting something of an after-party for the event that I had just cut out of early. Belinda is a healthy looking woman in – I would guess, and I have never asked – her sixties, with hair piled atop her head and her glasses then somehow mounted atop that. Luckily, what comes naturally to me is to head to the kitchen, where I got to chopping onions and filling potato skins. It turned out that Belinda had known Icke for many years and had helped run his 2008 political campaign.

We started to chat, initially about my research – although I did my best to talk about anything else. What about the recent high-profile paedophilia cases, I asked? Both Belinda and Caroline were certain that the Savile revelations were only the beginning of the exposure of widespread paedophilia among the power-brokers of UK Society. I was told that journalist, TV presenter and founder of the charity Childline, Esther Rantzen, 'was next', and that Childline was intended to locate vulnerable children for ritual abuse – a claim which surprised and unsettled me. I was chastised for referring to it as a 'scare' but managed to pull things back by pointing out that I had to remain impartial to all parties or else I was not being fair. They knew little about Strieber but were particularly intrigued by his connections to SRA. I told them about his Oprah Winfrey appearance, and of the similarities between SRA and the abduction narrative, and how strange that it had gone back into the mainstream as I was researching this book. Then I showed them some photos of my kids. I told them about how Ted (then aged 4) had just taught himself to read in a month by phonics songs on YouTube. Caroline and Belinda looked at one another knowingly and suggested that he might be an Indigo Child.[31]

It was almost eleven when the other guests began to arrive. I had been wrong in assuming the show was almost finished, it turned out. First to arrive was Dan, a friend of Caroline, who had, like me, been at the Wembley show but had left before the end. He was a nice chap, and interested in my research – presumably because he had heard from Caroline the difficulties of researching these kinds of subjects in an academic context. Others started to arrive before we could get too far into the conversation, however. Next were a couple made up of a blonde woman in her thirties and a man in his early forties, accompanied by an older, taller man. It turned out that the chap in his forties had been following Icke for a while, the new girlfriend had not; what I did not find out was if they had got together and then he'd introduced her to Icke, or if it had been something they'd had in common initially. The older chap sat next to me, and we spent the next hour or so talking about his long history of channelling spiritual and extraterrestrial entities. He and his wife ran a restaurant in Norfolk but travelled up to London once or twice a year to stay with Belinda. During the hour, two young working-class men arrived with a carrier bag full of beer, one bulky in a white t-shirt, the other smaller, dressed in darker gear and a cap. I named them George and Lenny.

Also present – and, it seemed, resident – was Tony Farrell, a former intelligence advisor for the Metropolitan police, who was currently suing them for unfair dismissal. He was allegedly fired after returning a report alleging that the UK government were responsible for the 7/7 London bomb attacks (Perrie 2011). Caroline became embroiled in a deep conversation with him, and although I was listening intently for tidbits, I didn't want to try to join the conversation uninvited.

About 1 am, pretty exhausted, a little drunk and aware that I was in an unfamiliar area and that I had a speaking engagement in the morning, I decided it was time to leave. Belinda insisted on driving me, which I was glad of, and Caroline came along too. I was told I must visit again and maybe even stay next time I was in London. I said I would think about it, more because I would not want to impose rather than any sense of discomfort. I liked Belinda and could see why she was so popular.

'David Icke Changed My Life'

The following day, I was to talk at the 'David Icke Changed My Life' meeting in the upstairs room of the George pub in the Strand. I was very nervous. This was a small and informal gathering – there were twenty-one people present, including Caroline, Dan who I'd met the evening before and Kate the organizer. A show of hands suggested that half had been at Wembley the previous day and the meeting began with a discussion of the event. One of them, Meg (a musician active in the industrial scene) was unusually challenging of Icke, claiming that he 'doesn't cite his sources', 'doesn't deal with criticism well' and 'is embracing celebrity, instead of railing against it'. She also referenced Alex Jones several times, interesting as she was the only American present. Her position was not widely supported in the room, however.

After this opening discussion, I launched into my presentation, based on my fieldwork with Strieber the previous month and talked a little about my broad field of millennial conspiracism, focussing on the ethnographic detail. However, I was at the same time making references to the similarities between Icke and Strieber, and their particular bricolages of popular millennial and conspiracist discourses and watching for dissent. I saw none.

As a result of my talk, I was able to orchestrate the discussion to some degree. Was Icke's admonition that 'We are all one' 'New Age', I asked? Almost everyone insisted no, which I was by now in no way surprised by. One black woman said that the 'New Age' was actually part of the NWO agenda – something I had come across frequently in the more overtly Christian US conspiracist milieu. Steven, a fairly posh chap who described himself as a filmmaker, gave me a link to Strieber's group by talking about out of body experiences (OOBEs) and the Monroe Institute. 'We are not humans having spiritual experiences', he said: 'We are spiritual beings having human experiences.' When I then asked what he meant by 'spiritual', he replied, 'religion is dogma . . . spirituality is the realisation that we are all one'.

I also took the opportunity to pass out a similar questionnaire to the one I had circulated in Nashville. Although I was only able to gather thirteen, I hoped that they might indicate whether Icke's audience were broadly ethnographically similar to Strieber's. Indeed they were. Gender was similarly evenly split, with age being mostly in the forty to fifty range. While there were not enough responses to gain any meaningful data on occupation, political and religious affiliation were both overwhelmingly identified as 'none', completely in keeping with Strieber's group. 'Spirituality' appeared a few times, interestingly as both a religious and political affiliation, and while two people identified as Christian, one of those added 'through family beliefs' in parenthesis. Interestingly, two people, both female, indicated their political identification as 'conspiracy theorist' or (that word again) 'conspiracy nutter'. More specific to Icke, most stated that the reptilian thesis was possible but were non-committal, although several claimed to have encountered reptilians, and one of the Christians stated that they were 'demons'. Most also believed that ETs had had some involvement with the early development of humankind, although slightly less committedly than the US group. Only one reported that the 'spiritual' aspects of Icke's work were other than 'very important' or 'somewhat important' to them, and only two reported that the 'conspiracies' aspect was less than 'very important'. About half expressed a liking for Alex Jones; seven had seen *Thrive*, although four of them were not particularly impressed; four were fans of Deepak Chopra. Interestingly, there was little interest expressed in either Strieber (one 'like', plus a few who said they would investigate further following my talk) or Wilcock (no 'likes').

I sat down and passed the chair back to Kate, and the conversation quickly turned back to the subject of child abuse. The general opinion in the room was that all the charges, from Savile to the most speculative, were true and indicative of widespread institutionalized abuse. They seemed genuinely convinced that this was the tipping point, after which the scales would tip towards complete disclosure of how, as they saw it, those in positions of power had engaged in ritualized, sexual and possibly satanic abuse with the most vulnerable among their charges. She had helpfully compiled a handout containing a number of newspaper reports that tallied with Icke's claims regarding Savile and others including Prince Charles and former prime minister Ted Heath. Among the images was one of Esther Rantzen.

I asked what they made of the Gnostic terminology Icke had introduced, in particular using 'archons' where he might have used 'reptilian' before. One Danish woman opined that the Gnostics were deliberately destroyed 'by the forces of evil' but now, 'the ancient wisdom is coming back', recalling Blavatsky's identification of the Gnostics as forerunners of the Theosophists in *Isis Unveiled* (1877 [1997], 140).

> Meg again: 'I'm just not comfortable with the term "evil".' Dan was. 'They don't want humanity, they want Earth.'

Jemima asked: 'Why do all these terrible things happen in the world?' – as neat a formulation of the need for a theodicy as can be imagined. The general impression in the room was that the universe was an equation. What the final result, I asked? 'Meaningful', Jemima replied.

As with Dreamland, the David Icke Changed My Life group were normal people. Male and female, working-class and wealthy, frequently highly educated and accomplished people. There was no sense of disfunctionality – everyone present was clean, sober and capable of polite discussion. While there was disagreement, it was accepted as being in the spirit of open-mindedness. There were no BNP or skinheads at Wembley and no-one at Belinda's or at the George professed Right-wing or racist views, far from it. Both groups seemed to be motivated principally by concern; for crimes and abuses going unpunished, for the inequalities of the state, for terrible things happening to innocents, at home and abroad. In short, they were decent, normal people who felt powerless and unrepresented.

That having been said, by the end, I was conflicted about how these people were dealing with the issue of paedophilia. While Meg stated that she thought she was being groomed in her experience in the music industry and found widespread support among the group that this was normal, I had my own experience in the industry and saw no evidence of any such institutionalized abuse. Childline founder Esther Rantzen was singled out for particular suspicion. While Dan could state: 'We are being conditioned to treat any contact with adults as potentially paedophile', the group seemed to revel in the details of reported abuse, something I felt uncomfortable with and continue to do so. There were claims that sodomizing a child under seven years old could open the kundalini. I wanted to go home and see that Ted was alright.

UFOs as discursive object in Icke's work

Icke began to see his ecological concerns in spiritual terms and his introduction to spiritualism came through contacts made in the environmental milieu. Environmentalism was a persistent concern of Strieber's also, and as Barkun points out, environmentalism often produces apocalyptic narratives, albeit of a scientifically framed kind (Barkun 2013, 17). As well as introducing Icke to teleological narratives, however, it convinced him that the political process was not driven primarily by concern for the best interests of the populous, as was claimed.

Icke's interest in the millennial was also driven by his desire to relieve the symptoms of his arthritis. The failure of his doctor to cure him and his experiences with acupuncture reinforced the idea that the claims of the authorities were not to be taken at face value (Icke 1993a, 103). As I have demonstrated, his early work unambiguously partook of 'New Age' discourse; his mentions of Rakorsky and the Seven Rays are clearly drawn from Alice Bailey, and Icke also uses 'Aquarian Age' tropes to indicate his millennial discourse (Icke 1991, 120–1). From 1993, however, he began to distance himself from 'New Age' discourse–or at least the term 'New Age'. He wrote of the 'spiritual arrogance' of the 'New Age', seeing it as a movement that was becoming 'dogmatic' and 'little more than another church' (Icke 1993a, 313). As with many others, as we have seen, by 1994 he was rejecting the *term* 'New Age' outright (Icke 1994b, 330), instead describing 'New Age' as part of the control system:

> Whenever I hear the term 'Masters', I cringe. Two organisations linked to Alice Bailey's work, the Lucis Trust and the World Goodwill organisation, are both staunch supporters of the United Nations...the New Age has inherited 'truths' over the decades in the same way that conventional religion has over the centuries. As the followers of Christianity have inherited the manipulated version of Jesus, so New Agers have inherited the 'Masters' ....

If New Age isn't careful, it will become Christianity revisited. It is already becoming so. (Icke 1995, 213)

The commitment to millennialism, however, continued (Icke 2003, 332). Yet it is clear that for Icke, occluded agencies were working to prevent this millennial transformation from occurring. This began with his earliest work – consider the quote from his *Wogan* interview above or the following:

[T]hey know this consciousness shift is happening and they want to stop it because they know the consequences of it for them…What better way than to feed a load of trash through channellers and 'gurus' to those who are being affected by that shift? (1994b, 331)

Unlike Strieber, Icke's interest in UFOs was secondary to his millennial concerns. Yet in common with Strieber and, as we shall see in the next chapter, David Wilcock, Icke's counter-epistemic position was grounded in an anomalous experience; in this case, channelled communications with ET 'masters'. During his Theosophical period, ETs are described as benevolent (1994a 75 ff.; 1991, 65). He writes:

There are many beings from other planets working to help the earth and its life forms through the years ahead. These beings are not aliens, but our brothers and sisters in the divine family. They have become known as extra-terrestrials. (Icke 1991, 102)

In keeping with the construction of extra-terrestrials in the Alice Bailey/ Findhorn genealogy, these beings are agents of the coming eschaton:

extra-terrestrials are arriving on earth in large numbers, to help us defeat these forces and make the giant leap in evolution into the Aquarian Age, when humankind, or those who are evolved enough to meet the challenge, will rise out of the abyss at last. (Icke 1991, 117)

Icke's movement into conspiracist narratives is, typically, driven by his belief in UFOs and that they must therefore being *covered up* for some reason:

What's for sure is that there's a whole library of information about UFOs and extra-terrestrials which the public is not being told about, including the background to human abduction and the mutilation of cattle and other farm animals all over the world, in ways that can only be done by technology not known to the public arena. Either it is the work of extra-terrestrials or of the human scientific elites at the underground bases in the United States ... Possibly even both, if the extra-terrestrials are working with the elite scientists. (Icke 1995, 291)

His research into this cover-up lead him to investigate UFO conspiracist material like *Behold a Pale Horse* (1991), and as outlined above, his references to the 'Illuminati Protocols' in *Robot's Rebellion* show that he was coming into contact with NWO conspiracism by 1994. Here again, the UFO narrative becomes the unit of discursive transfer between popular millennial and conspiracism. Yet as his conspiracist narrative develops, his extra-terrestrial narratives become much more malevolent. Once Icke has decided that the Illuminati dynasties originate in Mesopotamia and that, moreover, these societies were founded or at least influenced by prehistoric contact with extra-terrestrials, the conclusion is inevitable that the Illuminati are therefore extra-terrestrials. The most obvious and significant development of this is the reptilian thesis.

In his later works, however, are an attempt to reconcile these two positions, with human and non-human beings portrayed as parts of one greater entity; humans and reptilians, while 'real' within this Infinite Oneness, have forgotten that they are essentially parts of the same being (Icke 2003, 329–30). For Icke, then, although it appears from the everyday point of view that humanity has been enslaved by powerful, secret forces, from a higher level, this situation continues only because we allow it to. Nevertheless, Icke stresses that the possibility remains for individual human beings to see through the illusion that the world of four dimensions is all there is by gathering and ordering information and reconnecting with Infinite Oneness. When enough individuals realize this and choose love and oneness over fear and separation, the Time Loop collapses, and humanity is transformed:

Only by triggering and expanding a reconnection with our higher levels of being will we have access to the information and love that we so desperately need in order to heal ourselves ... We stand on the threshold of indescribable and incomprehensible change. (Icke 1994b, viii)

Icke's debt to Theosophy has been well established, but as far as I know, no one has pointed out his use of Gurdjieff. While Strieber had a long and acknowledged involvement with Gurdjieff's teaching, Icke's is rather more sub rosa. Firstly is the motif that the majority are spiritually asleep; in *Days of Decision*, he writes, 'So many on this planet ... have given up thinking' (5), and later coins the term 'sheeple' to describe the unthinking masses, a term which has unpleasant echoes of the 'goyim' (Hebrew: 'cattle') of the Protocols. Secondly is the notion of planets as spiritual beings and of a network of cosmic energy travelling from being to being, from the densest to the most refined, the Solar Logos, which plays a significant part in the narrative of *Love Changes Everything*. Thirdly, there is the identification of the moon as the reason for humanity's estrangement from the galactic spiritual network. For Gurdjieff, the moon feeds upon the psychic energy of those humans who have not become awake; 'Everything living on the Earth, people, animals, plants, is food for the Moon. The Moon is a huge living being feeding upon all that lives and grows on the Earth' (Ouspensky 1949 [1987], 85). While this motif is in *Love Changes Everything*, as noted above, it has become prominent again in his work of the 2010s and the narrative of the 'moon-Saturn matrix'. Gurdjieff's work owed a great deal to Gnosticism, and as I illustrate below, Icke has begun using Gnostic terminology in recent years, particularly 'archons' and 'gnosis'. In the previous chapter, I described how many of Strieber's circle used 'gnosis'. I return to this subject in the conclusion.

In the next chapter, I move into the present decade with a study of David Wilcock, a proponent of '2012' millennialism and alleged reincarnation of Edgar Cayce. The post-9/11 world is one in which the internet has become one of, if not the most important site for the dissemination of conspiracist narratives, and although both Strieber and Icke maintain a large online profile, Wilcock's career has focussed on using the internet to build his epistemic capital and establish himself as a millennial conspiracist prophet. The chapter will consider how millennial conspiracist narratives have adapted themselves to their contemporary situation, in particular the economic crash of 2008 and the resulting 'Othering' of the financial industries. Furthermore, it examines 2012 millennialism as an example of the continuation of popular millennialist discourse and its on-going connection to UFOs.

'The Science of Oneness':
David Wilcock and '2012' Millennialism

In 1939, Edgar Cayce – famous as the 'sleeping prophet' – provided a reading for a client who had asked if psychic or spiritual phenomena would ever be proven scientifically to exist (Free and Wilcock 2004, 28). The answer Cayce received from his 'source' was positive; when they were investigated in earnest, they would prove 'as meterable as any other phase of human existence' (Free and Wilcock 2004, 28). In the archives held by the Association for Research and Enlightenment, set up by Cayce and presently run by his sons, this reading is labelled '2012'. In 2003, his alleged reincarnation, David Wilcock – having argued that psychic phenomena were indeed scientifically meterable – announced that on 21 December 2012, the Earth would enter the 'fourth density' and achieve 'Ascension'.

This chapter examines the life and work of David Wilcock, a channeller, UFO enthusiast and jazz-rock drummer from California, who has become one of the most prominent figures in millennial conspiracist discourse in the late-2000s and 2010s. He actively promoted the '2012' narrative, a popular teleological narrative apparently drawn from the meso-American Maya people, which predicted an apocalyptic or millennial event on the 21 December 2012, and I here lay out the complex genealogy of '2012' millennialism and in particular its continuity with 'New Age' and 'Ascension' millennial narratives. Moreover, '2012' narratives have explicitly self-identified as scientifically verifiable; David Wilcock has gone further than most in mobilizing the scientific epistemic strategy, although as we shall see, his claims are predominantly drawn from channelled and synthetic sources. My examination of his life and work once again focusses on the role of UFOs in facilitating a discursive transfer between millennial and conspiracist narratives. I shall also consider the life and work of Edgar Cayce whose reincarnation Wilcock claims to be. Cayce, as we shall see, is frequently raised as an example of the efficacy of non-scientific knowledge and therefore of the value of counter-epistemic strategies. Wilcock's identification with Cayce is a clear attempt to increase his cultural and epistemic capital in the millennial conspiracist field. Bolstered by this claim, Wilcock's particular combination of '2012' millennialism and a conspiracist narrative centred on the financial industries quickly became one of the most popular in the milieu, without any publications or mainstream media appearances.[1]

In the ethnographic section, I examine his claims to be able to teach one – in emic terms – to make contact with one's 'higher self'. In etic terms, this means teaching techniques to expand the range of available epistemic strategies upon which one may draw, increasing one's epistemic capital as a result. Using Wilcock's online course, and thereby focussing on the medium which Wilcock has used so successfully, I tried David Wilcock's techniques for myself and suggest their continuity with Theosophical teachings.

In the previous chapter, we saw how the 9/11 attacks in New York were Icke's springboard into broader acceptance in the US conspiracist milieu, and to a significant degree, 9/11 dominated conspiracist discourse for the best part of the decade that followed. Organizations including Architects and Engineers for 9/11 Truth formed specifically to challenge the official version of events.[2] At least one arguably religious group (the Zeitgeist Movement)[3] emerged, and the narrative was adopted by several pre-existing groups. 9/11 conspiracy narratives also entered the mainstream to an unprecedented degree, with Michael Moore's *Fahrenheit 911* acting as a gateway into the more overtly conspiracist narratives of movies like *Loose Change* (2005) or *Zeitgeist* (2007).

By 2008, however, the so-called 'Truth Movement' had lost much of its momentum. There was infighting between the promoters of various theories, with the 'No Planers' (those who thought the towers had been brought down by missiles or a space-based energy weapon) coming in for particular criticism (O'Neill 2006). One of the most popular theories (perhaps because of its mobilization of scientific epistemic claims) was predicated upon the identification of evidence for the presence of 'nanothermite' in the wreckage of the towers, a military explosive producing controlled but intense heat. The theory was seriously criticized by the great majority of professional scientific bodies, however.

In conspiracist discourse of the 1990s, US foreign policy was aimed at covert control of the Middle East, in order to a) control the oil supply, b) control the opium supply, and/or c) to provide an ongoing 'war on terrorism' for the industrial-military complex. The United States and the Islamic states were the two sides in this battle over resources. For many including Icke and Alex Jones, the Illuminati were also orchestrating wars and terrorism in order to further restrict civil liberties in the United States and the UK. 9/11 fitted this narrative particularly well. In 2008, however, global financial markets collapsed, and in quite a short period of time, the financial industries became the occluded agency du jour. Alex Jones even claimed that 'Goldman Sachs funded the Bolshevik revolution' and that 'banksters' were behind the Kennedy assassination.[4] The combination of popular millennial narratives with popular concerns demonstrates both the malleability and vitality of conspiracist narratives.

'2012' Millennialism

The '2012' narrative demonstrates that popular millennialism remains popular, even if it no longer uses the name 'New Age' (Meyer 2013). In fact, '2012' – signifying a specific emic discourse concerning a belief in the immanence of a utopian world to come – is in complete continuity with the other popular millennialisms whose emergence, development and eventual abandonment we have traced through the book, 'New Age' in particular. Wilcock, as we shall see, has promoted a number of millennial narratives himself, although it is with '2012' he is most associated. Along with a number of other prominent writers, Wilcock has presented '2012' as validated scientifically, citing solar flare cycles, the Large Hadron Collider generating a black hole, volcanic eruptions and magnetic pole reversals being suggested as potentially causing an apocalyptic event (Larson 2013). Despite this strategic mobilization of the scientific epistemic strategy, in fact the '2012' narrative is drawn almost entirely from channelled and synthetic sources.

There was considerable variation in interpretations of the date allegedly predicted by the Maya. The first identification of the specific date 21 December 2012 as the end of the long-count calendar only appeared in 1983 and only became predominant in the mid-2000s (Whitesides and Hoopes 2011, 61–2). As the date drew closer, there was a steady stream of '2012'-related media – novels including Strieber's *2012: The War for Souls* (2007) and *The Omega Point* (2010); quasi-academic works like Daniel Pinckbeck's *The Return of Quetzalcoatl* (2006); numerous documentaries on the History Channel, the Discovery Channel and others (Whitesides 2013); and even a successful movie directed by Roland Emmerich, *2012* (2010).[5] At least 2000 books had been published on '2012' by February 2012 (Whitesides and Hoopes 2011, 53).[6]

The '2012' narrative developed from the combination of two initially discrete teleological narratives; Terrence McKenna's *time wave zero* thesis and Jose Arguelles' millennial reading of Mayan mythology. In the mid-1970s, following a trip to Columbia to study the use of ayahuasca and other native psychedelics (albeit largely through participant observation), writer and lecturer Terence McKenna (1946–2000) proposed a theory which he called 'time wave zero', which suggested that history described the interplay between order and chaos (Wilson, A. F. 2013, 225). In this model, history is interspersed with periods of high disorder, which engender increasing complex informational structures. Furthermore, McKenna thought that the speed at which these periods occur was accelerating, describing 'a long cascade into greater and greater novelty which reaches its culmination early in the twenty-first century' (McKenna 1975, 161). McKenna went on to develop this teleological narrative in subsequent works, and it was promoted by Robert Anton Wilson in *Cosmic Trigger* (1977 [1986], 217) which likely helped its dissemination in conspiracist discourse. McKenna presented the theory using scientific terminology and even had a computer programme written which enabled him to generate detailed graphs illustrating where order and chaos peaked. Nevertheless, the theory originated entirely from communications with entities encountered during his hallucinogen experiences. In essence, the 'time wave zero' theory was produced entirely from channelled sources but was presented with scientific terminology.

In 1987, José Arguelles (1939–2011) published *The Mayan Factor*, which presented a millennial narrative that incorporated an interpretation of the Mayan long-count calendar. Arguelles, a former professor of art history, had long been involved with popular millennial discourses. He was a key figure behind the *Whole Earth Catalog*, a major self-identified 'New Age' periodical published from 1968 (Wilson, A. F. 2013, 231), and was involved with 1987's Harmonic Convergence, an early example of the 'Ascension' narrative, detailed below (Mayer 2013, 264). Arguelles was certainly a 'seeker', investigating a wide range of spiritual practices and philosophies including astrology, mysticism and significantly, Alice Bailey (Meyer 2013, 264). Arguelles became aware of this Maya material around 1972, but it was only while preparing for the Harmonic Convergence in the mid-1980s that the parallels with 'New Age' and 'Ascension' narratives began to coalesce (Mayer 2013, 265).

The meso-American Maya civilization employed several calendars, one of which, known as the 'long-count', was used to measure long periods of time. It operated on a number of interlocking cycles of varying lengths, from the *k'in* of one day to the *bak'tun* of 144,000 days. Each of these cycles resets to one after reaching their maximum (generally twenty), as the immediately larger cycle counts one; so, twenty *k'ins* equals one *uinal* (twenty days), twenty *uinals* equal one *tun* (360 days), and so on (Whitesides and Hoopes 2011, 54). The final, and longest, cycle, the *bak'tun*, resets at the end of its thirteenth cycle. At this point, the entire system resets to zero after a period of 5125.37 years. According to one (or possibly two) archaeological sources, this cycle would reset on 21 December 2012 – at least according to some translations. The popular association between the end of the 13th *bak'tun* and a teleological event originates in Michael Coe's (1966) *The Maya*, although he identified the end of the 13th *bak'tun* as 24 December 2011 (1966, 149). Whitesides and Hoopes connect his use of apocalyptic language explicitly to Cold War-era fears (2011, 54–5).

Arguelles and McKenna's narratives seem to have fed off one another after they met at the Ojai Institute's 'Council of Quetzalcoatl' meeting in April 1985 (Whitesides and Hoopes 2012, 62–4). In his presentation at the event, McKenna acknowledged the closeness of the December 2012 date to the teleology of his time wave zero predictions; Arguelles' first published his theory in 1987 (Hoopes and Whitesides 2012, 62–3). Arguelles later wrote:

> My meeting with Terence McKenna...contributed greatly to this understanding of the Mayan factor...So it was that I threw myself with renewed abandon into the Mayan Factor. (Arguelles 1996, 39)

McKenna's vague 'early in the twenty-first century' became specifically 22 December 2012 in the second edition of *The Invisible Landscape*, published in 1994. This is clear example of rolling prophecy, as I defined in Chapter 2; consciously or not, by quietly revising his earlier predictions to bring them into line with those of others, McKenna lends his predictions greater credence. As a result, he increases his epistemic capital within the popular millennial field.[7]

'2012' narratives were incorporated into UFO and ancient alien discourses through the work of Nancy Lieder (1996) who identified 2012 as the date in which Sitchin's Nibiru would return and pass catastrophically close to Earth (Wilson, A. F. 2013, 232). *The X-Files*, having been instrumental in popularizing UFO conspiracism during the 1990s, fittingly incorporated '2012' into the show's final denouement, in a double episode entitled 'The Truth', broadcast in May 2002. In a secret government bunker, Fox Mulder discovers a message that states that the final invasion of Earth by the ETs will occur on 22 December 2012 (note the variation of the date, showing how late the narrative completely settled).

Icke initially embraced the '2012' narrative but later backed off, claiming that it was a distraction from other things. Strieber was also interested in '2012', publishing two novels on the theme, but like his abduction experience, never committed fully to it. David Wilcock however, as we shall see, embraced it wholeheartedly.

Life and work of David Wilcock

Wilcock's biography offers some interesting parallels with those of Icke and Strieber.[8] In each of these cases, there is an initial 'call to service' from extra-terrestrial beings, although in Strieber's case, he does not realize at first what it is. This initial contact is responded to with a demand for proof, which in turn leads to an ongoing relationship with what the individual understands to be a higher intelligence. This intelligence (Strieber's visitors, Icke's Racorczy and Wilcock's Higher Self) grants channelled information that apparently transforms the individual's view of the world and their place in it. This experience is their gnosis.

David Wilcock was born on 8 March 1973, in Schenectady, New York (Free and Wilcock 2004, 144). His upbringing appears to have been liberal and to some degree countercultural; his father was a music journalist, and his mother was a musician and lecturer with an interest in millennial ideas (Free and Wilcock 2004, 112–3). Wilcock later claimed that his father was affected by post-traumatic stress disorder after returning from the Vietnam War and was an overly authoritarian parent as a result. They divorced when Wilcock was in 6th grade (Free and Wilcock 2004, 117). His interest in counter-epistemological strategies seems to have originated with his mother; he was reading her books by the age of eight, and she may have believed him to have a talent for ESP (Free and Wilcock 2004, 112–3 and 116). He reports having had prophetic dreams and an out-of-body experience at the age of five and had a lifelong interest in UFOs and alternative archaeology, which, as we have seen, are frequently emblems of a concern with non-empirical sources of information.[9] He claims his interest in millennialism was triggered by encountering the work of Nostradamus around the age of seven, and he claims he was having lucid dreams in high school, where he would 'would end up on the main deck of UFOs and talking to beings' (Camelot 2007). His self-mythologizing account of his youth frequently veers towards the arrogant; 'I was unusually intelligent', he states, while describing reading a book aged seven as 'research' (Camelot 2007).

While in high school, Wilcock encountered Strieber's *Communion*, and as was the case with Mark at the Dreamland festival, the book appeared to stir up repressed memories:

> On the cover of the book was the classic Grey alien with the large, dark eyes. It was the first time I had ever seen this image in my life ... Somewhere in the back of my mind, I almost remembered the ongoing conflict that was being fought on Earth between positive and negative forces for the

control of the human soul. Not all 'Greys' were evil or self-serving by any means, but there were certainly negative ET's out there. (Wilcock 2000a, Chapter 3)[10]

Aside from establishing a direct connection to Strieber, this passage makes clear that Wilcock immediately construes the image of the ET in the context of a Manichaean cosmic war. The battle is between those who are working towards the millennium (here termed 'Ascension') and those who seek to prevent it. Moreover, there is an earthly, conspiratorial aspect to these negative forces:

These forces did not want third-density humans to Ascend, nor did they want the new Earth to be born, even though they couldn't stop it … They remained in contact with the *real* government of the Earth, according to sources I would later read. (Wilcock 2000a, Chapter 3)

Wilcock began a degree in psychology at State University of New York at New Paltz in 1991, a period he considers to have been particularly formative. He was a regular cannabis and alcohol user until September 1992, when he quit after several unpleasant experiences that left him with a sense of being unfulfilled. On the same day, he began recording his dreams, which he describes as part of his 'recovery process' – arguably another example of his self-mythologization.

In March 1993, Wilcock was told by a friend that his physics professor had said that it was common knowledge at NASA that UFOs had been recovered from crash-sites and that many recent technologies, including LEDs, microchips, fibre optics and lasers, were taken from them, in a process known as 'back-engineering' (Camelot 2007). This seems to have been Wilcock's introduction to the idea that there may be earthly conspiracies to keep certain knowledge hidden; and typically, UFOs were the discursive object.

In his final year, Wilcock began a passionate but stormy relationship with a Japanese woman named Yumi. Allegedly, while visiting a Shinto 'shaman-priestess', she showed the woman a photo of her new US boyfriend and was told that he would become a 'famous spiritual leader' (Wilcock 2000a, Chapter 7). Wilcock graduated in June 1995 and attempted unsuccessfully to gain entry to a 'Transpersonal Psychology' Master's programme at Naropa University (a private accredited institution with a strongly Buddhist-inspired approach), presenting them with a list of 'three hundred millennial/spiritual' books he had read (Free and Wilcock 2004, 21). Instead, he returned to New Paltz and began working in a psychiatric ward, from which he was fired after two and a half weeks 'for being "too friendly" to the patients' (Free and Wilcock 2004, 22). Lacking any finances, he returned home to Schenectady.

During this tumultuous period, he read a number of books that influenced his later thinking. These included *The Mayan Factor*, in which Arguelles first set out his version of the '2012' narrative and Scott Mandelker's *From Elsewhere* (1995), which concerns *wanderers*. Wanderers are described as extra-terrestrials who have volunteered to be repeatedly incarnated in human bodies in order to work towards the planet's spiritual development. Moreover, the book suggested that you, the reader, might be a wanderer; Wilcock certainly began to consider the possibility. Picking it up, Wilcock felt it was 'tingling, electrical' (Camelot 2007).

Most significantly, Wilcock began reading the *Law of One* series, consisting of four books in total and sometimes called the *Ra Material* (Free and Wilcock 2004, 23). The subtitle of the first book in the series is subtitled *An Ancient Astronaut Speaks*, suggesting that the publisher was making the connection with von Däniken's successful publications. Airline pilot Don Elkins, a UFO investigator until the early 1960s when his attention turned to contactees (McCarty, et al. 1984, 47), and Carla Rueckert, a channeller, founded the L/L Research group in 1970 to investigate the channelling of extra-terrestrial beings. James Allen McCarty became the third member of the group in 1980 (McCarty, et al. 1984, 47). The *Law of One* series presents conversations between Elkins and an entranced Rueckert, with McCarty recording and later editing the material thematically into the book series. Rueckert attempted to channel a being named Ra, a group mind representing the 'Council of Saturn', nine ETs who oversee the Earth and keep it quarantined from the larger galactic culture until humans become sufficiently evolved (McCarty, et al. 1984, 98). Elkins' suicide in 1984 ended the L/L Research Group's work, but the four volumes that collected Ra's communications have had a significant influence on popular millennial discourse in the period since.

McCarty had previously claimed to channel Edgar Cayce's source, as Wilcock would later claim (McCarty, et al. 1984, 47). Furthermore, the term 'Law of One' comes directly from Cayce (Johnson 1998, 63). Wilcock claims to have first become aware of Edgar Cayce through reading about Atlantis, presumably in the edited volume *Edgar Cayce on Atlantis* (1968). Either way, Wilcock joined the 'Search for God' study group in spring 1997, a course specifically designed to introduce Cayce's teachings (Free and Wilcock 2004, 121). During this period, Wilcock was, as he puts it, 'a direct full-time apprentice with beings of higher intelligence' (Free and Wilcock 2004, 25). These intelligences told Wilcock to move to Virginia, shortly before he lost his job, his flat and his girlfriend, events that he took as confirmation of the source (Free and Wilcock 2004, 26). Around this time, Skip Weatherford, leader of Wilcock's 'Search for God' group, pointed out to Wilcock his physical resemblance to Cayce and suggested he contact Cayce's Association for Research and Enlightenment (ARE) (Free and Wilcock 2004, 121–2). With the last of his money, he visited the ARE in Virginia Beach with the intention of applying to study 'metaphysics' there (Free and Wilcock 2004, 26–7).

Around November 1995, Wilcock sought proof that he might be a wanderer, and a musician friend suggested he try automatic writing. They interpreted the result as identifying a passage from Ecclesiastes, which Wilcock then interpreted as referring to his recent struggles to find employment and further education (Free and Wilcock 2004, 24–5). On 18 January 1996, a forgotten $200 phone bill arrived. Wilcock, lacking the money, decided to ask his source for assistance. 'I demanded an answer in as open and dramatic a fashion as possible: 'If I really am a Wanderer, then I need proof, and I need it right now"' (Free and Wilcock 2004, 24). That night, Wilcock's flatmate Eric had a dream in which Wilcock appeared alongside some extra-terrestrials:

> A robed and bearded man emerged from a UFO on a circular platform and spoke of the Earth being transformed into a paradise, and said that his group was our long-lost 'brothers' here to assist us. In Eric's dream I approached the man, and we suddenly seemed to know each other. The man threw his arm around my shoulder, looked at Eric, and with a serious expression on his face said, 'It is very important that you know he is one of us.' (Free and Wilcock 2004, 24–5)

In a later account, Wilcock quoted the bearded man thus:

> We are your brothers, your long-lost family…We are here now at this
> time because you are about to go through this amazing, fantastic, energetic
> enlightenment of your entire planet. Right now you're only seeing the bad
> part, where you have the earth changes and you have the upheavals in your
> government and you're starting to see the rottenness in your society, but
> what comes after is a golden age far more incredible than you could ever
> imagine, and we are here to help you through this transition. (Camelot 2007)

Now convinced he was a wanderer, Wilcock began to study the Law of
One series more seriously and claims to have achieved contact with his
'Dream Voice' or 'Higher Self' by November 1996 (Free and Wilcock
2004, 25). During this period he began noting 'synchronicities', often
numerical in nature, such as repeating patterns on clocks. Synchronicities
continue to be a concern of Wilcock up to the present, as do UFOs. In
October 2006, he attended a UFO conference in Connecticut, where he
met a government contractor who confirmed Ray's story and befriended a
second 'insider' identified as Daniel, who allegedly worked on the Montauk
Project, a popular conspiracist narrative concerning US military research
into time-travel (Camelot 2007).

In November 1997, Wilcock allegedly received confirmation from his source
that he was indeed the reincarnation of Edgar Cayce and that furthermore he
has 'to deliver an urgent message to mankind' (Free and Wilcock 2004, 27).
His researches in the Cayce archives at ARE convinced him of the connection
and further that many of his associates had also been members of Cayce's circle
(Free and Wilcock 2004, 126). He points out his own physical resemblance to
Cayce through carefully selected photographs. Furthermore, he consulted an
astrologer to confirm the similarity between the two men's charts (Free and
Wilcock 2004, 144–6). At some point, Wilcock became aware that Cayce had
predicted his own reincarnation.

Edgar Cayce

Edgar Cayce (1877–1945) was born on a farm near Hopkinsville, Kentucky,
to Leslie Cayce, a small landowner and Justice of the Peace, and his wife
(Johnson 1998, 3). Both were members of the Disciples of Christ (Christian)

Church, and the young Edgar was an active member (Johnson 1998, 3–4). According to an oft-repeated story originating with his sympathetic biographer Sugrue, Cayce had read the entire bible a dozen times by the age of thirteen (1942, 45). Less often mentioned by biographers desiring to construct a picture of an ideal Christian is that he later worked with his father selling insurance to Freemasons with the Fraternal Insurance Company (Cayce and Smith 1997, 56).

In 1900, aged 23, he suddenly fell mute and could no longer make a living as an insurance salesman. The following year, he was hypnotized by a local bookkeeper, and while under hypnosis he was able both to speak and to diagnose his own condition. He is alleged to have stated that his condition was a partial paralysis of the vocal chords brought on by 'nerve strain' (Sugrue 1942, 51). Not only did his voice return, he had a new career as a medical clairvoyant, which was to be his occupation for the remainder of his life. He was successful enough that the New York Times carried a story on him on 9 October 1910, entitled 'Illiterate Man Becomes a Doctor when Hypnotised' (Johnson 1998, 5). Nevertheless, in 1920 Cayce moved his family to Texas, where he launched an unsuccessful oil-prospecting career.

By 1922, his efforts had refocused on his career as a clairvoyant, and most of his influence on post-Cold War popular millennialism dates from these latter two decades of his life. He undertook a lengthy lecture tour that included at least one hosted by the Theosophical society, in Birmingham, Alabama (Johnson 1998, 6–7). In 1923, by which point he had already been giving medical readings for over twenty years, Cayce met Arthur Lammers, a printer from Dayton, Ohio, and a keen Theosophist (Johnson 1998, 6). Under Lammers' guidance, Cayce's readings began to diversify into distinctly esoteric areas not typical of the mainstream of Christianity, where his waking self preferred to dwell, including material on Atlantis, astrology and prophecy (Hammer 2001, 66). In particular, reincarnation became an important topic for Cayce, beginning with the unsolicited observation while in trance that Lammers 'once was a monk' (Johnson 1998, 6). Encouraged by Lammers and later Morton Blumenthal, Cayce would go on to describe a whole series of his own reincarnations, as well as those of his associates, who he claimed had often been his associates in past incarnations also. Cayce saw the purpose of reincarnation as part of a process of 'co-creation': individual souls, through their choices, moved towards their fullest potential and thus enabling other beings to do the same and ultimately all of creation (Bro 1989, 185).

Cayce was also very concerned with Atlantis, and his description is largely in keeping with those of Blavatsky and Donnelly (1817), although some features appear to have originated with Cayce (Johnson 1998, 63). Atlanteans had a life span of a thousand years (1968, 15), and practised the '[t]ransmission of thought through ether' (1968, 22). Their power-source was a crystal contained within a dome, which would ultimately be instrumental in the destruction of the island continent (1968, 45–7). Cayce also tracks his previous incarnations in the time of Jesus, with a portrayal of Jesus as an esoteric and mystically minded Essene that parallels later 'New Age' accounts (Johnson 1998, 69).

However, the largest proportion of Cayce's past-life recollections refers to Egypt. Cayce alleged to have been incarnated there around 10,500 BCE as a Caucasian Priest named Ra-Ta, who eventually became High Priest of Egypt (Johnson 1998, 65). Cayce tells us that Ra-Ta planned (but did not build) the Great Pyramid as an initiatory centre and that he guided the design of the Sphinx in a more symbolic direction (Johnson 1998, 66). Cayce also alleged that there was a 'Hall of Records' buried beneath the sphinx which contained records (and therefore evidence) of Atlantis (Johnson 1998, 67). Through these accounts, Cayce had a significant influence on the development of alternative archaeological narratives. The ARE have financed archaeological research in Egypt aimed at locating evidence of sites mentioned in Cayce's readings (Johnson 1998, 67–8). Hancock and Bauval, arguably the most influential alternative archaeology writers at present, cite him frequently, often without adequately identifying that the information comes entirely from channelled sources (e.g. 1996, 86–8, 95–101, 282; Hancock 2002, 519). Indeed, the central trope of their works focussed on Egypt – that the Giza pyramids were built (or at least planned) in 10,500 BCE – comes directly from Cayce's readings (Johnson 1998, 65). Sometimes one can detect an implicit millennialism in these works:

> We wonder if it is possible that the sages of Heliopolis, working at the dawn of history, could somehow have created an archetypal 'device', a device designed to trigger off messianic events across the 'Ages'–the pyramid age

when the vernal point was in Taurus, for example, the Christic Age in Pisces, and perhaps even a 'New Age' in Aquarius? (Bauval and Hancock 1996, 282)

Cayce never attempted to systematize his readings, which numbered 14,000 over a career of forty-seven years; that task was taken up by his secretary and son Hugh Lynn (Lucas 2006, 248). Cayce founded the ARE in 1931 to disseminate his readings and to promote research into 'spirituality, holistic health, intuition, dream interpretation, psychic development, reincarnation, and ancient mysteries',[11] with its headquarters in Virginia Beach, Virginia. Surviving him, it became a significant nexus for popular millennial discourses in the United States during the 1980s (Johnson 1998, 33). According to their official website, their mission remains

> 'to help people transform their lives for the better, through research, education, and application of core concepts found in the Edgar Cayce readings and kindred materials that seek to manifest the love of God and all people and promote the purposefulness of life, the oneness of God, the spiritual nature of humankind, and the connection of body, mind, and spirit'. [12]

Although never formally a theosophist, Cayce was certainly influenced by theosophy, particularly through Lammers and Morton Blumenthal (Johnson 1998, 6–8). Hammer writes that Cayce formed a link between theosophy and the nascent popular millennial milieu when the more formal post-theosophical organizations were experiencing declining membership (2001, 66). He was a significant influence on the later development of 'New Age' discourse, especially in the United States (York 1995, 60–2), primarily through the thematically edited collections of his readings published by his son which achieved a large counter-cultural readership in the late 1960s and 1970s (Melton 1990, 90–1). Most pertinently, Cayce had a great influence on those claiming to channel messages from extra-terrestrial beings. Furthermore, Cayce's term 'earth changes' has had continued usage in popular millennial discourse.

Cayce did not limit himself to the past, however; he predicted these earth changes would occur in 1998, ushering in the 'aquarian age' and the emergence of the 'fifth root race' (Johnson 1998, 9; c.f. Wilcock 2011, 111). Here, while he draws on Christian language and symbolism, his use of terminology is clearly drawn from the later Theosophical writings of Besant, Leadbeater, Kingsford, and others, in their desire to construct a millennial Theosophy that was less anti-Christian than Blavatsky's. Furthermore, Cayce prophesied a possible return in 1998 – in other words, Cayce's reincarnation heralds the eschaton:

> Is it not fitting, then, that [Ra-Ta and his associates] must return? As this priest must develop himself to be in that position, to be in that capacity as liberator of the world in its relationship to individuals in those periods to come, for he must enter again in that period, or in 1998. (Cayce reading 294–151, cited in Free and Wilcock 2004, 111)

Wilcock again

Wilcock argues that this return occurred in July 1998, when he began offering dream readings for money (Free and Wilcock 2004, 134). Clients would talk to him on the phone, and later he would dream about the client, dictating the dream and his analysis into a cassette upon waking (Free and Wilcock 2004, 127). This method is notably different from Cayce's, who would put himself into a hypnotic trance. Nor did Wilcock's readings tend to focus on medical issues as did Cayce's, although Cayce's previous incarnations are not described as giving readings in Cayce's manner either. Wilcock alleges that on 3 January 1999, his source identified itself to him as Ra, the entity from whom the Law of One channellings were alleged to have come and who furthermore was alleged to have worked with Cayce's previous incarnation Ra-Ta in Egypt (Free and Wilcock 2004, 131).

Those who endorsed Wilcock's claim would have been aware of Cayce's prophesied return in 1998. Wilcock's account presents himself as somewhat conflicted concerning his claims, but unlike Strieber, this seems to be more to do with hedging his bets rather than remaining unconvinced himself. While biographer Free describes how it 'took six months of negotiation before he was willing to trust the author's motivation and to perceive the element of service in allowing the story to be released', only two pages earlier he is describing Wilcock's efforts to identify his associates as members of Cayce's circle and post the comparisons on his website (Free and Wilcock 2004, 134–6). However, to date, the ARE have not officially endorsed

Wilcock's claim (Free and Wilcock 2004, 136–7). One reason for this may be a reluctance to associate themselves with 'parapsychology', stating that '[a]nything bordering on sci-fi or UFOlogy is strictly frowned upon by all of the official spokesmen for the Edgar Cayce Foundation... The critics of parapsychology are strident enough as it is, without providing them with additional grist for the mills of malice and mockery' (Bro 1989, 247). It is also possible, of course, that they simply disbelieved him.

At this time, Wilcock was gathering material that he felt could support his theories scientifically. In February 1998, Wilcock spent three weeks compiling this research into the first version of *Convergence*, which was published online the following month (Free and Wilcock 2004, 126–7). His website, ascension2000.com, went online in early 1999 (Free and Wilcock 2004, 127), becoming divinecosmos.com in December 2006.[13] Two more volumes followed in 2000 and 2002, which remain available free on his website, along with an autobiographical volume, *Wanderer Awakening* (2000a). Together, these three works present a millennial thesis of humanity's imminent 'ascension' to the 'fourth density', which is constructed as a less physical but more spiritual level of existence. They were furthermore presented as part of the research process for a movie, also entitled *Ascension*, which Wilcock has repeatedly claimed to have been working on since at least 1996 but has not appeared to date.

Wilcock seems to have gained considerable epistemic capital through his identification with Cayce. He appeared on *Coast to Coast AM* twice in 2004 and was interviewed on *Red Ice Radio* on 16 December 2007. His first non-self-published book, *The Source Field Investigations: The Hidden Science and Lost Civilisations Behind the 2012 Prophecies*, was published in 2011. Featuring a foreword by Hancock, the book presents the thesis 'that 2012 is a watermark for widespread acceptance of a greater reality' – put succinctly, 'a Golden Age' (2011, back cover). The 'source field' is constructed as 'the source of all space, time, matter, energy, biology and consciousness in the Universe', which he states we interact with through the pineal gland (Wilcock 2011, 5). Wilcock goes on to argue that time-space (the four dimensional structure identified by Einstein's Special Relativity) is mirrored by an opposite but complementary structure where time has three dimensions and space only one, which he calls 'time-space' (2011, 261–81). Travel is possible between these two structures, and Wilcock argues that Fortean phenomena are the result of spontaneous travelling between them (2011, 361–9). The book closes by arguing that crop circles represent communications from benevolent ETs (2011, 440–58; c.f. Strieber 2012).

The book presents itself as being drawn entirely from scientific sources – as well as the title, the cover reproduces a quote from Hancock's introduction which says that '[t]here is a tremendous amount of good science here, much of it new to Western readers' (2011, xx). Wilcock claims that between 1950 and 1996, more than five thousand papers on the 'source field' were published in Russia. However, he does not make it clear that none of these papers use the term 'source field' and that Wilcock himself decides which papers *really* mean the source field, without telling us his criteria. In fact, none of the scientific sources cited reach the same conclusions as Wilcock does. Wilcock argues that he presents 'hard scientific proof'; yet he frequently cites research by individuals whose scholarly credentials have been seriously questioned, including Rupert Sheldrake (2011, 71–2), Wilhelm Reich (2011, 190–91), Lynne McTaggart (2011, 33 and 167), Sir Alfred Watkins (2011, 316) and Zecharia Sitchin (2011, 3). Other times, he simply does not cite his sources at all – for example: 'Many scholars agree this twenty-five-thousand-year cycle ends in 2012, or thereabouts' (2011, 101; c.f. 135). However, the arrival of this 'Golden Age' has been perverted by the Illuminati, Wilcock argues, into the imposition of a 'worldwide dictatorship' known as the New World Order (2011, 136). Wilcock also questions Darwinian theories of evolution, arguably the paradigmatic case of scientific consensus today, suggesting that evolution is in fact directed by the source field (2011, 183–215). Interestingly, however, Wilcock accepts climate change but argues that it is evidence of a solar system-wide cycle (2011, 388–415). '[W]e have the tools to create the Golden Age', Wilcock concludes and adds – once again – '[a]s the old saying goes, 'the truth will set you free'' (2011, 460).

Despite the presentation, however, Wilcock draws from the full gamut of counter-epistemic sources. Channelled information from Edgar Cayce (and therefore, by extension, Wilcock's own source, although he chooses not to mention this here) is repeatedly cited with equal weighting (2011, 94–5, 97–8, 109–10, 115). Traditional sources including the Bible (2011,

108–9; 435–6) and the Mahabharata are cited, along with Blavatsky's *Secret Doctrine* (2011, 110). The 'insider' testimony of 'Mr X', who is alleged to have 'died suddenly of a massive stroke as he was getting ready to come forward', concludes the book, as experiential evidence that 'the ETs … will conduct a mass landing all over the world on December 21st or 22nd, 2012, whether our leaders like it or not' (2011, 459). As a whole, the book is an exercise in synthetic knowledge, drawing in any counter-epistemic phenomena to bolster his argument, including crop circles, UFOs, pyramids, stone circles, time-travel and ley-lines.

During this period, Wilcock had also begun to give weekend-long workshops, called *Convergences*, in cities around the United States and occasionally in Canada and Europe. Although they echo the quasi-collegial feel of the Dreamland festival, they are presented entirely by Wilcock. The first half is basically a presentation of the material presented in the online books and *The Source Field Investigations*, and the latter sections presents Wilcock's own method for 'accessing your higher self' – that is, to mobilize counter-epistemic strategies, and I return to this below. Wilcock began presenting *Wisdom Teachings*, a weekly TV show distributed through internet channel, Gaiam TV, in April 2013, which presented this material in thirty-minute chunks.[14] His second physical book, *The Synchronicity Key*, was published early in 2013 and continues the line of argumentation pursued in the *Source Field Investigations*. As a result, Wilcock reduced the number of live events he undertook and seems to have abandoned the Convergence events altogether.

Financial Tyranny

Following the publication of *The Source Field Investigations*, Wilcock began to prepare material under the title 'Financial Tyranny', which was published in several lengthy posts on divinecosmos.com between January and July 2012.[15] This material built upon the work of Benjamin Fulford, formerly Asia-Pacific Bureau Chief for Forbes magazine until 2005, now operating as an independent writer based in Japan.[16] Fulford claims to have been 'the first Westerner for 500 years to be admitted into the ranks of the Eastern secret societies', collectively known as the White Dragon Society (Fulford 2008, 11). The narrative that

Fulford presents is complex and novel. Unknown to the majority, a war for power is raging between competing secret societies, including the Illuminati (the Rothschilds, representing the old European royal houses), the Sabbatean Mafia or military industrial complex (essentially the Rockefellers, in control of the United States following a coup d'état in 1913) and the White Dragon Society, who promote free energy and an open press (Fulford 2008, 16). Fulford claims to have been elected as a spokesperson for the White Dragon Society, tasked with bringing the message to the Illuminati 'that they must recognise their time is over, step down without a fight and allow the world to thrive as it should' (2008, 11). Like Jim Marrs' Dreamland presentation, Fulford constructs a sweeping alternative history without appealing (explicitly, at least) to counter-epistemic sources. In his account, the Illuminati originate in Babylon, as Marrs' does, and there is a millennial drive to his description of the White Dragon Society giving the repressive Illuminati an ultimatum.

Wilcock's Financial Tyranny material draws heavily from Fulford but significantly adds two elements. Firstly, '2012' millennialism is brought in:

All of this leads back to ancient knowledge about the times that we're now in. This knowledge was inherited by these Illuminati New World Order people. I make a very compelling case that they are well aware of these ancient cycles. They know that the cycles end in 2012. They believed that this would result in some sort of catastrophic Earth change. This is a misunderstanding.[17]

Secondly, as Wilcock acknowledges, Fulford is not concerned with UFOs. As well as addressing this discrepancy, the following quotation is a good example of how agreeable testimony (especially when accompanied by scientific language) is accentuated, while disagreeing testimony is ignored or dismissed:

Fulford has no direct evidence that UFOs exist, and/or are piloted by extra-terrestrials. He has never seen one, and it does not appear that he has intensively studied the available literature on the subject ... However, Fulford has met with Pentagon sources who claim to have directly worked with gravity-shielding and stargate-type 'portal' technology, and who wish to release it to humanity. Fulford has not seen any of this himself, but said he would love it if it were true ... This was one of several ways in which the things

Fulford heard fit together very neatly with what I'd already encountered from other insiders … Fulford did also hear that the Chinese were contacted by ETs in the 1940s who were mistreated by the United States government – apparently in the Roswell crash … He was also told that this same ET group is apparently still assisting the Chinese – and others – to this very day. I have also had significant corroboration of this from my own 'insider' sources.

One of Wilcock's insider informants was referred to simply as Drake, who claimed to be an Illuminati insider who had defected and gone public. Drake claims that around 1979 he had come into contact with a 'five-inch thick' plan to restore a 'de jure' government to the United States – that is, one which fulfils the requirements as set out in the US constitution. Drake claims that the plan is (as of 2012) imminently to be executed, as evinced by multiple resignations by individuals whose positions of power are likely to be compromised, including the military, politicians and royals. He then predicts that in the G5 countries (UK, US, Germany, France and Italy), those who would not resign were imminently to be arrested en mass. The plan outlined by Drake is therefore a silent, bloodless coup and therefore resilient to falsification. Wilcock describes this as 'a very wide-spread effort to effectively give us, as a planet, a massive dose of antibiotics – against an infection that has been threatening to almost completely destroy its host.' In the interview, Drake even suggests that his participating of the interview itself anticipates these actions.[18] Wilcock would later claim to have received a death threat as he was preparing to publish these claims.[19]

Regardless of whether such an invisible coup took place or not, this account is a good example of how Wilcock and others combine counter-epistemic strategies to gain the capital of the millennial conspiracist field. Wilcock combines Fulford and Drake's narratives (experience/insider), multiple UFO reports (synthetic), scientific research papers (scientific) and his own channelling to create a millennial narrative on a cosmic scale.

When '2012' fails

Yet as we have seen, date-specific millennial narratives such as '2012', however constructed, sometimes require reinterpretation. Gordon Melton once told me: 'From an emic point of view, prophecy never fails. From an etic position it always does.'[20] For outsiders, '2012' came and went without any tribulation, but various strategies were brought into play by insiders to explain this apparent prophetic failure. Strieber, never having embraced the narrative without reservation, did not need to change his position. Icke, despite his earlier embracing of the narrative, decided that the '2012' narrative was part of the overarching plan to distract the masses from more tangible threats (Wilson, A. F. 2013, 234).

A roundtable on 6 April 2013, at the *Awake and Aware* conference in Glendale, California, organized by Project Camelot, saw a number of prominent figures in this milieu addressing the apparent failure of '2012' millennial prophecies. Along with others, the panel included Laura Eisenhower, granddaughter of the US president who claims to have travelled to Mars as part of secret CIA projects in the 1980s; 'Face on Mars' exponent Richard Hoagland; and Bashar, 'a multi-dimensional extra-terrestrial being who speaks through channel Darryl Anka from what we perceive as the future'.[21] The speakers employed many of the strategies of cognitive dissonance avoidance I outlined in Chapter 2. Hoagland and others, following the *miscalculation* strategy, argued that the 'timeline' had been meddled with and that therefore, '2012 is still to come'; alternative dates were proposed, including 2015, 2025 and 2036. Jordan Maxwell argued that humans move between different 'time-streams', and in some of those the date of 'Ascension' (note that it is again conflated with '2012') is different or moves further into the future depending on our level of awakening. There was broad agreement from the panel and audience for the *aversion* strategy – that the prophecy became incorrect because of the actions of the group. Sean David Morton, on the other hand, insisted that '2012' had in fact happened and that we were living in a 'post-Ascension' world, albeit unbeknown to most, which can be interpreted as either *spiritualization* or *privation*.

Wilcock's response, however, was novel and particularly interesting; 'I don't know. I was as surprised as everyone else'. Yet with an understanding of Wilcock's tradition of appealing to channelled authority, this makes sense; he does not claim authority from himself per se but rather, from the beings he channels. Therefore, that he does not suggest a specific solution to the failed prophecy underscores that his authority comes ultimately from someone else.

This is both a restatement of his unique epistemic capital and a sidestepping of the responsibility for making failed prophecies.

Online Convergence

The field-trips described in Chapters 4 and 5 actually constituted a relatively small part of the ethnography I carried out for this book. Traditionally, ethnography involves the researcher spending a more-or-less extended period (or periods) of time embedded within an ongoing community (e.g. Malinowski 1954, 145; c.f. Harvey 2011). On the other hand, my field-work consisted of only two short periods. However, these were the same short periods as the other members of the community gathered; which is to say, for the majority of the time, the community is loosely constituted, often through the internet, only coming together in person during these short periods. So my interaction with the community was actually fairly in keeping with the typical subscriber – mostly taking place at a distance, by listening to weekly podcasts, reading or watching interviews and following discussions on the websites. Each of these activities became part of my regular behaviour during the three years of research. I listened to Strieber's *Dreamland* podcast weekly and to others (particularly *The Alex Jones Show*, *Red Ice Radio* and *Coast to Coast AM*) two to four times per week, time permitting. Strieber, Icke and Wilcock were often guests on these podcasts (and others), particularly when promoting books. Finally, I signed up as a member of each of the 'member's areas' of the websites of the three groups discussed. In the case of Icke and Wilcock, this simply meant registering for access to the discussion boards, which are areas of the websites where the content is created by the subscribers responding to one another in response to specific topics. In Strieber's case, however, membership (which was paid for) included access to a large amount of archival material, some of which I have referenced in this book. Both Icke and Strieber have utilized the internet to disseminate their ideas, with Icke a notable early adopter. But Wilcock goes much further in using the internet to establish epistemic capital. Both Strieber and Icke were already public figures, whereas Wilcock's career has used the internet from the beginning.

As noted in Chapter 1, while many scholars and journalists continue to connect the popularity of conspiracist narratives to the growth of the internet, this is certainly an oversimplification. Nevertheless, Amarasingham makes two significant observations: firstly, that the *idea* of the internet as an alternative and uncorrupted source of information – a Wild West of the media – has considerable symbolic power; and secondly, that increased choice of media sources does not lead to a broader encounter with differing positions but quite the opposite (Amarasingham 2011). Which is to say that given the choice, people tend to stay with ideas they do not find challenging (thus avoiding cognitive dissonance), and as the internet increases that range of choice, it may actually increase epistemic seclusion (Baurmann 2007).

My concern here, however, is with how millennial conspiracists might use the internet to increase their epistemic capital. So, on 24 August 2013, I signed up for Wilcock's online version of his Convergence presentations. The idea of offering a stream of live events over the internet is becoming common, and Icke also offered a stream of his Wembley presentation (see Chapter 5; c.f. Coats and Murchison 2014). This had originally been a live event in 2010, but the live streaming video was of low quality, so Wilcock re-recorded it with a professional crew. The video was entitled 'Access your Higher Self':

> Millions of people are discovering that they have a Higher Self – an omniscient source of intelligence guiding their lives with meticulous care and wisdom, navigating the right people and situations into view for the highest and best learning potential, and perpetually trying to communicate directly through synchronicities, visions and dreams... As we move into increasingly challenging times here on Earth, it has never been more essential that we form a direct, stable and accurate connection with our Higher Self. David Wilcock has used his dreams as a daily source of guidance for 18 years, and has 14 years of experience bringing in verbal and visionary messages from his Higher Self, with stunning results – including hundreds of incredibly accurate future prophecies.

In the terms of my theoretical model, this meant that I would be paying Wilcock to teach me how to mobilize counter-epistemic strategies for myself, increasing my epistemic capital as a result. I resolved that I would try the techniques he was going to describe; Ted and Rex were packed off to their grandparents' for the weekend, and to get into the right frame of mind, I stayed off alcohol for three weeks prior, stocked up on herbal teas and got a long night's sleep. The following day, I downloaded the material, and prepared to begin working my way through it. At the same time, I logged into the discussion board of divinecosmos.com; although I could not take part in the event live, I hoped to follow the comments of those who had, gaining some sense of a collective occasion.

Like Icke, Wilcock rejects the term 'New Age', but his self-presentation is in line with traditional constructions of the discourse. Wilcock presented it sitting in front of a vista of sea and mountains, the background music was 'ambient' electronic jazz-rock and Wilcock's descriptions were complemented by 'visionary art' which generally employed imagery of nature (waves, mountains), 'ancient' cultures and outer space. As Wilcock describes it, the first section (of four) was intended to break down conditioning, particularly the idea that 'your thoughts are private'. It aims to teach 'protocols' to be able to remain conscious whilst under hypnosis. He repeats from the *Source Field Investigations* the story about hypnotist Cleve Backster (2011, 7–24), which was also recounted by Icke at Wembley and Strieber at Dreamland. Backster was alleged to be able to implant post-hypnotic suggestions (that is, commands given under hypnosis but which remain in operation during normal waking consciousness) that could cause an individual to be unable to see another individual in the room. The example Wilcock gives is that a person was caused to be unable to see an individual but could still see his cigarette floating in the air (why he could not see his clothing is never explained). Backster is also well-known for connecting plants to polygraphs and concluding that they responded to the emotions of other living beings in the area. To those in the millennial conspiracist milieu, this so-called Backster Effect suggests that living creatures including animals, plants and bacteria are all in communication with one another and therefore that the 'entire universe around us is made of living, conscious energy'. Wilcock suggests that we are all receiving these signals but screen them out, and he names this 'living, conscious energy' the Source Field.

He closes the section by talking about reincarnation. As well as explicitly identifying himself as Cayce's reincarnation, he describes reincarnation as an evolutionary process recalling Cayce's 'co-creation' – a process whereby sequential incarnations move gradually closer to identification with their 'higher self', finally leading to a teleological event which Wilcock, drawing from Solara, calls Ascension. For Wilcock, Ascension 'is a fundamental shift in the evolution of what it means to be human ... We are talking about the idea of literally being able to step into a light body, to step into a higher consciousness'.

However, not all the virtual attendees necessarily agreed that we manifested our own reality:

> I wish dw would address this issue using cancer as an example. he and [another forum member] state that thoughts become things and specifically, anger produces cancer. dw also says that everything is from the higher self. so anyone know the answer? ... also, if the higher self controls everything, does that mean praying for something is pointless? i personally pray – higher self, please allow me to ...'! [...] from david wilcock's post in fulford's may 10 blog; *beings with capabilities far vaster than any ets we might normally think of are making sure that we are never offered more on earth than what we are creating.* so is it the higher self or are we creating our circumstances by our thought?[22]

GAK replied (and note both the rejection of 'New Age' and the trope that physical existence is a 'school'):

> 'higher self' is just a new age term that ****** me off. as far as i'm concerned, if you don't already think you are your higher self [at all times] with constant access to this higher self [or god] then you are still stuck in high school and sol for now ...[23]

This line of argument continued into Part 2. Wilcock states that we learn lessons over multiple lifetimes and (again echoing Strieber) that 'the earth is a school for spiritual growth'. At the same time he echoed Icke by describing individuality as 'the Great Illusion', when we are in fact all one being experiencing itself subjectively. Furthermore, his statement that angels are ascended humans echoed William Henry's Dreamland presentation. As the video progressed, however, an implicit conspiracism began to emerge, again echoing Gurdjieff. Wilcock asserts that ETs are somehow shielding humanity from the totality of spiritual energies which other races take for granted: 'A lot of what they do in the higher realms is coordinating what they call the Great Illusion here on earth. They want us to believe it's an illusion; they don't want us until we're ready to break through and realise we're in a co-created reality.'

Disappointingly, most of the discussion on the boards concerned technical niggles; how to stream the event and when the footage would be available to rewatch. There was also some discussion of the price of the event. Mal, a long-time member of Wilcock's discussion boards, defended the price, saying:

> David gives away much of his stuff for free. you can see his conferences, interviews, knowledge and a lot of things other people require you to pay for in order to 'pay the bills'. i recall him saying that if you want to be prosperous as a spiritual teacher you have to give away 50% or more of your knowledge for free … i would have loved to be at his conferences, to see all the other people in person that i admire from afar. but, who knows, maybe that would have been a greater hindrance to me than being alone and working under my own direction? [24]

Interestingly, however, a narrative concerning whether a section of the talk as originally broadcast had been edited began to develop. It was rumoured that a section concerning the recollection of dreams had been removed surreptitiously, and a forum member called Transiten claimed that they had contacted the website operators on the matter but had received no reply.[25]

Up to this point, the material did not differ significantly from that presented in his books. Moreover, there had been little in the way of information regarding practical techniques, as the course had promised. However, this was rectified in the third section. Wilcock outlined several dietary guidelines intended to maximize your contact with your 'higher self': a largely vegetarian diet, although small amounts of meat is acceptable so long as it is not factory-raised; no processed food, including white flour and rice, dairy and sugar, which Wilcock argues actually absorb the source field and therefore actively prevent contact with our higher self; no alcohol or other intoxicants. Wilcock also advocates food-combining; for example, he suggests not eating meat and carbohydrates together nor fruit and vegetables. No water should be drunk for forty-five minutes before eating, and up to two hours afterwards, and he further advocates supplements of vitamin B and Omega 3 and 6 oils. These guidelines are important, as 'by purifying your body, you are purifying your instrument through which these messages will arrive'.

Despite the secrecy, however, it all seemed very familiar. Wilcock himself even admits that some might find it too simple but that there are no secret methods to be taught; it is the details and order that he is giving which are important. Consciously or unconsciously, his method repeated Theosophical ideas; for example, 'Ways to Perfect Health' by Irving S. Cooper (1912). This slim volume is number 2 of a series (according to the frontispiece intended to be at four volumes but eventually totalling three) entitled *Manuals of Occultism*. Volume 1 was entitled 'Methods of Psychic Development', and together, these books cover the same material that Wilcock's presentation does. The book offers twenty 'indictments against flesh-food' (23–36), including that it is 'unscientific' (14), 'fatal to psychic development and … spiritual progress' (14) and 'conflicts with the law of evolution and the law of love' (20). Similarly, the consumption of raw food is encouraged (62), white flour and rice are to be scorned (64–5) and alcohol is described as having 'caused widespread physical and mental degeneracy', with effects that 'from the occult standpoint … are equally disastrous' (76). I was disconcerted to learn that wool should not be worn, however, as having 'been shorn from the back of an animal … is saturated with unpleasant magnetism' (99). 'Patent medicines' also are to be shunned (83–4), although I wondered how this category applied to modern categories of 'mainstream' and 'alternative' medicine. I do not include this material in order to argue that Wilcock 'stole' the material; rather, I argue that Wilcock's practices are in complete continuity with a longer Theosophical tradition.

Wilcock also utilizes the Law of One material, which he describes as creating 'exponential' spiritual growth. First is to 'seek the love in this moment', which Wilcock describes as 'stepping out' of present emotions and instead 'stepping back into' love. Secondly, Wilcock's admonition to 'reflect upon the past for how it informs the present' certainly recalls Cayce's search for the roots of his own character failings in the lives of his alleged previous incarnations. Taken together, Wilcock suggests, these techniques allow us to turn trauma to our advantage for 'spiritual growth'.

The third part was the most practical of all. Wilcock suggests that Yoga, Callisthenics and other forms of physical relaxation can help access the 'Higher Self'. He suggests that meditation, whether contemplative or concentrative, is the most powerful technique of all, and he quotes

Castaneda's *Teaching of Don Juan* (1968) as evidence that bi-location and other powers can be gained through its practice.

However, the section on recording dreams, which continued into the fourth and final section, was the most detailed and unusual. Wilcock tells us that the higher self communicates in the language of symbolism and metaphor, through our dreams, which Wilcock believes contain messages of import for our spiritual development. This section showed a considerable debt to psychoanalysis, in particular Joseph Campbell's notion of the 'Guardian at the Threshold'. This Guardian is a personification of your 'shadow self', which is constructed from unresolved childhood traumas. Paraphrasing Jung's concept of reintegration, Wilcock states that embracing the Guardian allows us to experience growth in our waking consciousness.

Many of those on the forum were recounting the dreams they had had after taking part and were sharing them with the others. So I recorded my dreams. Aside from a morning cup of coffee, I was entirely clean, and as it happens, my partner is vegetarian anyway, so I seldom eat meat. I left my computer by the bed, as Wilcock suggests, which allows one to start with a few 'snapshots' which can be elaborated upon as more is recalled. Upon awaking wrote down what I could remember:

> Sunday, 25/8/2013 – 7:30
> Cars were travelling against us on the wrong side of the road – made a small error as we passed some police officers – this was at the bottom of kinmylies by my mum's house
> Travelling the bus with David Bowie, almost got lost in the terminal – looking for a bus named ratline

This is exactly what I wrote that first morning. How do we interpret it? To take a traditional approach drawn from Jung and Freud, we could note that it took place in Inverness where I grew up but have not lived for twenty years, but had visited recently. One might also point out that David Bowie was very much in the news at the time, due to the dramatic promotional campaign for his 'comeback' album, *The Next Day*. Finally, the 'ratline' – a term which refers to the mechanisms by which certain Nazi leaders are said to have escaped Germany before the 1945 defeat – had recently come to my attention due to interviews *Dreamland* and *Red Ice Radio*. So all of these elements already had a reason to be floating around in my mind.

If we follow Wilcock, however, then everything and everyone that appears in our dreams is an aspect of us ourselves – he terms it a 'psycho-cartography' or more prosaically, the 'You-niverse'. In which case, me, my girlfriend, the police, David Bowie and even Hitler all represent aspects of David Robertson. While I find this personally unpleasant, let's pursue it for a moment. According to this line of argumentation, David Robertson – presumably 'the real me', judging by the fact that I experienced the dream through this person – when with my family, feels nervous of making mistakes, or at least of being caught doing so. Yet, when away from my family, I am apparently more concerned with appearance, with Bowie, famous for playing roles and having a fluid sense of identity, perhaps representing my sense of how others see me – my super-ego, to use Jungian terms. There may be something to that; but why is my super-ego (Bowie) telling me about the Nazis? Is my playful side warning me about a fascistic side to my personality, which although apparently extinguished, actually survived, hidden away? Is my inner child concerned that my Bowie-esque super-ego too concerned with dark subjects? Or was it merely a jumple of half-remembered detritus from recent days?

The next night's results were similarly puzzling:

Monday 26/8/13
some mafia guys were trying to poison someone i knew with a poisoned sandwich – not sure why i was going along. somewhere very green and upmarket. there were two frogs one big and one smaller. One of the dons was friendly and knew about food. Scott from Tennessee was there and we had to climb a steep grass verge.

Again, this is exactly how it was written. Scott was a postgraduate student at the University at the time, so his appearance is perhaps not so surprising. Similarly, I have been working in restaurants for twenty-odd years, so the idea of bonding over recipes is not so bizarre. The mafia theme is perhaps more odd, as I'm not a fan of such films as a rule. Yet the dream followed a mafia-style narrative, we were crossing town presumably to assassinate someone, yet why Scott and I had to travel there across the lawns of neighbouring houses, including some which were a 70 per cent gradient, is far from clear. Again, each of these elements must also be me, by Wilcock's account. I am happy to accept that Scott may have represented a happier, more relaxed aspect of my super-ego, but what part of me the Mafia may have represented, I am less sure. Nor is it the case that any post-hoc recognition of these scenes has occurred to me as I redraft this chapter.

Curiously, on perhaps three occasions over the weekend, I noticed '11:11' on the clock on my computer. Perhaps my Higher Self was trying to contact me through synchronicities, as Wilcock had earlier suggested? I decided to try another of the techniques Wilcock had suggested, bibliomancy. The idea was that what was used for divination was not in itself important, rather that by asking for a communication from the Higher Self, one was 'encoding synchronicity', creating a situation in which the divined information must be interpreted meaningfully. I picked up the first book which caught my attention from a pile on top of my desk – *The Apocraphal New Testament* (Hone et al., n.d.) – opened it at random and stabbed my finger down. It was a line from *The Epistle of St Paul and Seneca*: 'And I wish to be in that circumstance or station which you are, and that you were in the same that I am' (Hone et al., n.d., 111). Was this a call for union from my Higher Self?

After three weeks according to Wilcock's guidelines – no drugs or alcohol, a predominantly vegetarian diet and no processed sugar or factory meat – I remained as bitter, cynical and materialist as ever, though perhaps somewhat healthier. During this and other similar periods, I have had no profound experiences. My dreams seemed more easily attributed to a random bricolage of bits of my everyday waking experiences than messages from my Higher Self. However, I do not want to suggest here that this brief foray into Wilcock's methods in any way disproves their efficacy. Indeed, as we have seen, his techniques are not in themselves particularly unusual and are in complete continuity with Theosophical teachings. However, I will suggest that Wilcock's prescriptions are not *in themselves* enough to generate a profound change in personality – or perhaps more accurately, an acceptance of a broader set of sources of epistemic capital. It seems as though the acceptance of this broader capital is a prerequisite for, rather than result of, Wilcock's methods. To take this further, what I was missing was the millennial conspiracist habitus – or episteme – predicated upon the acceptance of the full range of epistemic strategies.

UFOs as discursive object between spiritual and conspiracist narratives

As with Strieber and Icke, UFOs were central to Wilcock's millennial narrative. As with Icke, Wilcock posits a conspiratorial aspect to their communication with humans. In Wilcock's cosmology, the earthly conspiracy is a microcosm of a Manichaean cosmic battle between benevolent and malevolent ETs. Wilcock refers to these negative ETs as 'Orion Entities' and claims they are in control of Earth's political structures:

> the Orions had almost complete subconscious control over the leaders of our present world government, and were basically running the show ... This explained the shadowy, Luciferian doctrines I had read about as occurring in negatively oriented secret societies, such as Adam Weishaupt's 'Bavarian Illuminati.' Based on Ra's revelations, the whole 'New World Order' crew now pulling the strings and running the global military/political/corporate hierarchy is overrun with Orion in every possible way (Wilcock 200a, Chapter 10).

So in Wilcock's account, as with Icke's, the Illuminati is controlled by ETs:

> As time progressed even further, I came to realize that much of our modern consumerist, money-driven society, including television, media, entertainment, industry and food production, were all the byproducts of this self-serving Orion orientation ... Even if most of the CEOs of our corporations were not aware that the Orions were assisting them, they would essentially call on their services the more they indulged in their profit-motivated behaviors. (Wilcock 2000a, Chapter 10)

As with the other case-studies, Wilcock has become a prominent figure by presenting himself as possessing a high degree of epistemic capital, which he has pursued through several millennial tropes, including '2012' and 'Ascension'. The archaeology presented above demonstrates the continuity of these narratives with 'New Age' but, moreover, the continuity of all of these popular millennial narratives with earlier Theosophical writings.

As demonstrated by his response to the apparent failure of his predictions regarding '2012', however, Wilcock's mobilization of epistemic strategies in order to gain epistemic capital is particularly sophisticated. Wilcock's initial epistemic capital comes primarily from channelling; his autobiography recounts childhood channelling events, and his later exposure in the field comes from his claim to be a reincarnation of Cayce, arguably the most influential channeller in the history of popular millennialism. Moreover, it is through a channelled text (*The Ra Communications*) that Wilcock's involvement with UFOlogy develops. However, Wilcock goes to considerable lengths to validate his channelled knowledge and establish his authority through mobilization of the scientific epistemic strategy.

Wilcock has also used the internet with sophistication to accumulate social and epistemic capital. While Strieber and Icke have considerable profiles online, both began their careers pre-internet, and continue to focus on traditional media like books and personal appearances. Wilcock, on the other hand, has built up his profile almost exclusively through his website, going so far as to make four books available free through divinecosmos.com before publishing through traditional channels. Wilcock's live appearances have become increasingly infrequent as he channels his energies into TV and internet videos like *Wisdom Teachings*, *Ancient Aliens* and the Online Convergence.

In presenting methods of contacting the 'higher Self', Wilcock's *Online Convergence* underlines the importance of narratives of individualism and personal agency in these discourses. For Wilcock, the individual is paramount, yet the mobilization of that individuality is reliant upon information from outside the individual in question. This special knowledge – this gnosis – transforms the individual from being one of the passive, sleeping 'sheeple' into an active, autonomous agent of change.

In the final chapter, I draw these threads back together and 'connect the dots', to use an analogy from Icke. Why is it that UFO, millennial and conspiratorial narratives are so often found together? In particular, why are UFOs the object that has enabled this discursive transfer? Finally, how does millennial conspiracist discourse serve its subscribers?

The Counter-Elite/A Theodicy of the Dispossessed

In my introduction, I asked two interrelated questions. First, what is the common factor or factors which so often bring UFO, conspiracist and popular millennial narratives together? More specifically, why did UFOs become the primary discursive object between conspiracist and popular millennial fields? Secondly, how does millennial conspiracist discourse serve its subscribers? I shall attempt to answer these in this conclusion. I will argue the common factor is the mobilization of counter-epistemic strategies, as exemplified and symbolized by the UFO. The function of millennial conspiracist discourse, however, is that by proposing the existence of an occluded malevolent agency, it explains the disenfranchisement – culturally, economically and crucially, epistemologically – of its subscribers. In short, millennial conspiracism provides a theodicy of the dispossessed.

The preceding chapters demonstrated how Strieber, Icke and Wilcock mobilized the five types of epistemic strategies discussed in Chapter 2 in order to gain epistemic capital in the millennial conspiracist field. To complete my analysis of the common factors underpinning the convergence of UFO, conspiracist and popular millennial narratives, I briefly summarize these five types of strategy with examples from the case studies.

Tradition

Tradition may appear the least appealed to of the five strategies, as millennial conspiracist discourse tends towards an explicit rejection of tradition. Institutionalized religious traditions are particularly criticized, either as foolishly misguided (e.g. Wilcock 2011, 97) or as active participants in the conspiracy (Icke 2012, 100–3). Nevertheless, religious texts are frequently strategically cited, particularly Biblical texts including Genesis and Revelation but also the Vedas, Enuma Elish and Egyptian texts, and are furthermore accorded a high degree of authority in exchanges where epistemic capital can be acquired. Moreover, certain religious groups may be appealed to due to their perceived status as heretics: the Gnostics in particular are frequently referred to in this way. As with the self-proclaimed 'nutters' whom I encountered, 'heresy' is typically constructed positively in millennial conspiracism, as a counter-epistemic identity.

Implicitly, however, tradition plays a significant role in millennial conspiracist discourse. In particular, alternative archaeology is used to construct historical narratives which place the millennial conspiracist in a tradition of resistance against the conspiratorial Other. Indeed, appeals to Gnostic and other heretical groups are part of this construction, by positioning the contemporary millennial conspiracist in a tradition of perennial 'ancient wisdom', recalling Blavatsky's positioning of the Theosophical Society in *Isis Unveiled* (1877 [1997], 140; c.f. Lewis 2012, 218). Furthermore, narratives of reincarnation are a mobilization of the strategy of tradition, as also argued by Hammer (2001, 467–73), including Wilcock's claim regarding Cayce and Ra-Ta, as well as Icke's regarding Jesus. These are essentially appeals by the practitioner to the recognized social and epistemic capital of those individuals, capitalizing on their authority.

Scientific

Throughout the case studies, we were told that the scientific authorities are ignorant of, or deliberately suppressing, other forms of knowledge. 'Mainstream science', we are told, does not want to us to know the truth or cannot know the truth because it is limited to the physical world (e.g. Icke 2012, 64, 67). Universities and peer-reviewing are constructed as existing not to encourage but to limit free thought (Dyrendal 2013, 219).

Yet when a scientist publishes something which can be read as supporting telepathy, holographic universes or sophisticated antediluvian cultures (to take three examples encountered in the case-studies), their PhDs and the peer-review system are instead presented as supporting factors. Millennial conspiracist publications frequently include 'PhD' and other qualifications in the author credits; ironically, the academic authors they appear to mimic almost never do. Hancock is also described as having 'peer-reviewed' Wilcock's *Source Field Investigations* (2011, 112), adopting the language of an academic publication. It would be a mistake to argue that, therefore, millennial conspiracist discourses are 'anti-scientific'. Rather, what we find is a *strategic mobilization* of the scientific strategy, as one strategy among others. As Harambamm and Aupers put it, science is 'at once sacralised for its intentions but demonised for its manifestations' (2014, 12). 'Science' is not constructed as wrong in itself; rather, its epistemic hegemony in modernity prevents other strategies from being mobilized constructively.

In an important recent paper, Asprem writes:

> An affinity of the weird is characteristic of the fluid and playful engagement with subversive knowledge-claims that is fundamental to what sociologists of religion call the 'cultic milieu'... A staple element of engagement with representations spreading in these subcultural reservoirs is that individuals pick and mix to serve specific, situational needs–one person may invoke quantum mechanics to explain an event attributed to telepathy, while another seeks to justify a belief in immortality... It may be shared weirdness rather than shared stigmatization that is driving the process, fuelled by a linking of relevant mysteries. This can explain why we do not, after all, *only* see a trafficking with presumably 'stigmatized' representations, such as alien abductions, telekinesis, conspiracy theories or spirit possession, but also representations (in mutated form, to be sure) that originate in authorized scientific discourses. (2015)

Experiential

There were numerous examples of how individual experience is considered to override scientific epistemic authorities in the case studies. Wilcock 'proves' to himself that the Backster Effect is real after being able to affect a plant's polygraph reading (2011, 17). Icke's experiences came first through Betty Shine and other channellers but following his own journey to Peru, directly.

The importance of experience was particularly obvious in Strieber's case, as his apparent abduction led to him promoting a wide range of stigmatized narratives drawn from channelled, insider and synthetic sources. Many of the Dreamland attendees had had some sort of anomalous experience – not necessarily abduction per se but frequently involving entities or UFOs. One Dreamland attendee later told me:

> when a person realizes, through an interaction with the paranormal, that the 'normal' is in some sense a lie, the next step is to ask what other things you believe are lies. This is how the conspiracy thing becomes relevant. If the US Government IS actually lying about UFOs … then what else are they lying about? It doesn't take much digging to find they have been lying about pretty much everything from the Sinking of the Maine which led to the Spanish American War to a string of CIA involvement … right up to the Present wars in the Middle East which were based on lies …

Synthetic

Icke utilizes this approach most freely. Taking as an example his recent book *Remember Who You Are* (2012), he references NASA press releases (67), The San Francisco Chronicle (48), discredited academics including Castaneda (86), other conspiracist writers, often drawing on inadequately identified sources themselves (99–100, 179–80), the Bible (85), popular movies including *The Matrix* (30), unidentified internet articles (48) and channelled communications (40–2, 411, 149), giving equal weight to each and often failing to distinguish which is which.

Similarly, Wilcock describes *The Source Field Investigations* as 'not a book of philosophy, speculation or wishful thinking – it is a vast synthesis' (Wilcock 2011, 5). One chapter consists of a catalogue of images from religious iconography of pinecones, single eyes and pyramids, which he presents as collectively suggesting the importance of the pineal gland for cultures across geographical and temporal boundaries (2011, 40–56). With astonishing certainty, Wilcock concludes: 'When we put all these pieces together, it is obvious that the founding fathers of America clearly believed the return of the capstone on the pyramid symbolised the dawning of a new era in human history at the end of the Great Year [i.e. 2012]' (2011, 135).

Channelling

In each of our case studies, however, the central figure has been contacted directly by supernatural beings. Strieber frequently describes his abduction experiences as encounters with supernatural beings, and Strieber implies that the Master of the Key is more than human, perhaps even a theosophical Master. Icke's movement away from the mainstream media was triggered initially by contact with Wang Yi Lee and later Rakorczy, Jesus and others. Although the majority of his channelled communications came through an intermediary, he also claims to have received messages directly, first in Peru in 1990 and later during an ayahuasca trip. Most clearly, Wilcock's career began as a professional channel, and he later claimed to be the reincarnation of arguably the most influential channels of the twentieth century, Edgar Cayce.

Ultimately then, what distinguishes millennial conspiracist epistemology is *a broadened conception of what counts as knowledge*. Therefore, I argue that the answer to my first question – what is the common factor between millennial and conspiracist discourse? – is an epistemology which acknowledges strategies stigmatized by the epistemic authorities of the present Anglophone world.[1] From such a counter-epistemic position, the UFO is the perfect symbol, as it seems to offer proof that the hegemonic epistemic strategies of science and tradition are insufficient in themselves to explain the discursive object.[2] In fact, the other common themes in the field, including alternative histories such as the ancient alien narrative or alternative healthcare approaches, can all be seen as counter-epistemic to a large degree.

The second question I posed in my introduction was, what function does this discourse serve for its subscribers? In the section below, I suggest how this common factor of a broadened epistemology relates to the function of millennial conspiracist discourse.

The counter-elite

As outlined above and detailed in the case-studies in Chapters 4 through 6, I have shown how Strieber, Icke and Wilcock have each successfully mobilized counter-epistemic strategies to accumulate epistemic capital and therefore have established a relative degree of authority in the millennial conspiracist field. Each exerts a certain degree of formative authority upon their audience. Although certain assumptions are accepted in the field as a whole, there were also significant differences between the various groups, with for example Strieber's group broadly supporting the existence of alien abduction, but not Icke's.

Nevertheless, millennial conspiracist discourse stresses the importance of individual agency. Wilcock teaches how to embark on a quest for our 'higher self'; abduction narratives, with their accounts of anal probes, physical experimentation, implants and memory manipulation, describe the compromising of the individual as a physical being and hence contain at least an implicit invitation to take responsibility for one's fate; while Icke's NWO conspiracist narratives similarly concern the political disenfranchisement of the individual by global agencies. Moreover, it is frequently the framing of an experience which the individual considers inexplicable through scientific or traditional epistemic strategies which leads to an engagement with counter-epistemic strategies. Often, this transformational experience or encounter is described as gnosis and is constructed as a form of soteriological, experiential and importantly, personal knowledge. So for the millennial conspiracist, the individual 'self' is paramount; but the soteriological narrative that knowledge can liberate the individual brings concerns regarding the link between secrecy and agency to the fore (Dyrendal 2013, 223).

Furthermore, that individual is simultaneously represented as being embedded at a cosmic scale and often even as a 'subject-outside-history' (Maton 2003, 49). Millennial and alternative archaeological narratives present sweeping accounts of the present – as framed by the ancient past and anticipating a prophetic future – unavailable to those of us informed only by our socially constructed knowledge, lacking the channelled, synthetic or experiential knowledge they have access to. For the conspiracist sees subjects inside history and society as constructs of 'alien' information systems in which thoughts, values and beliefs do not originate with the subject (Maton 2003, 50). In contrast to the limited and impoverished 'everyday subject', the millennial conspiracist is constructed as 'a perfect autonomous subject who, despite being one of the majority outside the conspiracy's elite, remains unaffected by the conspiracy's operations and untouched by its disinformation – unlike the rest of society' (Maton 2003, 28).

However, the accounts of Strieber, Wilcock and in particular Icke ascribe a remarkable lack of personal agency to the majority of individuals, who are constructed as a sleeping, aquiescent majority whose every thought and action is determined by the conspiratorial agents. The irony then, is that these discourses simultaneously seek to empower the individuality of the subject while disempowering the masses. In claiming to address disempowerment, they in fact remove agency from the majority and restrict it for a special class: an epistemic elect.

Thus, the millennial conspiracist community is constructed as a third community; neither the controlled, acquiescent masses (Icke's 'sheeple', or more problematically, the 'goyim' of the Protocols of Zion) nor the conspiratorial elite but rather an elect minority defined by exclusive knowledge – gnosis. The elites are constructed as gaining power by restricting access to counter-epistemic strategies from the masses, but those who claim to see through these manipulations gain power for themselves. In essence, this makes them a *counter-elite*, predicated upon counter-epistemic strategies; rather than constituting an elite defined by the control of economic capital, they belong to an elite defined by control of epistemic capital. As Dyrendal notes,

> the revelation of 'secret knowledge' in conspiracy theory serves to delimit in-group from out-group, aiming in the same stroke to work as an 'initiatory' experience regulating the possibility of salvation through disclosure: adopt, and awaken, or reject, and join the black brethren (or the sheeple). (2013, 221)

My fieldwork revealed that the individuals in the field tended to feel disenfranchised, in terms of both economic and symbolic capital. Yet the one form of capital which they can potentially dominate (in emic discourse, at least) is epistemic. Whether aligned with left or right political values, millennial conspiracist narratives reframe Marxist critiques in terms of *epistemic* rather than economic capital. The liberation of the oppressed is reconstructed as being realized through a revolution in knowledge, a seizing not of the means of production but of the *means of cognition*. Knowledge is power. The truth will set you free.

As Benson Saler puts it;

> [W]hat ultimately is this gnosis or knowledge, the acquisition of which will enhance our dignity? It is knowledge, finally, that we humans are not the only intelligent beings in the universe and that we can hope for contact and communion with other intelligent beings. Hope is not in vain, because the others, who are presently alien, are not indifferent to us. (Saler, Zeigler and Moore 1997, 149)

A theodicy of the dispossessed

Millennial conspiracism discourse constructs humankind's spiritual and socio-economic disenfranchisement as caused by the occluded powers who conspire to deliberately suppress counter-epistemic strategies. This is different to previous popular millennial discourses, which construct disenfranchisement as the result of cosmic imbalances. An emic account of 'New Age' theodicy in the early 1990s is found in the work of prominent popular millennial writer Shirley MacLaine:

> negative didn't mean wrong. It simply meant the opposite polarity – the other end of the balance – of positive. Negative energy was as necessary as positive. It was the interacted combustion that produced and created life ... Understanding the basic tenets of that principle was helpful then in extending our understanding that 'evil' exists only in relation to point of view; if a child steals to live, if a man kills to protect his family, if a woman aborts a fetus rather than give birth to an unwanted child, if a terrorist murders because he has been raised all his life to believe that killing is his right and proper duty – who is evil? (1987, 144–5)

As I argued in Chapter 3, following the crisis of the 'New Age' in the mid-1990s, this theodicy seems to no longer have been satisfactory to many in the popular millennial field, and a new oppositional Other was sought at a representational meta-level beyond the thief, abortionist and terrorist constructed by MacLaine.

Typically, the Other has tended to have been found in the margins of the culture or group doing the Othering, and as a result there has been a tendency for the Other to be constructed from minority ethnic or national groups – the Jews in nineteenth and twentieth century Europe being a prime example. However, the increasingly multicultural and globalized culture of the contemporary West may mean that these minorities no longer seem as alien as they once would have, a point underlined by modern scientific understandings of humanity's common genetic and evolutionary heritage. The Other was traditionally found on the local margins, but when the societal group is increasingly constructed in a globalized society as including 'everyone', there are no outsiders who can be blamed when things go wrong (Beyer 1994, 72). Frisk hypothesizes that 'globalisation of society does not lead mainly to the death of God, but the death of the Devil' (2001, 35). However, I argue that my primary source material suggests that an Other can still be constructed, just not necessarily in terms of ethnicity or nationality:

> As these models of ritual once informed western understandings of 'primitive' religion on the cultural or historical periphery, so they have often (as now) been turned inward, to construe in religious terms the fear of subversive evil among us. (Frankfurter 2003, 112)

As I have argued, however, in the 1990s the need for such an oppositional entity upon whom to blame the perceived failure of 'New Age' millennial prophecies was keenly felt. As my case studies demonstrated, the narrative that the predicted 'New Age' or 'Ascension' was prevented from arriving by malevolent occluded agencies explains their adoption of conspiracist discourse in their later careers, as they increasingly search for evidence of this occluded Other.

Millennial conspiracist discourses echo historical constructions of Otherness, yet posit that Other as existing both within a globalized humanity (in the form of a conspiracy) and without (in the form of ETs). In doing so, a new popular theodicy emerges which does not contradict a sacralized, holistic view of humanity. By placing ultimate responsibility for the rapaciousness and iniquity of contemporary society with malevolent ETs, millennial conspiracist theodicy effectively removes the responsibility from humanity – for the Other is constructed as literally alien. In this way, millennial conspiracism reconciles a holistic view of humanity and a deterministic cosmos with a conspiracist narrative of unseen malevolent agency. Therefore millennial conspiracist discourse offers its subscribers a theodicy which constructs an occluded Other for a struggling 'universal humanity'.

By extension, this theodicy answers why these millennial narratives – 'Aquarian Age', 'New Age', 'Ascension', '2012' – apparently 'failed'. They were prevented from arriving by the machinations of an occluded malevolent counter-agency – the occluded Other. Yet in millennial conspiracist discourse, the millennial project must go on, now reconstructed as a continuing battle to identify and counteract the occluded Other rather than an imminent and decisive event.

'Connecting the dots'

My research suggests that conspiracist narratives spring from the same sources as narratives typically constructed as 'religious'. In fact, this fact may elucidate the growing appeal of conspiracist narratives in a society in which traditional religious institutions no longer exert hegemonic control. As Popper notes: 'The conspiracy theory of society … comes from abandoning God and then asking: What is in his place?' (1945 [1957], 95). This research suggests that the need to perceive underlying agency is not tied to a belief in the supernatural *qua* supernatural but rather a social function to which religions have historically aligned themselves. Therefore the idea of religious 'Othering' is challenged. Rather, there are multiple 'Otherings': when malevolent but external to our own society, we construct the Other as 'enemy'; when external but non-threatening, we construct the Other as 'primitive'; but when malevolent but within our own society, we construct the Other as a 'conspiracy'.

I suggest that Religious Studies might benefit from refocussing on the study of epistemologies rather than 'beliefs'. Despite a persuasive critique in recent decades that the focus on 'beliefs' and 'faiths' is a product of the discipline's Protestant heritage (McCutcheon 1997; Fitzgerald 2000), the terminology remains largely entrenched within Religious Studies. A refocussing on epistemology would offer a possible alternative approach, and would furthermore fit well with von Stuckrad's call that the discipline should cease trying to construct bounded definitions (particularly, and inevitably, of 'religion') and instead focus on analysing discourses, the epistemological strategies employed, and how they relate to their socio-historical context. Such a refocussing would ease issues concerning the boundaries of the discipline; by addressing social epistemologies rather than 'religions' per se, the discipline could more easily consider the functional similarities between 'religious' discourses and those of 'nationalism', 'political ideology', and so forth. While scholars of religion have become skilled at avoiding claiming that the apparently bizarre truth claims of cultures other than their own are irrational, we are less inclined to do so regarding the truth claims found on the fringes of our own society (Dolby 1979, 28). Yet, if we cannot acknowledge that there are multiple epistemologies in operation in the contemporary Anglophone 'developed' world, then I suspect we struggle to understand other contexts also, especially those we only receive through reified historical sources.

This brings me back to the first-level taxon, 'religion'. Given that this book exists within an etic discourse (Religious Studies), I am obliged to ask, who stands to gain if millennial conspiracist discourse is labelled 'religious' or 'religion'? Arguably scholars such as myself, who widen the category ever further, and perhaps secure some research grants and encourage a few PhDs. I hasten to add, however, that I do not see this research in that light; I come to bury the category, not to praise it.

Who stands to lose? Certainly there are many who would not be happy to see conspiracist or UFO narratives compared to or conflated with more familiar 'religious' traditions and categories – not only the caretakers of those traditions but the subjects of my case studies who construct their position as directly oppositional to such a construction of 'religion', which is to say that I see 'religion' as an empty category and the task of Religious Studies as deconstructing the category. I have here avoided using 'world religions', talking of 'religion' as a thing, continuing to use problematic terminology such as 'New Age' or even to talk of 'belief', and as such have offered an alternative approach, focussed on the analyses of socially mandated epistemologies.

As I wrote in the introduction to this volume, discourses are not neutral but reflect underlying ideologies and therefore power structures. This includes academic terminology and not only in Religious Studies. Too often scholars act as caretakers rather than critics of our *own* ideologies. We tell people who think and act 'correctly' (i.e. people like 'us') what the defects are which cause people to think and act 'wrongly' (i.e. 'them', 'the Other'). For example, no one is writing articles explaining why 'our' soldiers go off to shoot at people in other countries, but if someone wants to go and fight for *another* group, they must have been brainwashed or radicalized due to deprivation (McCutcheon 2014). In other words, *there must be a reason why they don't think and act like 'us'*:

> It is in the nature of many intellectual character traits that you don't realise you have them, and so aren't aware of the true extent to which your thinking is influenced by them. The gullible rarely believe they are gullible and the closed-minded don't believe they are closed-minded. The only hope of overcoming self-ignorance in such cases is to accept that other people–your co-workers, your spouse, your friends–probably know your intellectual character better than you do. But even that won't necessarily help. After all, it might be that refusing to listen to what other people say about you is one of your intellectual character traits. Some defects are incurable. (Cassem 2015)

The truth will set you free? Millennial conspiracism offers us an opportunity to redress that we do not in this field view all supernatural claims equally. If we cannot view Striber's abduction claims, Icke's reptilian thesis or Wilcock's spiritual science on an equal footing with the claims of the Catholic Church, then 'methodological agnosticism' has failed, and with it, the comparative project.

Notes

Chapter 1

1   The terms 'etic' and 'emic' were originally derived from linguistics by Kenneth Pike but were adapted for use in the social sciences. In Pike's original definition, emic refers to any 'item or system treated by insiders as relevant to their system of behaviour' (1990, 28). Such items or systems may include any concepts or objects which are recognized through naming, such as 'computer' or 'suicide' (1990, 28–9). Emic units can also be complexes made up of other emic units, such as 'games' or 'religions'. Etics, on the other hand, represent an attempt by an outsider to interpret those emic units by juxtaposing them against his own emic system, in Pike's understanding. Harris developed Pike's terms further, presenting a rather different understanding of etics (1990, 48). Harris constructs etic statements as those of the scientific community, 'trained observer familiar with several canons of scholarly and scientific inquiry'; therefore for Harris emics and etics represent 'two fundamentally different kinds of data languages' (Ibid., 49). In this thesis, I employ etic and emic in this latter sense of 'data languages'. Conceptualizations demarcated as etic are assumed to be using categories and methodologies that seek cross-cultural, reflexive and scientific validity. Those demarcated as emic, on the other hand, are assumed to be accounts of those who seek validity in terms of the capital of the field being analysed.

2   In this thesis, when I refer to 'New Age', 'Ascension', '2012', etc. (with quotation marks), I am referring to specific emic discourses. This intended to differentiate between etic and emic usages, which avoid much of the confusion which comes from the conflation of the two. See Chapter 2 for a fuller explanation of academic usage of 'New Age'.

3   Actually Dorothy Martin, who continued to have a successful career as a channeller in the popular millennial milieu (Wilson 2013, R. F., 230).

4   The two books are also implicitly a criticism against the academic discipline of Religious Studies for failing to take the subjective into account. Kripal does not seem to appreciate that in using these examples to challenge the methodology

of Religious Studies – that is, in not taking certain phenomena as seriously as others – he in fact undermines the entire rationale of the field. If we are to take truth claims evidentially, then we must take *all* truth claims evidentially, lest the field lose any cross-cultural analytic purchase. Kripal's argument, taken to its conclusion, would lead not to a more reflexive Religious Studies but an expanded and emboldened theology which defeats the very rationale upon which the discipline is constructed.

5   Silverstein (2002, 647), Sanders and West (2003, 6) and Pelkmans and Machold (2011), 73.

6   Faivre's definition presents 'western esotericism' as having four principal propositions: (1) that a complex of correspondences underpin reality, (2) that all life constitutes a single organism, (3) that the imagination can through ritual, meditation or symbolism access extra-mundane levels of being, and (4) that individuals, as well as nature as a whole, can undergo ontological transformations, or 'gnosis' (1998, 119–20).

7   Partridge's two-volume *The Re-Enchantment of the West* argues that detraditionalization – that is, the relativization of traditional religious authorities – has led to a profusion of novel religious narratives. In particular, motifs are drawn from what Partridge, again drawing from Campbell, calls *occulture*. Occulture is defined as 'an essentially non-Christian religio-cultural milieu' which includes elements of Eastern religions, esoteric traditions and popular culture (2004, 4). Christian and occultural narratives may be combined in eclectic combinations, while more conservative and traditionalist belief systems can passively absorb occultural motifs (2004, 317–8). I have doubts about the analytic purchase of the concept of cultic or occultural milieus. Firstly, they seem to reinforce the very power structures which I seek to problematize by using a discursive methodological approach; by using these terms, we essentially affirm that any non-authoritative epistemic position is 'cultic' or 'occult', with all of the negative connotations they carry. Secondly, they draw too strict a boundary; as we will see, there are in fact a great deal of Christian elements in millennial conspiracist narratives, and expanding the cultic milieu to include this and the many practitioners on yoga, for example, would render it so large as to include practically everyone. Thirdly, and perhaps most importantly, they act as a kind of 'black box'. By answering the question of where these ideas come from with the answer 'the Cultic Milieu', what have we answered? The cultic milieu is defined by its contents; to therefore analyse the field from this position can only reproduce the presuppositions of those who decided what is 'cultic' and what is

not. It does not in itself provide any analytical leverage but rather the question of the function and appeal of these narratives is simply deferred. Therefore, I will not be using Campbell or Partridge's terminology here.

8   He goes on to make the interesting comparison between this mingling of popular millennial and conspiracist ideas with the völkisch movement of the German-speaking countries of Europe in the late nineteen and early twentieth century, a loose affiliation of populist conservative groups whose eulogizing of nature and critique of modern society was accompanied by nationalism and notions of racial purity (299–300). The völkisch movement was a significant factor in the development of Nazism, which developed both a millennial narrative and a malevolent occluded agency. As I shall show in Chapter 5, David Icke has frequently been accused of promoting anti-Semitic ideas.

9   The present work has benefitted from several discussions with Ward.

10 See the gradual settling of the date 21 December 2012 in Chapter 6, for example, or Icke's abandonment of his early prophecies in Chapter 5.

11 http://www.infowars.com/ (accessed 7 November 2011).

12 See Rowbottom (2012), Sutcliffe (2003a, 174–80) and Singler (2015).

13 This was the tagline of an advert for vitamin supplements that ran daily on Jones' radio show from mid-2013 until early 2014.

14 It has proven impossible to get accurate listening figures for these shows. As they are syndicated programmes, they are broadcast on multiple (and constantly changing) local AM and FM stations, but this ignores the considerable listenerships gained over the internet, both 'officially' through their homepages and unofficially through YouTube and similar sites, which furthermore may have multiple versions of the files. *Coast to Coast AM* claims close to three million listeners per week (http://www.coasttocoastam.com/pages/about [accessed 21 May 2014]), and Alex Jones's advertising pack (http://static.infowars.com/ads/mediakit_public.pdf [accessed 21 May 2014]) claims a total of 11.5 million website hits per month, but these figures are unverifiable at present. I have therefore decided to use a vague but reasonably conservative 'millions' in the absence of firmer evidence.

15 http://www.glastonburysymposium.co.uk/ (accessed 16 July 2013).

16 Questions relating to religious and political affiliation were left open-ended to preclude any leading suggestion, as were a series of questions relating to specific propositions (including 'Is there an environmental threat to the planet, and if so how serious?' and 'Have you ever had a close encounter or other supernatural experience?'). Participants were invited to write as much or little as they

wanted. From the Strieber event, fifty-seven were returned in various states of completion, almost half the attendees, and from the Icke group fifteen out of twenty-one attendees returned questionnaires.

17 Data was unavailable for unknowncountry.com.

18 It should be remembered that 'none' was not an option out of several others; the respondents were free to answer in any way they saw fit.

19 I realize that I am making huge generalizations here in terms of the political 'left' and 'right' here. Nevertheless, I think the argument stands.

20 Various dates have been proposed for 'the End of the Cold War', including the USSR's unilateral commitment to disarmament in December 1988, the fall of the Berlin Wall in November 1989 and the dissolution of the USSR in December 1991. In this thesis, I have opted for the earliest of these dates, as it is closest to the publication for Strieber's *Communion* (1987).

21 The one exception here is Whitley Strieber; although he offered to discuss my research via email, I did not follow up. In part, this was because I had learned that his wife was extremely ill but partly also because by that point I had decided that the fieldwork was to be focussed on the subscribers of this material rather than its producers. For that reason, I did not pursue face-to-face interviews with Icke or Wilcock.

Chapter 2

1 It is perhaps surprising that Religious Studies has been slow to adopt discursive approaches (Wijsen 2013), as they would seem to be a good fit with the general phenomenological or 'methodological agnostic' positioning of scholarship in the discipline, which is intended to prevent scholars from making normative claims. Yet, as discussed below, Religious Studies has seemed unwilling to accept that its categories and theories may be historically and culturally specific constructions.

2 These are, firstly, the 'crisis of representation', that is, that the terms we use as scholars are more than historically and culturally contingent but 'mirror' an underlying reality or 'truth' (2003, 257–8). Secondly, and following from this, is the problem of 'the situated observer'; given that all theories and accounts are situated culturally and historically, none therefore can claim absolute impartiality (2003, 258–60). However, the recognition of this issue through reflexivity – that is, the explicit positioning of the author in relation to the object of study – leads to an apparently bottomless cycle of 'reflexive regression' in which the original

object is gradually replaced by the author (Maton 2003, 58–60). Finally, this creates a 'dilemma of essentialism and relativism', whereby if all narratives are socially and historically relative, then we cannot reify our terminology into *sui generis*, ahistorical categories (Maton 2003, 260–2).

3   Others have named this the discursive 'topic' (Reisigl and Wodak 2009), 'strand' (Stuckrad 2013, 13) and 'theme' (Taira 2013, 29).

4   This terminology is my own, although the distinction has been acknowledged in UFOlogical literature for many years.

5   For example, Pipes (1997), Byford (2011, 2014).

6   Hardly likely, it might be added, to counteract the belief that the government is out to silence your views!

7   In an interview with Alex Jones, Icke described the Occupy movement of 2011–12 as evidence of this 'global awakening'. Alex Jones Show, 3 November 2012. http://rss.infowars.com/20111103_Thu_Alex2.mp3 (accessed 16 December 2011).

8   For example, Blavatsky and other Theosophists received messages from the 'Mahatmas' in the form of letters, and Dorothy Martin received messages from extraterrestrials through the telephone (Festinger, Riecken and Schachter 1956 [1964]).

Chapter 3

1   The contemporary currency of the Roswell narrative is illustrated by the fact that Google recognized the 66th anniversary of the Roswell incident with one of their homepage animations but not the anniversary of Arnold's sighting.

2   Bailey went on to found the Arcane School in 1923, which did not survive her, and the Lucis Trust (originally the Lucifer Press), which operates to this day. Significantly, the Lucis Trust has been an aggressive promoter of globalism, and this has led to many conspiracists rejecting it, including Icke. For the more traditional Christian Right-wing elements of the conspiracist milieu, this is taken as evidence that 'New Age' is part of the globalist agenda. For example, Missler and Eastman have argued that the 'New Age' is specifically intended to undermine Christianity and inculcate the populous to (literally) demonic influences (1997, 143–60). This suggests a notable difference between UK and US genealogies of 'New Age', with the UK lineage deriving from Bailey occupying a position which, if not as anti-Christian as Blavatsky's theosophy, is

at least broadly ambivalent towards Christianity. On the other hand, while the Dreamland attendees largely refused to identify as Christian, one of them would later tell me that she had a relationship with Jesus, nonetheless. Perhaps there was a need in the US context for practices like reincarnation, channelling, etc., to be filtered through popular Christian theology in order to gain mainstream penetration.

3   This later formed the basic hypothesis of Linda Moulton Howe's influential 1980 documentary, *A Strange Harvest*. Howe's investigations led her to believe that the phenomenon was known to the government but was being covered up; I later saw her presenting at Whitley Strieber's Dreamland festival in 2012, described in Chapter 4.

4   Here retitled the 'Illuminati Protocols'; more on the possibility of anti-Semitic material in this field in Chapter 5.

5   Interview, 18 July 2005.

6   More on Solara at her homepage: http://anvisible.com/ (accessed 18 June 2013).

Chapter 4

1   Now the London Film School, a post-graduate-only accredited institute aimed at international students.

2   From an interview on www.unknowncountry.com but available only to members.

3   Dana described these events herself at the 2012 Dreamland festival.

4   This is similar to the 'criterion of dissimilarity' in Biblical Studies, utilized by the Jesus Seminar and others to argue that those words and actions attributed to Jesus in the New Testament which seem most anomalous are least likely to be later scribal additions and are therefore most likely to have historical basis.

5   I find it very interesting that Hopkins rejects the idea of benevolent ETs with an ad hominem attack on 'spiritualist cults'; he presents 'religion' (and interestingly, new religious movements in particular) as necessarily irrational and naive.

6   Strieber was certainly in contact with their main proponent, Stanton Friedman (Strieber 1988, 117), and later provided a foreword to Friedman's book on the MJ-12 documents, *Top Secret/MAJIC* (1997).

7   The full archive is searchable at the following link, although only the most recent episode is available to non-members; http://www.unknowncountry.com/ dreamland/all (accessed 9 December 2012).

8   Scarritt-Bennett Centre promotional leaflet.

9   'About William Henry'. At http://www.williamhenry.net/about.html (accessed 25 July 2012).

10 Personal correspondence, dated 8 January 2013.

11 Quoted from Strieber's 2012 Dreamland presentation.

12 See Ouspensky (1949 [1987]) for an explanation of Gurdjieff's cosmological theories.

13 Gurdjieff's influence on the popular millennial field is less often noted than that of Bailey and Cayce, yet his ideas have shown a significant influence on the case studies presented here, explicitly in the case of Icke and particularly Strieber and implicitly in the case of Wilcock. This is perhaps a result of his dualistic cosmology, which although not typical of 'New Age' discourses, is typical of millennial conspiracist discourse. Gurdjieff did not base his teaching on channelled messages; rather, the occulted masters to which he appealed were humans residing in ancient monasteries in the mountains of Georgia. Moreover, Gurdjieff did not obviously promote millennial narratives, although the argument could be made that there is an implicit millennialism (with Gurdjieff as Christ figure) in his work, for example, *Herald of the Coming Good* (1971). However, his teaching has had less of an impact on popular culture and popular millennial discourse simply because of its complexity, and that it was never fully explicated and systematized.

14 Personal correspondence, dated 8 January 2013.

Chapter 5

1   http://www.publicpolicypolling.com/main/2013/04/conspiracy-theory-poll-results-.html (accessed 5 April 2013).

2   Sources are extremely limited for Icke's early years, and I have been forced to rely upon his own account. Where there are several descriptions of an event, I have used the earliest.

3   He mentions Bob Dylan's 'The Times They Are A'Changing' and Thunderclap Newman's 'Something in the Air' as early favourites – both of which tellingly predict imminent societal change (Icke 1993a, 52–3) – and Donovan and John Lennon are frequently quoted in his later books and presentations.

4   Not that you would believe that based on the BBC's recent 25th anniversary reportage in which he is not named: http://www.bbc.co.uk/news/entertainment-arts-21040879 (accessed 30 November 2013).

5   Although most of this short piece is actually about someone entirely
     unconnected who attacked a police officer with a sock filled with glass and
     stones.

6   Nicky Campbell, *Into the Night* (BBC Radio 1,?/4/1991).

7   It is not for sale on his website and does not appear in the 'Other Books
     by ...' frontispiece of any of his works after 1994. Ironically, Wang Yee Lee had
     previously told him, 'The written word will be there forever. The spoken word
     disappears on the wind' (Icke 1991, 22).

8   The descriptions of Atlantis were channelled by Icke from a being called Magnu,
     who was supposedly later reincarnated as Edgar Cayce and, as we shall hear,
     David Wilcock.

9   Willings (2014, 587); Benn's (2014, 445).

10   Nexus magazine, Vol. 16, No. 2, February–March 2009. Front cover.

11   http://www.nexusmagazine.com/ (accessed 5 May 2013).

12   Interview via e-mail, 4 June 2008.

13   http://www.nexusmagazine.com/index.php?option=com_content&task=view&id
     =13&Itemid=28

14   Nexus magazine, Vol. 16, No. 2, February–March 2009. P. 2.

15   http://www.nexusmagazine.com/index.php?option=com_content&task=view&id
     =12&Itemid=27

16   http://flywithmeproductions.com/blog/?cat=765 (accessed 9 April 2013). Acorah
     is best known for his appearances on *Most Haunted*, broadcast on the UK's *Living
     TV* channel.

17   Editor Duncan Roads issued a letter to Icke, who then published it on his
     website; an archived version, complete with Icke's comments, can be read at
     www.http://educate-yourself.org/cn/duncanroadsreplytoickeongardner.shtml
     (accessed 5 January 2013). Roads' concerns appear to be that, firstly, he considers
     Gardner's work to present original ideas, unlike Icke; and secondly, 'because his
     research contradicts your own theories about the non-existence of Christ'. He
     continues: 'I, like many others, used to look up to you. You are very charismatic
     on stage, a powerful and motivated speaker, and very energetic. Your passion
     for what you believe comes through very strongly'. Icke replies by asking if,
     after reading his 'extremely childish' letter, '[a]re you REALLY the publisher of a
     magazine that has designs on being taken seriously?'

18   The intention seems to have been to create a legacy for his family by creating
     shares and distributing them to his children and former wife, perhaps driven
     by a realization that his marriage to Pamela was in difficulties. He was also in

conflict with his US publishing associate Royal Adams, who Icke alleged to have put the US rights to Icke's books into his own name and embezzled the profits. The process involved passing responsibility for much of the running of Icke's publishing, website and events from Linda and Pamela to Icke's daughter Kerry. Bridge of Love Publishing became David Icke Books (David Icke Books Ltd, 2007).

19 http://flywithmeproductions.com/blog/?cat=785 (accessed 6 May 2013).

20 Clarke (2012); http://flywithmeproductions.com/blog/?cat=785 (accessed 6 May 2013).

21 Like Icke, Nexus has frequently been accused of anti-Semitism, for example appearing in the February 1999 'Report of Anti-Semitic Incidents' by the Israeli Ministry of Foreign Affairs (MFA Report) and named by the Steven Roth Institute, based at Tel Aviv University (Roth Institute 1998).

22 Elsewhere, however, Barkun makes unconvincing attempts to construct the more typical 'gray' alien as derived from anti-semitism, writing that 'the Evil Grays are dwarfish with grotesque features – not unlike stereotypes of the short, swarthy, hook-nosed Jew of European anti-Semitic folklore' (2003, 144). This argument both ignores that such accounts typically describe an almost complete absence of a nose and that their colour is more often described as 'silvery' than anything similar to 'swarthy'.

23 An essay detailing Icke's accusations against Savile (including necrophilia) can be read at http://www.davidicke.com/articles/child-abuse-mainmenu-74/74874-jimmy-savile–doorway-to-the-cesspit (accessed 30 May 1975).

24 http://www.youtube.com/watch?feature=player_embedded&v=8jssCKpkcoM (accessed 28 May 2013).

25 https://www.youtube.com/watch?v=JoxrSJ-UttQ

26 Press & Journal, 18 November 2009. http://www.pressandjournal.co.uk/Article.aspx/1488131 (accessed 30 May 2013, but now dead; an archived version can be accessed at http://web.archive.org/web/20120627044349/http://www.pressandjournal.co.uk/Article.aspx/1488131).

27 Here is a perfect example of the frequent difficulty with a lack of secondary sources, described in Chapter 1; even to write a short paragraph, there are no reliable accounts from which to draw. Newspaper accounts are necessarily simplified and sensational, whereas insider accounts assume certain aspects as self-evident and therefore inviolable.

28 These included episodes of Richplanet, the web and cable show hosted by Richard D. Hall which, although originally concerned exclusively with UFOs,

has become involved with government cover-ups, notably 9/11, the 7–7 Tube attacks, 'global control', 'hidden history' and even such esoteric material as subliminal mind control through popular music videos. http://www.richplanet. net/ (accessed 24 December 2013).

29 http://www.starchildproject.com/team.htm (accessed 11 January 2013).

30 http://www.starchildproject.com/ (accessed 6 May 2013).

31 Originating with Nancy Ann Tappe's Millennial Concepts in Color (1982) and considerably elaborated upon in *The Indigo Children (1999)* and *An Indigo Celebration (2001)* by Lee Carroll and Jan Tober, the belief that a proportion of children are being born already highly spiritually developed has become widespread in popular millennial discourse since the 1970s (Whedon 2009, 61; Singler 2015).

Chapter 6

1 This is based on data mined by Charlotte Ward from Google advertising statistics (Ward 2012).

2 http://www.ae911truth.org/ (accessed 14 February 2014).

3 http://www.thezeitgeistmovement.com/ (accessed 12 February 2014).

4 http://rss.infowars.com/20130829_Thu_Alex.mp3 (accessed 30 December 2013).

5 Emmerich had previously directed *The Day After Tomorrow* (2004), based on Strieber and Bell's *The Coming Global Superstorm* (2000), for which Strieber was commissioned to write the novelization.

6 The rapidity with which '2012' millennialism emerged is perhaps best illustrated with a recollection from my own experience. While writing my undergrad thesis in 2006–7, my supervisor (Steven Sutcliffe, an internationally respected scholar of 'New Age') was unaware of '2012' millennialism but only three years later supervised Whiteside's Master's thesis on it.

7 Rolling prophecy can also be detected in Bob Frissell's *Nothing in This Book is True but It's Exactly How Things Are*, which in its original 1994 printing reads 'From 1998 to approximately 2000 we will most likely have experienced all of these events' (1994, 16). The same passage in the 2002 edition, however, is altered to 'Sometime between now and 2012' (Frissell 2002, 16; c.f. Whitesides and Hoopes 2011, 66–7).

8 Secondary sources for the following section have been even thinner on the ground than for Strieber or Icke, as Wilcock is still an 'up and comer'. As a result,

I have been forced to draw frequently on primary accounts in constructing his historiography. I have attempted to use the historical biographical information from these sources, without reproducing their assumptions about how the information should be reproduced – particularly their frequent attempts at mythologization – and to seek external verification where possible. Nevertheless, the account should be considered merely a first step towards a full biography of Wilcock's career.

9   https://divinecosmos.com/about-david-wilcock (accessed 26 December 2013).

10 This work is an online publication and as a result lacks page numbers. As the contents are arranged over nine webpages, chapter by chapter, I will adopt the protocol of identifying the quotations by their chapters. The webpage for the book is identified in the bibliography, but I include it here again for clarity: http://divinecosmos.com/index.php/start-here/books-free-online/25-wander-awakening-the-life-story-of-david-wilcock/138-wanderer-awakening-chapter-03-mystical-adolescent-experiences (accessed 26 December 2013).

11 http://www.edgarcayce.org/are/edgarcayce.aspx?id=1036 (accessed 28 December 2013).

12 http://www.edgarcayce.org/are/edgarcayce.aspx?id=1036 (accessed 28 December 2013).

13 http://web.archive.org/web/20051208040153/http://www.divinecosmos.com/cms/ (accessed 26 December 2013).

14 http://www.gaiamtv.com/show/wisdom-teachings-david-wilcock (accessed 28 December 2013).

15 http://divinecosmos.com/start-here/davids-blog/1023-financial-tyranny (accessed 28 December 2013).

16 Fulford has published several books in Japanese on secret societies including the Yakuza, but his introduction into the millennial conspiracist milieu in English was through an interview with Kerry Cassidy and Bill Ryan of Project Camelot, published by Nexus in July 2008 (interestingly, the cover of the magazine, drawing from Cayce, also predicts 'earth changes' in 2008). He continues to promote this narrative at the time of writing through a weekly commentary on the state of the occulted politics of the world under the title 'Geo-political news' at his blog, benjaminfulford.net (Fulford maintains several sites, but this is the only one which is entirely in English).

17 http://divinecosmos.com/start-here/davids-blog/1023-financial-tyranny (accessed 28 December 2013).

18 http://divinecosmos.com/start-here/davids-blog/1043-massarrests (accessed 28 December 2013).

19 http://divinecosmos.com/start-here/davids-blog/995-lawsuit-end-tyranny (accessed 28 December 2013).

20 http://www.religiousstudiesproject.com/podcast/podcast-gordon-melton-on-american-millennialism/ (accessed 28 December 2013).

21 http://www.youtube.com/watch?v=3viM4X1HFqw (accessed 19 June 2015).

22 http://divinecosmos.com/forums/showthread.php?14604-Access-your-higher-self-Online-conference/page5 (accessed 4 January 2014).

23 http://divinecosmos.com/forums/showthread.php?14604-Access-your-higher-self-Online-conference/page6 (accessed 4 January 2014).

24 http://divinecosmos.com/forums/showthread.php?14604-Access-your-higher-self-Online-conference/page2 (accessed 4 January 2014).

25 http://divinecosmos.com/forums/showthread.php?14604-Access-your-higher-self-Online-conference/page4 (accessed 4 January 2014).

Chapter 7

1 Interestingly, this is precisely the 'framework of analysis' which von Stuckrad presents for understanding 'esotericism' as a field of discourse between Christian, Muslim and Jewish mysticism, Neoplatonism, European philosophy and science, in which claims of and methods for accessing 'higher knowledge' are negotiated (2005, 93).

2 This is true for scholars like Kripal as well as abductees; while his asides that Méheust 'knew that in order to get a university position … he would have to mask his real thoughts' or that 'he put aside all of his bold speculations and true convictions and hid them behind the mask of scholarship and objectivity' (2010, 215) are open to interpretation, his statement in his foreword to Strieber's *Solving the Communion Enigma* that 'It is difficult to deny it any longer: UFOs are real' is not (2012, ix).

Bibliography

Primary

Books (Non-Fiction)

Argüelles, J. (1987, 1996) *The Mayan Factor: Path Beyond Technology*. Santa Fe, N.M: Bear & Co.

Baigent, M., Leigh, R. and Lincoln, H. (1982) *The Holy Blood and the Holy Grail*. London: J. Cape.

Bailey, A. (1925) *A Treatise on Cosmic Fire*. New York: Lucis Pub. Co.

Bailey, A. (1944 [1972]) *Discipleship in the New Age, vol. I: The Rays and the Initiations*. New York: Lucis Pub. Co.

Bailey, A. (1951) *Initiation, Human and Solar*. New York: Lucis Pub. Co.

Bailey, A. (1957) *The Externalisation of the Hierarchy*. New York: Lucis Pub. Co.

Barker, G. (1956) *They Knew Too Much About Flying Saucers*. New York: University Books.

Bauval, R. and Hancock, G. (1996) *Keeper of Genesis: A Quest for the Hidden Legacy of Mankind*. London: Heinemann.

Berlitz, C. and Moore, W. L. (1980 [1988]) *The Roswell Incident*. New York: Grosset & Dunlap.

Binder, O. (1968) *Flying Saucers Are Watching Us*. New York, NY: Belmont Books.

Blavatsky, H. P. (1887 [1997]). *Isis Unveiled: Secrets of the Ancient Wisdom Tradition, Madame Blavatsky's First Work*. Wheaton, IL: Theosophical Pub. House.

Blavatsky, H. P. (1888 [1974]) *The Secret Doctrine: The Synthesis of Science, Religion and Philosophy*. Los Angeles, CA: Theosophy Co.

Bohm, D. (1981) *Wholeness and the Implicate Order*. London: Routledge & Kegan Paul.

Bramley, W. (1990) *The Gods of Eden*. New York, NY: Avon Books.

Brand, S. (ed.) (1968) *Whole Earth Catalog*. New York: Stewart Brand.

Bro, H. H. (1989) *A Seer Out of Season: The Life of Edgar Cayce*. New York: NAL Books.

Butler, A. and Knight, C. (2005) *Who Built the Moon?* London: Watkins Pub.

Caddy, P. (1996) *In Perfect Timing: Memoirs of a Man for the New Millennium*. Findhorn: Findhorn Press.

Capra, F. (1975) *The Tao of Physics: An Exploration of the Parallels Between Modern Physics and Eastern Mysticism.* London: Wildwood House.

Carey, K. (1986) *The Starseed Transmissions.* Edinburgh: Starseed Pub.

Carroll, L. and Tober, J. (1999) *The Indigo Children: The New Kids Have Arrived.* Carlsbad, CA: Hay House.

Carroll, L. and Tober, J. (2001) *An Indigo Celebration: More Messages, Stories, and Insights from the Indigo Children.* Carlsbad, CA: Hay House.

Castaneda, C. (1968) *The Teachings of Don Juan: A Yaqui Way of Knowledge.* Berkeley: University of California Press.

Cayce, E. E. and Cayce, E. (1968) *Edgar Cayce on Atlantis.* New York: Warner Communications Co.

Cayce, E. and Smith, A. R. (1997) *The Lost Memoirs of Edgar Cayce: Life as a Seer.* Virginia Beach, VA: A.R.E. Press.

Chatelain, M. (1978) *Our Ancestors Came from Outer Space.* Garden City, NY: Doubleday.

Cooper, I. S. (1912) *Ways to Perfect Health.* Chicago: Theosophical book concern.

Cooper, M. W. (1991) *Behold a Pale Horse.* Flagstaff, AZ: Light Technology Pub.

Däniken, E. (1968) *Chariots of the gods?: Unsolved Mysteries of the Past.* London: Bantam.

Däniken, E. (1970) *Return to the Stars: Evidence for the Impossible.* London: Souvenir.

Dawes, C. (2005) *Rat Scabies and the Holy Grail.* London: Sceptre.

Donnelly, I. (1817) *Atlantis: The Antediluvian World.* San Francisco: Harper & Row.

Drosnin, M. and Vitṣtum, D. (1997) *The Bible Code.* New York: Simon & Schuster.

Ferguson, M. (1980) *The Aquarian Conspiracy: Personal and Social Transformation in the 1980s.* New York: J. P. Tarcher.

Fowler, R. E. (1988 [1979]) *The Andreasson Affair.* Toronto: Bantam Books.

Fowler, R. E. (1990) *The Watchers: The Secret Design Behind UFO Abduction.* New York: Bantam Books.

Free, W. and Wilcock, D. (2004) *The Reincarnation of Edgar Cayce?: Interdimensional Communication and Global Transformation.* Berkeley, CA: Frog.

Friedman, S. T. (1997) *Top Secret/MAJIC: Operation Majestic-12 and the United States Government's UFO Cover-up.* New York: Marlowe and Co.

Frissell, B. (1994, 2002) *Nothing in This Book Is Real, but Its Exactly How Things Are.* Berkeley, CA: Frog Books.

Fulford, B. (2008) 'An Eastern Ultimatum to the Western Illuminati, Part 1'. In *Nexus*, vol 15, no 4. June–July 2008, 11–17 and 79.

Fuller, J. G. (1966) *The Interrupted Journey.* New York: Berkley.

Gottlieb, A. (1987) *Do You Believe in Magic?: The Second Coming of the Sixties Generation.* New York: Times Books.

Gurdjieff, G. I. (1971) *The Herald of Coming Good: First Appeal to Contemporary Humanity*. New York: S. Weiser.

Hancock, G. (2002) *Underworld: Flooded Kingdoms of the Ice Age*. London: Michael Joseph.

Hopkins, B. (1987) *Intruders: The Incredible Visitations at Copley Woods*. New York: Random House.

Horn, A. D. (1994) *Humanity's Extraterrestrial Origins: ET Influences on Humankind's Biological and Cultural Evolution*. Altenkirchen: Silberschnur.

Howe, L. M. (1993) *Glimpses of Other Realities 1: Facts and Eyewitnesses*. Huntingdon Valley, PA: LMH Productions.

Icke, D. (1983) *It's a Tough Game, Son!* London: Piccolo Books.

Icke, D. (1989) *It Doesn't Have to Be Like This: Green Politics Explained*. London: Green Print.

Icke, D. (1991) *Truth Vibrations*. London: Aquarian Press.

Icke, D. (1992) *Love Changes Everything*. London: HarperCollins Publishers.

Icke, D. (1993a) *In the Light of Experience: The Autobiography of David Icke*. London: Time Warner Books.

Icke, D. (1993b) *Days of Decision*. London: Jon Carpenter Publishing.

Icke, D. (1994a) *Heal the World: A Do-It-Yourself Guide to Personal and Planetary Transformation*. London: Gateway.

Icke, D. (1994b) *The Robot's Rebellion*. London: Gateway.

Icke, D. (1995) *... And the Truth Shall Set You Free*. Wildwood, MO: Bridge of Love Publications.

Icke, D. (1996) *I Am Me, I Am Free: The Robot's Guide to Freedom*. Wildwood, MO: Bridge of Love Publications.

Icke, D. (1999) *The Biggest Secret: The Book That Will Change the World*. Wildwood, MO: Bridge of Love Publications.

Icke, D. (2001) *Children of the Matrix*. Wildwood, MO: Bridge of Love Publications.

Icke, D. (2002) *Alice in Wonderland and the World Trade Center Disaster*. Wildwood, MO: Bridge of Love Publications.

Icke, D. (2003) *Tales from the Time Loop: The Most Comprehensive Expose of the Global Conspiracy Ever Written and All You Need to Know to Be Truly Free*. Wildwood, MO: Bridge of Love.

Icke, D. (2007) *The David Icke Guide to the Global Conspiracy (and how to end it)*. Ryde: David Icke Books Ltd.

Icke, D. (2010) *Human Race Get Off Your Knees: The Lion Sleeps No More*. Ryde: David Icke Books Ltd.

Icke, D. (2012) *Remember Who You Are: Remember 'Where' You Are and Where You 'Come' From*. Ryde: David Icke Books Ltd.

Kemp, P. and Wall, D. (1990) *A Green Manifesto for the 1990s*. London: Penguin.

Leadbeater, C. W. (1925) *The Masters and the Path*. Chicago: Theosophical Press.

Lieder, N. (1996) *ZetaTalk: A Composite of Information Communicated Telepathically by Teams of Visitors from Zeta Reticuli to Their Emissary, Nancy, an Enhanced Contactee*. Foster City, CA: ZetaTalk.

MacLaine, S. (1987) *It's All in the Playing*. Toronto: Bantam Books.

Mandelker, S. (1995) *From Elsewhere: Being E.T. in America*. New York: Carol Pub. Group.

Marrs, J. (1989) *Crossfire: The Plot that Killed Kennedy*. New York: Carroll & Graf Publishers.

Marrs, J. (1997) *Alien Agenda*. New York: HarperCollins.

Marrs, J. (2000) *Rule by Secrecy*. New York: HarperCollins.

Marrs, J. (2006) *The War on Freedom*. Boyd, TX: Ares.

Marrs, J. (2013) *Our Occulted History*. New York: William Morrow.

McCarty, J. A., Elkins, D. and Rueckert, C. (1984) *The Ra Material: An Ancient Astronaut Speaks*. Norfolk: Donning.

McKenna, T. (1975) *The Invisible Landscape*. New York: Seabury Press.

McTaggart, L. (1996) *What Doctors Don't Tell You: the Truth About the Dangers of Modern Medicine*. London: Thorsons.

Missler, C. and Eastman, M. (1997) *Alien Encounters: The Secret behind the UFO Phenomenon*. Coeur d'Alene, Idaho: Koinonia House.

Mutwa, C. V. (1966) *Indaba, My Children*. London: Kahn & Averill.

O'Brien, C. and Phillips, M. (1995) *Trance Formation of America*. Las Vegas, NV: Reality Marketing.

Ouspensky, P. D. (1949 [1987]) *In Search of the Miraculous: Fragments of an Unknown Teaching*. London: Arkana.

Pauwels, L. and Bergier, J. (1963) *The Morning of the Magicians*. New York: Stein and Day.

Pinchbeck, D. (2006) *2012: The Return of Quetzalcoatl*. New York: Jeremy Tarcher/Penguin.

Randles, J. & Warrington, P. (1985) *Science and the UFOs*. Oxford & New York: Blackwell.

Robison, J. (1797) *Proofs of a Conspiracy Against All the Religions and Governments of Europe: Carried on in the Secret Meetings of Free Masons, Illuminati, and Reading Societies. Collected from Good Authorities*. London: William Creech.

Rogerson, P. (1994) 'Sex, Science and Salvation: Notes Towards a Revisionist History of Abductions – pt. 3: Sex, Science and Salvation' Magonia 49; June 1994. Archived at http://magonia.haaan.com/1994/notes-towards-a-revisionist-history-of-abductions-part-3/ (accessed 16 January 2014).

Ronson, J. (2001a) *Them: Adventures with Extremists*. London: Picador.

Schlemmer, P. V. and Bennett, M. (1994) *The Only Planet of Choice: Essential Briefings from Deep Space*. Bath: Gateway.

Sugrue, T. (1942) *There Is a River: The Story of Edgar Cayce*. New York: Holt.

Sher, B. and Gottlieb, A. (1979) *Wishcraft: How to Get What You Really Want*. New York: Viking Press.

Sitchin, Z. (1976) *The 12th Planet*. New York: Avon Books.

Sitchin, Z. (2007) *The End of Days: Armageddon and Prophecies of the Return*. New York: William Morrow.

Smith, M. and Pazder, L. (1980) *Michelle Remembers*. New York: Congdon & Latte's.

Stanmore P. Ober, C., Sinatra, S. T. and Zucker, M. (2010) *Earthing: The Most Important Health Discovery Ever?*. Laguna Beach, CA: Basic Health Publications.

Stratford, L. (1988) *Satan's Underground*. Eugene, OR: Harvest House Publishers.

Strieber, W. and Bell, A. (2000) *The Coming Global Superstorm*. New York: Pocket Books.

Strieber, W. (1987) *Communion*. New York: Morrow.

Strieber, W. (1988) *Transformation*. New York: Morrow.

Strieber, W. (1995) *Breakthrough: The Next Step*. New York: HarperCollins.

Strieber, W. (1997) *The Secret School*. New York: HarperCollins.

Strieber, W. (1998) *Confirmation: The Hard Evidence of Aliens Among Us*. New York: St. Martin's Press.

Strieber, W. (2001 [2011]) *The Key: A True Encounter*. New York: J.P. Tarcher/ Penguin.

Strieber, W. (2012) *Solving the Communion Enigma: What Is to Come*. New York: Tarcher/Penguin.

Strieber, W. and Strieber, A. (eds.) (1997) *The Communion Letters*. New York: HarperPrism.

Tappe, N. A. (1982) *Millennial Concepts in Color: Enhancing Your Life Thru Color*. San Diego, CA: Kairos Institute.

Valerian, V. (1990) *Matrix II: The Abduction and Manipulation of Humans Using Advanced Technology*. Yelm, WA: Leading Edge Research Group.

Vallée, J. (1969) *Passport to Magonia: From Folklore to Flying Saucers*. Chicago, IL: H. Regnery Co.

Vallée, J. (1975) *The Invisible College: What a Group of Scientists Has Discovered About UFO Influences on the Human Race*. New York: Dutton.

Vallée, J. (1988) *Dimensions: A Casebook of Alien Contact*. Chicago, IL: Contemporary Books.

Vallée, J. (1990) *Confrontations: A Scientist's Search for Alien Contact*. New York: Ballantine Books.

Vallée, J. (1991) *Revelations: Alien Contact and Human Deception*. New York: Ballantine Books.

Vallée, J. (1992) *Forbidden Science: Journals, 1957–1969*. Berkeley, CA: North Atlantic Books.

van Tassel, G. W. (1952) *I Rode a Flying Saucer!: The Mystery of the Flying Saucers Revealed.* Los Angeles, CA: New Age.

Velikovsky, I. (1950) *Worlds in Collision.* Garden City, NY: Doubleday & Co.

Wilcock, D. (1998) *Shift of the Ages: Convergence Vol. I.* Retrieved from http://divinecosmos.com/start-here/books-free-online/18-the-shift-of-the-ages

Wilcock, D. (2000a) *Wanderer Awaken: The Life Story of David Wilcock.* Retrieved from http://divinecosmos.com/start-here/books-free-online/25-wander-awakening-the-life-story-of-david-wilcock

Wilcock, D. (2000b) *The Science of Oneness: Convergence Vol. II.* Retrieved from http://divinecosmos.com/start-here/books-free-online/19-the-science-of-oneness

Wilcock, D. (2002) *Divine Cosmos: Convergence Vol. III.* Retrieved from http://divinecosmos.com/start-here/books-free-online/20-the-divine-cosmos

Wilcock, D. (2011) *The Source Field Investigations: The Hidden Science and Lost Civilizations Behind the 2012 Prophecies.* New York: Dutton.

Wilcock, D. (2013) *The Synchronicity Key: The Hidden Intelligence Guiding the Universe and You.* New York: Dutton.

Wilson, R. A. (1977 [1986]) *Cosmic Trigger: Final Secret of the Illuminati.* Tempe, AZ: New Falcon.

Wilson, R. A. (1995) *Cosmic Trigger III: My Life After Death.* Tempe, AZ: New Falcon Publications.

Zukav, G. (1979) *The Dancing Wu Li Masters: An Overview of the New Physics.* New York: Morrow.

Books (Fiction)

Brown, D. (2003) *The Da Vinci Code.* New York: Doubleday.

Bulwer Lytton, E. (1871) *The Coming Race.* New York: Routledge.

Gurdjieff, G. I. ([1950] 1999) *Beelzebub's Tales to His Grandson: An Objectively Impartial Criticism of the Life of Man.* New York: Penguin/Arkana.

Redfield, J. (1993). *The Celestine Prophecy: An Adventure.* New York: Warner Books.

Strieber, W. (1978) *The Wolfen.* New York: Morrow.

Strieber, W. (1981) *The Hunger.* New York: Morrow.

Strieber, W. (1982) *Black Magic.* New York: Morrow.

Strieber, W. (1983) *The Night Church.* New York: Simon and Schuster.

Strieber, W. (1989) *Majestic.* New York: G.P. Putnam's Sons.

Strieber, W. (2006) *The Grays.* New York: Tor.

Strieber, W. (2007) *2012: The War for Souls.* New York: Tor.

Strieber, W. (2010) *The Omega Point: Beyond 2012*. New York: Tor.

Strieber, W. (2011) *Hybrids*. New York: Tor.

Strieber, W. and Kunetka, J. W. (1984) *Warday and the Journey Onward*. New York: Holt, Rinehart, and Winston.

Strieber, W. and Kunetka, J. W. (1986) *Nature's End: The Consequences of the Twentieth Century*. New York: Warner Books.

Wolfe, T. (1968) *The Electric Kool-aid Acid Test*. New York: Bantam Books.

Films, Music, etc.

Avery, D. (2005) *Loose Change*. Onetara: Louder than Words.

Black Eyed Peas (2003) *Where Is the Love?* On *Elephunk* [CD]. Santa Monica, CA: A&M Records; Interscope Records.

Camelot (2007) 'The Road to Ascension: Interview with David Wilcock'. http://projectcamelot.org/david_wilcock.html (accessed 30 January 2014).

Conspirituality (2009) *Conspirituality* [CD]. Vancouver?: Inner Earth Music.

Emmerich, R. (dir.) (2004) *The Day After Tomorrow*. United States: 20th Century Fox Home Entertainment.

Emmerich, R. (dir.) (2010) *2012*. Culver City, CA: Sony Pictures Home Entertainment.

Gamble, F., Gamble, K. C. (2011) *Thrive: What on Earth Will It Take?* Soquel, CA: Clear Compas Media.

Gardiner, L., O'Brien, K. and Williams-Thomas, M. (2012) *The Other Side of Jimmy Savile*. London: ITV.

Howe, L. M. (1988) *A Strange Harvest*. Huntingdon Valley, PA: LMH Productions.

Icke, D. (2005) *Revelations of a Mother Goddess*. Venice, CA: New Science Ideas.

Icke, D. (2008) *Beyond the Cutting Edge*. (Video) Ryde: David Icke Books, 2008.

Hull, N. (dir.) (2006) 'David Icke: Was He Right?' Channel 5, 26 December 2006. http://video.google.co.uk/videoplay?docid=6860946590182985661&q=David+Icke+Was+He+Right%3F (accessed 9 July 2011).

Joseph, P. (dir.) (2007) *Zeitgeist*. GMP LLC.

Joseph, P. (dir.) (2008) *Zeitgeist: Addendum*. GMP LLC.

Joseph, P. (dir.) (2011) *Zeitgeist: Moving Forward*. GMP LLC.

Kaleka, A. (dir.) (2013) *Sirius*. Neverending Light Productions.

Landsburg, A. (1973) *In Search of Ancient Astronauts*. Alan Landsburg Productions & Xerox Films.

Landsburg, A. (1975) *In Search of Ancient Mysteries*. Alan Landsburg Productions & Xerox Films.

Landsburg, A. (1977) *The Outer Space Connection*. Alan Landsburg Productions & Xerox Films.

Marrs, J. (2012) 'Are Rocket Engines Obsolete?' Presentation at UFO Crash Con, 2012? Available at http://www.youtube.com/watch?v=AlhSS51ZGz4 (accessed 19 July 2012).

Megadeth (2009) *Endgame* [CD]. New York, NY: Roadrunner Records.

Moore, M. (2004) (dir.) *Fahrenheit 9/11*. Culver City, Calif: Columbia TriStar Home Entertainment.

Muse (2009) *The Resistance* [CD]. London: Warner Music UK.

Ronson, J. (2001b) 'David Icke, the Lizards, and the Jews', Channel 4 Television, broadcast 6/5/2001. Available at http://www.youtube.com/watch?v=3zVaOt_KYu8&NR=1 (accessed 3 May 2011).

Sonnenfeld, B. (2000) *Men in Black*. Columbia Tristar.

Theroux, L. (2000) 'When Louis met... Jimmy'. Channel 4, 13 April 2013.

Wachowski, A. and Wachowski, L. (2001) *The Matrix*. Warner Bros.

Newspapers & Magazines

Anonymous (1990) 'Protester David Icke Finally Pays Community Charge'. *The Guardian*, 14 November 1990.

Anonymous (1991) 'Icke Taunted'. *Times* [London, England], 27 May 1991.

Anonymous (1992) 'Why the Green Shoots Withered'. *The Guardian*, 28 August 1992.

Banks-Smith, N. (1991) 'Prophet with a Cauliflower Ear'. *The Guardian*, 1 May 1991.

Barker, D. (1990) 'Green Dusts Off Rebuff from BBC'. *The Guardian*, 17 August 1991.

Biddle, W. (2009) *Dark Side of the Moon: Wernher von Braun, the Third Reich, and the Space Race*. New York: W.W. Norton.

Bosquet, J. (1934) 'Lizard Peolpe's [sic.] Catacomb City Hunted'. *Los Angeles Times*, 29 January 1934.

Brown, P. (1995). '"Ex-nutter" Icke Rails at New World Order Mind Benders'. *The Guardian*, 19 May 1995.

Cadbury, D. (2005) *The Space Race: The Untold Story of Two Rivals and Their Struggle for the Moon*. London: Fourth Estate.

Chaudhary, V. (1994) 'Greens See Red At "Son of God's Anti-Semitism"'. *The Guardian*, 12 Sept 1994.

Christy, D. (1991) 'Crucifixion, Courtesy of the BBC'. *The Guardian*, 6 May 1991.

Clarke, N. (2012) 'He Once Claimed He's the Son of God and the World Is Run by Alien Lizards, but the Story of David Icke's Marriage Breakdown Is Almost as Weird'. *Daily Mail*, 9 January 2012. http://www.dailymail.co.uk/femail/article-2083287/

David-Ickes-marriage-breakdown-He-claimed-hes-Son-God-world-run-alien-lizards-story-marriage-breakdown-weird.html (accessed 10 November 2013).

Coe, M. D. (1966) *The Maya*. London: Thames and Hudson.

Ezard, J. (1991) '"Son and Daughter of God" Predict Apocalypse Is Nigh'. *The Guardian*, 28 March 1991.

Fielding, J. (2013) 'Savile Was Part of Satanic Ring'. *Scottish Sunday Express*, 13 January 2013.

Hofstadter, R. (1964) 'The Paranoid Style in American Politics'. In *Harper's Magazine*, November 1964, 77–86.

Honigsbaum, M. (1995) 'The Dark Side of David Icke'. *London Evening Standard*, 26 May 1995.

Hoyland, P. (1989) 'Speculation on Leadership Is Scorned by Lcke'. *The Guardian*, September 22 1989.

Kalman, M. and Murray, J. (1995a) 'New-age Nazism'. *New Statesman and Society*, 23 June 1995. 18–20.

Kalman, M. and Murray, J. (1995b) 'Icke and the Nazis'. *Open Eye*, #3. 7.

Kalman, M. and Murray, J. (1996) 'From Green Messiah to New Age Nazi' *Left Green Perspectives* #35. http://www.social-ecology.org/1996/01/left-green-perspectives-35/ (accessed 5 May 2013).

Kennedy, M. (1991) 'Icke Resigns Green Speaker and Parliamentary Roles'. *The Guardian*, 20 March 1991.

Linton, M. (1990) 'Greens tie their future to the world's'. *The Guardian*. 9 April 1990.

Linton, M. (1991) 'Greens Find Icke Factor Polluting Their Atmosphere'. *The Guardian*, 30 April 1991.

Nathan, P. (1987) 'When Is a True Story True?' *Publisher's Weekly*, 14 August 1987. 23–6.

Norton-Taylor, R. (2011) 'Iraq Dossier Drawn Up to Make Case for War – Intelligence Officer'. *The Guardian*,12 May 2011.

O'Neill, B. (2006) 'Meet the No-Planers'. *New Statesman*, 11 September 2006.

Perrie, R. (2011) '7/7 'Was a Plot by the Government, Bizarre Cop Expert Claims'. *The Sun*, 18 July 2011. http://www.thesun.co.uk/sol/homepage/news/3699907/77-was-a-plot-by-the-Government.html (accessed 20 January 2013).

Roswell Daily Record (1947) Interview with Mac Brazel, 9 July 1947.

Shaver, R. (1945) 'I Remember Lemuria!' *Amazing Stories*, March 1945. 12–70.

Sherwood, J. (1998) 'Gray Barker: My friend, the Myth-maker'. *Skeptical Inquirer* 22 (3). 37–9.

Sherwood, J. (2002) 'Gray Barker's Book of Bunk Mothman, Saucers, and MIB', *Skeptical Inquirer* 26 (3) May/June 2002.

Taylor, S. (1997) 'So I Was in This Bar with the Son of God ...' *The Guardian*, 20 April 1997.

Westcott, S. (1993) 'Back in Black'. *Comics Scene*. No. 33, May 1993.

Wintour, P. (2008) 'Tories Aghast as Davis Quits to Wage Lone War on 42 Days'. *The Guardian*, 13 June 2008.

Wood, N. (1992) 'Greens' Chairman Blames Resignation on Icke Invitation'. *Times*, 20 August 1992.

Archive

Air Force Regulation 200–2 (1954) 'Intelligence: Unidentified Flying Object Reporting'. Washington: Department of the Air Force. Available at http://www.nicap.org/directives/afr200-2_081254.pdf (accessed 26 December 2011).

Benn's media (2014) Vol. 1 (UK). London: WLR Media and Entertainment.

Chambers English Dictionary (1993) 'Conspiracy'. [New Edition] Edinburgh: Chambers Harrap.

Chopra, D., Elgin, D., Goodman, A., Hawken, P., Mitchell, E., Perkins, J., Robbins, J., Sahtouris, E., Shiva, V., Trombly, A. (2012) 'Letter of Dissociation'. Available at http://www.thrivemovement.com/thrive-movie-pioneer-letter-of-dissociation (accessed 26 January 2014).

Churchill, W. (1945) Hansard House of Commons, c84, 16 August 1945, Vol. 413. Available at http://hansard.millbanksystems.com/commons/1945/aug/16/debate-on-the-address#column_84 (accessed 29 May 2013).

David Icke Books Limited (2007) 'Appointment of Director or Secretary, Submitted to Companies House, 11 September 2007' (accessed 11 November 2012).

David Icke Books Limited (2008) 'Annual Report, Submitted to Companies House 18/11/2008'. (accessed 11 November 2012).

Eisenhower, D. D. (1961) 'Farewell Address' (17 January 1961). Papers of Dwight D. Eisenhower as President, 1953–61, Eisenhower Library; National Archives and Records Administration. At http://www.ourdocuments.gov/doc.php?flash=true&doc=90 (accessed 28 January 2014).

Gallup (2012) 'Trust in Government'. http://www.gallup.com/poll/5392/trust-government.aspx (accessed 2 August 2012).

MFA Report (1999) 'Antisemitic Monitoring Forum Report of Anti-Semitic Incidents – February 1999'. https://web.archive.org/web/20080705141035/http://www.mfa.gov.il/MFA/Anti-Semitism+and+the+Holocaust/Antisemitism+Monitoring+Forum/Report+of+Anti-Semitic+Incidents+-+Feb-99.htm (accessed 30 January 2014).

Oxford English Dictionary (1989) 'Conspiracy'. [Second edition]. Online version March 2011. http://www.oed.com:80/Entry/39766 (accessed 27 April 2011). Earlier version first published in New English Dictionary, 1893.

Roth Institute (1998) *Anti-Semitism Worldwide 1997/8*. Tel Aviv: Roth Institute for the Study of Contemporary Racism and Antisemitism.

United Nations (1945) 'Charter of the United Nations'. Available at http://www. un.org/en/documents/charter/index.shtml (accessed 30 July 2012).

Wile, A. (2012) 'David Icke on Terrorism Totalitarian Tiptoe and the Coming Post-Industrial Technocracy'. *Daily Bell*, 5 April 2012. http://www.thedailybell.com/ exclusive-interviews/3578/Anthony-Wile-David-Icke-on-Terrorism-Totalitarian-Tiptoe-and-the-Coming-Post-Industrial-Technocracy/

Willings (2014) *Willings Press Guide: The World's Leading Media Directory*. Vol. 1, London: Cision.

Winfrey, O. (1987) *The Oprah Winfrey Show* #W203, 24 June 1987. 'Witches'. Transcript at http://www.skeptictank.org/files//mys4/oprah.htm (accessed 20 July 2012).

Wogan, T. (1991) *Wogan*. BBC, 29 April 1991. Viewed at the British Film Institute, 19 February 2014.

Secondary

Amarasingham, A. (2011). 'Blackophobia and the Paranoid Style: Visions of Obama as the Antichrist on the World Wide Web'. In Robert Glenn Howard (ed.), *Network Apocalypse: Visions of the End in an Age of Internet Media*. Sheffield: Sheffield Phoenix Press, 96–123.

Asprem, E. (2015) 'How Schrödinger's Cat Became a Zombie: On the Epidemiology of Science-Based Representations in Popular and Religious Contexts'. *Method & Theory in the Study of Religion* (in press).

Asprem, E. and Dyrendal, A. (2015) 'Conspirituality Reconsidered: How Surprising and How New Is the Confluence of Spirituality and Conspiracy theory?' *Journal of Contemporary Religion* 30 (3), 367–382.

Aupers, S. (2012) '"Trust No One": Modernization, Paranoia and Conspiracy Culture'. *European Journal of Communication* 27 (1), 22–34

Baker, R. A. (1982) 'The Effect of Suggestion on Past-Lives Regression'. *American Journal of Clinical Hypnosis* 25 (1), 71–6.

Ball, S. J. (1998) *The Cold War: An International History, 1947–1991*. London: Arnold.

Barker, C. (2004) 'Habitus'. In Barker, C. (ed.), *The SAGE Dictionary of Cultural Studies*. London: SAGE, 82–3.

Barkun, M. (2003) *A Culture of Conspiracy: Apocalyptic Visions in Contemporary America*. Berkley, Los Angeles & London: University of California Press.

Barkun, M. (2013) 'Messages from Beyond: Prophecy in the Contemporary World'. In Harvey, S. and Newcombe, S. (eds.), *Prophecy in the New Millennium: When Prophecies Persist*. Farnham, Surrey: Ashgate, 17–26.

Baurmann, M. (2007) 'Rational Fundamentalism? An Explanatory Model of Fundamentalist Beliefs'. *Episteme: A Journal of Social Epistemology* 4 (2), Edinburgh University Press, 150–66.

Beyer, P. (1994) *Religion and Globalisation*. London: SAGE.

Bourdieu, P. (1977) *Outline of a Theory of Practice*. Cambridge: Cambridge University Press.

Bourdieu, P. (1980) 'Le Capital Social'. *Actes de la recherche en sciences sociales* 1, 2–3.

Bourdieu, P. (1985) 'The Forms of Capital'. In Richardson, J. G. (ed.), *A Handbook of Theory and Research for the Sociology of Education*. New York: Greenwood Press. 241.

Bourdieu, P. (1990a) *The Logic of Practice*. Stanford: Stanford University Press.

Bourdieu, P. (1990b) *In Other Words: Essays Towards a Reflexive Sociology*. Cambridge: Polity.

Bourdieu, P. (1998) *Practical Reason*. Cambridge: Polity Press.

Boyer, P. S. (1992) *When Time Shall Be No More: Prophecy Belief in Modern American Culture*. Cambridge, MA: Belknap Press of Harvard University Press.

Bratich, J. Z. (2004) 'Trust No One (on the Internet): The CIA-Crack-Contra Conspiracy Theory and Professional Journalism'. *Television & New Media* 5 (2), 109–39.

Brown, S. L. (1992) 'Baby Boomers, American Character, and the New Age: A Synthesis'. In Lewis, J. R. and Melton, J. G. (eds.), *Perspectives on the New Age*. Albany: State University of New York Press, 87–96.

Burr, V. (2003) *Social Constructionism*. London: Routledge.

Byford, J. (2011) *Conspiracy Theories: A Critical Introduction*. Basingstoke: Palgrave Macmillan.

Byford, J. (2014) 'Beyond Belief: The Social Psychology of Conspiracy Theories and the study of Ideology'. In Antaki, C. and Condor, S. (eds.), *Rhetoric, Idiology and Social Psychology: Essays in Honour of Michael Billig*. London: Routledge, 83–94.

Campbell, C. (1972 [2002]) 'The Cult, the Cultic Milieu and Secularisation'. In Kaplan, J. and Lööw, H. (eds.), *The Cultic Milieu: Oppositional Subcultures in an Age of Globalization*. Walnut Creek: AltaMira Press, 12–25.

Campbell, C. (2001) 'A New Age Theodicy for a New Age'. In Woodhead, L. with Heelas, P. and Martin, D. (eds.), *Peter Berger and the Study of Religion*. London and New York: Routledge, 73–85

Cassem, Q. (2015) 'Why Do Some People Believe Conspiracy Theories? It's Not Just Who or What They Know. It's a Matter of Intellectual Character', 13 March 2015, at http://aeon.co/magazine/philosophy/intellectual-character-of-conspiracy-theorists/

Chidester, D. (2005) *Authentic Fakes: Religions and American Popular Culture.* Berkeley: University of California Press.

Chryssides, G. D. (2007) 'Defining the New Age'. In Kemp, D. & Lewis, J. R. (eds), *Handbook of New Age*. Leiden: Brill. 5–24.

Clancy, S. A. (2005) *Abducted: How People Come to Believe They Were Kidnapped by Aliens.* Cambridge, MA: Harvard University Press.

Clarke, S. (2007) 'Conspiracy Theories and the Internet: Controlled Demolition and Arrested Development'. *Episteme: A Journal of Social Epistemology* 4(2), 167–80.

Coady, D. (2007a) 'Introduction: Conspiracy Theories'. *Episteme: A Journal of Social Epistemology* 4(2), 131–34.

Coady, D. (2007b) 'Are Conspiracy Theorists Irrational?' *Episteme: A Journal of Social Epistemology* 4(2), 193–204.

Coats, C. and Murchison, J. (2014) 'Network *Apocalypsis*: Recealing and Reveling at a New Age Festival'. In *International Journal for the Study of New Religions* 5(2), 167–88.

Cohn, N. (1970) *The Pursuit of the Millennium: Revolutionary Millenarians and Mystical Anarchists of the Middle Ages.* New York: Oxford University Press.

Conroy, E. (1989) *Report on Communion: An Independent Investigation of and Commentary on Whitley Strieber's Communion.* New York: Morrow.

Cox, J. L. (2007) *From Primitive to Indigenous: The Academic Study of Indigenous Religions.* Aldershot: Ashgate.

Culianu, I. P. (1992) *The Tree of Gnosis: Gnostic Mythology from Early Christianity to Modern Nihilism.* H.S. Wiesner & I. P. Culianu (trans.). New York: Harper Collins.

Davies, B. (2006) *The Reality of God and the Problem of Evil.* London: Continuum.

Dean, J. (2009) *Democracy and other neoliberal fantasies: Communicative capitalism and left politics.* Durham: Duke University Press.

Denzler, B. (2001) *The Lure of the Edge: Scientific Passions, Religious Beliefs, and the Pursuit of UFOs.* Berkeley and Los Angeles: University of California Press.

Dolby, R. G. A. (1979) 'Reflections on Deviant Science'. In Wallis, R. (ed.), *On the Margins of Science: The Social Construction of Rejected Knowledge.* Keele: University of Keele, 9–47.

Dyrendal, A. (2013) 'Hidden Knowledge, Hidden Powers. Esotericism and Conspiracy Culture'. In Asprem, E. and Granholm, K. (eds.), *Contemporary Esotericism.* London: Equinox–Acumen, 200–25.

Faivre, A. (1994) *Access to Western Esotericism.* Albany: State University of New York Press.

Fenster, M. (1999) *Conspiracy Theories: Secrecy and Power in American Culture.* Minneapolis & London: University of Minnesota Press.

Festinger, L. (1957) *A Theory of Cognitive Dissonance*. Stanford: Stanford University Press.

Festinger, L., Riecken, H. and Schachter, S. (1964 [1956]) *When Prophecy Fails: A Social and Psychological Study of a Modern Group That Predicted the Destruction of the Modern World*. New York: Harper & Row.

Fitzgerald, T. (2000) *The Ideology of Religious Studies*. New York: Oxford University Press.

Flaherty, R. P. (2010) 'These are They: ET-Human Hybridisation and the New Daemonology'. *Nova Religio* 14, 84–105.

Flanagan, K. and Jupp, P. C. (2007) *A Sociology of Spirituality*. Aldershot: Ashgate.

Foucault, M. (1965) *Madness and Civilization: A History of Insanity in the Age of Reason*. New York: Pantheon Books.

Foucault, M. (1969 [2002]) *The Archaeology of Knowledge*. London & New York: Routledge.

Foucault, M. (1970 [1966]) *The Order of Things: An Archaeology of the Human Sciences*. London: Tavistock.

Foucault, M. (1977) *Discipline and Punish: The Birth of the Prison*. New York: Pantheon Books.

Frankfurter, D. (2003) 'The Satanic Abuse Panic as Religious Studies Data'. *Numen* 50, 108–17.

Frankfurter, D. (2006) *Evil Incarnate: Rumors of Demonic Conspiracy and Ritual Abuse in History*. Princeton: Princeton University Press.

Frisk, L. (2001) 'Globalization or Westernisation? New Age as a Contemporary Transnational Culture'. In Rothstein, M. (ed.), *New Age and Globalisation*. Aarhus: Aarhus University Press, 31–41.

Fritze, R. H. (2009) *Invented Knowledge: False History, Fake Science and Pseudo-Religions*. London: Reaktion Books.

Gallup, G. (1972) *The Gallup Poll: Public Opinion, 1935–1971*. New York: Random House.

Giddens, A. (1991) *Modernity and Self-Identity: Self and Society in the Late Modern Age*. Stanford: Stanford University Press.

Goldberg, R. A. (2001) *Enemies Within: The Culture of Conspiracy in Modern America*. New Haven & London: Yale University Press.

Goodrick-Clarke, N. (2002) *Black sun: Aryan cults, Esoteric Nazism, and the Politics of Identity*. New York: New York University Press.

Gordin, M. D. (2012). *The Pseudoscience Wars: Immanuel Velikovsky and the Birth of the Modern Fringe*. Chicago: University of Chicago Press.

Hammer, O. (2001) *Claiming Knowledge: Strategies of Epistemology from Theosophy to the New Age*. Leiden: Brill.

Hanegraaff, W. J. (1996) *New Age Religion and Western Culture: Esotericism in the Mirror of Secular Thought*. Leiden: Brill.

Hanegraaff, W. J. (2007) 'The New Age Movement And Western Esotericism'. In Kemp, D. & Lewis, J. R. (eds.), *Handbook of New Age*. Leiden: Brill, 25–50.

Harambam, J. and Aupers, S. (2014) 'Contesting Epistemic Authority: Conspiracy Theories on the Boundaries of Science'. *Public Understanding of Science* 24 (4), 466–80.

Harris, M. (1990) 'Emics and Etics Revisited'. In Headland, T. N., Pike, K. L., Harris, M., *Emics and Etics: The Insider/Outsider Debate*. London: Sage, 48–61.

Harvey, G. (2011) 'Field Research: Particiapant Observation'. In Stausberg, M. and Engler, S. (eds.), *The Routledge Handbook of Research Methods in the Study of Religion*. London: Routledge. 217–44.

Heelas, P. (1996) *The New Age Movement: The Celebration of the Self and the Sacralization of Modernity*. Oxford: Blackwell.

Heelas, P. and Woodhead, L. (2005) *The Spiritual Revolution: Why Religion Is Giving Way to Spirituality*. Malden: Blackwell.

Hjelm, T. (2014) *Social constructionisms: Approaches to the Study of the Human World*. New York: Palgrave Macmillan.

Hone, W., Jones, J., Wake, W. and Lardner, N. (n.d.) *The Apocryphal New Testament: Comprising the Gospels and Epistles Now Extant that in the First Four Centuries were More or Less Accredited to the Apostles and Their Coadjutors, but Were Finally Excluded from the New Testament Canon*. London: Simpkin, Marshall, Hamilton, Kent.

Huss, B. (2014) 'Spirituality: The Emergence of a New Cultural Category and Its Challenge to the Religious and the Secular'. *Journal of Contemporary Religion* 29(1), 47–60.

Introvigne, M. (2001) 'After the New Age: Is There a Next Age?'. In Rothstein, M. (ed.), *Religion and Globalisation*. Aarhus: Aarhus University Press.

Jameson, F. (1990) 'Cognitive Mapping'. In Nelson, C. and Grossberg, L. (eds.), *Marxism and the Interpretation of Culture*. University of Illinois Press, 347–60.

Johnson, K. P. (1998) *Edgar Cayce in Context: The Readings, Truth and Fiction*. Albany: State University of New York Press.

Jones, J. H. and Tuskegee Institute (1981) *Bad Blood: The Tuskegee Syphilis Experiment*. New York: Free Press.

Jung, C. G. ([1958] 1991) *Flying Saucers: A Modern Myth of Things Seen in the Skies*. Princeton: Bollingen.

Kay, J. (2011) *Among the Truthers: A Journey Through America's Growing Conspiracist Underground*. New York: Harper.

Keeley, B. L. (2007) 'God as the Ultimate Conspiracy Theory'. *Episteme: A Journal of Social Epistemology* 4, 135–49.

Knight, P. (2000) *Conspiracy Culture: From Kennedy to The X-Files*. London & New York: Routledge.

Kripal, J. (2010) *Authors of the Impossible: The Paranormal and the Sacred*. Chicago: University of Chicago Press.

Kripal, J. (2011) *Mutants and Mystics: Science Fiction, Superhero Comics, and the Paranormal*. Chicago: University of Chicago Press.

Kruglanski, A. W. (1987) 'Blame-placing Schemata and Attribution Research'. In Graumann, C. F. and Moscovici, S. (eds.), *Changing Conceptions of Conspiracy*. New York: Springer, Verlag.

La Fontaine, J. S. (1998) *Speak of the Devil: Tales of Satanic Abuse in Contemporary England*. Cambridge: Cambridge University Press.

Landes, R. (2006) 'Millenarianism and the Dynamics of Apocalyptic Time'. In Newport, K. G. C. and Gribben, C. (eds.), *Expecting the End: Millennialism in Social and Historical Context*. Waco, TX: Baylor University Press.

Larson, K. (2013) 'Viral E-mail and the 2012 Apocalypse Contagion: Seven Reasons Why the World WON'T End in 2012'. In Harvey, S. and Newcombe, S., *Prophecy in the New Millennium: When Prophecies Persist*. Farnham: Ashgate, 239–54.

Levy, N. (2007) 'Radically Socialized Knowledge and Conspiracy Theories'. *Episteme: A Journal of Social Epistemology*, 4 (2), 181–92.

Latour, B. (2004) 'Why Has Critique Run Out of Steam? From Matters of Fact to Matters of Concern'. *Critical Inquiry* 30 (2), 225–48.

Lewis, J. R. (1992) *Perspectives on the New Age*. Albany: State University of New York Press.

Lewis, J. R. (ed.) (1995) *The Gods Have Landed: New Religions from Other Worlds*. Albany: State University of New York Press.

Lewis, J. R. (2012) 'Excavating Tradition: Alternative Archaeologies as Legitimisation Strategies'. *Numen* 59, 202–21.

Lewis, J. R. and Hammer, O. (eds.) (2007) *The Invention of Sacred Tradition*. Cambridge: Cambridge University Press.

Lewis, T. and Kahn, R. (2005) 'The Reptoid Hypothesis: Utopian and Dystopian Representational Motifs in David Icke's Alien Conspiracy Theory'. *Utopian Studies* 16, 45–75.

Lucas, P. C. (2006) 'Cayce, Edgar'. In Hanegraaff, W. J. (2006). *Dictionary of Gnosis & Western Esotericism*. Leiden: Brill, 247–9.

Malinowski, B. (1954) *Magic, Science and Religion: And Other Essays*. Garden City, NY: Doubleday.

Mason, F. (2002) 'A Poor Person's Cognitive Mapping'. In P. Knight (ed.), *Conspiracy Nation*. New York: New York University Press, 40–56

Maton, K. (2003) 'Pierre Bourdieu and the Epistemic Conditions of Social Scientific Knowledge'. *Space & Culture* 6(1), 52–65

Mayer, J.-F. (2013) '2012 and the Revival of the New Age Movement: The Mayan Calendar and the Cultic Milieu in Switzerland'. In Harvey, S. and Newcombe, S., *Prophecy in the New Millennium: When Prophecies Persist*. Farnham: Ashgate, 261–76

McCutcheon, R. T. (1997) *Manufacturing Religion: The Discourse on Sui Generis Religion and the Politics of Nostalgia*. New York: Oxford University Press.

McCutcheon, R. (2014) 'Move Along, Folks, Nothing to Explain Here'. At http://edge.ua.edu/russell-mccutcheon/move-along-folks-nothing-to-explain-here/ (accessed 19 June 2015).

Melanson, T. (2009) *Perfectibilists: The 18th Century Bavarian Order of the Illuminati*. Walterville, OR: Trine Day.

Melley, T. (2000) *Empire of Conspiracy: The Culture of Paranoia in Postwar America*. Ithaca, NY: Cornell University Press.

Melton, G. (1990) 'Edgar Cayce'. In Melton, J. G., Clark, J., & Kelly, A. A. (eds.), *New Age Encyclopedia: A Guide to the Beliefs, Concepts, Terms, People, and Organizations that Make up the New Global Movement toward Spiritual Development, Health and Healing, Higher Consciousness, and Related Subjects*. Detroit, MI: Gale Research, 89–91.

Melton, J. G. (2007) 'Beyond Millennialism: The New Age Transformed'. In Kemp, D. and Lewis, J. R. (eds.), *Handbook of New Age*. Leiden: Brill, 77–97.

Merker, D. (1993) *Gnosis: An Esoteric Tradition of Mystical Visions and Unions*. Albany: State University of New York Press.

Moberg, M. (2013) 'First-, Second-, and Third-level Discourse Analytic Approaches in the Study of Religion: Moving from Meta-theoretical Reflection to Implementation in practice'. *Relgion* 43(1), 4–25.

Montemaggi, F. S. (2011) 'The Enchanting Dream of "Spiritual Capital"'. *Implicit Religion* 14 (1), 67–86.

Moore, D. W. 'Three in Four Americans Believe in Paranormal' (16 June 2005), at www.gallup.com/poll/16915/Three-Four-Americans-Believe-Paranormal.aspx (accessed 24 March 2014).

Moore, J. (2006) 'Gurdjieff, George Ivanovitch'. In Hanegraaff, W. J. (ed.), *Dictionary of Gnosis & Western Esotericism*. Leiden: Brill, 445–50.

Newport, F. 'In U.S., 77% Identify as Christian'. (14 December 2012), http://www.gallup.com/poll/159548/identify-christian.aspx (accessed 2 September 2015).

Newport, F. and Strausberg, M. 'Americans' Belief in Psychic and Paranormal Phenomena Is Up Over Last Decade' (8 June 2001). Available at www.gallup. com/poll/4483/Americans-Belief-Psychic-Paranormal-Phenomena-Over-Last-Decade.aspx (accessed 24 March 2014).

O'Connor, D. (2008) *God, Evil, and Design: An Introduction to the Philosophical Issues.* Malden, MA: Blackwell Publication.

Olmsted, K. S. (2009) *Real Enemies: Conspiracy Theories and American Democracy, World War I to 9/11.* Oxford: Oxford University Press.

Palmer, S. J. (2004) *Aliens Adored: Rael's UFO Religion.* New Brunswick, NJ: Rutgers University Press.

Palmer, S. J. (2010) *The Nuwaubian Nation: Black Spirituality and State Control.* Farnham: Ashgate.

Partridge, C. (2003) 'Understanding UFO Religions and Abduction Spiritualities'. In Partridge, C. (ed.), *UFO Religions.* London: Routledge, 3–42.

Partridge, C. (2004) *The Re-enchantment of the West: Alternative Spiritualities, Sacralization, Popular Culture and Occulture Volume 1.* London: T. & T. Clark International.

Partridge, C. (2005) *The Re-enchantment of the West: Alternative Spiritualities, Sacralization, Popular Culture and Occulture Volume 2.* T. & T. London: Clark International.

Partridge, C. H. and Christianson, E. S. (eds.) (2009) *The Lure of the Dark Side: Satan and Western Demonology in Popular Culture.* London: Equinox.

Pearson, B. A. (2007) *Ancient Gnosticism: Traditions and Literature.* Minneapolis: Fortress Press.

Pelkmans, M. and Machold, R. (2011) 'Conspiracy Theories and Their Truth Trajectories'. *Focaal* 59, 66–80.

Pigden, C. (2007) 'Conspiracy Theories and the Conventional Wisdom'. *Episteme: A Journal of Social Epistemology* 4 (2), 219–32.

Pike, K. L. (1990) 'On the Emics and Etics of Pike and Harris'. In Headland, T. N., Pike, K. L., Harris, M. (eds.), *Emics and Etics: the Insider/Outsider Debate.* London: Sage, 28–47.

Pilkington, M. (2010) *Mirage Men: A Journey into Disinformation, Paranoia and UFOs.* London: Constable & Robinson.

Pinkus, J. (1996) 'Foucault'. http://www.massey.ac.nz/~alock/theory/foucault.htm (accessed 18 December 2013).

Pipes, D. (1997) *Conspiracy: How the Paranoid Style Flourishes and Where It Comes From.* New York: Free Press.

Popper, K. R. (1963 [2002]) *The Open Society and Its Enemies,* 4th revised edition. Princeton: Princeton University Press.

Popper, K. R. (1945 [1957]) *The Open Society and Its Enemies*: Vol. 2, 3rd revised edition. London: Routledge & Keagan Paul.

Popper, K. R. (1959) *The Logic of Scientific Discovery*. London: Hutchinson.

Popper, K. R. (1963 [2002]) *Conjectures and Refutations: the Growth of Scientific Knowledge*. London: Routledge & K. Paul.

Potter, J. and Alexa Hepburn (2008) 'Discursive Constructionism'. In Holstein, J. A. and Gurium, J. F. (eds.), *Handbook of Constructionist Research*. New York: Guilford Press, 275–93.

Putnam, R. D. (2000) *Bowling Alone: The Collapse and Revival of American Community*. New York: Simon & Schuster.

Reisigl, M. and Wodak, R. (2009) 'The Discourse-historical Approach'. In Wodak, R. and Meyer, M., *Methods of Critical Discourse Analysis*. London: SAGE, 87–121.

Repp, M. (2004) 'Aum Shinrikyo and the Aum Incident'. In Lewis, J. R. & Petersen, J. A. (eds.), *Controversial New Religions*. Oxford: Oxford University Press, 153–94.

Rey, T. (2007) *Bourdieu on Religion: Imposing Faith and Legitimacy*. London: Equinox.

Robertson, D. G. (2013) '(Always) Living in the End Times: The 'Rolling Prophecy' of the Conspiracy Milieu'. In Harvey, S. and Newcombe, S. (eds.), *Prophecy in the New Millennium: When Prophecies Persist*. Farnham: Ashgate, 207–19.

Robertson, D. G. (2014) 'Transformation: Whitley Strieber's Paranormal Gnosis'. *Nova Religio* 18 (1), 58–78.

Robertson, D. G. (2015) 'Silver Bullets and Seed Banks: A Material Analysis of Conspiracist Millennialism'. *Nova Religio* 19(2) (in press).

Rothstein, M. (2013) 'Mahatmas in Space: The Ufological Turn and Mythological Materiality of Post-World War II Theosophy'. In Hammer, O. and Rothstein, M. (eds.), *Handbook of the Theosophical Current*. Leiden: Brill, 217–36.

Rose, S. (2005) *Transforming the World: Bringing the New Age into Focus*. Oxford: Peter Lang.

Rowbottom, A. (2012) 'Chronic Illness and the Negotiation of Vernacular Religious Belief'. In Bowman, M. and Valk, U. (eds.), *Vernacular Religion in Everyday Life: Expressions of Belief*. London: Equinox, 93–101

Saler, B., Zeigler, C. A., and Moore, C. B. (1997) *UFO Crash at Roswell: The Genesis of a Modern Myth*. Washington and London: Smithsonian Institution Press.

Sanders, T. and West, H. (2003) 'Power Revealed and Concealed in the New World Order'. In West, H. and Sanders, T. (eds), *Transparency and Conspiracy*. Durham: Duke University Press, 1–37.

Sapountzis, A. and Condor, S. (2013) 'Conspiracy Accounts as Intergroup Theories: Challenging Dominant Understandings of Social Power and Political Legitimacy'. *Political Psychology*, 34, 731–52.

Silverstein, P. (2002). 'An Excess of Truth: Violence, Conspiracy Theorizing and the Algerian Civil War'. *Anthropological Quarterly* 75 (4), 643–74.

Sinason, V. (1994) *Treating Survivors of Satanist Abuse*. London: Routledge.

Singler, B. (2015) 'Big, Bad Pharma: New Age Biomedical Conspiracy Narratives and their Expression in the Concept of the Indigo Child'. *Nova Religio* 19 (2).

Smart, N. (1996) *Dimensions of the Sacred: An Anatomy of the World's Beliefs*. Berkeley: University of California Press.

Smith, R. (1988) 'Afterword: The Modern Relevance of Gnosticism'. In Robinson, J. H. (ed.), *The Nag Hammadi Library in English* (Revised Edition). San Fransisco: HarperSanFrancisco, 532–49.

Smith, T. (2000) *Little Gray Men: Roswell and the Rise of Popular Culture*. Albuquerque: University of New Mexico.

Spanos, N. P. (1996) *Multiple Identities & False Memories: A Sociocognitive Perspective*. DC: American Psychological Association.

Spiro, M. (1966) 'Religion: Problems of Definition and Explanation'. In Banton, M. (ed.), *Anthropological Approaches to the Study of Religion*. London: Tavistock, 85–126.

Stewart, K. and Harding, S. (1999) 'Bad Endings: American Apocalypsis'. *Annual Review of Anthropology*, 28, 285–310.

Steyn, H. C. (2003) 'Where New Age and African Religion Meet: The Case of Credo Mutwa'. *Culture and Religion* 4, 67–91.

Stringer, M. D. (2008) *Contemporary Western Ethnography and the Definition of Religion*. London: Continuum.

Sunstein, C. R. and Vermeule, A. (2008) *Conspiracy Theories*. Harvard Public Law Working Paper No. 08–03; U of Chicago, Public Law Working Paper No. 199; U of Chicago Law & Economics, Olin Working Paper No. 387. Available at SSRN: http://ssrn.com/abstract=1084585.

Sutcliffe, S. (2003a) *Children of the New Age: A History of Spiritual Practices*. London: Routledge.

Sutcliffe, S. (2003b) 'Category Formation and the History of New Age'. *Culture and Religion*, 4 (1), 5–30.

Sutcliffe, S. (2007) 'The Origins of 'New Age' Religion Between the Two World Wars'. In Kemp, D. and Lewis, J. R. (eds.), *Handbook of New Age*. Leiden: Brill, 51–76.

Taira, T. (2013) 'Making Space for Discursive Study in Religious Studies'. In *Religion* 43 (1), 26–45.

Thalmann, K. (2014) '"John Birch Blues": The Problematization of Conspiracy Theory in the Early Cold War Era'. *COPAS-Current Objectives of Postgraduate American Studies*, 15 (1), 1–17.

Thompson, K. (1991) *Angels and Aliens: UFOs and the Mythic Imagination*. Reading, MA: Addison-Wesley.

Trompf, G. and L. Bernauer (2012) 'Producing Lost Civilisations: Theosophical Concepts in Literature, Visual Media and Popular Culture'. In Cusack, C. M. and Norman, A. (eds.), *Handbook of New Religions and Cultural Production*. Leiden: Brill, 101–32.

Tumminia, D. G. (2005) *When Prophecy Never Fails: Myth and Reality in a Flying-Saucer Group*. Oxford: Oxford University Press.

Tylor, E. B. (1958 [1871]) *Religion in Primitive Culture*. New York: Harper.

Underwager, R. (1994) 'Book Review: Treating Survivors of Satanist Abuse'. In *Issues in Child Abuse Accusations* 7 (1). Available at http://www.ipt-forensics.com/journal/volume7/j7_1_br7.htm (accessed 16 January 2014).

Verter, B. (2003) 'Spiritual Capital: Theorizing Religion with Bourdieu Against Bourdieu'. *Sociological Theory* 21 (2), 150–74.

Victor, J. S. (1996) *Satanic Panic*. Chicago: Open Court.

von Stuckrad, K. (2003) 'Discursive Study of Religion: From States of Mind to Communication and Action'. *Method and Theory in the Study of Religion* 15, 255–71.

von Stuckrad, K. (2005) 'Western Esotericism: Towards an integrative model of interpretation'. *Religion* 35, 78–97.

von Stuckrad, K. (2010) 'Reflections on the Limits of Reflection: An Invitation to the Discursive Study of Religion'. *Method & Theory in the Study of Religion* 22 (2), 156–69.

von Stuckrad, K. (2013) 'Discursive Study of Religion: Approaches, Definitions, Implications'. *Method and Theory in the Study of Religion* 25 (1), 5–25.

Wagstaff, G. F. (1984) 'The Enhancement of Witness Memory by 'hypnosis': A Review and Methodological Critique of the Experimental Literature'. *British Journal of Experimental & Clinical Hypnosis*, 2 (1), 3–12.

Ward, C. (2012) 'The Extent of Millennial Conspiracism – A Quantitative Study'. SOCREL Annual Conference, University of Chester, 28 March 2012.

Ward, C. and Voas, D. (2011) 'The Emergence of Conspirituality'. *Journal of Contemporary Religion* 26 (1), 103–21.

Waters, A. M. (1997) 'Conspiracy Theories as Ethnosociologies'. *Journal of Black Studies* 28, 112–25.

Webster, J. (2013) *The Anthropology of Protestantism: Faith and Crisis Among Scottish Fishermen*. New York: Palgrave Macmillan.

Whedon, S. W. (2009) 'The Wisdom of Indigo Children: An Emphatic Restatement of the Value of American Children'. *Nova Religio: The Journal of Alternative and Emergent Religions* 12 (3), 60–76.

Whitesides, K. (2013) 'From Counterculture to Mainstream: 2012 Millennialism in Your Living Room'. In Aston, J. and Walliss, J. (eds.), *Small Screen Revelations: Apocalypse in Contemporary Television*. Sheffield: Sheffield Phoenix Press, 74.

Whitesides, K. A. and Hoopes, J. (2011) 'Seventies Dreams and 21st-Century Realities: The Emergence of 2012 Mythology'. *Zeitschrift für Anomalistik* 12, 50–74.

Wijsen, F. (2013) '"There are Radical Muslims and Normal Muslims": An Analysis of the Discourse on Islamic Extremism'. *Religion* 43 (1), 71–89.

Williams, M. (1996) *Rethinking 'Gnosticism': An Argument for Dismantling a Dubious Category*. Princeton: Princeton University Press.

Wilson, A. F. (2013) 'From Mushrooms to the Stars: 2012 and the Apocalyptic Milieu'. In Harvey, S. and Newcombe, S. (eds.), *Prophecy in the New Millennium: When Prophecies Persist*. Farnham: Ashgate, 225–38.

Wise, D., and Thomas B. Ross (1964) *Invisible Government*. New York: Random House.

York, M. (1995) *The Emerging Network: A Sociology of the New Age and Neo-pagan Movements*. Lanham: Rowman & Littlefield.

Index